PUNISHMENT

PUNISHMENT

a novel

LINDEN MacINTYRE

RANDOM HOUSE CANADA

PUBLISHED BY RANDOM HOUSE CANADA

Copyright © 2014 Linden MacIntyre

www.penguinrandomhouse.ca

Knopf Canada and colophon are registered trademarks.

Excerpts from the poem "And after we damned each other"
by Anna Akhmatova, from *Three Russian Women Poets: Anna Akhmatova,
Marina Tsvetayeva, Bella Akhmadulina*, Mary Maddock,
editor and translator (Crossing Press, 1983).

Library and Archives Canada Cataloguing in Publication

MacIntyre, Linden, author
Punishment / Linden MacIntyre.

Issued in print and electronic formats.
ISBN 978-0-345-81390-9
eBook ISBN 978-0-345-81392-3

I. Title.

PS8575.I655P85 2014   C813'.54   C2014-905224-3

Book design by Terri Nimmo

Cover images: (figure by truck) © David et Myrtille / Arcangel Images;
(leaves) © Mattwatt / Dreamstime.com

Printed and bound in the United States of America

2 4 6 8 9 7 5 3 1

Penguin
Random House
RANDOM HOUSE CANADA

IN MEMORY OF

Ernie Hayes,

AKA TYRONE W. CONN,

1967–1999

Rat (rat) *n. interj., v.* **rat-ted, rat-ting** 1. Any of several long-tailed rodents of the family Muridae, of the genus *Rattus* and related genera, distinguished from the mouse by being larger. 2. *Slang.* **a.** a person who abandons his party or associates, esp. in a time of trouble. **b.** an informer.

Kingston Penitentiary, May 2000

I REMEMBER IT CLEARLY, all the details except the date, which really doesn't matter. Before the incident, it was just another day. I know it was mid-afternoon on a Saturday. I remember that because we had a barbecue on Sunday. We were in the bubble, eyes and ears of the institution. I try to avoid calling it "the joint." I don't mind "pen." It is a prison, a place where people are confined, cons and pigs alike. Everybody in it, more or less incarcerated. The bubble is a prison inside a prison, but just for us, a place to hide if necessary.

From the bubble you should be able to see everything and everybody—when all the systems function properly, which they didn't on that afternoon. You could imagine Upper G range empty if it wasn't for the noise. No sign of inmates in the monitors, but you could hear them, the shouts, the cheers, the jeers.

The gladiator sounds. Now and then a figure hustled past the camera, face hidden.

"Jesus, Tommy, I just saw someone hang a blanket." Smith was pointing urgently at nothing. "Guys in control can't see out."

"Who was it?"

"Couldn't tell, he was running with the blanket up in front of his face."

We all stared. A phone rang. Tommy Steele said, "Yeah, yeah ... we're lookin' at it." Hung up. "Tony, come with me." Tommy the Keeper, unit super, senior officer that day.

We clattered up the iron staircase to Upper G, where we found Meredith and Wilson watching monitors that showed an empty range. Large window at the front of control now blocked by the blanket. One monitor showed sturdy tables bolted to the floor. A wall phone. Inoperable washer-dryer at the far end. No human form. But vivid sounds, substantiated by experience and fear, projecting images on the imagination, embedding permanent sensations. Deep trauma for tomorrow.

"Fuckin animals," said Meredith, as if to himself.

"They're in the blind spot," Wilson said.

Now Tommy Steele was leaning toward an empty screen, all quiet, asking, "Whad'ya see, before the blankie?" Shrug. Coffee and a crossword puzzle on the console. "I was out taking a piss and when I came back ..." Wilson shrugged again. Meredith displayed his empty hands. "It was quiet, then in a split second ..."

"Where's the other camera?" asked Steele. Wilson looked at Meredith.

"Been out for two days. We put in a report ..."

"There you go," said Steele. "Fuckin bean counters."

Then a figure appeared, backing into the shot, now a horrified face turned, looking upward toward the one remaining camera, appealing. Then the camera was dead, blinded, an old eye darkened by a cataract. "What's that?"

"Toilet paper," Wilson laughed. "Cute! Can you believe it? Direct hit." Soaked in a toilet bowl, wadded and hurled like a snowball from the upper gallery into a camera lens. Now everything gone from all monitors. "What happens when you let them have their own toilets," said Wilson. Distracted chuckles. "If it was up to me they'd be pissin' in their . . ."

"That was Pittman," said Meredith.

"Ah, Pittman," Tommy said. "Go Pittman."

Sound escalates. "I remember Pittman once in Collins Bay . . ."

"Jesus Christ someone," I said.

"Calm down," Tommy, laying a reassuring hand on my shoulder. "Just a normal Saturday on Upper G. What were you gonna say about Pittman in Collins Bay?" He was interrupted by a scream.

All four of us crowded toward the empty monitors. Toilet paper suddenly dropped off the lens leaving a smeared image, vague figures roiling in a group. Wilson, Meredith and I watching Tommy Steele, corrections manager, waiting for the cue.

"Somebody's getting killed in there," I said.

"Nah. Let them work it out."

"We gotta go in."

"Hey. You want to go in there, Tony?"

Then more screaming, a hard man screaming like a child.

"Aw fuck," sighed Meredith, picking up the phone.

"Just another minute," said Tommy, stopping him. "Give them another minute. Let them have their fun."

The shouting died and in the silence, whimpering. Blurred figures on the monitor, shrinking back. A dark mass squirming on the floor.

Finally the banging, heavy boots and plastic shields, men in black, helmeted and visored shouting, hammering the shields. Loud-spoken, metallic urgent voices. "Clear the range . . . clear the range." Inmates back in cells, shouting loud abuse. Whirring sound, then clank of cell doors locking shut. Pittman, face down on the floor, life pumping out of him, his blood, so like my vital blood, running free, a wasted viscous puddle spreading. Tommy, face bloodless white, staring not at Pittman, but at me, seeing through me, penetrating all my screens, into the depths of my fear and nausea.

"You there, Breau?"

"I'm here."

"Solid?"

"Solid, Tom."

"I didn't hear you, Tony!"

"I said I'm solid."

"Stay solid, man."

"They lost Pittman," said Meredith.

"Big loss."

"He was a human being, Tommy."

"We're all human beings, Tony. Everybody has to go sometime. And Pittman was about to go to Joyceville. You know what that means—he was slithering back toward the street."

"That's the system. They come, they go back out."

"And if one of them doesn't make it back out, what the fuck, one less problem for society . . . you gonna lose sleep over this, Tony?"

"Not likely."

"Got any plans for tomorrow?"

"Nothing in particular."

"You and Anna come by. We'll have a barbecue. Sally found this new butcher . . ."

"Sounds good, Tommy."

"Everybody take it easy. Book off a couple of days for stress. I'll write it up. Everybody good?"

Everybody good.

Then Tommy called me back. Draped an arm across my shoulder. "We've known each other longer than I care to think, Tony. I didn't want to get into this in front of the others. But I know you, Tony. I can read you like a book. And I always respected you, man. You got goodness and that ain't easy after all the years in this racket. And I know—*hang on, hear me out*—goodness means marchin' to your own drummer sometimes. *Just listen, Tony. Don't say nothin'.*"

Now he was in front of me, hand raised, voice low and urgent, close to my face. "There's an old saying, Tony. Hang together or hang separate. I'm just sayin'. We survive this place by sticking together, staying on the same page of the same hymn book. It's a rough world we're living in. I'm not suggesting anything here, Tony, but . . . *wait* . . . you want to go it alone? Great. But there'll be consequences. For all of us. Including you."

"I'm listening."

"But are you *hearing*, Tony?"

"I'm hearing."

"Okay. Tomorrow then. Say after three. And there'll be no talk a' this tomorrow, okay? Tomorrow or ever."

"I hear you, Tommy."

one

And after we damned each other,
whitely passionate,
We still didn't understand
how the earth can be small for two people,
how, strong as we are,
memory punishes us, is our disease.

ANNA AKHMATOVA

1.

St. Ninian, September 2002

The scuffle at the courthouse made the metro papers and I should have known from past experience how the validation of a headline can unleash the hounds of vengeance in all their myopic savagery. *Angry Relatives of Dead Teen Confront Accused Killer.* There were obviously other factors driving what unfolded in the months that followed but as I look back I see that headline as a catalyst for passions that inflamed the public mind, causing reason to evaporate. But let me start at the beginning.

It was a balmy late summer day in 2002 and I'd gone to the county courthouse to pay my taxes. The business finished, I was walking to my car when the sheriff's van arrived accompanied by two RCMP vehicles. They drove around behind the old brick building and I decided to follow. I suppose I'm like an old soldier—at the sound of a parade I stop, I listen, I remember. I had a hunch that I already knew what this parade was all about.

When I rounded the corner I noticed a small group waiting near the back entrance to what once had been the county jail but now was just holding cells for people awaiting court appearances for more serious offences. The new regional facility for longer-term incarceration is hours away.

There were four burly men, a grand-uncle and three older cousins of the victim. They were of a more recent generation than mine but I knew them all, their names and genealogy and status. They were all solid, decent citizens. I could feel the tension, the potentially explosive mix of grief and anger. But there was also the awkwardness of normal people in the presence of the law.

They were silent as the vehicles pulled up. Three were tradesmen who mostly worked in distant places. The grand-uncle was a seasonal fisherman. There were two women, one of them the dead girl's grandmother. I knew her well from long ago and felt a sudden rush of recollection. She looked startled and distracted when she noticed me.

Five officers assembled near the back door of the van. One unlocked and opened it to reveal young Strickland, shackled, pale and blinking in the sudden flood of daylight, hunched over, staring out. A reporter started the disturbance by shouting at him as he walked, handcuffed, amidst the little scrum of lawmen toward the entrance to the cells. *"Do you have anything to say to Mary's family?"*

Strickland lifted his face and stared at the reporter with an expression that was both defiant and contemptuous. He smiled briefly and seemed to wink at her.

That was when one of the cousins, a tall man about forty years of age, stepped forward, face furious, and reached into the moving knot around the accused only to be quickly seized and wrestled down by the two RCMP. Two other men then raised their voices in protest and moved toward what was now a squirming struggle on the ground. A sheriff's deputy blocked them, a cautionary hand raised.

"Come on now, boys," he said.

The younger of the two women then shouted *"Bastard!"* and spit at Strickland. He saw it coming and ducked as the sheriff hurried him toward the door. The Mounties were by then on their feet, still restraining the angry cousin. It was while the sheriff fumbled with a clump of keys that Strickland noticed me and raised his eyebrows in surprise just before the sheriff grabbed his elbow and half-shoved him through the doorway. He stumbled on the threshold, and was gone.

I knew a little bit about the victim from the papers and the talk. She was seventeen years old, an athlete (distance runner, soccer player), a dancer and a prodigious student. She'd been missing for five days before they found her body at Dwayne Strickland's place. The early speculation was about hard drugs and rape, so it was probably for the best that he had been nowhere to be found at first.

There were conflicting reports about what happened but the one consistent factor was Strickland. I had avoided the community formalities, the wake especially, which would have been abuzz with speculation and inflamed emotion. Three days before the courthouse incident I'd almost blundered into the funeral, which I'd been determined to avoid, too, given what I knew about the man everyone was blaming for the tragedy. I was probably the only person in the village who didn't go—the other absentee was Collie Rankin who ran the local store. He saved a daily paper for me and I was on my way to get it when I saw the cars and trucks lining both sides of the road that runs past the ancient sandstone church. The large back door of the hearse was open wide, the undertaker and his helper hovering.

Collie looked up from a newspaper as I entered. Just inside, on a corkboard festooned with notices of sales and schedules of social functions, there was a photo of the dead girl, Mary Alice Stewart, and a request for contributions to a memorial scholarship fund. She had a smile that revealed both shyness and a sense of mischief.

"I hear they got young Strickland," Collie said. "He was at the airport. Making a run for it by the look of things."

"I see."

"You must remember Strickland."

"I was gone from here by his time."

"You knew he was adopted . . ." It must have been the expression on my face—he stopped, then added quickly, "Not that that means anything, Strickland is in a class all by himself."

"The papers are in?" I asked.

"Yes." He carefully folded the newspaper he'd been reading before handing it to me. "Awful about young Mary Alice."

I nodded, paid and left. I could see people trickling out of the church and as I turned my car onto the highway, six men of varying ages, faces all deformed by sorrow and exertion, were carrying the coffin to the hearse.

The Mounties, back in their cars, sat for a few moments eyeing the group still standing just outside the lockup door. The men seemed angrier now with the crisis passed. I could hear their voices raised, loudly venting afterthoughts, regrets about what seemed now to have been a moment lost—words unsaid, deeds undone. I turned to leave. Then the grandmother was at my side. Years ago we called her Caddy. She still retained the basics of her youthful prettiness, clear blue eyes, strong cheekbones, but she seemed haggard now, face grim. "I saw the look he gave you," she said. "How do you know that piece of garbage?"

"It's a very long story," I said.

I wanted to say more but felt the weight of strangeness. She said: "You haven't changed much, Tony."

"I was devastated when I heard ..." I said, embarrassed by the banality but at a loss for anything more meaningful. She didn't seem to notice. She was looking toward her relatives who were now walking away slowly, still muttering. Then she met my eyes, searching. "We'll never get over it, you know, something like that. People like that Strickland are ruining the place."

"What's happening here today?"

"The arraignment," she said. "I had to get a look at him. Don't ask me why."

"I'll come and visit," I said. "When things settle down."

"Please do," she said, touched my hand briefly. She walked away, then stopped as if remembering, turned and smiled.

She waved again and disappeared around the corner of the courthouse.

In those early days of my retirement I found a disproportionate sense of satisfaction in completing little obligations, even paying taxes. Former colleagues who had retired were always telling me how much they had to do. *Never been so busy. Not enough hours in the day.* A load of crap, as I had learned in the first five months I'd been back here. Days spread out in front of me as vast uncultivated plains. So my expedition to the courthouse had been something to look forward to. The unexpected drama was a bonus.

I thought of Caddy all the way home and about how strange it was that in spite of nearly forty years and all the living in between I'd still feel this nagging adolescent mix of sadness, anger and embarrassment just from seeing her. I had thought about calling on her since I'd moved back but, each time, had been restrained by memory and a cautious nature. Considering my confused reaction on seeing her at the courthouse, I realized that my caution had been prudent.

After I filed away the tax receipts in a drawer I sat back to contemplate the ancient desk I'd brought with me from Kingston. It's an old roll-top from an age when ideas turned more slowly into words, when words were written by hand. I'd also taken books, although there had been some tension over texts that Anna said she needed for her legal practice, dense volumes that mostly dealt with deviance and criminology, which were, I pointed out, my specialty as well as hers. I'd also somehow ended up with the conjugal bed. All sentiment aside, it was a good bed and when she indicated her intent to send it to the dump I said I'd take it. She kept almost everything else.

We'd sold the Kingston house and split the equity. I kept the place in St. Ninian, the coastal village I'd grown up in, and where Anna always seemed to be vaguely miserable. Now I was here alone, for good. It was a disturbing thought–being at a dead end, in a way–but I was vaguely comforted by the desk's connection with a time when I was relevant and busy. And I admired its obvious antiquity and quality as I sat in front of it with my fingers laced across my stomach the way an old man sits. The stomach, I noted with some chagrin, had become substantial.

I'd been told the upside of divorce is often weight loss but, if anything, I'd gained. The Kingston doctor had cautioned me that two life changes close together–retirement and divorce– might constitute a psychic overload and to be careful with the comfort food and booze. He offered pills. I'd never needed pills before, even in the most stressful periods of my working life. I didn't trust pills. He said I needn't worry. The pill he had in mind would be innocuous–it might cause some dryness in the mouth, a fuzzy brain at first and perhaps, occasionally, an inappropriate erection which, at my age, might not be entirely a bad thing.

"At my age," I asked rather sourly, "what would you consider 'inappropriate'?"

He laughed. "You'll have to be the judge."

I've been on the pills ever since, with no apparent side effects.

———

I remembered that I had a photograph of Dwayne Strickland buried somewhere in a desk drawer, a coloured eight-by-ten that I found easily. A friendly inmate snapped it for us on the day I introduced young Strickland to my wife, back in 1998. It was August, I believe. The backdrop was a whitewashed prison wall and they were crouched while I was standing. I was frowning slightly, which was appropriate for my status as an institutional parole officer. Anna was still building up her practice at the time. They, being much younger than I, were more flexible and so looked quite relaxed, squatting in what I would have found to be an awkward pose. Anna was smiling like a girl and afterwards she gushed about the con—Strickland was so engaging; "a waste," was how she put it. What was he like once one got to know him?

I had pointed out to her that one rarely ever gets to "know" an inmate but as far as I could tell he had no discernable personality disorders. He had a fairly high opinion of himself. He wasn't especially violent, just a garden-variety drug dealer who had strayed beyond his expertise by robbing banks for which he was serving eight years. He was in Kingston Pen, far more custody than he required, but only for a psychological assessment before a likely reclassification to medium security. His case managers were also trying to assess the fallout from an incident that might have got him labelled as a rat—a fatal designation in the world we occupied. All that aside, he had a lot of life ahead of him if he had the character to rise above the consequences of his past behaviour.

She had shrugged. "He's awfully good-looking anyway."

Four years had passed since that sunny day in 1998 but I remembered quite clearly how young and carefree Anna seemed back then. It's amazing how anger strips away a woman's youthful qualities. She *was* beautiful, even squinting in the sunshine that was bouncing off the glaring walls, her fine auburn hair ruffled by the August breeze.

I'd had to visit Strickland there that day and Anna had asked to come along. She'd acquired her interest in criminals quite naturally. Anna grew up in or near a lot of prisons. Her father was an officer who had worked his way up the corrections food chain to warden in another institution. She'd heard me speak of Strickland, and the fact that he and I were from the same small place in Nova Scotia seemed to excite her curiosity. Maybe I was mildly flattered by this rare and unexpected show of interest in where I'd come from.

"If we had a son," she'd once said, after she'd become better acquainted with Strickland, "I'd have been happy with someone just like him. In any case, the way he turned out has everything to do with his family background. Discipline without love. Being adopted."

"Take him and everything he tells you with a grain of salt," I'd warned her.

I put the photo back in the drawer. The telephone saved me from another slide into the wasteland of remorse.

The caller asked if I was Mr. Breau. I told him that I was. "*Tony* Breau?" he stressed, sounding friendly. I confirmed it by staying on the line.

He told me that his name was Sullivan, Stanley Sullivan, and that he was a lawyer representing Dwayne Strickland.

I said I was acquainted with his client. Sullivan then proceeded to assure me that he was calling me at Dwayne's request. Strickland wanted to reconnect, given all our history.

"It's all behind me now and I'd like to leave it there," I said.

"I understand," he said. "But I think you were friends."

Naïveté annoys me. "I know him," I said at last. "We both grew up around here and we had some other things in common. We talked occasionally when he was inside but the relationship was hardly personal. Given my line of work, 'friend' would be a bit of an overstatement."

"Whatever the relationship was," Sullivan said, "even if you weren't friends, you were friendly. Let's say he respects you. And for people with his background it's rare to see respect for someone in the so-called system. He'd like to talk to you. That's why I'm calling."

"Did he tell you what he wants to talk about?"

"You've heard about the allegation, the death of the young woman. I think he'd like to present his version of events. He said he wants to tell you exactly what happened."

"And why would I believe him?"

There was a pause, then he said, "It would be as much for my benefit as his. Given your history with him and your background I think it might be helpful to hear him tell it again. There might be small details, even inconsistencies."

"From my point of view," I said, "I'm not sure what I could contribute."

"Mr. Breau, you and I have been around long enough to understand these kinds of situations."

"He got himself in a jam. He wants to get out of it. There's really nothing I can do."

"Look. It's my job to help him deal with his predicament. How to do that isn't clear yet. Do we go for broke or cut our losses ..."

"Around here he's already guilty ..."

"I don't give a shit about 'around here.' He's innocent until the system says otherwise. So will you help or not?"

"Let me think about it."

"Here's my number," he said. "We don't have a whole lot of time."

I wrote down the number, thanked him, said goodbye. I've learned from long experience the peril of a hasty answer to a lawyer or a con.

After hanging up the phone I reopened the desk drawer, looked again at the photograph of Strickland and my former wife, then slammed it shut again. I stared for a while through my living room window at the sunny afternoon. It was a surreal vista of bucolic loveliness, the amber fields, the blue sea glittering.

I first met Anna at an evening class at Queen's. I remember it was sociology. I was still a CX-2, a guard, and after nearly twenty years, nearing burnout. My long-term ambition had always been to upgrade my career. Now or never, I decided, then signed up for classes.

She was trying to enrich an undergraduate degree to improve her chances of getting into law school. We were both older

than the others so we'd often sit together and during breaks
share little insights over coffee and, over time, bits of personal
disclosure. When she learned that I was single she seemed
shocked. I was forty-three. She was thirty, also single, but she
had lived a fairly vivid life, lots of travel, a hippie phase, several
intense relationships, any one of which in more conventional
circumstances would have qualified as marriage. She had, she
confessed, a mild aversion to commitment and a fear of bear-
ing children. She didn't tell me right away that her dad was
also in my line of work, at that time assistant warden in a
medium-security establishment called Warkworth. I stepped
back a bit when she did tell me later. Her father had a reputation in the system—an old-timer, feared equally by con and
copper. But looking back, the outcome of our chats and coffee
seemed preordained.

I don't recall a swell of orchestral accompaniment as our
friendship crystallized, or when on a pleasant weekend trip to
Montreal in 1991 (during *le Festival de Jazz*) we broke through
the barriers of caution, entering what we both acknowledged
to be "a relationship." But that weekend would, in my crooked,
two-faced memory, mark the true beginning of a nine-year
phase of unrestrained (some would call it reckless, even self-
ish) happiness.

Oh Anna. Where are you now? Are you alone? Unlikely.

And then as I watched the sun go down I thought of Caddy.
Anna and Caddy, the end and the beginning of my journey
from here to there and back again—an emotional odyssey, I
suppose, if I wanted to sound grand. I had banished Caddy
from my consciousness decades earlier. That's the way it often

happens when you're young. In time the pain and passion are forgotten. But today, when she turned and smiled, the protective ice just melted, leaving me exposed, and Anna, at least temporarily, forgotten.

2.

A month passed before I summoned up the nerve to visit Caddy. Why not, I reasoned. After all, at the courthouse she'd invited me and it had been more than thirty years since our last meaningful communication, if you want to call it that. I think there had been one encounter since, a superficial social moment long since lost in the confusion it had caused. We were different people now, I told myself. But I'd already made it my business to find out where she lived—a tidy bungalow in what I remembered as a hayfield, not far from Collie's store.

Though Collie saved a metro daily for me faithfully, I frequently forgot to pick it up. Faraway events didn't seem to matter much anymore. But that day I remembered to get the paper. Or maybe I was having second thoughts—I hadn't had the nerve to call her in advance. A call to set a time would sound too purposeful. Best if I just dropped by unannounced. Or maybe not at all. Or maybe she'd not be at home.

There were cars and pickup trucks in front of the store. Inside, half a dozen men were gathered around his complimentary coffee urn. Neil Archie MacDonald was among them. I'd have recognized him anywhere though I'd not set eyes on him for decades. He was just as tall and straight as he'd always been, the shoulders still formidable. Obviously meatier around the middle and he still had the aggressive confidence of an all-American big-city cop, Vietnam War vet, local hero.

He was expounding on Iraq as I was paying for the papers. Collie said, "It's starting to look bad for Saddam. Neil thinks the Americans are on the warpath over nine-eleven." He nodded in Neil's direction but Neil didn't seem to notice.

"I didn't realize Saddam had anything to do with nine-eleven," I replied, loud enough for Neil to hear.

I could feel his eyes, the sudden silence, measuring the moment. "There wouldn't 'a been a nine-eleven if they'd done what they had to do in '91," he said carefully.

I pretended to be scanning the front page of the paper. "You were in Vietnam, weren't you, Neil," I said. I could feel that he was struggling to remember who I was.

"Two tours." His tone communicated the unspoken *who-the-fuck-is-this?*

"Two tours," I repeated, nodding. "Well, well. And you still believe in war?"

He was smiling but the face-flush and eye-glitter were warnings that I remembered from a long time ago.

Then he laughed. "Ahhhhh. Now I remember. Tony Mac-fucking-millan." And he walked over and threw an arm over my shoulder. "This guy and I . . . he's just pullin' my leg. Tony, you know and I know that Saddam is only a part of a bigger problem. Like the whole fuckin world is a jungle now. I'da thought you of all people would know that."

"The name is Breau," I said. "Maybe you've got me mixed up with somebody else."

"No chance of that." And he walked away and out the door.

"Where did he come from?" I asked, struggling to seem amused.

"You didn't know?" said Collie. "He's been home for about a year. Runs a bed and breakfast for tourists, down the road. Ever since the shooting in Boston."

"Shooting?"

"Well, you knew he was a cop?" said Collie. "I hear he's still got a bullet in his body somewhere. It was big in the American papers. They made it sound like the O.K. Corral."

I realized Collie and the others were waiting for a comment–sympathetic or sarcastic–but I knew how, in quiet places like St. Ninian, memorable commentary travels. So I gathered up my papers, smiled around and left.

Caddy hadn't heard my footsteps as I crossed the patio to her back door and she didn't notice that I now stood paralyzed, hand raised to rap on the sliding glass between us. I almost turned away, she looked so sad. She was seated at her kitchen table, one elbow resting on it as if balancing her cup of tea, the other forearm on her thigh. From where I stood it looked as though she might have been examining the decorative detail of the cup. It was elegant, a fragile mug made of what appeared to be fine china with small blue flowers, violets maybe. But she was staring past it, through a window just above the kitchen sink.

It was a lovely day, early October, the sky cobalt with fluffy cloud. The cool wind rustled dried leaves in a nearby maple tree. In the few moments I stood there I noted that her hair, once chestnut, was streaked with a steely grey I hadn't noticed at the courthouse. Her eyes, of course, were always her most distinctive feature—the palest blue I'd ever seen in a human face, but somehow warm and always, always searching, seeing through me. Hard to imagine she was only seventeen back then. I rapped lightly.

I was worried that she'd flinch, maybe spill her tea, but she turned her face slowly toward me and smiled and waved me in. She didn't stand, there was no embrace of greeting and I was somehow pleased. It felt a little like a welcoming reserved for someone who had never really gone away, someone who was still familiar. "Pour yourself a cup," she said, nodding toward the stove. And, reading my uncertainty, she pointed. "The cupboard, there, beside the fridge."

I fetched a mug from a shelf and poured. She held hers toward me and I refilled it. "Milk?"

"In the fridge," she said. "I'm fine with mine the way it is. Then sit."

I was suddenly speechless. The reality of why I'd come rose like a wall between us along with a flood of memories. After we had sat in silence for what felt like minutes, she said, "I doubt if you ever met her. I'll get a picture." Then she stood and left the kitchen.

She returned with the photo that was on the poster in the store. She placed it on the table and we sat silently before it.

"Does anybody know what happened?" I asked finally.

She shrugged. "How can anybody ever know? She died. Why did she die? Isn't that always the question? And there are probably so many answers. I'm not sure any of us want to know." Her voice quavered slightly. "I'm sorry," she said. "I have to find a way to be stronger."

I placed my hand on hers. "Don't be sorry."

She nodded, still staring at the photograph. Then she smiled and stood up. "You must think I'm a wreck, making you pour your own tea. Get up and give an old woman a hug for God's sake." And so I did.

With my arms around her, face touching hers, I was nineteen years old again–away from here, at university and very lonely, staring at a glass and metal wall, row on row of mail slots, looking for a letter. In memory it seems she was the only one who ever wrote to me.

She let me go, and said, almost whispering, "I was a grandma when I was only thirty-five. Isn't that a hoot? My Rosalie was only seventeen when she announced that she was pregnant."

I'd always read her letters upstairs in the dining hall in the clatter of cutlery and dishes, the clamour of adolescent student voices. Before the last one, the closest that her letters ever came to intimacy was "I miss you, xo, Caddy."

I stepped back. Our eyes locked briefly. "I know what you're thinking," she said, then looked away.

I asked, "Are there more pictures?"

"Of course," she said. "Come, and I'll show you some of Rosalie too."

I hesitated, afraid of this journey back in time. "Come," she said gently, and looped her arm through mine. We passed through a darkened hall, past the bottom of a stairway, and into a parlour where everything seemed new. "Poor Jack," she said. "He'd just finished the renovation when he went." She stopped by an old upright piano. "He promised me that he was home for good. Little did he know." There was a photo on the top of the piano, a pretty woman with a careful smile.

"Rosalie," she said. "She was eighteen when the child was born, way too young for motherhood. Abortion was out of the question. Especially around here, back then. Even now, it would be difficult. Jack and I told her up front, 'If you want to give her up, it's okay with us. But if you want to keep her we'll do everything we can.'

"I couldn't imagine myself as Grandma and anyway, Maymie—we called her Maymie—she seemed to think of me as Mom, right from the start. Rosalie went to live in Windsor right afterwards. She's married now, you know. A nice man who works at Chrysler. They have three of their own. They were all here for the funeral. I don't think you ever met Rosalie, did you?"

I shook my head. "Remind me, what year was Rosalie born?"

"1966, October 29," she said, and looked away again, toward a window and the cobalt sky, a contrail streak behind a speck.

"This was Jack," she said, removing another photo from the top of the piano and handing it to me. "I don't think you knew Jack, did you?"

I shook my head, surprised by a feeling similar to resentment. Jack was conventionally handsome, mostly because of the smile that transformed his entire face, the kind of smile that made everybody smile, even looking at a picture of it, even knowing that he could never smile or laugh again. I handed back the picture. Caddy was nodding, rubbed a finger across the glass. "I must dust someday," she said.

She guided me across the room. "And here's our little gallery." I counted eight photographs of her dead granddaughter: a high school graduation, various grade school poses, one of her juggling a soccer ball on her right foot in the middle of a little scrum, hair flying. Crossing a finish line, arms high in exultation. Step dancing on a stage. Wearing a tiara and a fancy dress.

"She had perfect teeth. No need for those braces they're all wearing now."

"She was very pretty," I said.

"Jack would tell her she should get the braces anyway, half-joking. Smooch-prevention, he called braces. That's the way Jack was. His big concern was sex."

She looked away again, toward the window, but not before I saw the crimson on her cheeks. She crossed her arms and sighed. "Drugs never crossed his mind, poor Jack. Not for an instant. But I had my suspicions."

I leaned close to the photograph of Maymie wearing the tiara, looking for a resemblance. "I think she had your eyes," I said.

Caddy smiled. "Princess in the Homecoming, just last summer," she said. "It was around then himself resurfaced. You knew him, from before?"

I nodded. "A terrible waste."

"She was something else," Caddy said quietly. "In her personality, she reminded me a lot of yourself at that age, how she loved to laugh. And she had a smile just like . . ." she clasped my wrist, looking stricken. "That was thoughtless of me."

"No, no," I said. "Not at all."

"I can't imagine what you thought when you found out that I was . . . that Rosalie was on the way. Your Caddy up the stump." She studied me.

It was my turn to look away. "I can't remember exactly how or when I heard. It was sometime afterward, I recall. You were wise to go away. To Windsor, was it?"

"Yes, Windsor. I had an aunt there. In those days you just had to disappear. I often thought I should have told you. Just let the chips fall where they may. But I didn't have the heart."

"It all worked out for the best," I said, and instantly regretted it. We both studied the dead child for a moment. Rosalie's daughter. Caddy's grandchild.

"For the longest time, it did work out," she said. "She was like an angel in the house."

Another silence, broken by the distant roar of a passing truck.

"We'll go back to the kitchen, then?"

She'd refilled the teapot. "You became a prison guard?"

"Sort of."

"You always planned to be a cop, I think."

I shrugged. "It was complicated."

"Yes. Tell me about complicated. I wish you were a cop, in a way. So many things I'd want to ask you. Though I never thought that you were cut out for that kind of work. You were too nice."

Then there was more silence for a while. "You have a lovely place here," I said to end it. "I understand that Jack built it, from the ground up."

"Yes," she said. "He was great at the carpentry. It's hard to believe he's been gone two years now. Almost exactly. I'm almost glad he wasn't here for this latest. He worshipped her. She was all we had, you know. Rosalie was like his own, in spite of everything, God bless him. But Maymie, the sun rose and set on her. They were inseparable. She took it awful hard when he died. I think that was when she started to get a little wild."

"It was a heart attack, I heard. Jack."

"Yes. He never knew a thing. I hope, when it's my time, it'll be like that."

I had not anticipated struggling for words. So I sat there studying the face I once knew so intimately, surprised by how familiar it remained. Some crinkling in the fine skin just below the pale, pale probing eyes, microscopic lines above the upper lip.

"Jack wasn't from here, was he?"

"I met him in Toronto. I moved there right after Rosalie was born. Then he turned up here to work at the heavy water while it lasted. After that he set up a small construction outfit. We did well for a while, but there was a lot of stress. Especially when Rosalie came home to live with us."

"She came back here from Windsor?"

"Yes. Ten she was. Spoiled. I hate to say it but it's true. My aunt spoiled her rotten. It was tough on Rosalie, coming here from a place like Windsor. But Aunt Sadie and her husband were getting old and they couldn't handle her. We thought we could. Then, when she was only seventeen, she dropped the bombshell. Knocked up. It must run in the family." She laughed.

"A shock, I'm sure."

"Well, yes, been there, done that." She laughed again and I imagined she was waiting for some generosity from me.

"Poor Jack nearly had a stroke. But then the baby, Mary Alice–I told you we always called her Maymie? She turned out to be such a joy. A gift from God, Jack always said. How's your cup?"

"It's fine."

"After his business went under poor Jack had to go away like everybody else. To Alberta. That was hard on him. And the timing was bad, especially as far as Maymie was concerned. I have to say it, they need a man around."

I nodded. Another truck roared by on the nearby highway.

"So how well do you know this Dwayne Strickland? He grew up here you know."

"I knew that, but I first met him in Millhaven, four years ago I guess. He was there for robbery."

"He's always been a piece of work, that fellow. I know it wasn't always easy for him, but there's no excuse."

"No," I said. "There's no excuse."

"You must have met a lot of evil people in your work."

I studied my tea mug for a moment. "Once you get to know them you realize that 'evil' is a complicated word . . . more an adverb than an adjective." Realizing instantly I sounded pompous.

"I'm glad you think so," she said, and got up and walked toward the stove. "Can I freshen you?"

I shook my head. "I'm sorry," I mumbled. "I didn't mean that the way it came out. It was something somebody I worked with used to say. I'm still not entirely sure what it means."

Her expression was suddenly weary. "I hope he knew what he was talking about, the fellow who came up with that."

"It was a woman," I said. "A psychologist."

"Ah. One of those."

She sat down. She sipped.

"You never had any, yourself? No kids."

"Not that I'm aware of," I said.

She laughed. "Isn't that the way."

"So you're here alone now?"

"I am," she said. "Alone with the memories."

"That makes two of us."

"Ahh," she said. "I'm sorry to hear that. Death or divorce?"

"Divorce," I said. "I suppose there's worse things that can happen." And again I felt infinitely stupid. And so I stood. "Anyway, I just wanted to drop in. Say hello."

In the sudden silence I heard a clicking sound. "Well look who's here," Caddy said. I followed her eye line and found a small dog standing in the door to the hallway leading toward the parlour. He was grey with irregular black patches. "Come over here," she ordered. The dog just stood, then gave a small brief bark.

"Listen to yourself," she said. "The first sound out of you in weeks. So you came out to see the visitor."

The dog walked toward me, stopped and nosed my knee.

"Honest to God," she said. "That's the first time he's come out of the parlour since the funeral. Except to do his business outside the front door. Then he's right back in, God love him."

"I didn't see him there."

"He stays behind the couch. We had to move the couch out for the casket at the wake. So that's where he stays, right where the casket was, poor little fellow. Come here, say hello to Caddy." But the dog stayed put, staring at me as if trying to remember something, someone.

"He looks like a Jack Russell," I said, stooping down to scratch his ears.

"Is that what he is?" she said. "Somebody in Halifax gave him to her when he was just a puppy."

"He's mostly Jack," I said. "I had one. What's his name?"

"She called him Birch, because of the colour of him. Mr. Birch Bark."

The dog yapped once again. "There you go," Caddy said. "That was their trick. When he hears the B word, he does that. You had one like him?"

"Yes," I said. "I named him Jack Daniels because everybody was calling him that anyway." I squatted, ran a hand along the ridge of his back. He sat.

Caddy tipped her face, eyes asking the unspoken question.

"Anna got custody," I said, smiling. I stood.

"Anna," she said. "Now I remember."

"I don't think you met."

"Once," she said. "It was at an outdoor concert. I remember thinking how glamorous she was."

"I don't recall."

"You had a bit of a *sgleo* on. It was the first time I'd seen you since . . . ages. You looked happy. I was glad. I always wanted that, Tony, no matter what you thought." Her hand was resting lightly on my wrist.

"*Sgleo,*" I said. "I can't remember the last time I heard that word."

"So you're home for good now?"

"You never know."

"Come back sometime," she said. "I promise to be happy."

"Don't make promises you can't keep."

"We're both single now," she said. "You come back and we'll give them something to talk about at the store." She smiled and again I saw the teenaged face, the captivating eyes.

"Ah yes," I said. "The store."

She laughed lightly and pushed me toward the door. "You know where I live. Don't be so long before coming back."

The little dog was at my heels. I slid the door shut as he looked up at me.

Another day was fading fast. The amber evening light emphasized the polished oaken desk in front of me. I opened the drawer, fished out a slim packet of letters. She wasn't much for writing, Caddy. They were usually one page long, brief little chronicles from home. And then the last one, Holy Week, 1966.

> *I'll be short and to the point. There isn't any easy way to say this but I have to try. I won't be here when you come home this weekend. I promised myself that I wouldn't say I'm sorry even*

though I am. It's such an easy thing to say, sorry, such a common little word. Too, too easy. But being sorry really hurts more than such a little word implies. And you deserve to know why I'm going but I just can't bring myself to tell you because I know how you'd react and your reaction would be such a big mistake in the long run. You'll find out soon enough at any rate. And maybe you'll hate me then. I hope so. It'll make things so much easier for both of us. Goodbye Tony. Love, Caddy.

And I sat staring at that unfamiliar word. Love.

3.

I was awake most of the night. The ATVs, the ubiquitous four-wheelers, didn't help. Young people, boozed up, smoked up, invading private property, the entitlement of darkness, anonymity—as if anyone in this place could ever be anonymous. Finally, sometime after four, silence. I fell into a groggy slumber and I dreamed of Strickland.

We were in the woods across the road from the high school and we were smoking cigarettes. "You're adopted too," he said. "Who told you that?" I asked, irritated. "Everybody knows," he said. And then we were walking deeper in the woods and Caddy was there but she was holding Strickland's hand and I seemed to have been excluded and the day was growing darker. "We should go back," I said. "We'll be late for chemistry." But then Caddy was Anna and she was saying, "We can't go back, we're already late for chemistry, we've gone too far."

I woke then. Through my dormer window I could see a flaming red horizon, smeared as if by smoke. And I resolved to call the lawyer Sullivan and to tell him that Dwayne Strickland could go to hell, which is what I'd said back in '96 when Clarke, his case manager in Millhaven, first told me that the inmate Strickland was asking to meet me.

"He claims the priest back home suggested that he connect with you. It's a good sign that he wants to."

"I don't have time for this," I'd said. "I really don't. Trust me, I've been there once. I'd be wasting his time and my own."

"Maybe if you had a word with him," Father MacIsaac had said, clutching my sleeve. *A word?* I'd been gone from the place for years and I was home on a hard-earned vacation in the summer of 1988. Even so it was hard to say no to the priest. He gave my arm an insistent little shake, speaking softly: "Maybe give him the facts of life from your point of view."

"My point of view."

"Inside the prison system. What it's really like. A lot of the young ones see crime as glamorous. TV and the movies. I'm sure you have a different perspective."

"So, Father, what you're really asking is that I try to scare him."

"I wouldn't go that far, Tony. But it wouldn't hurt to sit down with the boy, just talk. People here look up to you. You're quite the success story."

I laughed. "I'm doing life in prison. Some success story."

And he laughed with me. "I can relate to that," he said. "Life is a prison of one kind or another for most of us." And then he seemed a little bit embarrassed. "But I feel bad for his poor parents. They've tried hard to give the boy a chance to make something of himself."

"Well, how bad can he be? He's what?"

"Fifteen, I think. You heard about the store?"

"They found the stuff he took . . ."

"Yes. The poor little fellow–I gave him credit for having more brains. He had everything in his room. Of course it was the first place they looked."

"One-kid crime wave" I'd overheard someone saying in the store. First time in perhaps a hundred years anybody'd ever violated the village store. It had been a co-op in the early days, everybody's business. Had to be someone who knew the place, but not belonging to the place, not really. Someone inside from the outside. Mostly movies and cigarettes gone missing. Didn't have to look far for the culprit.

"I'll see what I can do," I said.

I called and told his mother that I'd be dropping by and she seemed glad but when I got there the kid was nowhere to be found.

"Dwayne got called out this morning," she said.

"Called out?"

"Some days he helps with the hay. Somebody called this morning and he took off."

"And where would they be making hay?"

"He didn't say."

"Maybe I'll try again."

"Yes. I'll tell him." She looked old and tired, her heavy body propped up by the doorframe. "I'm trying to place you," she said.

"MacMillan," I said. "Tony."

"Tony MacMillan from the mountain road?"

"The one."

"But the name you said on the phone . . ."

"I changed my name," I said. "Back to what I was born with."

"Ahhh. That's right," she said. "You were adopted too. Can I offer you a cup of tea?"

"Thanks just the same, but I have to be somewhere."

"Ah well." She sighed. "It's never easy, is it?"

"What's never easy?" I said.

"Growing up nowadays, with all the pressures."

"I'll call again," I said, and squeezed her hand.

"We'd be awful grateful if you would."

And when he wasn't there the second time I visited, I confess I felt relief.

"Still haymaking?"

His mother seemed uncomfortable at the door. "Who's out there," a gruff male voice called from inside. She turned her head slightly. "It's young Tony MacMillan," she replied. "Looking for Dwayne." There was no answer. She shrugged.

"No problem," I said. I told her I'd be going back to Ontario soon, probably wouldn't get a chance to call again. "Give him my best," I said.

She nodded and shut the door.

———

The store decided to not press charges. Restitution, Mary said. She'd been hired to help to run the place after the co-op went under and Collie became the owner. There were rumours Mary was a silent partner.

"He'll pay for everything and clean up around here for a few months," she told me just before I headed back to Kingston. I thought that seemed fair, being cautious with my opinion. It was Collie's decision, she said. "I'm just sayin', but if it was up to me. Then again I suppose he's got enough going against him without a record."

So first it was the priest. Then, in 1996, it was Clarke, Strickland's case management officer. "Maybe if you had a word with him. You might get through to him where others are failing."

"A waste of time," I said.

"Just hear me out," Clarke said. He told me that Strickland was withdrawn, vulnerable, but simmering. He was terrified of the chicken hawks hovering around him, pretending to be his guardians. He was much too pretty. Would I oblige before he broke? He'll survive, I said.

More curious than concerned, I asked, "What's in the file? What'd he do?" Guy from home, vaguely familiar, normal interest, but casual.

Clarke was browsing. "Hmmm ... some minor shit back in the eighties, selling dope back in ... where you guys come from, Tony."

I shrugged, and Clarke looked back at the file.

"Sentenced to three years in 1992 ... holdup in a convenience store in ... Toronto. Hey, looks like he walks into a little 7-Eleven, hand in his pocket, threatens the owner—some Lebanese guy—who hands over a wad of bills. Strickland runs for it, storekeeper in hot pursuit, armed with a *bayonet* ... catches him a block away ..."

"Don't fuck with the Lebanese. Guy probably from the civil war. Strickland's lucky."

Clarke laughed.

"Now," he said, flipping through the document, "doing eight for a bank job last year, Bloor West. Taken down two hours later counting his haul in a Lakeshore motel room. Don't fuck with the banks, eh?"

I laughed, and thought no more of it.

Then Clarke brought his name up again, two years later.

"Christ," I said. "What's with this guy?"

"You must know him pretty well," Clarke said.

"Don't you think I've got enough to do without taking on one of your Millhaven problems? And for the record, I don't know him at all."

"You're mentioned in a profile report as a possible personal contact. You know his home life."

We were all around the boardroom table, case managers and support staff from around the region, five institutions from minimum to max. Meetings bored me and I was doodling an AK-47, trying to ignore what my gut said was an entanglement I didn't really need.

"He might be worth a visit," Clarke said.

Strickland had potential to reoffend but there was hope for him, Sophie said. She was the psychologist. Earnest Sophie.

I used to ask myself, *How did she get in here?* Too pretty and too soft.

"So let me get this straight," I said. "You're all thinking: Two guys from the boondocks, two guys with murky origins and all the psychological and social hang-ups associated with adoption—a perfect therapeutic fit. Is that what I'm hearing?"

Sophie sighed. "I can't imagine what you're hearing. What's *being said* is that there's a chance you might be able to give a little bit of support to this guy. I think there's something decent in the core of him." This was the same Sophie who had brought one of our meetings to a halt with the stunner: *Evil is an adverb.*

But I never forgot those words, or her smile, the flicker of the deep blue-hazel eyes dancing on my face.

"You're laughing at me," she'd accused.

"I would never laugh at you."

It was Sophie who talked me into seeing him.

Looking back I can understand how Dwayne Strickland could charm Anna and Sophie, or any woman, really. To them he'd represent a wealth of possibilities for improvement. The nurturing instinct: take bad boys and make them good men. To me he was just another good-looking, fairly articulate young con. There are lots of them inside, contrary to popular belief. They don't all have low foreheads and knuckles scabbed from dragging on the ground. Of course there are the losers and the predators, more than a few lost causes. But what kept me in the system for so many years was the obvious potential that I saw in so many like Dwayne Strickland, the possibilities of "rehabilitation"–a word that makes me sick and angry now that I'm out of it. Strickland was bright and presentable enough to have had a shot at making it in any walk of life, but maybe he'd wanted too much too soon, and maybe he was not quite so clever as he thought he was.

I met him for the first time just after the first 1998 riot. Millhaven went through a bad stretch in the late nineties, inmate agitation for reforms exacerbated by ineffective management. They were rough times and maybe that's why I finally succumbed to his requests to see me. Nothing to lose, I thought.

I arranged to meet him in a quiet corner of the woodwork shop where we wouldn't draw too much attention.

"I don't remember you from home," he said. "I only heard of you from my ma. She told me that you came to the house a couple of times, looking for me. The teachers mentioned you, what you did for a living. So I guess I ducked you." He was smiling.

"So why did you stop ducking?" I asked.

He shrugged. "A couple of years ago I had a letter from the priest, Father MacIsaac. Said maybe I should contact you if I ever needed anything. Somebody to talk to. He said you went by 'Breau.'"

"Growing up I used my adopted name," I said. "MacMillan. I guess there was confusion when I changed it back."

"Ah," he said. "I remember hearing that. We probably know a lot of the same people."

"I'm sure we do." Of course I'd always been aware of him, even before the crime wave. Someone else adopted in the place.

Someone's sister's cousin's bastard being brought up somewhere decent. "How do you like the wood shop?"

"A Unit is too fuckin close. Every minute of every day is a problem. Going to work, going to eat, going back to my house for counts." He was talking about a reception range, basically a holding facility where inmates were assessed for the most appropriate incarceration.

I shrugged. "They're just here for processing, just passing through. What's your problem?"

"They try to talk to you, man, but you don't know who they are. Seen talking to the wrong guy here and you're dead meat." There was a loud clang and he cringed.

I liked the woodworking shop, the way the fragrances of sawdust and glue and machine oil overwhelmed the disinfectant and the staleness of old cigarettes and bodies. But always loud sounds clanging off the tile and steel and concrete surfaces, inescapable. Loud ego voices, reminding us of where we were.

"So what year did you leave?" he asked.

"In '65," I said. "Went to university."

"Wise choice."

He looked away, couldn't hold eye contact for more than a few seconds. He had stood out in the village in a way I never did. I just folded in, Tony MacMillan from up the mountain road, almost like I belonged. He was different. After the store incident, there was a car accident, a sixteen-year-old Strickland driving crazy, two young people dead. People saying: after all the old MacInnises did for him, he never even took their name. What the hell kind of a name is Strickland anyway? Adoption, always a crapshoot, never knowing what you're getting.

Sophie the psychologist had warned me. Issues about rejection, alienation, also guilt that had morphed into deep-rooted, textbook anger. Aren't they all textbook angry, I had said.

To Dwayne I pretended ignorance. "I don't remember any Stricklands around home."

"There aren't any. I was raised by the MacInnises. Shore Road. But I guess you'd know that." He coughed, fished for a cigarette.

"You can't smoke here," I said.

"Right," he said, staring at the floor, palming the cigarette.

Something else remembered: He cleaned up his act after the horrific accident, took a trade at the community college in town, small engines someone at the store had said; the store, the clearing house for news, better than the radio. Plans to open up his own shop on the old place. Growing dope on the old place more like it, someone else had opined.

Then he went away.

"Pretty common name, MacInnis," I said.

"Our MacInnises were called Big Rory's," he said, and I laughed.

"Big Rory's—long time since I heard that."

"After some old-timer called Big Rory, I guess. You know them?"

"I went to school with the older ones, Margaret and Jimmy. But I haven't seen them for years."

"Maggie's married in Boston. Uncle Jimmy lives in Sudbury, shaft contractor there, did very well in the boom times. Drives a Lincoln."

"You worked in the mines?"

"No. I wish." He laughed.

I knew but asked him anyway: "How did you end up in the 'haven'?"

He shrugged. "I won't make any excuses. You can read about it." Good answer.

"What's your plan?"

"I'm in substance abuse, anger management, trying to finish high school. Maybe start working on a degree."

"I heard you had a trade."

"A while ago. Small engines. Did nothing with it." He shrugged again. "You know the way it is at home. Hard to get anything going. Nobody wants to pay for anything. Fixing lawn mowers for fuck all. Eventually took off for Toronto. Land of opportunity." He spread his arms wide. "And here I am."

"Well, keep at it," I said. "The studies. The shop. There's decent money in the shop."

"Just FYI," he said, now looking around nervously. Then he had the cigarette in his mouth, hands cupped around a flame. Dropped an extinguished match, exhaled a billow of smoke straight at me: "There's talk of another smash-up. The warden started confiscating money from our welfare fund, for broken food trays. The food here sucks. They wheel it over in metal carts from next door at Bath. Garbage by the time it gets to us. Guys have been breaking the trays, to protest."

I nodded at the cigarette, smiled. "You'd better be careful with that."

"I'm always careful," he said. "The secret of survival."

"Good to know."

"Maybe you should pass it on. Any night now. They'll know

who–the gang on J." He was rock steady, now held eye contact, bold and brave. A calculated risk, I thought–a small investment. He drew deeply on the cigarette, looked away, then pinched the ember, pocketed the butt.

I said nothing and he seemed puzzled, wondering if I'd paid attention. Which is how you deal with them, how you both survive. I left him there.

"Where'd you get this, Breau?" I was standing in the doorway at Institutional Protective Security. The IPSOs, as they're known. The officer was looking skeptically at the typed-up page I'd handed him, a copy already in my files.

"Confidential source."

"Come on, Tony. Give. We need to know how credible this is."

"Can't. Confidential. But I have reason to believe . . ."

"Just tell us if he's one of yours."

"I can't do that . . ."

"Well just confirm that it's from a con in Millhaven . . ."

"Confidential source," I repeated.

"We'll take it under advisement," the officer said as he turned away.

And Millhaven blew up just the way Strickland said it would. First the inmates blocked access to the ranges with those steel food carts they were complaining about, then they sabotaged the mechanism for the cell doors, making it impossible to close them. It went on for days, smoke and water, noise and violence everywhere as it spread to all the other units, except A. They tried to break into A, but the guards drove them back with pepper spray and fists and boots and batons. Then they managed to get into the pharmacy. It was on day three that two psychotic inmates stoned on Percocet killed the Italian. There was no reason in particular. Someone found him annoying. Someone thought he was a rapist. He was a from-Italy Italian, no friends in the joint. So they killed him slowly, carving on him for most of an afternoon. Finished him off when they heard the emergency response team breaking in. Had a pillowcase over his head so he couldn't see who did it, just in case he survived.

After it was over, the IPSOs wanted me to sniff around since I had such super confidential sources there.

Sophie had set up the second meeting in her Millhaven office. No eyebrows raised, no questions asked. Strickland off to see the shrink. He was surprised and obviously frightened to find me there.

"I need to know who did the Italian," I said. I kept my voice low.

"Why do you care about the Italian? He was a fuckin skinner. Anyway, you had your chance. I warned you."

"He wasn't a rapist."

"Yeah? How would you know?"

"I know for a fact. He was an okay guy. So just tell me what you know."

"You're trying to get me killed."

"Nobody knows you're talking to me."

"I'm no fuckin rat, man."

"I'm not asking you to rat."

"Even if I knew for sure I wouldn't tell you," Strickland said. "I was hiding under my blankets."

"Did you know what was going on?"

He laughed. "They were skinning him alive. What do you think?"

"Who did it, Dwayne?"

"Can I go back now?"

I sighed. "If you change your mind, get the word to Sophie. She'll pass it on to me."

"If I change my mind you'll know because I'll be a corpse."

Come on, Tony, I said to myself. *Enough with the navel gazing. Time to face the day.* Through my dormer window I could see the sun climbing up the slippery slope of the sky. It was nearly nine o'clock. I got up, pulled on a pair of sweats, resolved again to start an exercise program, maybe take up running once again, maybe buy a bicycle, get some weights for a bit of upper body. Upper body used to be impressive, bench press two hundred pounds, no sweat. I filled the kettle. Remembered how I once was passable at judo.

At 9:15 I called Sullivan's office but he wasn't there. I left a message, asking him to call me back. Then I put a jacket on, found my car keys. I'll soon be like the rest of them, I thought. Gravitating to the store for the coffee and the gossip. No goddamned way. Kill me first.

I noticed Neil MacDonald's Lexus parked close to the door. He still had a Massachusetts plate on the front, a little status symbol that said a lot about his ego. A Bush-Cheney bumper sticker prominent on the back.

Neil was on the way out as I was entering. I nodded but he asked me to step back outside for a moment. "You and I should get together, have a beer someday. There's lots to talk about," he said.

"Where are you living?"

"I thought you knew. I opened the Seaside B and B a year or so ago."

"So you're living there too?"

He nodded.

"I hear it's quite the posh establishment. How's business?"

"Slow," he said. "But it gives me something to do. You bought an old place on the Shore Road?"

"Years ago."

"You were a prison guard in Ontario?"

"Prison guard, parole officer—'case manager' they call them nowadays. Part of the system. But I'm out now."

"I got to hand it to you," he said. "Jesus, working among that crowd."

I shrugged. "No worse than your job, I suppose."

"I always thought you wanted to be a cop, like I did. I remember, you were saying that after the Mountie came to grade eleven and gave the talk about careers."

"How did you get into it?"

"After the war, I was released in California. I liked California. The weather, eh. Took out citizenship, but after a while I wanted to be closer to home. Moved up to Boston. Bunch of relatives there. Then got on the police."

"And how was that."

"A living," he said. "Quite a good living, actually. I'm comfortable. And what about yourself."

"Getting by," I said. "Took a package and a pension."

"Aren't you a bit young for that?"

"Burned out, you could say." I tried to laugh. "It was complicated."

"Same for me," he said grimly. "But a different kind of complicated burnout. Burned by a gang of niggers . . ."

"Please," I said, holding up a hand.

He laughed. "You know that's what they call each other."

"Just humour me," I said.

"Tony," he said. "I got a bullet four centimetres from my spine. It'll go into the grave with me. That's my permit to use any fucking word I want, okay?" He shook his head. "Fuck me. So what burned you?"

"Ah well. It's a long story."

"Bad guys got to you?"

"Actually, no . . ."

He was waiting. I looked away. Enough said. He cleared his throat, pulled car keys from a pocket. "By the way, we should talk sometime about that quiff Strickland."

"What about him?"

"About what if he gets off."

"What's it got to do with us?"

"You know what was going on there, don't you?"

"Not really."

"Well I'll tell you. And it's from a solid source. He was exploitin' the young folk. Drugs. I understand they found porn there.

Christ knows what he had in mind for the poor kid that died before he got at her . . ."

"Neil, Neil," I interrupted. "You know better than this. You're trained . . ."

"I'm trained to put two and two together." He hesitated, gave a kind of laugh. "You're always fuckin with me, Tony. Just tryin' to get a rise out of the old cop. But I know where your heart is. I know you as well as I know myself. What was it old Abe Lincoln said? We hang together or we hang separate."

He walked away shaking his head and climbed into the Lexus, peeling rubber as he drove away.

Sullivan called five minutes after I got home from the store. "Mr. Breau?"

I hesitated. "I've been giving it a lot of thought."

"Good," he said. "What'll I tell Dwayne?" And in a flash Strickland's face was there in front of me, pale and frightened, and he was saying *You owe me, man*, and then Sophie's voice, dear Sophie who was always too persuasive: *I think you owe him that much, Tony.*

"Okay," I said. "You tell Strickland that I'll be down to see him tomorrow. You make the arrangements to get me in to see him. Tell him I'll be there to listen . . . nothing else."

The sense of self-betrayal was instantaneous.

"Thank you," said Sullivan, "he'll be pleased."

That night, I called Anna. I figured it would be useful to get some advice from her before seeing Strickland, as in the end she got to know him better than I did. We hadn't talked for ages and she sounded wary when I mentioned him. "I'm surprised he ended up back there," she said.

"His lawyer wants me to talk to him. I said no at first. But you know how lawyers are."

There was a long silence on the other end of the line.

"It's pretty serious," I said. "A young woman was found dead in the place where he's been living and it looks like they'll go for second-degree murder."

"Second degree? Wow."

"He's definitely looking at criminal negligence. He wants to see me. I could use your advice."

"God, Tony. I don't know what to tell you. What were the circumstances?"

"It isn't clear yet. She was missing for five days. She was probably there all the time. He was gone when they found her, which looked bad. Looked like he was running away."

"I can't imagine Dwayne mixed up in anything violent. He'll probably say that he was gone when she died. Have they come up with a time of death?"

"Not that I've heard."

"The cause?"

"Drug overdose. It seems he's been dealing serious drugs around the place. Maybe it's a mistake for me to talk to him. People here are pretty stirred up about it. I know the victim's family pretty well."

"You'll have to be the judge of that because you know the way they are down there," she said. "But he always looked up to you."

"That was then," I said. "When he was inside and I was part of the system, part of his survival."

"Say hello from me if you see him," she said. "But you know what?"

"What."

"I'd be very careful. It's bound to get messy."

"You're probably right."

"How are you otherwise?"

"I was thinking about you the other morning," I said. "Just lying in the old bed, remembering."

Silence on the other end.

"It sounds stupid, but I can't help wondering how life would be if I could just push pause and rewind. Go back to where the story got confused, where I lost the thread."

"So how far would you rewind it, if you could?"

"Good question."

"Tony, I should tell you, you'll hear it anyway–I'm involved with someone."

"That's great," I said. "I'm glad."

"Are you?"

"I suppose that depends."

"Depends on what?"

"I think I'm going to hang up now."

"Tony, before you do. About Dwayne, he'll probably remind you that you were partly responsible for the fix he got himself into at Millhaven, over that Italian. Surely you can't forget that. It's probably why he'd turn to you now."

"Thanks for that," I said. And I put the phone down.

—

Looking back, the third encounter with Strickland was inevitable. Sophie was the catalyst for that one too. She was nervous when she called. "Someone needs to talk to you," she said.

When I got there, Strickland was sitting in her office smoking a cigarette, something he only did when he was under pressure. He liked to run, was worried about his body.

I acted surprised to see him. I made myself sound hostile, impatient. "What's up?" Pretended to be reading something in a file.

He looked at me, head slightly angled, eyes on mine, a smile threatening. "I think you know."

"You're here to tell me about Vito?"

"I need to make a deal."

"Let's not play games. What kind of a deal?"

"I need to get out of here."

I laughed. "That'll happen, eventually. What's your rush?"

"Two goofs come up to me in the yard, an hour ago. One gets right up in my face. I could smell what he ate for breakfast. 'There's a rat,' he says. 'About Vito. And we're real close to him now.' His forehead is almost up against mine. What am I supposed to think he means? 'Great,' I say. 'Keep me posted.' And he says, 'Ooooohhh yeah. You'll be one of the first to know.'"

"Who was that?"

"Can you get me out of here?"

"Doesn't sound like you're in any position to negotiate. Who are you afraid of?"

He hesitated, looked toward Sophie helplessly, spread his hands in resignation.

"Were they the guys who did the Italian? The guys who threatened you?"

"I can't say. I didn't see."

"Okay. Who made the threat?"

"They call him the Horse. The asshole right up in my face was Jimmy Driscoll."

"Have you been talking to anybody?"

"Only you." The look and the tone were accusing. "Only you, Tony. Who you been talkin' to?"

"Come on," I said. "What was there to talk about?"

"There's this fuckin rumour in the unit that you and I are related. People making jokes. Then the IPSOs comin' around," he said. "Assholes, those guys. Comin' right up and talking to me in front of everybody. You told them."

"I told them nothing."

"Someone talked to them because they've been all over me."

"And you told them . . . ?"

"What I told you . . . just fuck right off. But there's talk around the unit, people looking at me funny. Tony, just get me the fuck out of here. You owe me, man."

Sophie was nodding in agreement, face downcast, her expression almost accusing.

By the next morning he was on his way to Kingston Pen.

The call to Anna made for a long sleepless night. When she had asked, *Depends on what?* I might have answered: *Depends on* when *you started seeing someone. Depends on* whom. *Depends on what you mean by "involved."* The mental math and lurid speculation were inevitable. By two in the morning I'd drifted off but then the nightly roar of traffic to the shore had started up, the ATVs on the nearby gravel road sounding like they were passing through my living room.

It hadn't occurred to me that I might have been too hasty in my rush to assume the full burden of blame and the hangover of guilt when our marriage hit the rocks. What if she'd had someone waiting in the wings? For sure it would explain how quickly she'd accommodated our new reality, and how efficiently she removed me from her life. *Involved with someone else*–a gentle phrase, evasive substitute for real disclosure. How about: *Fucking someone else*. Let's try that on for size. Sounds of distant engines filtered through the pillow on my head. What if Anna ... but then the images of Anna as I knew her intervened, Anna when everything between us was new and vivid. It was probably merciful that the roaring came closer then, the nocturnal ATVs. *Tonight they're early,* I said aloud. There was rumbling and revving as they paused outside my kitchen door, it seemed. In my fantasy I had a rifle pointed out the upstairs window. Like nutty what's-his-name out west. Ludwig Wiebo or whoever. And I thought of Pittman then, and something else I should have said: I don't owe Strickland *anything*.

Finally I got up and switched on a light. After another moment I could hear them roar away, wheels spinning in the gravel, the crack of stone bouncing off my car.

4.

I was technically impaired, driving in my exhausted state. The regional correction centre was about two hours away and I had to make two stops for coffee. It was raining, the autumn leaves collecting in the ditches and the fields. Winter wasn't far away and I was dreading it, remembering the dreariness of childhood. Of course the isolation wasn't only caused by weather but the winter climate was a factor, for sure. I should buy cross-country skis, I thought.

I turned on the car radio. Another American talking about weapons of mass destruction. I clicked it off. Every morning at the store it seemed Neil would be front and centre, holding court, delivering the latest propaganda from the Bush cartel. · Saddam this, al-Qaida that and nine-eleven, mixed up in a crock of speculation. More than once I'd come close to saying exactly that–it's all a crock. A few years back I would have wiped the floor with Neil using logic, humour, facts, but now I just ignored him, even when he tried to draw me in. In the rearview mirror I could see the eyes of a sad old man who'd lost his appetite for conflict. *What would Sophie think if she could see me now?*

At the top of Kelly's Mountain the rain briefly turned to sleet.

Sophie was standing in my doorway, arms folded, something clearly on her mind. Strickland had been in Kingston for nearly nine months by then and was complaining to anyone who'd listen. Obviously Sophie had been listening more sympathetically than I had been.

"I'll be recommending reclassification for Dwayne," she said.

"That's nice," I said. "So he's 'Dwayne' now, is he?"

She ignored that. "If I have my way he'd be in minimum. But I could use some help from you."

"I'll think about it."

"He doesn't belong here, Tony. They're fucking him around."

Her face was pink. She never used obscenity. People commented on that, her calmness.

"Come on," I said.

"He's been here for more than *eight* months. He was in the hole for three of them. He doesn't belong here, Tony. It's having a bad effect on him."

"He's considered a rat," I said. "It's for his own good he's here. Any other place would be a risk. You know that."

"I want him in Warkworth. He wants to be in Warkworth. They have decent programs there. And please–this rat business. You know better."

"I know what?"

"You know the circumstances."

"I know that circumstances don't cut it in that world. A rat's a rat."

"Circumstances matter, Tony, more than anything. *Come on.*"

I shoved my chair back from the desk and stared at her for a while. I suppressed a resentful comment, and said instead, "You're sticking your neck out, don't you think?"

"It's what we have to do sometimes," she said. "I'm a bit surprised by your attitude. I'd have thought . . ."

"It's the world we live in. It's reality."

"Reality," she said, obviously holding back her anger. "Reality can change. It's up to us . . ."

"I think you should stick to your knitting," I said. "You want to go out on a limb for this fellow . . ."

"'Stick to my knitting'?" she said. "An interesting analogy." She walked away.

I studied the empty doorway, surprised by a deep, deep sense of disappointment.

An hour later I called her to apologize and to ask if I could buy her lunch.

She surprised me and said, "I understand Strickland isn't your problem and it was unfair of me, trying to draw you in just because of personal history. You don't have to buy me lunch."

"I'd like to," I said. "I'd like to have lunch. What do you think?"

"Pick a day," she said.

Lunch with Sophie was near the waterfront. A small hotel dining room fashionably cluttered with large antiques that created little nooks for privacy. She accepted a glass of wine but didn't touch it for a while, holding the stem of the glass between her fingers, twirling it slightly, deep in thought.

Finally she spoke. "I met someone a while back who said he knew you when you were just starting out. Lou something."

Lou was long gone, burned out. "Where did you run into him?"

"In a liquor store," she said and chuckled. "He lives near us, retired. But he mentioned you. And he talked about how some of you came in with such great intentions. You were going to turn the system inside out. Full of progressive ideals."

I drank from my glass, tried not to squirm. Shrugged and looked out the window.

"What happens to idealism, Tony? That's a real question. I see it all the time. People losing their ideals."

"I suspect you know the answer," I said. "You're the psychologist."

"Strickland doesn't belong in max," she said.

"Where would you put him?"

"Medium for sure. Probably Warkworth. Maybe minimum, Bath or Archambault. He grew up on a farm, didn't he?" She sipped her wine now, staring intently into my eyes.

And by the end of lunch I'd told her that I had already agreed to put in a good word for Strickland, to help him on his way to Warkworth. She reached across and grasped my hand. I remember the expression, the smile, the eye-warmth.

"Thank you, Tony. You won't regret this."

Two weeks later Sophie called me. "My turn to buy lunch," she said.

"What's the occasion?"

"I've just come out of a meeting," she said. "Dwayne Strickland will be moving to Warkworth any day now."

In Strickland's final weeks in Kingston Pen, while Sophie worked the system to get him out of there, he and I established a rapport of sorts, talking about the place we knew as home– whatever that means–and "normal" people that we knew.

"Maybe we could change your name to MacInnis," I told him. I was trying to be helpful.

"Nah," he said. "Why would I do that?"

"Word will be out in the system, you ratted out the Horse and Driscoll."

"I didn't fuckin rat out anybody." His face was flushed. So much for anger management.

There had been no formal charges in the death of the Italian as the only evidence was circumstantial. So corrections punished the suspects as best we could. Mess up their miserable lives a bit more. "Fuck them up," was how we put it in our private justice system.

"They're being shipped out," I'd informed him. "One to the

Special Handling Unit at Ste-Anne-des-Plaines, one to the max in Renous. Let's just say life is gonna be a bit more complicated now. Their families are back here, Ste-Anne is infested with bikers, and Renous is in the middle of nowhere. They'll know there's a reason for the change and they'll know what the reason is. You'll get the blame, just based on the rumours."

"So what help would that be, turning me into a MacInnis?"

"Strickland kind of stands out. Why not make it easy on yourself?"

"Thanks but no thanks. I always kind of got off on being who I really was."

"Suit yourself," I said.

Rat. How glibly I had used the word. I knew that I was taunting him, knowing every time how that simple word would get a rise, briefly knock his irritating cockiness aside. Dealing with them is a constant struggle for control.

The rain was pounding down when I got to the corrections centre, and I ran from the parking lot to the reception area, folded newspaper over my head. Sullivan was waiting for me, impatiently, I sensed. He wasn't what I had expected. He was tall with squared-off shoulders and maybe fifty years old. His face was smooth and tanned and his hair was prematurely silver. He had a white mustache, a crushing handshake.

They put us in a tiny room with a small table and three chairs, a door with a wired window. We made small talk waiting for Strickland. I noticed from Sullivan's ring that we had gone to the same university, at different times of course. But it turned out we knew a lot of the same teachers. I'd just mentioned that my ex was a lawyer, practicing in Kingston when the door opened.

Strickland was wearing baggy prison green but he seemed relaxed, self-assured. He might have been holding court in a high-end hotel. His smile was unreserved and boyish. I felt a sudden pang of pity, but then I thought of Caddy and her sorrow and the pity turned to guilt.

"Hey Bro'," he said, reaching out to shake my hand.

"I think '*Mister* Breau' might be more appropriate," said Sullivan.

"It's okay," I said. "It's a little inside joke from Kingston Pen. The dark complexion, I guess."

"It's a Cajun name, Breau?" said Sullivan.

"Yes," I said. "My biological background is Acadian."

"Biological?"

"It's a complicated story."

"The black guys started it," Strickland said. "And of course it suited–this was one of the rare human beings in the joint."

I felt the heat in my face.

"It's true," said Strickland, sitting down. He folded his hands and studied me. It's how they psych themselves, I thought–the facial calm, the bold assertions, the silences. They're never in a hurry when in custody. Sullivan slid his chair back slightly.

"I think you've lost weight," Strickland said.

"On the contrary." I laughed. "I've been putting it on since I retired."

"So you've gone to pasture."

"In a manner of speaking."

"There was talk in Warkworth. Then someone said something about you being back in St. Ninian. I'd been meaning to look you up. You're on the Shore Road too, the old MacDougall place. When did you get that?"

"Years ago," I said. "Fixed it up. Been there since late spring."

"And Anna. How is Anna?"

"Fine," I said.

"She's here with you?"

"No. She's still working in Kingston."

"That must be tough on both of you."

I studied his face for evidence of knowledge.

He was nodding. "A loss for the system," he said. "I'm not just saying that. What did it for you? Surely it wasn't the Pittman thing . . . or was there just a point where you said . . . ?"

You never know how much they really know. I laced my fingers, rubbed my thumbs together. "Spur of the moment thing," I said at last. "They were looking for new blood, new ideas. Offered a nice package. I had the numbers. It was time, when I thought it over."

"I seem to remember the last time we talked, maybe two years ago. I think it was about Billy Pittman . . ."

I nodded. "Yes. I think so. But in the end it was the big picture." I smiled.

He went silent, and our eyes locked. Then he looked away, as if remembering his lawyer.

"Pittman," he said. "That was—fuck. Tragic." Shook his head.

Sullivan's eyes shifted from me to Strickland, back to me, inquiring.

"Long complicated story," I said. "Irrelevant."

"Yeah," Strickland said. "Probably." He was studying his hands, face grave. Then he looked up. "I remember Anna saying how there were only a few guys like you left. Frustrated idealists, I think she said. Guys who went in during the early seventies, full of big ambitions. Then getting them beat out of you."

The little voice kept saying: *Don't engage.* My head was bobbing, noncommittal agreement.

"Anna would say you'd have had to be more like her old man to make it for any length of time. The old-timers, being tougher than the cons, learned to think like inmates. It's all about your own survival."

"The cons are usually passing through," I said, the little voice now hissing, *Don't engage.* "Most of us are there for life."

He laughed. "Exactly. How often I thought exactly that."

Sullivan intervened then. "Why don't you guys talk about how you first got to know each other? I'd be interested. There's quite a difference in your ages."

"How do we know each other, Dwayne? You start. I'm trying to remember how old you are anyway."

"Twenty-nine," he said. "Heading for the big three-oh. What about yourself? I think you said you were in school with Aunt Maggie. But if you're retired . . ."

"Went out early," I said. "I'm fifty-five."

"Wise." Strickland was smiling at me, a private and communicative smile. We are from the same world, I thought. And not just home. I have more in common with him than with the lawyer in the suit.

"How are you passing the time here?" I asked.

"The usual," he replied. "Reading a lot. Watching way, way too much television. You following that shit in the States?"

"Not really," I said. "I haven't got a TV. I read what's in the papers. And of course it's all they talk about in the store."

"Ah," he laughed. "The store. But you must have an opinion."

I shrugged.

He tilted back in his chair. "For my money it's all about the oil. The Americans will do anything to get control of oil. It'd be the same for us if we had oil they wanted."

"We have tons of oil," said Sullivan. "They're buying it as fast as we can pump it."

"My point exactly," said Strickland nimbly. "You'd see how quick they'd be in here with their Marines if we ever decided not to sell it to them."

Sullivan patted a jacket pocket, retrieved a pen and a folded wad of paper, unfolded what appeared to be notes, studied them briefly. "Now," he said. "Let's get down to it. You guys knew each other inside, I gather."

"Not really," I said, studying Dwayne's face for some indication of how much I should reveal. "We had some dealings back in '98 and '99 about a particular situation. I didn't see a lot of Dwayne after that."

"But Anna, Mrs. Breau–after I went to Warkworth–became my salvation." Dwayne was talking straight to Sullivan. "Her father was the warden there and I had a few little privileges. Nothing unusual. But like, for access to books and such. I was thinking of taking some university courses. Anna and her father helped me big time. I started. English lit. Made good marks, found I had a talent for stories. Wrote a few, actually.

Nothing you'd show anybody other than, say a friend, like Ann–Mrs. Breau."

"She never used my name," I said. "Always went by Moroz. Like her father."

"There you go," he said. "I just took it for granted. She was always Anna as far as I was concerned. The once I called her Mrs. Breau she corrected me. 'Just Anna,' she said. And that was that. You'll give her my best?"

"For sure."

There was a movement on my right and I realized that Sullivan was looking at his wristwatch.

"So the here and now," Sullivan said. "Maybe you can tell Mr. Breau about why we're here. All off the record–just to be clear. Let's start with how you knew the deceased."

Strickland studied his hands, furrowed his brow, looked up at me. "You know her family, I guess. Her mom, really her grandma, would be closer to your age."

I nodded.

"If you're talking to any of them, not that it would do any good . . . I um . . ." He shook his head and looked away briefly.

"How did you know her?" I asked.

"I didn't really," he said. "She was just a kid I saw around. I was living alone in the old place, the old home, and they'd drop in. There isn't much around, no place for the teens to hang. The store, I suppose. But that's discouraged. So they'd come to my place. I guess they felt comfortable there. It started with just one or two. Then there would be maybe a dozen regulars coming around when they wanted to get out of the house or didn't want to go home. To tell you the truth, it got to be a bit of a pain.

They seemed to think they could come by at any time." He paused, studied my face. "I suppose you heard all the rumours."

"What rumours?"

"That I was dealing drugs, that I was a fag. You know the way the place is."

I shook my head. "I keep mostly to myself."

"Good policy," he said.

"So Mary Alice, she was one of the regulars?"

"Not at all. It was mostly boys–kids from families that don't care or don't know their youngsters are hanging around with an ex-convict. Or kids who don't give a–don't care what their parents think. I don't want to try to make myself sound pious, but I was actually trying to get through to them. A lot of the dads are away, out west, working."

"How were you trying to get through to them?"

"You can imagine. They wanted to hear stories from the inside. Or about the crimes I'd done. The holdups. Like I'm Jesse fuckin James. Like there was something glamorous about crime and prison. I cleared that up, for sure. Couple of stories about the skinners and the chicken hawks and what happens to pretty kids like them inside."

His tone and his expression projected a kind of sorrow.

"So how did someone like Mary Alice end up at your place?"

"She came maybe once with some young fellow who was one of the regulars. I thought a boyfriend, but I asked him later and it wasn't like that. She was from a good family but was acting up a bit, wanting to hang out with the rougher guys. Anyway she landed in with one of them one night, I think in August. It was late. They had a six-pack. Wanted a place to sip a few beers, watch a video. I said make yourself at home. I went to bed before they left."

"This was in August?"

"Early August, I think."

"Who was the guy?"

"I can't remember. They all kind of blur together in my memory."

Sullivan interjected. "We have the name of the young lad he's referring to. I've spoken to him on the telephone and he's able to confirm what Dwayne is telling us. He's on an oil rig somewhere in northern Alberta, but he'd come back."

"So imagine my surprise," Dwayne continued, "when she arrived alone, maybe a couple of weeks later, looking kind of wrecked. I was getting ready to go to bed but I let her in—one of those moments I'll spend the rest of my life thinking about. One tiny little action—you step aside, hold the door open, she walks in and, you don't know it yet, but the rest of your life just flew out through that same open door."

We sat in silence, Sullivan and I processing his words for truth.

"Anyway," Dwayne said, clearing his throat. "She was a pretty girl—in a wholesome way, not at all sexy or anything. But she looked like shit that night. She told me that she'd had this big blowup with somebody at home. She said she needed a place to crash. I sympathized. I've been in her position a hundred times myself. I got a blanket and I put it on the couch, along with a pillow. I went to bed."

"You didn't talk to her at all?"

"Nothing that I can remember. Oh—she asked if I had

anything to drink. I think I had a heel of rum and she asked if she could make a toddy to help her sleep. 'Sure, go ahead,' I told her."

"A heel."

"It was a forty-ouncer. There might have been maybe four or five ounces in the bottom. At the most."

"Had you ever seen her drink?"

"A beer or two on that other visit. After they'd been there a while I realized that what they really wanted was to smoke a little weed. I suppose I should've drawn the line at that. But, anyway, I didn't."

"Were you aware of any drugs that second time?"

"Nothing. She wanted to make a toddy and that's what she was doing when I left her. I can still see her standing by the kitchen counter with her arms folded, watching the kettle."

"Then what?"

"Then what? Not a thing. I went to bed. Slept. In the morning I had to drive to Halifax. I left at six a.m. The living room was kind of dark but I could see that she was there, curled up under the blanket. Sound asleep, I thought."

I let the silence hang.

"And that's the God Almighty truth," he added.

"There will be toxicology, I assume . . ."

Sullivan interjected. "The toxicology–and this is confidential until it comes out in court–the toxicology revealed the significant presence of a narcotic, possibly oxycodone, in her system. The official cause of death was cardiac arrest."

"She was seventeen."

"We're trying to get her medical records to determine if there was any prior history of coronary disease, for her or near relatives. I believe her grandfather died quite young of a sudden heart attack."

"He wasn't a blood relative, as far as I know," I said.

Strickland said to Sullivan: "He'd know." The tone was neutral.

Sullivan said, "I see. Well, given the circumstances, Dwayne is in a strong position to get the charge reduced and a reasonable outcome. Obviously the Crown will want to be seen to pursue this aggressively because of local sensitivities. Her age and background. Being a young woman with a promising future, one way or another related to almost everybody in the place from what I hear. But the facts speak for themselves."

I studied Strickland's face. "Oxycodone?"

He made a face and shrugged. "Don't look at me. God knows where she got it. She could have got it from home, for all I know. She told me she lived with old people. They get it real easy."

"So you have no idea where she got it?"

He raised his right hand, looked me directly in the eye. "Swear to God, on my mother's grave."

Our eyes were locked, and he didn't blink. I let the silence grow.

Finally I said, "So what were you doing for five days?"

Strickland shrugged. "A bit of business. Met some friends. Enjoyed the city. I have a female friend up there. She can confirm everything."

"And how did they trace Mary Alice to your place?"

"No idea," he said. "I assume one of the regulars said try there. Anyway, I hadn't even locked the door behind me when I left." He laughed. "Some murderer, eh?"

"The fact is," said Sullivan, "the Crown knows they have an extremely weak case. This murder charge is a knee-jerk reaction to the local mood. I think they came on strong because they're as anxious as we are to settle this without a trial. We're talking about an agreed statement of facts and some kind of a saw-off on sentencing for a guilty plea. They're pushing for criminal negligence causing death. I think we can hold out for bodily harm. Get off with time served."

"Sounds like they don't have much of a case at all," I said.

"My thought exactly," Strickland said.

Sullivan waved his hand. "Look. Let's be realistic. Dwayne here has a serious record. They're gonna try to make the case that he was a drug dealer and the source of the OxyContin that's been showing up around the place ..."

"That's all horseshit," Strickland interrupted.

"I'd rather play it safe, argue for probation. A period of house arrest. Community service."

"Right," said Strickland. "I can imagine the community service ..."

"What *would* be helpful," said Sullivan to me, "would be someone of your background and obvious stature to give us an affidavit for pre-sentencing. Talk a bit about how Dwayne grew up, the things he was up against, kind of an outsider in a tight, dare I say, inbred community. What he was like as an inmate, how he worked to turn his life around. You know his institutional history, which was pretty positive, I understand. What do you think?"

"An affidavit," I said. "I could be called then, and cross-examined?"

"Technically."

I suppressed a smile. Technically? "I'm not sure that I could be very helpful. We grew up in the same place, but at different times. I never met him here. I think the Crown would argue that any insights I achieved in prison would have been affected by the circumstances."

"That I was putting on an act?" said Strickland.

"I wouldn't say that, but someone else might."

"I think your words would carry a lot of weight," said Sullivan. "We'd be before a judge and I think he or she would pay attention to anything you had to say."

Nobody spoke for what seemed like a full minute. "What do you think, Dwayne?" I asked.

"I hate putting you on the spot," he said. "You're probably thinking about how you gotta live there. What they're going to think. But you've always been one for doing the right thing, eh."

His eyes were steady, unblinking, a slight smile at the corners of his mouth. "Plus, I think you probably owe me one."

"Owe you?" said Sullivan. "Owe you what?"

I cocked my head. "Where have I heard that before?"

"I'm just sayin'."

"Do we really want to talk about that again, Dwayne?"

"What's the downside?"

"About the Italian? You're sure."

"What Italian?" Sullivan was puzzled.

"There was a situation," I said carefully, "when Dwayne had a choice to make, whether to respond as a convict or as a citizen."

"I see," said Sullivan. "I'm assuming he made the right choice."

"I couldn't say for sure," I said. "I couldn't swear to it."

"How about if I tell you up front," Strickland said. "I ratted out some guys for a murder in the joint."

Sullivan seemed to jerk backwards, face surprised.

"You did?" I said. "Not to me."

"No. I kept you out of it. I told the IPSOs. I also told the shrink, the cute one, Sophie. You can check it out."

"I don't work there anymore."

"You still have contacts."

I shook my head. How much should I disclose? How much does he already know? "It's pretty sensitive," I said.

"Mr. Sullivan put his finger on it," said Strickland. "Comes a moment in everybody's life when you gotta pick a side. Right or wrong. Even if everything is on the line. You know what I'm sayin', Tony?" His eyes were briefly anxious.

"I'll have to think about it," I said, suddenly too warm. "You'd really want that on the record, Dwayne? Public testimony that you informed on a couple of other inmates? Guys like the Horse and Driscoll? The media would be all over it."

"If it would get me off I wouldn't have to worry, right? They're both doing life twenty-five. Maybe facing dangerous offender. We'll all be old people when they get out. Anyway, if we can keep it from going to trial, who'd ever hear about it?"

"I'll think about it," I said.

"Oh. And you should know Mr. Sullivan plans to get in touch with Anna. You can maybe let her know."

"Anna and I aren't together anymore," I said.

"Oh, really?" Dwayne's surprise was genuine. "Christ. That must be tough. Since when?"

"It's not really relevant," I said. "Suit yourself about getting in touch with her, though I can't imagine how she might help."

"Character," said Sullivan. "She can talk about his character and how hard he worked to improve himself."

"Anna was the best friend I ever had, for a while there," said Strickland, face now slightly flushed. I asked myself if I was imagining some insinuation in his tone.

"I envied you," said Strickland. "I really did. I'm really sorry to hear that you two split. Anna is one of a kind." His eyes were actually misty.

I stood, reached out a hand. He clasped it. "I'll think about it," I said. "You think about it too—about me bringing up the Vito business." I shook my head. "Give it some serious thought."

"Thanks for your time," Dwayne said. "And be sure to remember me to Anna, if you're talking to her." Was there a hint of mockery in the tone? "Come back sometime," he said, all smiles.

"We'll see."

"I'll do the paperwork. Get you on my visitors' list."

"Sure thing."

"It's a really, really short list." Smiled again, calm and handsome, confident.

"Oh, and the kid's family," Strickland said. "Really. I really mean it. I can only imagine what they think."

Driving away, the wind and rain were delivering a full-bore autumn storm, a preview of the coming winter. Imagine this as snow, the groaning windshield wiper seemed to say. But I was still with Strickland, weighing his sympathetic words for honesty, some evidence that he grasped the reality of his situation. The legal case was weak, almost non-existent. But he didn't seem to understand that in the court of public sentiment, he was in deep, deep shit.

5.

The rumour spread that Strickland was going to plead guilty, save everybody a lot of heartache. At the store, there was general approval. I didn't ask, "Guilty to what?" Or comment, "We'll see how pleased you are when he pleads out on negligence causing bodily harm or less and gets what you'll consider a free pass." Time served because he'll have been in jail for months by then; community service, whatever that might be.

Caddy called the night before Strickland was to appear in court for a plea and pre-sentence arguments. She told me she had to be there and asked if we could go together. She needed moral support. "I'll pick you up," she'd said. "Be ready, I'll not come in."

The next morning I watched the lane, nervous as a boy, for half an hour before I saw her car.

We showed up at the courthouse early, and already the parking lot was full. Caddy had warned me there would be a crowd and the seating would be limited. Maybe thirty people filled the chairs, some standing at the back, Neil Archie among them. Caddy sat beside me, thigh and shoulder warm on mine.

Nearly half the courtroom was a large enclosure separated from the public seating by a rail; pale maple panelling, long tables, chairs for lawyers. A bench behind the lawyers' tables, reserved for the accused. A jury section, witness box. A lectern. At the front a kind of altar for the judge, the high priest of the business; a high-backed chair flanked by flags; above the flags a flattering portrait of the Queen. In the front rank of the spectators, young reporters were laughing, chatting, clasping notebooks. Coming in, one of them attempted to engage with Caddy but she just looked down, hurried by. When I realized she'd looped her arm through mine, I smiled.

Lawyers sauntered in, stood inside the enclosure, posed thoughtfully organizing files on tables. Sullivan was there, talking to a prosecutor who was frowning. Then a door clicked open and everyone went silent. Three men in uniforms, bulky in protective vests, flanked Strickland. He was wearing a pale green shirt and a dark tie, black dress pants. He'd had a haircut. I thought with a slight twinge of resentment that he was the best-looking man in the room. Young, trim. He could have been an actor in a movie drama. Brad Pitt maybe. He looked straight ahead, face grave. They ushered him toward the bench behind his lawyer where he sat, one of the officers beside him. The other two withdrew to stand like sentinels at the back of the room.

Caddy gripped my arm, just above the elbow, followed every move he made. He stood, nodded to the officer beside him, bent to talk to Sullivan briefly, then sat again, leaning back and looking around, frowning. Sullivan turned to him, talking rapidly, but Strickland was just staring straight ahead.

"What's going on?" Caddy whispered.

"I'm not sure."

Then another door opened and a woman's voice called, "All rise." Everybody stood and suddenly it felt like church. A bulky older man in robes entered, looking grumpy. He made his way to the high chair. The woman loudly made another proclamation: Court was formally in session. The judge sat, reading glasses on a nose that seemed to be enlarged and unusually red. He peered quickly at a sheet of paper, then leaned forward and looked down, spoke directly to the Crown. "You're ready to proceed?"

The prosecutor stood. "Your Honour." He paused and glanced with what appeared to be disdain toward Sullivan. "My friend has just informed me that he has a brief statement he wishes to make to the court, a matter that could affect proceedings here today." And he sat.

Sullivan rose, thanked the Crown. His voice was muted by what seemed to be uncertainty. I had to strain to hear.

"Your Honour, this is a little bit awkward but I find myself in the position of having to ask the court for an adjournment."

He was shifting nervously from foot to foot, shuffling papers. The prosecutor sat with his elbows on the table, hands on either side of his face.

The judge looked angry. "My understanding was that we

were here for a plea and pre-sentencing arguments. Are you telling me that this has changed?"

Then Strickland was on his feet. "I want to say something."

Caddy grabbed my hand. Strickland turned, as if to address the room. His guard was standing, too, looking confused.

"Sit down," the judge said firmly. Strickland faced him.

"No. I'll sit down when I'm finished—"

"Sit down, and shut up," the judge enunciated with forced calmness.

"I'm not pleadin' guilty for the convenience of the court. I've seen too much of that."

"I'll have you removed," the judge said, voice rising.

"Not until—"

"Officer, remove the prisoner."

The burly deputy reached for an elbow but Strickland snatched his arm away. He swept his hand around the room, half-turning toward us. I realized I'd abandoned Caddy's hand, was on the edge of my chair. They don't understand the situation, I thought, heart racing. They don't get it, not even the officers. This is new to them, this defiance. Then Sullivan was on his feet, speaking quietly to Strickland.

Loud enough for all to hear, Dwayne said, "I'm not going to lie because you want everything nice and tidy. I'm not going to play that game. I know the ending . . ."

He didn't get to finish the sentence, as three officers overwhelmed him. There was the rattle and the click of a handcuff and he was being roughly quick-marched away.

Sullivan turned back to face the judge, shoulders slumped. "Your Honour, I can only offer my apologies to the court . . ."

"Am I to take that as a not guilty plea?" the judge asked. Perhaps I imagined that he was now actually holding back a smile. There was a nervous chuckle from the crowd.

Sullivan seemed speechless. Then he said, "I'd like a moment to confer with the Crown."

The prosecutor turned and stared in mock amazement, held up his hands and shook his head. The room was silent. The judge studied the lawyers for what felt like a full minute. Then he said wearily, "I'd like to see you gentlemen in chambers." He stood.

"All rise," the woman cried.

I turned to Caddy. Her face was blank. "Come," I said. "Let's get out of here."

"Do you know what just happened?"

I shook my head. But of course I knew. Strickland didn't trust the lawyers, didn't trust the court, backed out of a plea bargain. He could feel the public appetite for punishment. And maybe it was true: maybe he was innocent, unwilling to put himself at risk. He used the word "convenience." I knew exactly what he meant.

Neil stopped me as we walked out. He nodded at Caddy. "Hello Neil," she said and continued on without me.

"If you have a sec," he said to me, then leaned close. "What did you make of that?"

"Who knows," I said, and tried to move on.

He caught my arm. "Hang on a minute." He looked around, then dropped his voice to a whisper. "There was a rumour going around that you were going to testify for that fellow. Put in a good word for him, so they'd go easy on him. I didn't believe it for a minute, knowing how close you and Caddy were." He laid a hand on my shoulder, squeezed. "Anyway, he saved us all a lot of trouble."

"Not sure I follow, Neil," I said. I was genuinely puzzled.

"After that performance? They'll throw the book at him."

"We'll let the system do its job," I said.

He laughed. "Yes, the system. We know all about the system, don't we, Tony."

Outside Caddy was waiting in her car, engine running, windows up as reporters tried to get her to speak to them. There was a television camera. I pushed through but the car door was locked and I was trapped for a moment. "Sir, is it true you knew Strickland in prison?" someone shouted. The door lock popped and I climbed inside. The car was moving even before I had the door closed.

"They're like vultures," she said.

"Just doing a job," I said.

"What did he want?"

"Who?"

"You know who. That Neil."

"He heard a rumour that I was going to go to bat for Strickland, before sentencing." We drove in silence. She was staring straight ahead.

"So aren't you curious?" I asked at last.

She shrugged. "I can't imagine what you could say."

"His lawyer thinks I could help him. He got involved in something when he was in prison."

"I can imagine."

"Anyway, I said no."

"I see."

We drove away in silence. Then she sighed. "So where does this leave everything?"

"In limbo for a while," I said. "They'll have to prepare for a preliminary hearing. The Crown was hoping to avoid that. Just to get it over with."

"Weren't we all," she said.

I stared out the window at the leaden sky. There was so much I could have told her, so much I could have predicted about the weeks and maybe months ahead. But I realized that we were strangers, she and I. Estranged by time and life, our only link a distant, painful memory. Childhood, really. I studied the dark spruce trees that lined the road and was taken by surprise when I felt a surge of grief I'd long assumed to have gone cold, like an old volcano. I almost spoke but caught myself. Tears welled. She turned down a gravel road.

"Stop the car for a minute," I said, and opened the door while the car was still moving. She hit the brakes and looked at me, alarmed. "Is there something wrong?"

I walked behind the car and just stood there, breathing deeply, saying to myself, "Get a grip for Christ's sake." Then I blew my nose. Then went back, sat, looking straight ahead. "I'm okay now."

"If you ever want to talk . . ." she said.

———

Standing at my door as she drove away I watched the car diminish in the lane. It's a long lane that disappears in a turn that is obscured by spruce and juniper and tangled hawthorn. The engine sound was gone before I lost sight of the car and it seemed almost ghostly, floating off in silence. I became acutely conscious of a gathering breeze, and of a stinging on my face, granular snow thickening the air around me. Then the wind sound hushing trees, the caressing *whoosh*, and in the distance, beyond the field, the dark sea rumble. It was like I'd never been alone before.

I told myself: *This is what you wanted. You wanted solitude. And how many days did you imagine this peaceful emptiness, this liberation from the grim ugliness of the limestone walls, chain-link fences, barbed wire, grimy institutional pastels.* The names rolled through my head: Kingston, Joyceville, Millhaven, Collins Bay. Once proud, lovely place names now appropriated by the purpose they've obtained. Penitence and punishment. The false promise of redemption.

So what caused this sudden sense of abandonment? Perhaps the way it all ended–a marriage, a career. So much untruth, so much misunderstanding, so much unfinished business. Strickland's futile gesture said it all: How deals get made; the convenience of the system; the perversion of justice.

I unlocked my door. It sticks, still unaccustomed to frequent opening and closing. *I'll have to get somebody to look at it,* I thought, but then realized there isn't anybody. Everybody useful to the place has gone out west. Heartland of prosperity and anger. Years and years resentful of the east's prosperity; now prosperous, but angry still; resentful of resentment. I felt a smile on my face but nowhere else.

Tea maybe. Too early for a meal. I thought court would eat the day. There was a musty smell, ooze from the muddy cellar. Something else to fix.

When did I start longing to be liberated from the prison world? I remember it was fairly early on, before Anna. Ten years at least before Anna, I'd become disillusioned with all the platitudes about the potential for "correction" of deviant behaviour. Then Anna opened up another life, a healthy life I thought, insulated from the violence and hypocrisy and hopelessness I saw around me every day. I could go to work each morning with a smile, look forward to her comfort and perspective. I could, for long periods of time, forget the reality of where I worked, with whom I worked, forget that work had once been a vocation.

Somewhere in the remnants of my early, optimistic life I still have the book the sociology professor was reading aloud the first time I noticed Anna in the classroom: *The more effective any individual or group of individuals is in getting the categories of deviance and crime imputed to others, the more effective he is in getting the categories of morality and law-abiding citizen imputed to himself.*

The professor let the words sink in, pacing back and forth, index finger buried at the page. I realized that I was staring at Anna. She caught my gaze, held it for a moment, smiled and winked. "There you have it folks," the professor said dramatically, "the Manichean motivation for our justice system. Classification, depersonalization. Good and evil, black and white, them and us."

Then, staring out the window at the sunny day, sunlight on his face, he said, "At least the Manicheans were honest—they believed in killing anybody who didn't fit the proper category. We isolate and dehumanize them, and then we turn them loose expecting them to act like normal humans."

He turned full face to the room: "And it doesn't. Fucking. Work."

Light tittering agreement.

"What did you think?" I asked Anna afterwards.

"I think he's on the right track," she said.

After that we always sat together.

I stared into the glare of the refrigerator. Too much empty space. Too much shelving, bare and shiny, too much light in there. Remembering the fridge at home in Kingston. Things piled on top of things. The cottage-cheese tubs stacked. I must remember to get cottage cheese for moments like this. Kingston freezer jammed with steaks and chops. The frozen vodka. Deli drawer neatly packed with cheese and spicy meats. Nothing in my deli drawer but a hard plastic piece of cheddar, stored too carelessly. At the back of a shelf, six cans of Keith's. Snapped one. Stood, staring at the emptiness.

The wind was rising outside, snow or hail or sleet or all three ticking on the windows, damper scraping in the oil stove, wind bumping in the stovepipe. I closed the fridge, not really hungry anyway. In the living room I went through the CD pile she left for me. Rachmaninoff. She couldn't stand him. She'd complain about his heavy hands. *"Moody Russians, dark and tragic."* Flicked through the titles. Some Bach, perhaps. Nothing heavy or morose. *"Anna Moroz morose, I used to tease. You call Chopin jolly?*

Slavs invented dour." Maybe Brandenburg, merciful timeless music blocking out the moment and the storm the way the beer blocks hunger.

Strickland had caught everybody in the courtroom by surprise and I couldn't suppress the flicker of respect. Caddy wasn't even breathing when he spoke. I'm sure I felt her shudder when they marched him out. We expect people like Strickland to be stupid because so much of what they do, in retrospect, seems pointless. But think it through: You only know what they get caught for. You only know their failures. This is what you learn: their world is upside down. Out here, success is noted publicly and celebrated. But only they know the scores they got away with, the little victories that justify the next big risk. We think the system always wins. Of course, we must believe that. We must believe that everybody on the inside lost. But their successes must have brought enough rewards and satisfaction to motivate the failures that we punish.

In the courtroom I'd watched the faces of the law-abiding citizens as they watched Strickland, earnest, honest faces imputing categories of deviance and crime to him and people like him, reinforcing their own morally secure positions in society. Lawyers' faces calculating where this was going, planning how to get there first, to intercept and thwart. Strickland held everyone's attention because his gesture had inherent eloquence. He had a point to make: I'm not going to play the convenience game; I'm not going to make it easy for the system; I don't owe the system anything.

———

Next morning in the store, five familiar faces leaned over the daily paper, crowded close. "There he is," said one of them, smiling as I walked in. "The man a' the hour."

They were studying a photograph–me trapped outside Caddy's car, smiling. Or was that the look of fear?

"What did you think?" John Robert asked. "Did you have any clue that he was gonna pull a stunt like that?"

"No," I said. "It looked like a last-minute thing on his part."

"So what does it mean?"

"It means that he wants the judge to hear the Crown's case against him. Let a judge decide if the evidence is worth a trial."

"Going for the publicity," said John Robert. "Gonna get his fifteen minutes of fame no matter who it hurts."

I made a face, walked to the newspaper rack.

"You were probably gone when he was growing up." This was from someone else I remembered from long ago. A MacKinnon. Paul.

"Yes, Paul," I said. "Long gone."

"You missed all the excitement. The time he broke in here. And then the accident. Killed the Graham boys. But I suppose the poor fella never had a chance, all things considered."

Silence fell. I wanted to ask: "What things considered?" But I knew the silence was the sound of civility, the consciousness of the unspoken gaffe–*Well, he wasn't really from here, was he?*

I had another vague memory of one of the others, a quiet boy in school, still quiet. "How is your mother, Jake?"

"Good, Tony. Still in her own place. Still driving."

"She'd be what?"

"Ninety-two."

"And still driving?"

"Got her licence renewed for five more years."

"Sharp as a tack, Christy is," said John Robert. I considered the coffee urn. Then the door opened and Neil walked in. The door closed loudly. I imagined a drum roll.

"What's new in the world, Neil?" Collie asked from behind the counter.

"Don't get me going about the fuckin world. You heard what happened in that courtroom yesterday."

An uncomfortable murmur in reply.

Collie picked up the newspaper: "Hey, I see where Saddam is accepting the terms of that resolution they passed at the UN."

"Fuckin UN."

"It says right here . . . Saddam says they can inspect all they want. Won't find a thing."

"You believe that? You believe Saddam? I wouldn't trust that fucker as far as I could throw him."

I turned to Collie, put down a bill to pay for the papers.

"What do you have on today, MacMillan?" Neil asked, his tone suddenly playful.

"Never stuck for things to do in an old house, as you well know, Neil."

"What did you make of yesterday. That Strickland. Some gall that fella."

I shrugged. "We'll see how it plays out."

"Right." Neil was standing with his arms folded, eyeing me, words piling up inside his head, unsaid for now.

6.

It was mid-December. Caddy hadn't told me she was coming by and I was just as glad. No time for nervousness. No time for compulsive tidying, obsessive watching of the lane. I hadn't seen her since our day in court, had happily stopped the memory-meandering.

She stood in the kitchen, a hand on her hip, looking around. "I'm trying to remember the place," she said. "When I was in the CWL, we'd come here to check on poor old Charlie MacDougall. Make sure that he was eating." In her free hand she had a plastic bag.

"I brought a little something," she said, and put the bag on the table. "Fresh out of the oven." She looked around some more. "You're going to have to get a little Christmas spirit in this place."

I laughed. "Hard to remember about Christmas, living by yourself."

"Tell me about it," she said.

"Let me take your coat," I said, but she quickly slipped it off and dropped it over the back of a kitchen chair. She was wearing a mauve cashmere sweater with a loose turtleneck, some kind of heavy chain that dangled down her front, sculpting breasts I hadn't noticed earlier. Jeans. She's kept her shape, I thought, then felt ashamed.

"Well here you are," she said. "You'd never know it was the same place. I think Charlie had a lounge over by the window, where he could watch the lane."

"Got rid of it," I said. "Charlie was on it for a few days before they found him."

She laughed. "Poor Charlie. Sad way to go. But probably in his sleep. Did you know Charlie?"

"Just to see around."

"Poor old fellow. No harm in Charlie. So you bought the place from who?"

"His sister and her husband. They lived in Boston. She worked at Harvard, in the library."

"I didn't know that."

"Can I make you tea, Caddy?"

"Well, I suppose. Just to see you do it." She was teasing.

The tea was poured. She'd brought fresh biscuits that were still warm and so I offered her one. "I'll just have the tea," she said, and sipped. "Very good. You can't go wrong with the orange pekoe." Then: "Actually I'm here to ask a small favour."

"Sure," I said.

"I'm not sure if I told you, but I'm going to go away for Christmas, up to Windsor. I decided to spend Christmas with Rosalie and her family."

"That makes sense," I said, surprised by my disappointment.

"I thought it would just be too much, here alone for the first Christmas after Maymie. It was bad enough, just the two of us, after Jack. I don't want to put myself through that, not this year. Not so soon. Does that make sense to you?"

"Perfect sense," I said. I studied her face, fighting a sudden urge to go to her, stand her up, put both arms around her.

"It was the worst day of my life, when they came and told me ..." Her eyes flooded but didn't overflow. She had trouble speaking for a moment but didn't look away, didn't blink.

I took a deep breath. "You'd come back in the New Year?" She had a tissue then and blew her nose.

"No. I plan to be back before that. They're going to Mexico for the New Year's break. Giving themselves a treat, after everything. They were after me to go with them, but I drew the line at that. Mexico. Couldn't see it myself."

"So," I said. "Whatever I can do."

"I have someone in the car," she said, and put her cup down. When I glanced out the kitchen window the car was empty. She saw the questions in my face.

"Just wait."

Through the window I watched her walk to the far side of the car, open a back door, then bend. She seemed to be struggling and I stood, prepared to go to her assistance. But then she straightened and I could see that she was carrying the little dog, the one Maymie had called Birch.

"I thought I'd kill two birds with one stone," she said. "You by yourself here over Christmas just didn't seem right. And I could tell he took to you the day you met. Maybe he sensed something from when you had one of your own. What do you think? You wouldn't mind looking after him for me, would you? He's good company. A little walk now and then, mostly to let him do his business. I have his food in the car. And his special blanket. Actually an old coat that Jack used to wear in the shop."

The dog was squirming now, and she put him down. He walked toward the door, sniffed the floor, then came back and sat between us, head cocked. I reached out. He sniffed my fingers, then licked them.

"He likes you," Caddy said. "Dogs have a sense about people. Jack would always say that. Let a good dog be the judge of people, he'd say. What do you say, Birch Bark?"

The little dog yapped once then curled up on the floor, chin resting on his paws.

"The other thing," said Caddy. "You're going to have to break down and get a television set. Unless you have one upstairs."

I shook my head. "I was never much for watching TV."

"Well let me tell you," she said. "You're going to find on those long winter nights that in spite of all the crap that's on it, the TV will be good company. At least it'll let you stay on top of the news."

I was smiling. "We'll see."

"Never mind with the 'we'll see,'" she said. "I want to see a nice big TV in here when I get back. And if you're wise you'll also get a generator. We'll get a big power failure here probably in January and you'll end up talking to yourself. You'll end up like poor old Charlie."

"And will I be able to count on you to see that I get fed?" I asked.

"You'll be able to count on me for anything you need," she said. She picked up her coat, smiled, then looked away, some private thought unsaid.

And after she was gone I tried to remember the angry letter that I wrote way back, the one I never sent to her, full of wounded vitriol and speculation. I remember it was autumn when I heard the reason for her sudden flight to Windsor. But the letter and the memory are mostly a blank space now, details in a larger washed-out tapestry. But I do remember one thing: before I tore the letter up, I had signed it Tony Breau, the MacMillan gone for good.

Why did she have to mention Charlie? I've owned the place for at least ten years. Actually twelve, but it will never in my lifetime belong to me. An old house remains the property of the departed, and until I'm gone I know that I will live in Charlie's place. Fair enough. Some young couple will one day bring up a family at Tony's.

Anna would have talked me out of it for sure, but I bought it before I met her. It felt right to me even though people made wisecracks about Charlie and how the place was haunted by his spirit, never mind the cheesy musk of his decaying corpse. But Charlie, for all his loneliness and poverty, had a priceless view. Hills to the east, a long meadow that slopes to the west where on a clear day you can see the bulge of sea pressing up against a pale abstract horizon. Sunsets are memorable, even in the winter when the light seems just as hard and still as frozen water.

I bought Charlie's when I sold the old MacMillan place on the mountain road after Ma went off to her reward. No ambiguity of title there. It had always been MacMillans. Four generations, big teeming families, mostly bound for emigration or self-destruction, common destinies in these parts, until my father came along. Barren Duncan inherited the place. Of course they blamed his wife for the lack of children, as was the tendency. Eventually, they went to the Little Flower orphanage and picked me, a kid already five years old, the way you'd go into the woods, cut down hardwood for warmth. And because I've never been a MacMillan, not in the real sense that is so essential and all-defining here, when the title passed to me I had no qualms about selling the old farm to a couple of dreamy young Americans.

I'd never liked it up there and I haven't driven up that road in years. I always had a trapped feeling and the deer flies in the summer–godawful. The old man would say: they perch in the trees, then swoop down, take a piece out of you and fly back up and sit there eating, just to piss you off. He said so little in his lifetime, Duncan, that I think I remember every word.

I wish I had a clearer memory of Charlie. That way I could more easily dismiss the creepiness I get at nights when I feel his presence, or hear the disembodied sounds that still persist in spite of all the changes I've made. But how can a sound be disembodied? How can absence make a sound, or make a presence felt? On second thought, I feel a lot of absences.

Charlie sure as hell was disembodied when they got through with him. The relatives in Boston ordered up cremation in spite of Father MacIsaac's feeble protests about the inevitable Judgement on the Final Day, the bodily resurrection. They dumped Charlie's ashes down in Graham's Cove, not far from the pioneer cemetery, near where he'd once worked in a lobster cannery, a fact remembered only by a few old-timers among whom, I guess, I now am numbered.

Caddy phoned before she left for Windsor. Just curious, she said: How were we getting along, the dog and I?

I pretended to be hearty. Famously, I told her. He really was great company. I didn't tell her that for a day he'd been lying in the middle of the kitchen floor, on Jack's old coat, snout resting on his paws following my every movement with his eyes. If I left his field of vision, the eyes would close and he'd sleep. I considered it substantial progress when, the next morning, I found him sleeping on my couch. But when I sat beside him and spoke to him, he seemed surprised, jumped down and returned to the coat. I didn't tell her how the presence of another living creature, man's best friend allegedly, actually made old Charlie's place feel lonelier.

Late that afternoon I realized that I was talking to the dog a lot. I heard myself say: "Birch, old buddy. If we're going to be living here together, we're going to have to establish some form of communication."

He stood up, whined softly, walked to the door, then looked back at me.

"I know that you're depressed," I said. "Tell me about depression! I could write a book about it. Anything you want to know, just ask. Pills? You want pills and all their side effects?" He barked once.

"A walk," I said. "Of course. Let's go get some fresh air."

Caddy had brought a leash but I left it hanging in the porch. I thought he'd settled in. My mistake. The moment we were outside, Birch raced off up the lane and promptly vanished. I shouted after him but he was gone.

"Ah, for Chrissake," I said. Then went back inside to get my car keys.

He wasn't hard to find. He was shivering on the back deck at Caddy's. When I walked around the corner he whined briefly, then trotted toward me, his sorrow instantly dispelled by a familiar face. And somewhere near my heart, I felt a surge.

"Let's go home, Birch Bark."

He yapped in the affirmative.

I didn't know there was so much choice in television sets. Cathode ray and liquid crystal, flat screens of all sizes, some bigger than a picture window. RCA, Toshiba, Sony. I can't remember what I bought in 1991, after Anna and I got our first place together. It was mostly for watching movies but for a while we were, like everybody else it seemed, addicted to news of that other Gulf war. Saddam. Bush. Baker. April Glaspie. Kuwait. Oil. Everyone at work an instant expert, everyone a hawk, officers and inmates alike, cheers for carnage caused by smart bombs.

But mostly I remember a hotel room on a summer evening. I

am on the bed, remote in hand watching the long columns of American soldiers in a desert, flashes like lightning in a distant sky. And charred wreckage on a highway, blackened shrivelled bodies; a reporter breathless, face distorted by a too-close camera lens in a too-small room somewhere in Baghdad. Turning to Anna: *Do you believe this?* Anna nodding: *Someone had to do it. Look at what he was doing to his own people. And then what he did to Kuwait. All those dead babies.*

I remember it so clearly: that hotel room in Montreal during *le Festival de Jazz*. She was just out of the shower, her hair still wet. And I said: *Speaking of babies.* And the towel falling to the floor.

We can talk about our babies some other time, she said, walking toward me slowly. *But just us, for now.*

And the TV screen in sudden darkness, ghost images of death decaying.

The appliance store was busy with the Christmas shopping surge. Couples murmuring in front of stereo equipment, dish-washers and refrigerators. "They're still working out the bugs in the flat screens," the salesman said. "This one here's a tried and true. All you'll need. And we can have it down there this afternoon. There's a truck going out in a couple of hours."

The satellite man came the next morning and in spite of myself I felt a mild elation as I studied the impenetrable instruc-tion book. Even the dog seemed interested.

"I hate to admit it, Birch, but this sucker is going to trans-form our lives."

———

I hadn't been to the store in days and knew there would be a backlog of papers there, and questions. People around here notice absence, alteration in routine, which is probably a good thing. Charlie didn't have a routine anyone could follow and so he died alone, quietly decomposing until he was discovered thanks to someone else's routine—some good neighbour looking in, making sure that he was eating. Only to find he definitely wasn't. "We gotta stop thinking about Charlie," I said as I snapped the leash on. I removed it once we were inside the car, engine running. He sat up straight in the front seat. Briefly I wondered about the seat belt, then secured it just to stop the nagging buckle-up alarm. Birch's mouth was open, smiling I imagined, as he watched the passing landscape.

"Good boy," I said, rubbing his neck when we stopped in front of the store. "You wait here." But the moment I opened the car door, he was across me in a bound, and out, trotting down the road toward Caddy's place. I watched him go, a mix of anger and resentment rising. Fidelity and dogs? A myth like everything I've ever heard about fidelity. Go and be damned, I said silently.

But at the door I looked down the road after him and to my surprise he was heading back toward me at a gallop. He arrived, panting, paused briefly at the bottom of the steps, head cocked, then as I opened the door he bounded up and followed me inside.

Collie's business partner, Mary, was behind the counter. "Hey, look who's here," she cried.

"That's Caddy's dog," said a man I recognized, the name Lester floating to the surface—Caddy's brother. And I remembered the September courthouse scene, the struggle with the Mounties. "Lester?" I said.

And he nodded. "It's been a while."

"Yes," I said. "It's been a while."

Then there was a long silence.

"I heard she went away," said Mary.

"The daughter in Windsor," Lester said. "Rosalie. Maymie's mother."

"How much do I owe you?" I asked Mary, as she loaded newspapers on the counter. It had been about five days since the last visit. "Thanks for saving them."

"Noooo problem," said Mary.

"That's nice, you looking after Caddy's dog," said Neil. He'd been standing at the back of the store, almost out of sight, elbow propped on the chip rack. "You and Caddy used to be a number years ago I think."

I laughed. "Christ, Neil. You keep saying that. It was another life altogether."

"The dog was always with little Maymie," Lester said. The silence returned, this time heavier. Then he asked, "What do you think will happen to Strickland?"

I shrugged. "I don't know much about the case."

"I'm betting he's gonna walk," said Neil. "Crooked lawyers will always find a way. Remember where you heard it first, guys. People like that know the system, know how to play it. You saw him in court. An ordinary person would have been shitting in his pants. But not that one. Cool as a cucumber was that son-of-a-hoor."

I knew I was being watched, commentary waited for. I studied the front page of the paper. Iraqi foreign minister saying something. Weapons inspections. Hans Blix skeptical. Considered diverting the conversation to Iraq. Second thoughts. Christmas coming.

"Caddy went away for Christmas," I said. "I agreed to take care of the dog. He's pretty low maintenance."

"I'm surprised you aren't going away yourself," said Neil, tension suddenly evaporated. "Must be pretty quiet over around Charlie's. It isn't easy being alone at Christmas."

I studied him, trying not to show surprise at hearing something close to empathy.

"It's just another day for me," I said.

Nods around, floor being studied. Thoughts unsaid. Always the loner, Tony was. Adopted, what would you expect. Never had any kids himself, even though he was married a dozen times, wasn't he? Thick as thieves with Caddy years ago, until someone knocked her up. Someone not Tony. Suppressed smiles.

Mary said: "Let me get you a little treat, Birch Bark . . ." The dog barked. "That's the boy."

Lester squatted, scratched the dog's head. "They were together all the time, Maymie and this here little guy."

"You must have got to know that Strickland pretty well," said Neil. "Seeing him every day, in the joint."

"I didn't see him every day, Neil. He was mostly in a different institution. It's a pretty large population, as you know."

"Not fuckin large enough," Neil said to laughter. I laughed too.

"It looks like things are finally sorting themselves out in Iraq," I said, holding up the paper. "Should take the pressure off Neil Archie and George W. to invade. Let them focus on the real enemy." People glanced at Neil, expectantly.

"And who might that be?" Neil asked.

"Oh, I don't know. Al-Qaida. Bin Laden. The people who blew up the towers."

"They're all one and the same," said Neil. "As long as that fuckin Saddam is there, it's just a matter of time. You wait and see."

"What do you think, Birch?" Mary said. "I suspect your opinion is worth as much as anybody's."

"Did you call him Bitch?" Neil asked, pretending innocence.

"You're an asshole, Neil," Mary said. And everybody laughed in what I took to be unanimous agreement.

It was pleasant returning to the house with someone in the car, even if that someone was a dog. I left the papers where I dropped them, on the kitchen table. Told myself: you're wasting money, buying papers that end up mostly unread in the blue recycling sack at the end of the lane with all the cans and bottles. Buying papers was mostly a habit from Ontario—a public servant had to keep on top of things. What am I now, private servant, self-servant? The dog sat by the door and whimpered, looking at me, head atilt. Ah. Dog-servant.

"Let's take a hike, Birch." He stood and smiled at me, nodding. "You'll soon be talking back to me," I said.

The trail through the trees was once a railway track-bed. Birch dashed ahead of me, chasing creatures that I suspect were figments of a rich imagination, activating killing instincts from the wild. He always came back for reassurance, trotting by my side until another interesting diversion sent him dashing once again. With a pang of sorrow that was tinged with guilt, I remembered another dog and how, for a long time he resented me, the small intruder who threatened to steal his place in the heart of the MacMillan household. I know this from my Ma, who'd laugh remembering how the dog, who was the same age as I was–five when I'd arrived– would slink out of a room if I was in it, looking back at me with frank hostility.

But he had a kind soul and an instinct for fairness and over time he seemed to realize that the heart of the MacMillan household was large enough to accommodate two needy pets. He lived long for a dog, into my adolescence. And when he vanished I hardly noted it, I was by then so mesmerized by the girl that everybody knew as Caddy.

It was Christmas Eve. Our excursions on the trail had become the highlight of our mornings. The ditches had a skim of ice and among the trees there were patches of dirty snow but the trail itself was bare. I heard the distant sound of a motor long before the ATV raced into view. I stepped to the side of the trail and shouted for Birch, but he'd already taken refuge in the woods. The machines were a common sight and sound on the trail, usually meandering. This one skidded to a stop beside me, and when the driver removed his helmet it was Neil, face flushed, smiling.

"How's the hammer hangin'," he shouted, high on what for him was physical activity. He turned the machine off and the trees resumed their whispering. Birch was back and sniffing around a wheel, then he lifted his leg and pissed against it. Good dog, I thought.

"So," said Neil. "I was thinking after the store the other day. You being by yourself over there for Christmas just doesn't seem right to me. I was telling the wife and she agrees."

"Neil . . ."

"No, the wife told me. 'Call him,' she said. You never met the wife. Girl I found in Boston. A good American who doesn't take no for an answer. And she told me to make sure you come to our place for Christmas dinner tomorrow. Come early, say three in the afternoon. We'll have a couple a cocktails."

He started up the machine again and the dog dashed to the woods.

I shouted: "That's awfully good of you, but I wouldn't want to leave the dog . . ."

"Bring him with you," Neil shouted back and spun away from me.

That night I stood at the kitchen window, drink in hand, sound of people singing on the television in the other room. Outside it was bright from a fattening moon but there was snow falling. I was tempted to walk over to the end of the long meadow and just stare at the sea. In Kingston, I'd often walk to the shore of the lake and stare out, pretending it was the ocean. In the early days Anna would come with me and we'd walk hand in hand, words now unnecessary. But one night she said simply, "It doesn't work for me."

"What doesn't work?"

There was a long pause before she said, "You name it."

"Okay," I said. She took her hand away and folded her arms across her chest, a gesture I always associated with distress or anger. But she wasn't angry, it seemed to me.

"That, for instance," she said, nodding toward the lake. It was flat and still and there was a splash of blue from the moon and glitter from the streetlights, the sound of someone laughing somewhere in the darkness. "I don't know how you can be satisfied with that, pretending it's the ocean."

Anna's family was from Gdansk, which they'd fled in 1971 because of the disturbances after Gomulka. She remembered the Baltic. "A lake is just a lake," she said. "It doesn't matter how big it is."

"Depends on how you look at it," I said

"I suppose," she said. "It depends on what you need, how bad you need it." Then: "If you miss back there so much, why do you stay here?" In retrospect, that was how the end began. Or how I remember it.

I drained my glass. The drink wasn't doing a thing for me. It would be nice, I thought, to walk out to where I could stare at the gulf, feel the gentle kiss of snowflakes melting on a cheek. Get the dog out. But the dog was unconscious on Jack's old coat, on his side, legs stretched out, one twitching, dreaming of the chase, the kill. I couldn't bring myself to disturb him.

Then I heard the newscast theme from the other room. I took the whisky bottle with me, sat down to watch. More about Iraq, quiet streets in Baghdad. Commentary about sanctions, poverty, shortages, people sick and dying. Whether or not this was a country we should fear. Someone on a panel was certain there were weapons stockpiles hidden somewhere. Saddam was starving his own people, using petro money to buy weapons to attack his neighbours. I struggled to retain the information, sift the speculation out of it, the politics and posturing. The way I'd learned when I was working. Listen for the facts, draw your own conclusions, act accordingly.

The phone woke the dog. I could hear him scrambling to his feet. It was Caddy.

"Just checking in," she said. "How are you guys doing anyway? Merry Christmas, by the way."

"Doing good," I said. "Everybody happy. How are things there?"

"Okay," she said, "all things considered. I just wanted to wish you guys a Merry Christmas."

"Same to you and yours," I said. "No worries here. We're great." I held the phone out. "Aren't we Birch Bark?"

"Yap," he said and Caddy laughed.

"Oh," I said. "I've been asked to go to dinner tomorrow. And I was wondering how my housemate would feel about being by himself."

"That wouldn't be a problem," she said. "Leave a light on, and water and some munchies. And maybe the TV. You did break down and get a TV?"

"I did. I'm becoming addicted."

"I'll believe that when I see it. So where are you going to dinner?"

"Neil's place," I said. "He asked me earlier today."

I wondered for a moment if she was still on the line. "I see," she said.

"It wouldn't be my first choice but he wouldn't take no for an answer. The hard part will be avoiding arguments. Neil likes to stir things up."

"He does that," she said. "Anyway the dog will be just fine. I often left him by himself."

"I hope everything is okay with you, Caddy."

"It was the right thing to do, coming here," she said. "But I'm missing my own place."

"Yes," I said. "It'll only be a few more days."

Then she said, "Well, I'd better get back to them. I just thought of you guys there. I'm glad you aren't alone, Tony. Even if it's just a little dog."

"Hey," I said. "It's hard to beat a dog for company. Growing up my best friend was a dog."

"Yes, I remember Bingo, and how upset you were when he disappeared."

"Jesus. You remember? Even his name?"

"I remember lots of things, Tony. Lots and lots of things."

"I don't remember being that upset."

"I remember it," she said. "I remember you were upset."

For a moment, after she was gone, I considered midnight Mass. How long has it been? I poured a drink. An old movie was beginning, *It's a Wonderful Life*. Christmas Eves Anna and I would watch it, ironic and sarcastic. Now something about the familiarity brought a kind of peace. The dog hopped up and lay beside me on the couch, head resting on my thigh.

"Let's watch this, shall we?"

He rolled an eye and it seemed to me he winked. I scratched his head.

"There'll be more about justice in this story than you'll ever hear in any church, eh Birch."

He yawned.

"What's your real name, Tony?"

"What's *your* real name, Caddy?"

"You know my real name. Catherine Anne Gillis. Now tell me." She had grasped my hand and was shaking it playfully.

We were in the red Ford truck, parked near the shore. We had opened the Christmas gifts shyly. Mine was shaving lotion. Old Spice. I dabbed some on my neck. She sighed over the small plastic camera I gave her. "It uses flash cubes," I said. "There's some in the package and a roll of film."

"I'm going to try it out," she said.

"Don't you dare. And you know my name anyway. It's MacMillan," I said.

"I mean born with. Ma said your real name sounds French."

"What's the difference?" There was a low moon, three-quarters full, off to the left, the sea to the right, swishing in the loose shore gravel.

"Tell me!"

And I took the camera from her hands and placed it carefully on the dash, and drew her to me and kissed her deeply and she responded, lips moving gently, arms tight behind my neck. Then she pulled away. "Tell me."

"What'll you give me if I tell you?" I was trying to draw her back, my free hand now between her thighs. "How bad do you want to know?"

She broke free, slid away to the far door, arms folded. "You make a joke about everything."

"Breau," I said. "B-r-e-a-u. Like beau, with an 'r.'"

She was looking in my direction again. "Tony Breau. Neat."

"I wouldn't go that far," I said, fishing for the cigarette pack.

"It could be a singer's name, or an actor."

"What's wrong with MacMillan?" speaking to the stinging smoke, blowing out the match.

"Everybody here is mac-something. Who ever heard of a famous mac-something?"

"There's lots of them I bet. There's a prime minister of England, isn't there? Or was. A MacMillan, actually."

There were little ragged flurries of snow settling around us. I rolled the window down, flicked the cigarette away into the darkness. I felt a chill, started up the truck to get us warm. Grabbed her hand and drew her back to me. She still seemed far away.

"Neil MacDonald is home from the States," she said. "Neil Archie. I saw him this afternoon at Confession."

"You went to Confession?" I said. "That explains it."

"Stop," she said. "Don't be making jokes. You mean you didn't go to Confession?"

"Nothing to confess," I said. "You've made sure of that."

She gave me the sideways look, mouth twisted in mock disapproval. "You're hopeless."

"What's the look for?" I said.

"Christmas Mass and you won't be able to receive? It'll be a scandal. They'll all think you must have committed a mortal sin. And they'll be after looking at me."

"But you'll be receiving . . ."

"Yes, but they'll be wondering just the same."

"Okay, for your sake, I'll go to Communion anyway. My soul is pure."

"You're sure?"

"Nothing a good act of contrition can't repair."

"Okay," she said.

"So were you talking to Neil Archie?"

"Briefly. You should have seen him, in his army uniform. I have to say, he was something to look at. Out of the movies, he was. He was asking about you."

"And what was he asking?"

"What you were up to. I told him you were slaving away at the books."

"And that was it?"

"Well." And she tilted her head and looked at me with mischief in her face. "He wanted to know if I'll go out with him while he's home. He said he'll probably be ending up in Vietnam soon."

"And you said?"

"I said I'd have to check with you first."

I laughed. "You didn't."

"No. But isn't that what you'd have wanted me to say?"

I stared out into the night. The snow was thickening. Then a puff of wind scattered it around.

"There'll be carols before the midnight Mass," she said at last. "The choir has been practicing for weeks."

I nodded. "So what did you say, really?"

"Say about what?"

"About a date with Neil."

"A date with Neil Archie? You're cracked in the head, Tony MacMillan."

Then she slid up close beside me, snuggled, grabbed my hand and draped my limp arm over her shoulder, pressed her cheek to mine.

"I think 'Tony Breau' is neat."

The wind outside was rising and along the shore white foam was rolling farther up the gravel.

"Hey," I said, and pulled her even closer.

"What?" she said.

"When did you start saying 'neat'?"

When I awoke Christmas morning for once the silence of the house struck me as a measure of my privacy and not a reminder of my exile. When I stretched I felt a weight on the bed near my feet and realized that the dog was there, head up, watching me.

"Hey," I said. And he rose unsteadily, moved carefully toward me and licked my face. The sudden emotion that I felt was shocking. Then he jumped to the floor and left the room. I could hear the click of claw on the wooden stairs. The room was awash in a pale light and from what I could see of the meadow through the window the snow had carried on overnight.

Downstairs the dog barked. I swung my legs over the side of the bed. The floor was cold as ice. I imagined other houses, people stirring to the sounds of children already mobilized. Christmas trees and wrappings, music, fragrant kitchens noisy.

I had considered a tree but there's something pathetic about a Christmas tree in a silent house.

Briefly I let myself imagine Sophie with her children. Christmas morning chaos and Sophie's face transformed by the exclusive ecstasy of family and celebration. Odd how easily I could imagine Sophie there among her darlings even though I'd never seen her in her home, never known her children or her husband except as happy images in plastic picture frames.

The dog barked again, a bit more urgently. I knelt on the cold floor, looking for socks under the bed. Realized I hadn't vacuumed in a month. Finally went downstairs in bare feet, opened the door for Birch and felt the cold fresh blast of winter.

He darted pointlessly around the yard sniffing the ground as if in search of some lost treasure, then stopped by my car, lifted a leg briefly at a wheel, then ran into the field and squatted. No need for little plastic bags and poop-scoop here. Then he dashed up the long driveway until I could no longer see him. There were rubber boots near the door and I slipped my bare feet into them. So clammy I winced. Plucked a hooded jacket from a nail and stepped outside.

There was a patch of blue above the far end of the meadow and on the horizon the flutter of what might have been the banners of an approaching army, or another blizzard preceded by a cavalry of prancing cloud. Where was the damned dog? I shivered, squinted up the lane and there he was, trotting resolutely back. Amazing that I should feel such affirmation from a dog who isn't even mine.

The hardest aspect of disintegration is all the ordinary things we have to relearn in the aftermath. Time and toilet seats and toothpaste, the solitary life. So much becomes instinctive when a person lives alone. Reason and reflection become imperatives only when we must accommodate another.

When we went back inside, he went straight to his water bowl, slurping noisily. I fetched three Oreo cookies from the cupboard, tossed them toward him. "Merry Christmas, fella," I said. He pounced, gobbled them, then stared at me expectantly. I retrieved the electric coffee pot and plugged it in, half-filled the urn with water. The dog whined.

"Uh-uh," I said. "You've had your Christmas."

I doubt if I'll ever quite recover the ability to make a decent cup of coffee. In my pre-Anna existence, my coffee would be remarked upon, my bean selection, my technique for grinding, how I frothed the milk so it delivered the texture, taste and visual appeal of cream. I was proud of my coffee. But then Anna usurped the coffee making, as she did so much of my domestic independence, and my skills atrophied. And soon I came to think of coffee the way my former colleague Tommy Steele referred to it: stage-one urine.

Smell of brewing coffee, smell of life awakening for most. Smell of death to me. Death of a life I knew, a life presumed to be endless. The name hit me like a diagnosis—Pittman—a forgotten lump, now revealed to be malignant. We were in a coffee shop, summoned by the Keeper, Tommy Steele.

"What the *fuck*," Tommy said, slapping down the tabloid paper. "Pittman! No mention about what *we* put up with. Makin' him sound like a fuckin martyr."

Everybody was silent. Meredith picking at a fingernail. The mindless morning coffee shop around us clinking, chattering.

"You okay, Tony?"

"Yeah. What's this about Pittman?" My stomach churned. "That was last May!"

"It's in the papers. Look at the headline: *Execution on Upper G.* For Chrissake. It makes it sound like *we* killed him."

"Well . . ." I said. They ignored me.

We'd only faced routine questions in the immediate aftermath. Another inmate rumble on the range, which had been noticeably quieter since Pittman's death. Con-on-con violence resulting in another one of scores of inmate deaths that go unremarked in the outside world, barely noticed on the inside except in paperwork that goes unread.

"Christ," said Meredith. "Isn't there anything else to write about?"

We huddled round, studying the picture of a younger, pleasant-looking Pittman. "Anybody remember the cunt looking like that?" asked Tommy.

"It's the family," Wilson said. "Goin' on about brutality."

"Well," said Tommy leaning back and folding his arms. "One thing I know is we better remember what we said at the time and get on the same page and stay there when the new questions start."

There was a quiet murmur of agreement around the table. I see that moment now as a point of no return.

I returned shaken to my office and after sitting for what felt like an hour just staring at the wall, I picked up the phone.

Sophie answered on the second ring.

"I need to talk to you," I said.

———

I shut her office door behind me. Then I locked it. She seemed to stiffen. "I don't want anybody walking in here," I explained.

"What happened?"

"It's about Pittman," I said.

"Ahh." She stood and came from behind the desk, sat in the chair beside me and clasped my hand. "That was a year ago. What happened?"

"I'm not sure. It got in the papers. The family . . ."

"But you guys are okay, right? You did what you had to do."

"No," I said. "I'm afraid not."

"Tell me what you need to tell me, Tony."

I did, making sure to emphasize my own responsibility. "I could have stood up to them," I said. "But I went along with it. I chickened out. I hid behind the power structure. Tommy was the boss and it wasn't up to me to intervene. But it *was* up to me, wasn't it, Sophie? Any one of us could have called him on it. But nobody did. And now there's going to be accountability."

She folded her arms. Her legs were crossed at the knees and her foot was bobbing. She seemed to be studying her shoe. I stood to go. "I just wanted you to hear it from me before it gets around the place."

She caught my hand again. "Sit," she said. So I sat and the silence closed in around us.

Finally she said, "There can be no going back. There's only going forward now. The issue isn't what happened. It's what's going to happen. You know what I'm saying, Tony?"

I nodded.

"You can't make a bad thing better. But you can keep it from becoming worse. How you do that will be up to you. But I'm sure you'll do the right thing. I know you will."

"What's the right thing, Sophie? Pittman is dead. There's no bringing him back. "

"It isn't about Pittman anymore, Tony. And it isn't about you and Tommy and the rest. It's about a whole lot of vulnerable people. Vulnerable to each other, vulnerable to us. And it's about how the system works to protect them from each other. And from us. You know that."

I didn't know what to say to that.

"Have you spoken to Dwayne?" she asked.

"Dwayne?"

"He might have heard things. Just a thought."

"I'll think about it."

She stood then. "You need a hug, Tony." I stood, too, and she put her arms around me.

"I could happily become dependent on hugs like this," I murmured.

She stepped back and stared at me for some moments. Then she went to a bookshelf. "Do you read poetry?" she asked.

"Only when I have to. And it's been a long time since I've had to. What do you have there?"

"A poem," she said. She had the book open to a page she'd bookmarked. "I don't suppose anybody made you read Anna Akhmatova."

"I'd probably remember a name like that."

"I'll copy this one for you," she said.

"What's it about?"

"It's called 'And after we damned each other.'"

———

The phone rang and the dog barked almost simultaneously. I picked up to a cheerful "Merry Christmas." It was Neil.

"I was thinking I'd stop in on the way home from Mass," he said. "It'll be about noon. Unless you want me to pick you up on the way there." He laughed.

"I'll pass on Mass," I said. "Why don't I just drive myself to your place a little later in the day?"

"Nope," he said. "We're going to have an early dinner, about mid-afternoon. I thought it'd be nice for you and me to do some catching up beforehand. You can stay the night. But if you really want to go home I'll drive you. I know the local constabulary pretty well, in case they happen to be out."

I was surprised by a tiny tickle of elation, perhaps the Christmas spirit that we used to talk about.

"See you soon," I said.

7.

The Seaside B and B was set back off the road at the end of a long lane through trees, mostly evergreens. It had been a farmhouse once, perched on a hilltop and surrounded by fields that were now grown over. I remembered it as distant, derelict, abandoned. Neil had obviously spent a lot of money to restore it. There was a new section attached that almost doubled its size.

"Got eight guest rooms," he said, "set up so we can close up six of them come winter when there isn't much business."

"Do you get a lot of business in the summer?"

"She pays for herself. It's basically something to do and a way to meet people. You get some pretty interesting folks passing through. You wouldn't believe some of them. Movie stars.

Hockey players coming around for the golf and the scenery. You can't beat the scenery."

I hadn't expected such a view. You could see the shore, waves breaking silently and the sprawled gulf writhing, flecked with anxious whitecaps.

"Some view, eh," said Neil. "This was all farm in my father's time. In the family for generations, came down to an uncle but there was always a lot of friction. Passed to a cousin of mine but he got a little careless with the taxes and it went up for sale by the county back about twenty-five years ago. I got a tipoff from the courthouse and bought it at the tax sale. Good thing too. Some big real-estate outfit from Toronto was going after it but I had first dibs because of the family connection."

"And what about the cousin?"

Neil shrugged. "I guess he learned to pay closer attention to his mailbox after that. There was a bit of legal hassle but it's done now. Let's go in."

We were met by a blast of warmth laden with the fragrances of cooking. On the left of a large reception area was a living room dominated by a richly decorated Christmas tree, ablaze with multicoloured lights. A central stairway led up.

"We redid all this," Neil said, "but you'd never know it. I used local carpenters, old-timers not afraid to work with an old place like this. *Hannah!*"

A woman materialized, wiping her hands on an apron. She was small and thin, dressed stylishly, modestly pretty but with a head of over-bothered blonde hair that I found distracting.

"Hannah," Neil said. She extended a small hand and I grasped it.

"This guy and I go back a hundred years. You've heard me talk about him I'm sure. Tony MacMillan."

"Welcome," she said.

"How's the dinner coming?" Neil asked loudly. "Hannah stayed home to cook. Can't get her to darken the door of a church anyway, not even at Christmas. Figured I might as well put her to work getting a head start on the dinner."

He was struggling out of his overcoat. Hannah was smiling at me. "Don't listen to him," she said. "I'm Jewish."

"That's not the point," Neil said, pretending to be cross. "It wouldn't kill you to go to church."

"Lovely to meet you, Hannah," I said. "And for the record, my name is Breau. Tony Breau."

She stared from me to Neil.

"Long, long story," he said, waving a dismissive hand.

He gave me a quick tour of the house, stuffed with a surprising number of antiques, large beds with too many pillows, mass-produced landscape prints on a backdrop of busy floral wall-paper, and the overwhelming artificial scent of potpourri. "If worse comes to worse and you stay the night," he said, "this'll be your room."

"I'd love that," I said. "But there's the dog, home alone in a strange house."

"Right," he said. "Caddy's dog. You should have brought him."

The tour ended in the kitchen where Hannah was monitor-ing the progress of a large turkey in a vast gas-fired oven. The kitchen was impressive, with granite countertops and stainless steel appliances. The contrast to my own sparse, musty quarters, Birch brooding on his coat, was stark.

Neil went to a cupboard and opened a door revealing an array of bottles.

"What'll it be?" he asked. He moved some of them around before extracting one. "How about a nice single malt. This sucker is twenty-one years old, old enough to drink himself." He laughed and grabbed two glasses. Hannah was already sipping on a glass of wine. In the harsh light of the kitchen she looked considerably older than her husband.

"You've done well," I said.

"Not bad for a cop," he said. "Being married to a Jew helped. Right, Hannah? Hannah has the brains in this place."

She met my eyes, brows raised, over the top of her large wine glass. "Was he always such a motormouth?" she asked.

The whisky was mellow and I complimented him on his selection. When Hannah basted the turkey the aroma caused a wave of hunger. I hadn't eaten breakfast, had only coffee in my stomach. I felt the whisky fumes caress my brain.

"So I wonder what they're feeding Strickland today. I bet he'll be eating as good as we are," Neil said. "But he won't have this." He raised his glass and clinked it against mine.

Hannah stood up and closed the oven door, waved the turkey-baster in our direction. "Two subjects that will not be tolerated here today," she said. "Dwayne Strickland and Saddam Hussein."

We ate mostly in silence, bathed in Christmas ballads. I realized that it had been months since I'd eaten like this. Sitting down to a heaping plate, loaded with what Anna used to call "food groups." Everything hot, delicious. I felt myself filling prematurely so I slowed down, listened to the old songs. Earlier it was Jim Reeves. Now Anne Murray.

"Lovely sound," I said. "You must have a great system."

"Top of the line," Neil said. "Professionally installed. We love our music, me and Hannah. I said if we're going to be living here where there isn't much to do we're gonna have technology to enjoy whatever is available. My four-wheeler. A Ski-doo. Satellite TV and the best goddamn audio system money can buy."

"No point scrimping on technology if you like music. It's all in the technology nowadays." I was listening to myself, commenting privately: *You're so full of it. You know SFA about technology.*

"First thing a burglar would head for," Neil said, waving his fork for emphasis. "So'm'a bitch would make a pretty day's pay in here, just that stereo and Hannah's computer." He turned to his dinner, face low over the plate. "When I think of some of the places I worked back in the States. This place would be cleaned out while we're sitting here eating."

"Too bad you couldn't get a good security system," I said. "Something wired for quick response. I was noticing your antiques."

"Hah. I got all the security system I need upstairs in the bed-side table drawer," he said. He took a mouthful of wine. "All the security I need, right there." Suddenly he sounded angry.

I laughed. "I don't have to tell you that the gun laws are a bit different up here, especially for hand guns."

"Don't get me going on that bullshit," Neil said. "Canada's gun laws. The true north strong and free to do whatever the government tells you."

I looked at Hannah. She held her wine glass to her mouth, but met my eyes and winked. She lowered her glass. "There, there now," she said.

"Anyway," Neil said, "it's unlikely to get used around here, but if I ever need it, the last thing I'll be worrying about is the gun laws."

"Why don't we talk about something nice," said Hannah. "You guys reminisce. I love the old stories." She poured herself more wine, then refilled our glasses.

And so we did. Specific boundaries of time and place soon fell away, releasing us to wander.

"The last time I remember seeing you," Neil said, staring at the ceiling, "was I think Christmas, around '65. It was just before I went to Vietnam. I seem to remember talking after midnight Mass."

"I remember you in uniform," I said. "But I'm not sure what year it was."

"Had to be Christmas '65," he said. "I went over in early '66. February it was, in the middle of Operation Masher. That was my baptism." He shook his head, looking grim. "We won't go into it tonight, but I know I got home on leave for a few days, I think in late January. You wouldn't have been around then. In college I think you were."

Hannah returned from another room with a photograph. "This was Neil back then," she said.

He was tall and very lean, his expression stern, hair shorn. I had a quick flashback to that expression, how he'd gripped my hand on that Christmas Eve so many years ago, then lightly tugged my shaggy shoulder-length hair. "Barbers gone on strike?" he'd asked. And then he was gone to war. It was the talk of the place at Easter when I was home. Easter alone, Caddy gone away to Ontario. Easter was near the middle of April that year but it had felt like dead of winter.

"Sure," I said, when Hannah offered to refill my wine glass.

"I was surprised when I heard that you went back for a second tour, to Vietnam," I said. "I'd have thought once would have been enough for anybody."

"I actually considered making a career of the military," he said. "Figured a couple of tours would get me promoted faster. But I soon realized that without an education it wouldn't be much of a life."

"We corrected that though, didn't we, dear," Hannah said.

"After I met Hannah here, she insisted that I finish off my high school, at night school. It was that and the military record that got me on the police. So it was all good in the end. I became an American citizen, the whole shebang. Married Hannah and lived happily ever after. Strange how quick it all goes by."

"Very strange," I said.

"I was surprised when I heard you were after moving back."

"Ah well," I said. "When my marriage broke up I wanted to get some distance from where I was." I instantly regretted the disclosure.

Neil and Hannah were both studying me, waiting for more.

"That would have been tough," Neil said. "That and retirement. That's a lot to cope with all at once. But you're still a young man, Tony. You need something to do."

"Same age as yourself, Neil."

"I have this place, and Hannah here. Hey, did you hear old

Alex MacFarlane got one of those mail-order brides? You could always look into that."

"For God's sake, Neil," Hannah said, and stood. She moved some pots noisily around on the stovetop.

"Ah well," said Neil. "We're all screwed when we lose our sense of humour."

"I couldn't imagine being here with nothing to do," Hannah said, as she started gathering the dinner plates. "The winters, my God. Maybe it's different when you have roots in the place."

Neil was studying my face.

"What makes you think I have roots here?" I asked. Neil looked away.

"I assumed . . ." she said.

"No roots anywhere," I said. "I was adopted. Age five."

Neil stood then, helping Hannah to distribute smaller plates and coffee mugs. "It's quite the story, Hannah. How Tony came here. I don't know if I have it straight. Tell Hannah, Tony."

"You go ahead."

"You'll correct me if I'm wrong. Tony's dad, Duncan MacMillan, had a cousin working in the Little Flower orphanage over in Sydney. And he was visiting her one day and there was this little gaffer hanging around and Duncan spots him and asks about him. I'm not sure of the details. But isn't it correct that on a later visit he got permission to take you home with him for Christmas? And he just never took you back. Wasn't it something like that?"

"Something like that," I said.

"Things were pretty informal back in those days. It worked out great."

"It did," I said.

"And did you ever find out about your birth parents?" Hannah asked.

"Yes," I said. "Eventually I found out about them. Not much to tell." I shrugged. "A couple of youngsters. I heard that my birth dad was killed in a coal mine accident later."

"So that was when you changed your name back," Neil said.

"At some point I realized I never really was a MacMillan, right? Never having been legally adopted."

"That's so strange," Hannah said.

"I remember being around here years later and people talking about this Tony Breau and I didn't have a clue," said Neil, placing the whisky bottle on the table. "We'll have a small one to help settle the turkey. It was a great dinner, Hannah."

"It was a wonderful dinner," I echoed. "Thank you."

"You guys take it easy, we aren't finished yet."

Neil was pouring. "I've never got used to that Breau business. You'll always be Tony MacMillan as far as I'm concerned. As much a part of the place as I am."

"Thanks, Neil. But the truth is I always felt like a bit of an outsider."

"Tell me about it," Hannah said. "They're practically tribal here."

"Ah, get away with the both of youse," said Neil. "We're in God's country."

After dinner Neil excused himself, announced that he was in need of a catnap. "Twenty minutes, max," he said. "I'll be fresh as a daisy. You two can talk."

I actually welcomed the prospect of a break from conversation. There was music in the background again. I recognized a sad violin and another wave of longing leaked out of memory: 1966, young and so unaccustomed to such sorrow that you think it's permanent.

"I understand you went to university," said Hannah.

"Yes," I said. "Not far from here."

"I wanted Neil to keep going with the night courses, work on a degree. But he wasn't much for the books."

"He did well without them," I said. "He must have been quite the policeman."

"He loved his work," she said. "It was a terrible adjustment when he had to give it up."

"It must have been a big adjustment for you, too, moving here," I said.

She sighed. "I miss home. I get back now and then, but it isn't the same."

"I'm surprised Neil didn't consider retiring in the Boston area, where you're from."

"Outside Lowell is where I'm from." She stood, suddenly nervous. "I'm afraid we didn't have much choice in the matter."

"Oh," I said.

"You make a lot of enemies doing your job as a policeman. The danger never ends. You'd know that, working in the prisons. I think Neil told me you were a corrections officer."

"Yes," I said. "I heard that he had a close call, on duty ... before he retired."

She folded her arms across her chest and studied the floor. "He spent his entire service in Roxbury. It was hard, especially in the seventies and eighties. I'm sure he'll tell you all about it himself. If you'll excuse me I'm going to do some cleaning up. You'll be okay by yourself? I could get you something. Another drink, more coffee?"

"I'm fine," I said. "I'm getting good at being by myself."

Her sad, thin smile made me instantly sorry I'd said it.

While she was gone I drifted off to a distant Christmas near the shore, waves gently rippling through gravel, moon beaming through the swirling feather flurries and faces softening, disintegrating, dark sea endless, rolling out of darkness, shushing, Caddy Gillis telling me that Tony Breau was "neat."

"Ma, do I look like a nigger?"

Forks dropped, Ma's eyes wide, jaw hanging, no sound from her gaping mouth.

Duncan was standing, furious. "Who said that? Answer me!" But I couldn't get the words out and now I can't remember who said it or if anybody said it or if I just conflated my own isolation with a word describing otherness.

"I'm not going to ask again. Who?"

Tears sliding, tears of fear.

"Don't tell me then because I fuckin well know."

He wheeled away then, grabbing his coat from a peg. Ma blocked his path to the door, and was roughly shoved aside.

"Get out of the way. You can't let something like that go— somebody like that has to be dealt with."

And it seems in memory that he was gone for days, long enough that when he returned his bruises had begun to fade, but not the words. The words have never faded: Something like that has to be dealt with.

"You're snoring!" The hand was rough on my shoulder. "Look at the expression on him, Hannah. I'm trying to imagine what he was dreaming about. Come on, Tony. I'll drive you home. You got a dog to think about."

He was still laughing when he returned with the coats.

On the shore road he pulled over and stopped the car, turned the motor and the lights off announcing, "I've got to take a slash." He got out.

The night was still, silent. Then he was back but he didn't start the car, just sat there staring into the darkness. He plucked a cigarette package from his shirt pocket, a soft, fat little American pack of smokes. He shook one out, held it toward me. "You smoke?" he asked.

"Not in thirty years," I said.

"Wise."

Now the Zippo lighter, cap snapped and wheel turned on flint, Neil bent over the flame, face pink and puffy, lined in shadow, eyes squinting. "We picked on you something wicked growing up," he said. He exhaled loudly. "No, it wasn't fit, the way we'd pick on you."

"I don't remember much," I said. There was a chill fingering the darkness.

"Mentioning the orphanage, the Little Flower, back at the

house, reminded me." He was staring straight into the night.

He towered over me, leaning. I was sitting in my desk, staring down. Shrieks and cackles, laughter all around. It was like he was leading a singsong: "Duncan gave Christy a little flower for Christmas and it smells like a stinky lily." Then the teacher's sudden voice, ancient Mrs. MacIsaac, large and grey, grasping an ear, dragging Neil away: "That's quite enough. One more word out of you Neil Archie MacDonald and it'll be staying after school for you."

"Kids can be wicked mean," he said. "But there was no harm in it. You were no different from anybody else."

Ma saying: "That Neil, he's nothing but a bully anyway. You tell him that your mother and father got to choose you. His didn't have a choice, they got the first droighneach *that came along. And it's the truth."*

"I remember this time your dad, Duncan, landed at the house. It's vague now. He had a wild temper, Duncan." He puffed the cigarette, eyes narrowed. Cleared his throat. "He was ... anyway, I can't remember what it was all about. Ahhh Jesus, I was only about fifteen. But big. Anyway, the old man got in between us before Duncan got ahold of me. And fucked if *they* didn't go at it.

"Only lasted seconds I suppose. But this is the best part. The two of them took off together. Gone for a couple of days in that old red truck of yours. On a tear. That's the way they were, eh. There was nothin' personal. A dying breed they were. Duncan was a war vet too, I think."

"He was," I said.

"I just wanted to say, once and for all, how bad I felt when I realized the way we tormented you." He rolled the window down. Smoke rushed out and the cold night air refreshed the car. There was a high pale distant moon, stars glittering. He rolled the window up until there was just a small gap at the top. "I actually confessed it once. I went to the chaplain and we talked about it. Things like that bother a fellow when you're seeing people blown to pieces every day and figure it could be you next. You think about all the shitty things you done. Anyway the padre said I should one day tell the person how I felt. Meaning you. So."

He laughed and drew on the cigarette. The ember lit his face again. "I said to that padre, 'You're assuming, Father, that I'll survive this shithole.' He just laughed. He was a good guy, that padre. You could talk to him like that."

He looked away for a while and there was a long silence. "So here I am. Talkin' about how I felt. Who'd'a believed it?"

"I hardly remember anything from then," I said. "But I appreciate the thought."

He reached into an inside pocket and pulled out a flask. "A *dileag* for the old-timers," he said, uncapping it and passing it to me. I swallowed. It was warm from the heat of his body.

"But by Jesus you put me in my place eventually," Neil said, laughing again, coughing on the smoke.

"I did?"

"You sure did. You're not telling me you forget that scene?"

"I'm not sure," I said.

"It was in the old co-op store. You're full a shit if you're telling me you don't remember."

I remembered.

He'd knocked my cap off again. I lost count of how often. But they'd laugh every time. I'd bend down, put it back on, stand up, look him in the eye. He'd do variations. Feint with one hand, then sweep up with the other, knock the cap off. He was fast with his hands, already widely known for his aggression. A bad man on the ice. Played hockey with the men. Fought with the men. He was a head taller than I was, which was convenient for knocking off the cap.

"We're hanging around the co-op one noon hour, the way we always did, and I was picking at you as usual, and you just poled me, in front of everybody. There wasn't a thing I could do. I had it coming. Nobody bothered you after that."

"I don't think I poled you."

"Sure as I'm sittin' here. Cold-cocked me. It was the surprise that did me in. It wasn't much of a punch, if you don't mind me saying."

I'm bending to pick the cap off the floor again and I notice, just behind his heels, a wooden crate full of empty pop bottles. As I'm straightening up I see his gut at the level of my face and without a thought I drive my fist into it, just below the belt buckle where it doesn't take much to do a lot of damage. I drove that fist in without a thought. And he goes backwards over the pop case, crashing down arse over tea kettle. And I stand above him, watching as he rolls, doubled up, face all scarlet with the pain and shame. "You cock ... sucker," he says. "I'll fucking kill you." But he can't get off the floor. And then it's Big Frank, the co-op manager shouting: "Everybody out ... You two, MacMillan, Neil ... I don't want to see either one of you back in here for a week." And all the way back to the school, he's goading, threatening, pushing. But I ignore him and he knows by the silence of the moving mass of spectators surrounding us that it is over. Mercifully frigging over.

He blew a stream of smoke through the small open space at the top of the car window. "All's I remember is you put me in my place. Best thing that ever happened to me. You had balls, my friend. Whatever else you had, you had that going for you. Big ones. Took shit off *noo-body*. It's what we all admired about you, from day one. Not like this piece of shit."

When I followed the line of his arm I noticed for the first time that we were parked near the end of a long laneway.

"Who lives there?" I asked, pretending not to know.

"Your man Strickland," he said. "There was a piece of work . . . from day one."

"But you and I were both gone long before he got here, right?"

"Ah but I heard plenty. I'm surprised you didn't. Total arse-hole right from the get-go. You say you've never been up there?" Neil's voice was now tinged with a skepticism that might have been deliberate.

"Can't say one way or the other," I said.

"Cuz somebody at the store was saying how you once went out of your way to straighten him out, saying how the priest or somebody asked you to weigh in."

"I'm not sure what they're talking about," I said.

"More power to you if you did. Sure someone should have taken him in hand while there was still a chance." He was studying the lane and in the light of the moon I could see a pulse in his cheek, near the jawbone, as if he was chewing gum. He puffed on his cigarette in silence, then he turned to me and smiled.

"There's also talk—I think I mentioned this already—that you were thinking of going to bat for him, come the trial. Word is they were going to try to get a soft sentence. Time served or some other slap on the wrist. And you'd have some influence, being from here and also knowing his situation from when he was inside."

He was staring at me, smile gone, and I wondered how familiar all this seemed to him, a darkened road, a silent car, him in the driver's seat exuding power and moral certainty; some lesser being sitting where I am, light slowly dawning in the brain.

I chuckled. "The store. Wherever this stuff comes from, I'd love to know."

He looked away then. "I hear you," he said. "People without half enough excitement in their lives. I got first-hand experience with how things get garbled by folks with too much idle time and not half enough factual information. You take what happened to me."

"I don't think I heard anything, Neil, apart from what you told me yourself. How you've got a bullet in you."

He laughed. "There's a half a dozen versions of how that bullet got there, Tony. But here's the only one that matters: me and my partner stumbled on a drug deal and before you could shit yourself or say a word everybody in the room was trying to shoot everybody else. Pure chaos, and I'll be honest—pure terror. You hadda be there."

He reached into his pocket for the cigarette pack, lit another. "To hear some of the horseshit afterwards: It was me trying to rip off the drug dealer. It was me and my partner running a protection racket, or we were slum landlords. You name it. In the papers even, a couple of nigger-hating cops run wild. They kind of brushed aside the fact that my partner was a so-called nigger himself. And that he was *fuck-ing dead.*"

I didn't look but I knew he was staring at me intensely.

"I know you think I'm just a redneck, Tony, but I'm not. I know those people. The good ones and the bad ones. So you don't have to say what you're thinking."

I sighed, squirmed for warmth. "We should move on, Neil. It's not good sitting here. We can continue the conversation at my place. Have a nightcap. Or a cup of tea."

At the mention of the nightcap he produced his flask again and drank from it.

"Even after the official report—even after everything was cleared up, no wrongdoing found. Not even what happened to poor Donnie. Never mind what happened to me. Guys in that room had records as long as your arm—but you should have heard the garbage. You'd think I shot Martin Luther King. So here I am."

He chewed his lip. "Poor Donnie never had a prayer."

He was staring at me again, handed me the flask. I just held on to it.

"I'll be honest with you," he said. "I'm here because me and Hannah sat down and figured it was the only safe place for us. Word on the street was that somebody put a contract out, fifty grand to put another bullet in me. Think of that, Tony. A sanctuary is what this place is. I got half a notion that it's the same for you. A safe place. And that's why I'm saying to you that it's going to be up to guys like you and me—you and me, Tony—to keep it that way."

I screwed the top off the flask and drank, gasped, screwed the top back on. "That's not bad," I said to the flask.

"The very finest," he said. "No more second class for Neil Archie MacDonald."

He looked at me again. "So what do you think? Tony. Here we sit, just the two of us. Two old guys with a lot of history and a little bit of future. Not a lot we can do about the history. But what are we going to do about the little bit of future we got left?"

"I don't know, Neil. There's only so much a fella can do to control the future."

"But you gotta do what you gotta do. Take that fuckin Saddam Hussein, over there in Iraq. He's sitting there, one great big threat to all our futures. Which is why they gotta take him out. Weapons 'a mass destruction, you name it. It's only a matter of time he turns them on us. Look at what happened on nine-eleven. That's what you get when you don't make the first move. And then there's this asshole, up that lane, if he ever gets back there . . ."

"You're covering a lot of ground, Neil," I said. "I think we should call it a day. We're getting tired. We aren't the men we used to be."

"No, that's for sure. But here's the thing. My partner there, Donnie Turner was his name. Black as the ace of spades he was. You couldn't have found two different fellas on the face of the planet, me and Donnie. But we were like one man, Tony. No black, no white. We were two parts of a machine. Five fuckin years. I never had a brother but Donnie was close. Closer, I think. Brothers got their issues. But Donnie and me, man." He went silent, voice thick with emotion.

"I know what you're saying, Neil."

"I'm only glad he wasn't there to see what happened afterwards. The goddamn media, liberal politicians . . . the bastards crucified him, and him dead. All they could talk about was the piece of shit he blew away in self-defense, and the other two who survived to my everlasting regret. Moanin' and groanin' about the one with his arm blown off. Arm blown off, my arse. It should have been his fuckin head. But that's not the point I'm making here, Tony. The point is, for all our differences, when push came to shove, black Donnie and white old Neil Archie MacDonald were one man. And that was because of values, man. We shared the same fuckin values. We stood for the same things. You're an educated man. You know what I'm talking about."

"Values," I said.

"Yes, values," he echoed. "You think about it. It's values holds us all together. Keeps us civil. It's values I fought for in the war, on the police. And it was fuckin values kept you in the prison system all those years. We got values to uphold, Tony boy, and don't you fuckin forget it."

He started the engine, turned on the headlights. In the glow of the car interior his face was grim. He turned to me once more before we drove away.

"I just know the kind of a man you always been, Tony. I know the kind of man you are now. And when the old bugle blows, I know in my guts that you're gonna be on the right side of things."

"That's for sure," I said. And he put the car in gear.

Turning down my lane, he asked: "Surely it wasn't just the marriage breakup got you thinking of early retirement. You must have just got tired of babysitting bad guys, I bet. Christ, I wouldn't last a week at that. If I had my way we'd go back to the old days, send them off to some place like Australia. Some other planet maybe."

I laughed. "That might work."

We were driving down the lane slowly, trees close around. "You got a few enemies yourself, eh Tony?" he said with what I took for grim sympathy. "You see that's the trouble. We put the bad guys in jail but then they let the bastards out and it's us who end up lookin' over our shoulder. Strange, strange, strange. Then you got your Strickland."

When the car stopped, I knew I should just thank him and get out. Say good night. Maybe it was fatigue, or the liquor, or maybe it was studying my darkened house. But I sat there pondering his homily about values and I came within a whisker of saying what I really thought, that some of the worst people in the system never get out, that they fester there, day after day, until the bureaucracy permits them to retire. Cops and prison guards. And how the one thing that sustains them is the power they wield, the power to control the smallest details of the incarcerated life, to bully and abuse people in poverty and prison in the name of institutional security, public safety, righteousness and values. And how we are so, so corrupted by that attitude and by our power. I came *that* close to saying it aloud. But was silenced by an overpowering feeling of futility.

"Good night, Neil," I said. "It was a lovely dinner. Thank Hannah again for me. You lucked out there, pal."

"You got that right," he said. "I got a feeling we're going to be seeing a lot of each other. Us old-timers gotta stick together, Tony. Aren't many of us old-school fellas left, buddy."

———

The telephone was winking red in the darkened kitchen. I was exhausted and wanted to ignore it. The dog was leaping on my leg making small whiney sounds. "Sorry, Birch," I said. "Didn't mean to be so long." Then I realized his bladder was probably exploding. I opened the porch door and he shot out. I flipped on the kitchen light. Then I listened to the message.

"Hey, Tony. Been thinking about you."

It took a moment for the voice to register. I'd been anticipating Anna. But it wasn't Anna. And it wasn't Caddy.

"Hope you had a nice Christmas." There was a short laugh. "It's Sophie, by the way. Remember me?" A pause. "Anyway Tony, I just wanted you to know that I was thinking about you, hoping that the day wasn't sad for you. Call sometime, or write. I miss you."

The dog was back at the door and so I saved the message and let him in. Then I listened to her words again, this time for tone. *I miss you.* I took the words to bed with me, played them over and over in my head. They were spoken quickly, shyly. *I miss you.*

8.

My roommate at the university in 1966 was Mark somebody from Halifax and he wanted me to spend the Easter holiday in the city. I was tempted. I had never been there. Had never been anywhere. Wanted to be anywhere but home. Mark's father was a jail guard who worked at Rockhead Prison in the north end. Mark said he could arrange a tour now that the old place was to be shut down. His old man had claimed he met Hank Snow in Rockhead years ago—Hank in there over a domestic fracas. He said I'd get a charge out of his father's stories. Talking to Mark was probably when I first became interested in corrections. But I took a rain check, told him I had to go home, help out on the farm. Didn't tell him how confused and bruised I was.

You could hardly call it a farm, the old place up the mountain road. A couple of hundred acres, mostly woodland; two cows and a garden. When I was younger we had a horse for the ploughing and the haymaking and most years a pig for slaughter. By then my father was away most of the time, working in a mine out west. He'd been a miner in his younger days and went back to it around the time I started talking about university. He wasn't going to be home at Easter, which meant the old red half-ton would be at my disposal, not that there was much to do with Caddy gone. I had to keep reminding myself: Caddy is gone. *I won't be here when you come home.* A pretty simple statement but it took a while for the meaning to sink in. We were never closer than at Christmas when I couldn't have imagined life without her. And I would have bet my life she'd felt the same.

They used to call them "Dear John" letters. I think it was because of a popular song by that name—*Dear John, oh how I hate to write*—a saccharine song about a soldier somewhere getting a letter from the girl back home who was going to marry someone else. Dear John letters were common in university and the people who got them would be teased and mocked until they'd be laughing at their own despair, no matter how they felt.

You deserve to know why I'm going but I just can't bring myself to tell you because I know how you'd react and your reaction would be such a big mistake in the long run.

Caddy and I had never talked about much beyond the moment or the next weekend. Being together seemed so natural and comfortable that I guess I just assumed that it would go on indefinitely. There had been no declarations; the normal passions, which at times became intense, were managed by her. Recently we'd found ways to achieve a certain embarrassing relief on my part. Enough to calm me down, at least temporarily. Mortal sin just the same, I suppose, but a minor kind if such a distinction was possible. It was something else we didn't talk about; something else that, like so much in those years of curiosity, was exciting mostly for the progress that it promised. I thought that we were happy together.

You'll find out soon enough at any rate. And maybe you'll hate me then. I hope so. It'll make things so much easier for both of us. Goodbye Tony. Love, Caddy.

The word sat there. "Love." It was stunning, a discovery. But right after "Goodbye Tony"? There was something cruel about it. I didn't know the words "gratuitous" or "juxtaposition" back then but the effect of those two words, "goodbye" and "love" almost side by side, induced a kind of paralysis. Anyone watching me in the dining hall that day would have seen a puzzled look as I folded up the letter and shoved it in my pocket, stood and walked away from the table. I left my tray behind, food untouched. That was out of character and they'd have wondered about the letter. Bad news from home; Dear John. Looking back now, nobody knew me well enough to read my expressions or to safely mock, not even Mark, my roommate. Some things you never talked about to anybody.

I hitchhiked home on Good Friday. I walked the last two miles and arrived just after noon. Ma was in the middle of the sacred silence, one of the Good Friday traditions, and just hugged me and pointed to the clock, a reminder of the church service at three. I nodded and went to my room and sat there studying my hands. Then I read the letter again. *You'll find out soon enough at any rate.* Find out what? Probably for the first time in my life, I was looking forward to the grim Good Friday service, all purple and slow with medieval dirges making everybody think of hell instead of the redemption it was supposed to promise. For a moment I was sure that I'd see Caddy in the usual place, among the Hector Gillises, three pews back on the right side where they always sat.

She wasn't there. *Ecce lignum crucis.* It seemed to take them a frigging hour to peel the shroud off the wooden cross. Maybe she was sitting somewhere else, among friends. But I had plenty of opportunity to search the crowd during the Stations, when the priest and altar boys circumnavigated the church and we followed the progress, kneeling, standing, praying along. She wasn't there. *Ecce lignum crucis.* Coming back from the rail after the Adoration, near the end, when everybody goes up front to kiss the exposed cross, I caught her mother staring at me with a sad, sympathetic look that told me everything but why.

Saturday and Sunday I spent at the books. Finals would be starting shortly after the Easter break. The history section was about the U.S. Civil War and was unusually well written so that kept me focused. English lit was another matter, all the poetry and essays about love and longing left me staring out the window for much of the time. When you're young each remarkable moment obscures everything before it, becomes a foretaste of forever. Which is mostly good since, for the lucky ones, so much of youth is happy. But it's also why youthful grief, at least for those who are unlucky and unwise, can be so dangerous.

Late Saturday afternoon I went for a walk and on an impulse took a rifle from the rack in the back porch. It was just a .22 but there was something reassuring in its heft, its light fragrance of oil, the smoothness of the stock. Of course that time of year there was nothing left to hunt since anything worth eating had been eating badly for so long or had been eaten by another predator. I think now the rifle was a test. Is life worth living any longer? I had to force myself to seriously consider what it was that generated this feeling like congestion that sometimes made it hard to breathe, that worked up into my head and pressed behind my eyeballs, that sometimes caused my breath to catch and then release in ragged sobs. Is this how I will always feel? Because if it is … *Jesus Christ,* I said more than once. *What's the matter with you?*

I sat on a stone in a clearing and from there I could see out over the water, silvery beneath the pale sun. There were still clumps of granular snow in the woods, darkened and dirty from falling leaves and tree needles. I thought of a distant relative of Caddy's, a Gillis, who went off into the woods somewhere up near the strait the day that Kennedy was shot in 1963. Sitting in a place like this they say he drank rum for a while, then he shot himself with a .303. Or maybe a 30-06. Made no mistake. It was talked about everywhere, lots of speculation. Women trouble, booze, that sort of thing. Then it came out that he had shell shock from the war. War and its aftershocks, you hear about it all the time. And then I thought of Neil Archie MacDonald and the war that everyone was talking about in those days. Indo-China, or Vietnam. In the co-op, people huddled over the newspapers. "God help him, his timing couldn't a been worse," someone would invariably say. Or: "Poor Neil, he's got a lot of the old man in him, couldn't stay out of a fight if his life depended on it." Ma said that at Mass the previous Sunday they prayed for his safe return.

What would that be like? I wondered. Just go to the States and join the army. One of the Americans at the university was saying it would be a piece of cake. They love recruiting foreigners and poor people. No political downside losing folks like that in a controversial war. I could go out in glory, not like this, alone in the darkening woods on Holy Saturday, an instant scandal, like Caddy's distant cousin. They'd never suspect woman trouble. They'd blame the books I bet, blame the pressures of university. I studied the rifle, looked down the barrel. With a .22 you'd have to stick it in your eye, or right up against the roof of your mouth.

I spit out the bitter taste of oily metal and discharged gunpowder.

Then I went home.

Monday morning Ma was looking at me with an expression that spoke of hard questions held back. I didn't help her, offered no entry point. Now that I was sure of things, that Caddy really had gone away, I just wanted to go back to the university, hit the books, lose myself in the finals. Then think of summer work to help with another year's tuition. Or not. Maybe drop out for a year or two. Just after the noon meal she drove me to the highway. I slid out and slammed the truck door quickly, before she could ask. When I was standing on the road, she rolled her window down. "I heard from your father last week. He proba- bly won't be home before Christmas."

I nodded, thinking of his absence for the first time.

She said, "It's lonely with you both gone."

I said, "It'll only be a few weeks though, I'll be back."

"Uh-huh. Then what though?"

"Where is it that he's working?"

"Saskatchewan," she answered. "Some place called Estevan."

I just shrugged. Yes. Then what? "Bye, Ma."

Later, waiting for the next ride, I studied the leaden sky. The air was warm, heavy with moisture. After a series of passing cars, drivers resolutely staring straight ahead as if I was invisible, I channelled disappointment and impatience into that dark place where the grief was and it all fused as in a chemical reaction. Suddenly I wept. No sound. Just tears flowing down my cheeks, around the corners of my mouth. It was a relief in a way. But that was the only time. And then a car slowed down. I wiped my face on my sleeve and trotted toward where it was paused, passenger door swung open, offering a temporary sanctuary.

I spent that long summer in Saskatchewan, working with my father in a potash mine. Duncan never talked much but one evening in the cookhouse he said, "I hear that the young Gillis one gave you the heave-ho." And he smiled. It was a warm smile, free of mockery and I could feel the creeping flush in my face, a sudden heaviness.

"Oh yeah?" I said, all nonchalant. "Where'd you hear that?"

"I don't know," he said. He made a harsh throat-clearing sound, which usually signalled that he was finished talking. But then he said, as if from a great distance: "You're better off. There's a bad streak in those people."

"What people?"

"Those Gillises."

"That's a lot of people," I said. "There's nothing but Gillises."

"That crowd is different from the rest of them. There's lots of good Gillises."

"So what's wrong with that crowd?"

"Oh, I could tell you things."

It was as if the noisy cookhouse had suddenly emptied. "Ah well," he said. "Best left where it is."

I nodded, focused on my plate of food. "You mean the one who shot himself, up near the strait. He was related?"

"Yes," he said.

"How did you know him?" I asked.

"The war," he said. "I saw him near the end of the war. He was never the same. Got wounded bad. I was there."

"You were there?"

"Shortly afterwards. Himself and his buddy named MacAskill got into something. I was military police, which was why I was there. It was Holland we were in. Just before the end."

"I didn't know," I said. "That you were . . ."

"Anyway, it's best not talked about. It was a long time ago. I was just saying, there's a bad streak in that crowd. You're best out of it."

And the billow of sorrow rolled over me again.

And then it was September. There was merry laughter in the co-op. It stopped when I closed the door behind me, but not before I heard Caddy's name.

"What about Caddy?"

"When did you come home?" Big Frank, the manager, was watching me, face tight.

"What about Caddy," I repeated.

"Caddy's expecting," he said quietly.

"When did Caddy get married?" I asked.

"Who mentioned marriage," a voice behind me said. I turned.

Big Frank said sternly, "Tony ..."

His name was Peter. Older than I was by at least ten years. That's all that I remember. Except for the expression on his face as he said, "It would've took some kind of a man to get into Caddy's ..."

And the rest is a lot of confusion, things toppling, and me suddenly on top of that fucking Peter, strangling his fucking neck until the eyes bulged, face turned purple.

And being jerked to my feet by Big Frank who was behind me.

"Jesus Christ, Tony ... he was only kidding ..."

"*Fuck you all. Fuck every one of you.*" And the door slam.

———

But it was true. Ma said: "I suppose you heard about Caddy." She shook her head in sympathy or disapproval or some combination of the two.

"It's such a shame," she said. "There's her life, gone. And for what?"

I couldn't suppress the question. "When?"

"Her mother told me, it'll be sometime late October. They're just devastated."

There was a long silence then, or all senses paralyzed. I waited for the mental math and the speculation that was irresistible, but it only hung there, silently, expanding until it filled the room. "I think I'll go out for a while," I said.

Nobody talked about Caddy Gillis around me after that. Which is not to say that there wasn't a lot of talking about Caddy going on, especially inside of me. Mostly questions. If it wasn't me, then who? I was working backward in my mind, trying to remember how far she let me go and when. I told myself: It doesn't take much. When you're young and inexperienced it can happen pretty much without you knowing. But if it was me who got her pregnant in some freak accident, why would she go away without telling me? Maybe to spare me? Probably to give it up without me knowing. That would be like her. But then I had a flash of anger at that thought. *You deserve to know why I'm going but I just can't bring myself to tell you.* This wasn't just about her. It took two to create that life that was now a problem she was trying to solve alone. No. She wouldn't do that. But, then, maybe, for noble reasons—she'd want to spare me the grief and scandal.

A friend of mine from younger days—I'll call him Dave—arrived home unannounced in March one year. He'd been working far away so there was much speculation about what brought him home at that unlikely time. He kept to himself for the week he was around and it was said that he seemed grim. Was he in some kind of trouble away? Was there someone sick at home? Then he went away again. The reason for his visit remained a mystery until May when his girlfriend who was still in school began to show. It was a major topic of discussion.

Caddy knew her well and told me how it happened. One night while he was home for the Christmas holidays they were necking on a couch after her parents had gone to bed. And before she knew what was happening he'd slipped it in. Caught her totally by surprise, she told Caddy. It was her first time but it didn't hurt, she said. She'd been pretty turned on herself, from all the fondling. He was only in for like three seconds when she panicked and he pulled back, squirting stuff all over her and the couch. What a mess! Caddy was blushing telling it.

They got married in June, right after high school graduation, because that was what you did. You did the right thing and the right thing was for the community, upholding standards that held the place together even if it was at some painful cost for the individuals involved. Values. Civility. Doing the right thing was never the wrong course of action, not in those days. You sinned and you were sorry. You owned up and did your lifelong penance after an act of contrition called marriage. Everything was okay then. I was ready for that but Caddy spared me.

And then I did the math again: I hadn't seen her from the Christmas break until the end of February. So if it was true that she was due at the end of October it was someone else who'd sinned. Someone who'd just run away, turned his back on values and civility.

Duncan had it absolutely right. *I was just saying, there's a bad streak in that crowd. You're best out of it.*

It was mid-November when I heard a baby had been born a few weeks earlier. A girl. Catherine Rosalie. No shame there, I thought. Maybe they'll call her Caddy too. But she went by Rosalie, according to the scraps of gossip I'd hear from time to time. Everything was clear and simple then and my reaction was unambiguous. The hurt confusion had by then grown thin. I was profoundly and permanently angry. And there would be moments of cold elation. What a lesson! I should get in touch and thank her. To learn something so revealing about human nature was worth more than anything I was learning from the university professors. I looked at girls and women differently, saw them for the perils and complications that were always festering within their complex needs. After Caddy I could still be friendly, even passionate in particular situations. But I always held something back and, perversely, it seemed to make me more attractive. Women seemed to be obsessed by the idea that there were things they couldn't know about me, places I wouldn't let them go, things they couldn't have. I was like that right up until I met Anna.

In time I learned that Caddy had given up the child to a relative in Windsor. And that she had moved to Toronto where she worked for several years, creating distance from her daughter so the little girl could bond, I guess, with the new parents,

Caddy's aunt and uncle. And at some point when it didn't matter I heard that she was home for good and married to a lovely man named Jack Stewart. Salt of the earth, Ma said of Jack.

There was inevitable speculation that Jack was the father, especially when at the age of ten, Rosalie came to live with them. But anyone who thought it through would realize that couldn't be the case: Jack wasn't even from around here, never met Caddy 'til after she had gone away herself. And they never had children of their own so it was clear that there was something wrong with Jack in that department. For a long time it was considered odd and tantalizing that Caddy never gave the slightest hint about the father of her baby. There were predictable jokes about the Immaculate Conception and even I could, eventually, ignore the crude insensitivity and smile a little. There would come a time when no one talked or thought of it at all. But I always knew that someday, somewhere I'd come face to face with the reality.

9.

December 29, coming back from our walk along the trail I saw Caddy's car at the house. Birch saw it too and dashed off to sniff a wheel. Then he barked twice and trotted to the door. I felt a combination of elation and disappointment.

Caddy was at the kitchen table, sitting with her coat on, car keys in her hand. She smiled when I came in but didn't stand. Birch jumped up, placed forepaws on her thigh. She scratched his head. "None the worse for wear," she said.

I started pouring water into the kettle. "So how are things in Windsor?"

"It was lovely," she said. "A relief to be away."

"Everybody fine up there?"

"Everybody coping. It was sad just the same."

"I'm making tea," I said.

"None for me," she said. "I just wanted to take this fellow off your hands. I got in late last night. I'm beat."

The kettle was whispering. I stood, back to the counter, arms folded. The dog was lying on the floor, on his side, looking up at her while she scratched his ribs. Her face was sad, the dog reminding her of loss. "I didn't know he liked that."

"Loves his belly being scratched," she said. "I hope he wasn't any trouble."

"He's great company," I said. "Went AWOL once but he was easy to find, looking confused on your back deck. Other than that, he settled right in."

"I can't thank you enough," she said, and stood. "It was a great break."

"Too bad you couldn't have stayed longer."

"It was long enough." She seemed to hesitate.

"I could keep him for a few more days, 'til after New Year," I said. "Just a thought."

She laughed. "Look at the face on you. I think he stole your heart too."

"No," I said, feeling the heat on my cheeks, "It's just I . . ."

"I'll bring him back for visits." She moved toward the door. "Come on, Birch Bark," she said. He yapped and followed her. Passing by me, Caddy caught my hand and squeezed, then leaned in and quickly kissed my cheek. "You're a dear," she said.

I slept late the next morning. No reason to get up. And I'd stayed up too late, well into the wee hours, watching an American channel where people on a panel were haranguing one another about Iraq. I thought: So this is where Neil is getting all his big ideas. Staying up late, watching American TV.

One man on the panel was a skinny, balding, whiskery academic, whose name was also Tony, I noted. He was talking about the United Nations, how non-violent measures were achieving the security everybody seemed to be concerned about. But he was mocked and shouted down. And I wished that I had told Neil the Pittman story, about what happens when we grow cynical about the law, abandoning the civility the laws protect, unleashing our own violent, fearful demons. The price we ultimately pay for chaos.

After I turned the television off and went to bed, I couldn't sleep for all the sounds and images: Hussein, Strickland, Pittman, thudding feet, violent noise and someone's life a bloody puddle spreading on a dirty floor. And all the people who will die because of a consensus shouted by some lucky people on a television panel, people sleeping, eating, laughing at this very moment, and unaware that they will soon be dead. And Tommy's voice, *Stay solid, man*; and why I couldn't have told Neil what happened when I wasn't solid, how I succumbed to weakness, ended up alone, in an old house on the edge of nowhere.

I swung my legs out of bed, stood staring out the window. The sun was shining and the wind was out of the northwest. There was fresh snow on the ground and it was lifting and shifting, phantom dancing on the meadow. The agitation of the night returned briefly then faded in the relaxed murmuring of wind. The word "finality" occurred to me, the way that lawyers use it. It wasn't weakness. It was strength. *You did the right thing,* I told myself again. And, *This is the finality, the isolation that is also peace.* And I thought of the poem by Anna Akhmatova: *Strong as we are, memory punishes us, is our disease.* Be on guard, I thought. Too much memory is toxic.

I was watching coffee dribbling into the urn when I heard two sharp yaps just outside my door. I laughed out loud. Dog memory—memory without moralizing—a blessing.

"The little bugger," Caddy said impatiently when she picked up the phone. "I'll come and get him."

"No," I said. "I needed motivation to go out for a walk. This is good. I have to go to the store later anyway so I'll bring him by." On a sudden impulse I said: "Then again ... what are your plans for tonight? I just realized it's New Year's Eve ..."

"You can imagine," she said. "I'm picking up the new ball gown in a few minutes. Then the beauty parlour for the rest of the day." She laughed. "What the heck do you think my plans are? Sitting in front of the TV watching a bunch of Mr. Bean reruns, waiting for the magical midnight moment."

"Okay, why don't you come over here and I'll make dinner. And you can take your little friend home with you when you go."

"I didn't know you were a cook."

I almost said *there's a whole lot you don't know about me,* but I caught myself and said instead, "Well you can be the judge of that. Besides I've got a bigger TV than you."

She sounded wary when, after a long pause, she said "O-*kay,*" a kind of query on the second syllable.

———

The phone rang at three o'clock that afternoon. Caddy was already laughing when I picked it up. "You're serious about this?" she said. "You're sure now?"

"What?" I said, pretending to be hurt. "You don't think I can cook a dinner?"

"I'm sure you can, but I was thinking, why don't you come over here?"

"No," I said. "I'm baking a ham right now. I have the fixings for a salad. I even found a nice baguette in town. And an expensive bottle of wine. There's no turning back now."

"Ham," she said. "I'm impressed. But I have to do something. How about I whip up a casserole of scalloped potatoes? You plan on that."

"My mother used to make it with lots of onions and cheese," I said.

"I have the same recipe."

She arrived at seven sharp. I had music on low, some Brahms. Making the selection I was reminded of how little I knew about her. I tried to recall if she drank alcohol. I thought I remembered Dixie cups of rye and ginger but it might have been like the cigarettes she'd smoke more out of curiosity than desire. I realized that I was nervous and badly needed something strong to drink.

Her chestnut hair, thick and rich, faintly greying, was gathered up high on her head, giving prominence to forehead, eyes and cheekbones. Her face, I noted with a pang, was still extraordinary. She seemed slimmer than she was before she went away. She was wearing a long loose pale blue sweater that hung to her hips, tailored blue jeans, boots almost to her knees. She handed me a heavy object in a plastic bag—the casserole. It was warm. "Put that in the oven, on low," she instructed. From a large shoulder bag she extracted a bottle of wine. One question answered. She sat then on a kitchen chair and struggled with the boots.

"They're new," she said. "I did some cross-border shopping."

"Let me help," I said, and knelt in front of her, seizing the heel of a boot, one hand on her calf. When I looked up she was staring at me, half-smiling, hands gripping the edges of her chair. Her eyes were shining. "Just look at you down there."

Boots off, she reached back into the shoulder bag and produced a pair of shoes.

"And oh yes," she said, reaching in again. "I brought dessert." She was holding a small plastic container. "Some brownies," she said. "They'd be great with ice cream."

"Ice cream I have," I said. "I'm going to have a drink while the wine is breathing for another little while," I said. "How about yourself?"

"I'll have some breathless wine," she said.

I poured myself a very large glass of Scotch.

We were playful preparing dinner. Anybody watching through the window would have seen an extraordinarily attractive woman, age irrelevant, busy in a kitchen that was not unfamiliar to her. I guess all kitchens are more or less the same. Occasionally, though, she'd have to ask me where she could find something or other. "This place could use some organizing," she said, then blushed. "Will you listen to me?"

I checked my image in the window of the microwave. Hairline holding, hair steely grey on the sides, but still black on top. Swarthy face too fleshy. I regretted the shirt that I was wearing, an old denim thing that was a bit too tight around the middle.

"If you don't mind me asking," I said. "How do you keep in shape? You look fantastic."

She cocked her head, "Thank you," she said. "I don't mind you asking at all." She turned back to the counter where she was squeezing garlic for the salad dressing. "It's mostly in the genes."

"That's a part of my problem," I said. "I don't know much about my genes."

She let the comment pass and I resisted the temptation to pour another Scotch.

"How's the wine?"

"Lovely."

I couldn't see her face. I refilled her glass, poured one for myself.

Dinner conversation was mostly catching up with the lives of people we once knew: who was dead, who was happy, who was married and unmarried, brief references to the children of old acquaintances who were doing well, or badly. Sketchy details of our own lives.

"You and Jack met in Toronto," I said.

"We knew each other there," she said concentrating on her fork. "Then after I moved back home, he turned up here." She smiled. Enough disclosure about Jack.

"And you. How did you meet up with–Anna, if I remember?"

"Yes, Anna," I said, feeling awkward. "We met taking night courses at Queen's. She was hoping to be a lawyer."

"Wow," she said, and daintily placed a slice of potato in her mouth, eyes interested and searching mine.

"She pulled it off," I said. "Now in a practice. Successful criminal lawyer." I fell silent, caught in a warp between the two of them.

"Funny about relationships," I said. "One of the things that attracted me was that we didn't seem to have much in common. It was kind of disappointing that we had more in common than I realized."

"How so?"

"She more or less grew up in prisons. Her father was in the system, he'd worked his way up from guard to warden. He was running Warkworth when Strickland was there ..."

She stopped chewing for a moment, then looked down at her plate, stuck her fork into a morsel of ham, looked up and met my eyes.

"I'm sorry to have mentioned him," I said. "I'm an idiot."

"No, no," she said. "It's okay. So Anna would have known Strickland too?"

"She took an interest in him, trying to help him through some university courses. We never really talked about how that worked. Things were kind of strained between us by that point."

"Thank God I was spared all that," she said. "I couldn't imagine the grief of that kind of situation."

And then there was a long silence.

"It's funny, looking back," she said eventually. "New Year's Eve we always remember. A year ago I went to bed before midnight. Maymie was out with a gang of friends. There was a big dance in the hall and they all went. Boys and girls together, no dates or anything like that. Not like when we were young and everybody would be paired off. Do you remember where you were?"

"In an empty house in Kingston. Just about everything cleared out but boxes of books and a big old bed. I went to bed early too." But I couldn't remember going to bed. Just that I woke up there, head and body throbbing from an alcohol-induced unconsciousness.

"I was just thinking," she said, "how it's kind of pathetic the way we indulge ourselves in hopeful expectations at times like this and, of course, on birthdays. I think you're what, Tony, fifty-five?"

"Yes."

"Two years older than I am," she said.

"You'd never know to look at us," I said. "You look twenty years younger than me."

She laughed. "Now you're just trying to get around me." She looked away, face pink. "It's kind of like a kid's game, isn't it. All the resolutions and predictions and expectations. Pretending that we can know one day to the next what's going to happen, that we can actually have influence, somehow prevent the bad things by being optimistic. 'Look on the bright side,' they used to say."

She sighed. I placed my hand on hers. She studied my face and hers softened and became the face of many years ago, eyes searching. I was afraid to make a sound. After what seemed to be a very long silence I said, "It took me years to stop thinking about you."

She looked away but didn't move her hand. "I can't imagine what you thought. But believe me, I knew what you were going through. I must have written a hundred letters, then tore them all up."

She shrugged, raised her eyes to mine. "I admired your silence," she said. "The word I used to think of all the time when I thought of you was 'dignified.'"

I laughed. "Dignified! I had lots of questions, lots of times I had to struggle to hold them back. I'd tell myself a day will come when I'll have answers. Or maybe not. Maybe there will be a day when the questions and the answers don't matter anymore."

"And so?" she said. "The questions? Now?"

I hesitated, took a sip of wine. "For a while I thought it was me. I remember one night we were parked in the old truck. I think I got a bit carried away."

She looked off as if at something above my head. "I remember that little truck," she said at last. "It was red."

"Is that all you remember about it?"

"It was a red Ford F-100. I'm thinking 1955."

"My God," I said, surprised. "I think you're right."

"For the longest time I'd see a little red Ford and I'd be wondering what became of you."

I shrugged. "It's one of the few great things about time passing. Everything diminishes. And then nothing matters anymore."

"Oh stop," she said. "Jee-zus." She pulled her hand away from mine but she was laughing. "Let's just do the dishes."

"No," I said. "Let's sit in the living room and listen to the music. And wait for midnight. I promise, no predictions or resolutions."

"But we're allowed to hope," she said.

"I can live with that."

So we went to the living room and we sat side by side. "I didn't ask if you enjoy classical music."

"Actually, it isn't classical," she said. "It's the Romantic period I think."

"Wow," I said. "An authority on music. So do you like Brahms?"

"I like all serious music," she said. "But my personal taste runs more to the baroque. You know our local fiddle music is essentially baroque?"

"I didn't know that," I said. "And where did you pick up your expertise?"

"Maymie," she said. "She could play anything. Piano, guitar, fiddle, you name it. She could step-dance like nobody's business. There was a great music teacher at her school. I got interested in the music books she'd bring home, theory and history and all that." She sighed, retreated briefly into silence then said: "Something else I miss."

I took her hand and she moved closer. After a while she put her head on my shoulder and eventually we fell asleep like that.

It was shortly after midnight when I woke up. She was curled up beside me, head resting on my thigh. The dog was on the other side of me. I was afraid to move. But she popped up quickly, rubbing at her eyes.

"We missed all the hoopla," I said.

"What time is it?"

I looked and said, "Twelve twenty-five."

"Yikes."

"Hey. I think that was the first time we ever slept together." I squeezed her hand.

"Better late than never," she said, sounding groggy. Then it seemed to register and she stood up.

"You don't have to leave," I said. "You can stay 'til the morning."

"I don't think so," she said. "Not now." She leaned down and kissed me swiftly, softly, on the forehead.

The dog was sitting up, watching us intently. She scratched between his ears. "I think I'd like to leave him here, if that's okay with you. I think it's better all around. I was hoping that his little holiday over here would change some things but the minute he got home it was back to his old spot, where the casket was." She shook her head. "There are things I'm not ever going to get over as long as he keeps reminding me. So, would you mind?"

"Of course not," I said. "He's no trouble. Maybe another little spell here and he'll be ready."

"As long as I have visiting rights," she said, smiling.

On January 2 the store was busy with people emerging from their privacies. Pulling up I noted Neil's Lexus in its usual spot, close to the door. Inside I felt the unfamiliar warmth of inclusion as people greeted me. "All set for '03 are you Tony?" Mary said from behind the counter. "Lots of big resolutions I bet."

"I don't believe in resolutions," I said. "How about you, Neil?"

"Been making the same one for thirty years and sticking to it. No booze 'til Easter. Secret of my survival in the rest of the year, cleaning out the system in the winter."

"That's admirable," I said. "And thanks again for Christmas."

He nodded, then picked up a newspaper and scanned the headlines.

Mary said, "Maybe you should make one more resolution and start paying for the newspapers you mess up every frigging day."

"Huh," said Neil, perusing headlines over the top of his glasses. "What are you saying, sweetheart?"

"I'm saying buy the friggin' paper if you want to read it, that's all."

"No need to buy the paper when I've got the satellite, honey. Two hundred channels, clickety click. Anything I want to know at my fingertips."

"I have the satellite," said Mary, "and it's all crap that I see there."

"You're just not lookin' in the right places. You're lookin' for amusement. Soap operas and sitcoms and the like. I'm lookin' for information about the world. About the human condition. Right, Tony?"

"Whatever you say, Neil." I winked at Mary.

"See, me and Tony here have been out in the wider world and we know the importance of keeping informed because the world is all connected now, folks. Everybody in the same boat, more or less."

The older man I vaguely remembered–Donald something– said, "I wonder what resolutions old George WMD Bush made for the New Year."

Neil snorted, dropped a section of the paper on the counter in front of Mary. "George WMD Bush. That's a good one. Says right here, about fifteen thousand fresh troops from the third infantry division heading for the Gulf. Now that's a New Year's resolution. And all this country can do is dither over doing the right thing,"

"And what do you think the right thing is, Neil?" asked John Robert, agitating.

"Everybody in the world seems to know what the right thing is," said Neil, "except France and this fucking excuse for a country. Don't get me goin'."

After a nervous silence, which even Neil seemed to register, he said, "Time to change the subject. I was thinkin' about the poor little girl who got murdered last summer. Mary Jane or whatever."

"Murdered?" I said. "I think you're jumping the gun a bit, Neil. And her name was Mary Alice."

He raised a hand. "Whatever. Just hear me out. I was saying to the wife this morning that it would be a nice idea to hold a benefit of some kind in her memory. Something in the hall. Raise money for a memorial, a scholarship or something."

"How do you think Caddy would feel about this?" I said carefully.

He shrugged. "I can't see the downside."

"There already is a scholarship fund."

"So we'll have two."

"Maybe you should talk to Caddy." I reached for the newspaper that was reserved for me.

"I was thinking *you* should talk to Caddy, Tony," Neil said. "I think she'd like to hear it coming from yourself."

I laughed. "You're about forty years out of touch, Neil."

"I'm just sayin'. It wouldn't hurt to run it by her."

"I think it's a bad idea for half a dozen reasons. The timing for one. There's going to be a preliminary hearing in a few weeks. Maybe a trial. The court might take a dim view."

"The court's got fuck all to do with it. This is about the community, Tony. The place hanging together, trying to get some good out of something wicked."

John Robert asked, "So what were you thinking, Neil?"

"Nothing major. A social event, music, food, a liquor licence. Maybe Caddy could say a few words about the kid. Get the priest involved."

"It could be fun," John Robert said. "There isn't much going on in January. What do you think, Tony?"

"I'll have nothing to do with it."

Silence then while everybody stared at me. Finally I said, "Caddy and the family are struggling to put what happened behind them. Going through the trial will be bad enough."

"If there ever is a trial," said Neil. "That's another thing."

"What's the real agenda here, Neil?"

"Whoa, Tony. What are you talking about? It's just an idea. Fuck me."

I walked out with my newspaper, realizing outside that I'd forgotten to pay for it.

I became an obsessive television watcher, staying up late at night, surfing through the channels for discussions about Iraq. Maybe I was trying to prepare myself for a showdown with Neil.

Collie, from behind the counter, had commented, "You have

to admit, Neil makes a good point now and then." I was shocked. Sensible Collie agrees with Neil?

"What good point?" I asked. "Name one."

"Well, if they *have* managed to hide serious weapons in the desert somewhere, who knows ... ?"

"They haven't been able to find any evidence of weapons. And the country is hardly functioning after all the years of sanctions."

"Maybe. But you can't be too careful dealing with those kinds of people."

"Come on, Collie," I said.

"I'm just sayin'."

Around the middle of January Sullivan called to tell me Dwayne wanted to talk to me again.

I told the lawyer that I hadn't changed my mind since the last time we talked.

"I think he understands your position," Sullivan said. "I'm just passing on his request. Maybe he just wants a visitor. He's pretty much alone in the world, as you know."

I said I'd consider it. Sullivan told me they were expecting a firm date for the preliminary hearing any day, probably in early February.

"I think we're in pretty good shape," he said.

After he hung up I sat for a while in the silent house. Alone in the world? When all is said and done aren't we all alone in the world?

But soon enough I decided I'd go to see Strickland. I would do it for Caddy and the community. Maybe learn something useful. Perhaps he trusted me enough to disclose what really happened the night the girl called Maymie died.

The sky was dark and the air still as I stood at my kitchen window the next morning waiting for the coffee water to boil. And then large feathery flakes of snow began to float straight downward. I stood, hypnotized, and it was only when the first gust of wind sent the gentle snowfall into a swirling fury that I realized that I was witnessing the birth pangs of a snowstorm. You aren't going anywhere, I said to myself. Not even to the store. I watched, with my coffee, as the rising wind wrapped the snow around the house, softly flinging it against the windowpanes.

By noon the schools were closing, according to the radio newscast. Authorities were warning people to stay off the roads. Late afternoon I learned from CNN that the British were sending twenty-six thousand soldiers to the Persian Gulf, including part of the armoured Desert Rats brigade. The Americans were sending sixteen thousand more from bases in Texas and Colorado. Colin Powell was pressing the United Nations to stand firm against Iraq. Standing firm against what seems to be inert is ridiculous, I thought. Mental note to Neil: give me one scrap of evidence that the government of Iraq represents a threat to anybody but Iraqis and I'll take you seriously.

Boredom set in by early evening. I poured a Scotch. Somewhere around nine o'clock all power failed ominously. Lights, television, suddenly gone with the subtle background sounds we never seem to notice until we can't hear them anymore.

Now only the creaks and protests of the naked house, the sighs and moans of nature, ragged snow flapping at the windows. The phone rang.

"Everything copacetic over there?" Caddy asked.

"Yes. What about you?"

"I have a generator," she said. "You're welcome to come over if you can make it."

"I'm sure the lane is blocked."

"If you get desperate I'll send someone with a snowmobile."

I laughed. "How bad can it get?"

"Sometimes these things can go on for days. You have lamps?"

"They're all over the place," I said. "I was going to get rid of them but I kept them for decoration."

"Get them ready, you're going to need them," she said.

After I put the phone down I did a mental inventory. The lamps; stove in the living room is fuelled by oil; I have a pro-pane camp stove somewhere; enough canned food for days; nothing to go bad in the refrigerator; I have a powerful flash-light (property of the Correctional Service of Canada). I real-ized that I was speaking aloud and that the dog was listening; the sound of my voice and the sense that it was being heard and understood was comforting. He came close, placed his snout on my knee. "I know you're wondering about Strickland," I said. "Whether I'm setting myself up for trouble, engaging with him. But you'd have to know the whole story, Birch."

He licked my hand and clambered up beside me on the couch, turned in a full circle, then lay down, head resting on my thigh. "Go on," he seemed to say.

"You're the expert on loyalty," I said. "You'd understand better than most people what Strickland and I really have in common. Something deeper than the fact that we were both adopted. We're traitors, Strickland and me. I hate admitting it, Birch, but in the world we come from, we're both known as rats."

The dog lifted his head from my knee and stared up at me.

"That's right. We're rats. In the world that did so much to shape what we've become, where everyone is more or less a prisoner of the system—there are two distinct cultures, two breeds of animal, if you will. Each breed has rules so rigorous you wouldn't believe it. Or maybe you would, actually. Maybe you would. Because rule one, the absolutely most important, is loyalty—you are unquestionably loyal to your own breed. Anyone who betrays his own is dead, one way or another. And that's how Strickland and I both ended up back here, back where we started from, both more or less in hiding. His problem is that he got noticed. I want to know: Was your young friend's death an accident? Or did he do something bad or stupid that night when Maymie showed up at his place. If he brought it on himself, he'll have to face the consequences. That's the way we see things, Birch. I know you understand."

The dog yawned assent. I was relieved he couldn't ask the obvious.

I'd known what the letter was about before I opened it. There is something ominous about an administrative summons. And over coffee we'd compared them. Me, Meredith, Wilson and Tommy Steele.

"*Roger* William Pittman," Tommy scoffed. "Anybody know his name was Roger?" We all laughed.

"He was twenty-eight," said Meredith. "Christ, I thought he was a lot older than that. Just from his record. Busy boy, he was."

"Okay," said Tommy. "This ain't gonna be pretty. But we're ready for it, right guys?"

There was a murmur of agreement from Meredith and Wilson.

"See, here's the situation. We've all been through this before. People come along after the fact with twenty-twenty hindsight, right? Like we're supposed to know what's gonna happen *before* it fuckin happens, right? Just the way the brains trust knows after everything is done and all the reports are in. We were supposed to be fortune tellers."

He was shaking his head sadly. Then he was looking straight at me, smiling at the mouth. Oh, but not the eyes. Eyes hardened by his insight and his certainties. "Something on your mind, Tony?"

"Maybe we should talk about this," I said.

"What's to talk about?"

"Maybe coming clean."

Tommy didn't move. He was sitting with his arm hanging over the back of his chair, expression wary. The coffee-shop din suddenly seemed far away.

"So you're gonna strike out on your own," he said at last.

"That's not what I said."

"Amounts to the same thing. You going rogue on us?"

"I'm just saying the simplest and safest thing is to explain exactly what happened."

"Okay, Tony. Exactly what happened?"

"We waited too long ... it got out of control. There were four of us. We could have gone onto the range, we could have got security in sooner. It was a wrong judgement call, by all of us. And so there's a guy dead. I don't care what he was, Tommy. He ..."

"Great," he said. "Just hand them an excuse to hang someone out to dry. And who do you think that someone's going to be? Not you, Tony."

"I'll take my share ..."

"Don't go getting all sanctimonious on me. Just do what you feel you gotta do."

And he got up from the table and walked away, shaking his head. But then stopped, turned. "We're all counting on you, Tony."

I sat alone in my office. *There can be no going back. There's only going forward now. The issue isn't what happened. It's what's going to happen.*

I opened my desk drawer, extracted the folded sheet of paper I'd almost memorized by then. *Strong as we are / Memory punishes us / Is our disease ...*

I folded the poem and placed it in my inside jacket pocket. This I'm going to need, I thought. And you, my wise dear Sophie.

I dialed her office number but she wasn't there.

I fell asleep to the howls of wind and whispering of trees. Sometime during the night I awoke to what sounded like the splattering of rain. Early morning I looked out on a glistening landscape, trees drooping with the weight of crusted snow. The power was out. The battery radio reported trees and lines down, all across the province, tens of thousands without electricity.

I took advantage of the daylight, read a lot, resolved to read more. Coffee on the camp stove tasted lovely. Beans and wieners spooned from heated cans. Birch slept mostly and I envied his ability to drift off at will.

Just after four a machine roared in the lane and I thought at first it was a snowplough but it was a snowmobile, rider lost in heavy winter clothes, a helmet. The sudden and unexpected appearance of strangers still makes me nervous, even here. But this was Mary, delivering newspapers accumulated since my last visit to the store.

"I thought you'd be in bed when I was going home last night so I didn't want to bother you."

One of the papers seemed disorganized, as if it had been read. "I see Neil got out in spite of the storm," I said, smiling.

"No, that was me. I won't charge you for that one."

She turned to leave and impulsively I said: "Is there room for two on that machine of yours?"

"Sure," she said. "Where do you want to go?"

"Caddy's," I said. "She has a generator. She's offered supper. And I think the dog is missing her."

"You'll have to make your own way back, unless you want to wait there until I'm coming home."

"What time will that be?"

"About nine tonight."

"Surely Caddy can put up with me 'til then."

———

Bundled in my warmest coat, the dog wrapped in a blanket clutched to my chest I teetered on the back end of the machine as we roared through a deserted countryside. Wood smoke curled above silent blank-windowed houses, here and there cars were abandoned on the roadside or in ditches, half-buried. A snowplough passed us carefully, wheel chains clanking, as we seemed to hurtle down the road. The dog squirmed and I held him tighter. The setting sun seemed briefly to have paused between a bank of purple cloud and flexing sea.

I could see Caddy smiling in the kitchen as we thumped across her back deck; the dog had his head protruding from the blanket and was struggling to be free. I dumped him through the sliding door and she quickly stooped to hug him. "Well look what the cat dragged in," she said. Then she stood, eyes gleaming and touched my face. "You're half-frozen," she said. "Give me that coat. You're too much, the both of you."

Over a hot drink I said, "Last night I started talking to the dog. Then I was thinking that poor old Charlie probably started out like that. Talking to himself or to an animal."

"Storms do that," she said. "Especially when the power fails. I overheard someone at the store telling the gang that during the last big storm he caught himself talking to the wife. That was when he bought a generator, mostly to keep the TV going."

"When did you buy yours?" I asked.

"That was Jack's doing," she said. And became silent for a while before she stood and fetched the kettle from the camp stove, the bottle from the sideboard. "Let me strengthen that."

At the refrigerator door she said: "The generator keeps the

fridge on, and of course the television. I hope you don't mind leftovers."

Fork poised in mid-air, she frowned, then lowered it. "I hear that there was talk at the store about some kind of benefit, a memorial for Maymie."

"So what did you hear?"

"Just that. Do you know anything about it?"

"Doing it for the family, they say."

"You'd think they'd have discussed it with the family."

"Well, actually, that was supposed to be my job."

She studied me, face slightly tilted. "So?"

"Obviously I didn't do my job. I think it's a bad idea. Especially now."

She sighed. "I agree with you."

"I think Neil is trying to stir people up. He's behind it. I heard him use the word 'murder.'"

She shrugged, pushed a bit of food across her plate. "So what?"

"It's a loaded word and he knows it."

"I just want it all to go away," she said. "Nobody knows what happened and even if they did it won't bring her back."

I placed my hand on hers. "Even Strickland says he doesn't know what happened."

She bit her lower lip. "I suppose he would, wouldn't he."

"Do you really want to hear this?"

She shrugged. "Ignorance, I've learned, is anything but blissful."

"His story doesn't add up to much–just that she was alive

the last time he saw her, as far as he knows. She was fine. A bit down maybe. But otherwise, normal."

"Down?"

"He didn't elaborate."

"And you believed him."

"I'll be interested in the evidence."

"What evidence could there be? There was just the two of them."

"Yes. But there will be forensic stuff. It won't be easy to listen to, Caddy."

She stood up. "I'm going to make tea."

"I'll have some."

With her back turned, she said, "Nothing can be worse than what's already happened. Nothing can make it un-happen."

"He wants to talk to me again."

She turned, studied me for a long moment. "That doesn't surprise me."

"I'll probably go."

"Fair enough," she said and turned back to face the cupboard.

I could hear the wind rising outside. We sipped our tea. I noted it was nearly eight o'clock. "Mary said she'd come by around nine to give me a lift home."

She studied her cup for what seemed like a long time. "You don't have to go so soon."

"How would I get home?"

"I can get you home," she said. "There's a snowmobile in the garage. I know how to drive it. So you're not stranded."

"One of us will have to call Mary at the store, tell her I've made other arrangements."

"Let me do that."

"When she returned from the telephone, she said, "I'm glad you're here, Tony. When I talk to you, it's like . . ."

"It's okay . . ."

"No, I want to say it. It's like having another life, where things really are okay."

After a long silence, she said, "Come. Sit."

We were sitting on the couch, side by side, my arm behind her on the back of it. Then she turned slightly and nestled closer and plucked something from the front of my sweater. "How did you get into that line of work anyway, Tony?"

"Random circumstances," I said.

"I could never picture you in a penitentiary, among that sort."

"What sort?"

"Crooks. Convicts."

"Ah Caddy, there's worse than them walking around free."

Now she was examining my hand. "So how did you end up there?"

"Back in '66 I had a roommate. I'm sure I talked about him, when we were . . . His father was a prison guard in Halifax. Full of stories. They were supposed to be comical, or philosophical. I found them grim. The prisoners he talked about sounded a lot like me. Outsiders."

"Oh stop," she said.

"You asked."

Now her forehead was against my cheek, hair tickling.

"So I took some post-grad courses in sociology and crimi-nology. And ended up working for a professor who eventually got a government contract to look into the causes of the 1971 riot in Kingston Pen. I don't know if you remember. It was a big story for a while. The inmates trashed the place, took hostages. It was a kind of turning point for the prison system. He sent me to Kingston for the field work, interviewing people, researching for him."

"I often wondered where you got to."

"One of his recommendations was better screening for people going into corrections. He thought guards and other staff in the system generally should be more … educated, I guess. He thought that a lot of the trouble started with atti-tudes among the people who run the system. I agreed with him and at some point decided that I wanted to get into it, make a difference."

I blushed at the sophomoric words. Then laughed.

"What's so funny?"

"I don't know," I said. "I guess there's nothing funny about naïveté, or where it gets you."

"I know something about that," she said. "So what made you quit?"

For a moment I considered telling her, but then she took my left hand in both of hers, stroked my fingers. The wind was battering the house again. "Thank God for the oil stove," she said and snuggled closer.

"Thank God for body heat," I said. There was a blanket on the back of the couch and I dragged it over us and soon we were lying down, me on my back, she with her head on my shoulder, eyes closed. We drifted off to sleep like that.

It was after midnight when I woke. I realized her eyes were open, that she was studying me. "I was just thinking," she said. "How natural this feels."

I swung my feet to the floor and she did too. She yawned and stretched, then took my hand. "Come," she said. And she stood and led me toward the stairs. "We aren't going out in this."

I looked toward the window where snow was hurtling, horizontal. I followed her.

When she came back from the bathroom she was wearing a man's shirt, top buttons open. She had long slim legs and with one hand she modestly gripped the bottom of the shirt to stretch it down in front. But when she bent to turn off the bedside light I saw her breasts suspended briefly. "Can't we leave the light on?" I asked. She laughed. "I don't think so." And then she was beside me, soft and warm. I snuggled closer, deliberately pressing my erection against her leg. She reached down and touched it. "What's that?" she said. I slipped my hand inside the shirt, felt the full softness of a breast. Kissed her neck. "Let's take it slow," she said.

And so I slowly undid the buttons on her shirt, kissed her breasts, pressed my face between them, licked a nipple, savoured a faint taste of salt. "You never used to let me do this," I murmured. "But now and then I could . . ." and ran my hand along her flank, and into the warm place between her thighs, ". . . do this."

She placed her hand on mine, guiding my fingers, sighed. "You never were very good at that," she said.

I chuckled. "It takes practice. And a bit of co-operation. You weren't much help." She turned her face away.

"What's wrong, Caddy?"

"I don't know," she said.

"It's okay. We don't have to."

"I started thinking," she said. "It's always a mistake, in bed. Thinking."

"It's all I ever do in bed anymore, actually."

"Yes, that, and say my prayers. Do you say prayers, Tony?"

"I gave up praying when I realized that nobody was listening."

"There's that," she said. "But it's a nice habit anyway. Like meditation."

"Except when it gets in the way of other things."

She drifted off for a bit. And then, after a long pause, she asked: "What ever happened to the little red truck?" I rolled onto my back. Game over.

"The old man traded it, eventually," I said. "I was glad. It was always a reminder." Then I noticed that she was staring at the ceiling. I touched her cheek and it was wet. "I'm sorry," I said, and I wrapped my arms around her, held her close.

She slipped a hand between my legs. "Your friend has gone away."

"Old age," I said.

"No," she said. "It's my fault. Thinking. Remembering. Talking."

"It's nobody's fault," I said quickly.

"Or maybe everybody's fault," she said.

"What do you mean?"

"Too many people in the bedroom," she said, and kissed my forehead.

"How many can you count?"

"Two besides us," she said.

"Hmmm. Just two. Do they have names?"

"Jack and Anna," she said.

"Mmmmhmmm."

"Listen to that wind," she said. "Aren't you glad we didn't go out?"

I listened to the storm, now amplified by silence. A vehicle drove by, lighting the window briefly. The wet streaks glittered. And then she said: "So how many by your count?"

"Offhand, four," I said.

"My, my. Four. That's a crowd. Do they have names?"

"Two of them you know already, Jack and Anna. There was a third whose name wouldn't mean anything."

"Interesting. She must have been very special."

"Who said 'she'?"

She rose up on an elbow, staring.

"Just joking," I said quickly. "She *was* special, maybe because it couldn't go anywhere . . . except emotionally."

"Yes," she said. "That would make it special. And number four?"

"That's the big mystery, isn't it," I said. And she became silent again.

Then she said: "So number three was like a little fling."

"Some people might call it that. But I wouldn't."

She kissed me. "Don't be sad," she said.

"Did you ever have one of those, Caddy? A little fling that went wrong on you?"

She pressed her face against my shoulder. "No," she said. "No flings for me. There was only Jack." The wind was shrieking. "Just listen to that," she said.

"So there really isn't a number four then," I said, "if there was only Jack for you."

The wind emphasized the sudden silence in the room, and I wanted to rewind the conversation.

"I know what you're thinking," she said after a while. "I never counted that as anything. Just an accident, one of those mistakes you don't get away with. Did you ever make a mistake you didn't get away with, Tony?"

"A few," I said.

"I want to go to sleep now," she murmured, an arm lightly across my chest. "Okay?"

"I loved you, Caddy," I said.

"I know you did."

And in a little while she was breathing quietly in a deep, untroubled sleep.

10.

It could have been a dream but I know that I was wide awake, processing the reductive thought: number three was like a little fling. A little fling that went wrong. Little fling. Storm outside flinging snow and sleet and hail and rain against the window. I could have told her that there were many flings. But only one I remember now, Caddy's stillness, her soft breathing a reminder.

When Sophie had informed me she was going to the conference in St. John's to be on a panel on the effectiveness of rehabilitation programs, I had a momentary panic.

"You mean the one sponsored by the Judicial Institute?"

"Yes. What's wrong?"

"Sophie, they just asked me to go to replace someone who's dropped out."

"Who asked?"

"Someone in the minister's office. I didn't even ask who else was on the panel."

"I could beg off," she said. "If you think it's going to be awkward."

"God no," I said, suddenly elated. "Have you ever been to St. John's?"

"No, never," she said.

"You'll love it," I said. "The weather can be rotten but it should be nice in June."

And the weather was nice, a sunny balmy day with high white clouds and a light cool breeze. On the panel, Sophie and I, as usual, ended up saying basically the same things. We were discreetly critical of the status quo, referring to the over-crowding, suicides and recidivism that offer too much evidence of our professional failures, our historic inability to turn felons into citizens. The other panel member was a journalist and author who had written widely and with admirable passion about the flaws in the system. His radical views gave me the space I needed to seem, from time to time, to be defending the establishment just enough to satisfy the bureaucratic spies and knuckle-draggers I knew were in the room. The audience was mostly lawyers and a sprinkling of judges but there were also academics and corrections managers, not to mention media.

We stayed on for a talk by an American psychiatrist who spoke about his personal experience with repeat offenders and his insights into the clinical causes that doom certain people to spend much of their time on earth incarcerated. But after coffee we slipped away, into a sunny afternoon. We considered climbing Signal Hill but opted instead for a stroll along the waterfront, inspecting deep-sea draggers, offshore service vessels, cargo ships. Inevitably we were waylaid by the bustle of a pub. The time and place became exceptional, an experience that would forever stand apart from all that came before and after it.

Had I given it the rational consideration it probably deserved I'd have recognized that, based on past experience, we were naive. But there is a certain beauty in naïveté when it is honest and spontaneous, as in childhood. There was something childish in our pleasure that evening, in the laughter and the intimacy that was, until a certain moment, pure. Reality intervened only once—a quiet moment near the end. "The Pittman thing," she said. "Where does that stand?"

"Let's not talk about Pittman."

"You didn't talk to Dwayne?"

"I called him. Asked him to let me know if he thought of anything that could explain why Pittman would have been a target."

"You called him?"

"At Warkworth. I kept it formal and superficial. Anyway, he said he'd think about it. Only knew Pittman vaguely. I don't believe him, but that's what he said. I don't expect to hear back from him."

"I'm sorry," she said. "I didn't mean to ..."

"It's okay," I said. And walking back to the hotel she slipped an arm around my waist. I put my arm around her shoulders and we walked like that, perfectly in step, in a moment that was singular, complete and self-contained.

I was wide awake, no sense of time. And yet we had exhausted our capacity for wandering and eating and for the hilarity and music of the crowded bars we visited. In the hotel lobby I asked: "What floor are you on?"

She had to check the little packet that contained an electronic key. I was almost precisely one floor below. And I asked with pretend formality, "May I see you to your door?"

And she replied, "That would be very gallant of you."

But outside her door we just stood, staring at each other, smiling faces flushed, until I said, unoriginally, "I really hate to see this day ending."

"I could offer you a nightcap from the mini-bar."

And it was that simple.

It seemed to me that I lay awake most of that night too, fascinated by the silence of a woman sleeping. Her breathing was almost imperceptible, her face was still. It was the face of an exhausted child and I was profoundly reassured by the innocence I saw there, no trace of guilt or the anxiety that would inevitably follow.

We were up early. I returned briefly to my room, had a quick shower, changed my clothes. Then we met in the lobby and set out to explore a walking trail around a nearby lake. About an hour into the stroll (we were holding hands), Sophie stopped and said, "Oh my, look at that."

There was a sign that told us we were in a place called Cuckold's Cove.

"Why would anybody . . ." she began. Her distress was immediate and real.

I tried to lighten the moment. I told her Newfoundlanders are famous for their profane sense of humour. Odd place names abound: Conception Bay, Dildo . . . Cuckold's Cove.

We continued walking. My hands were in my pockets now. Her arms were folded. Finally I said, "I suppose the merciful thing about being a cuckold is that you can go through your entire life without knowing it."

She was nodding even though I knew she wasn't listening.

"It was lovely, Tony. But it was a mistake." She'd stopped and her eyes were searching mine.

"Yes," I said. "I know."

Caddy drove me home on her snowmobile early on the morning after my storm stay at her place and I felt uncomfortably dependent, sitting there behind her, the dog crushed between my chest and her back, constrained within a blanket.

Before we left I'd asked: "What about him?" Pointing at Birch.

"My God, I think you two have become a couple," she said

But I didn't believe her when she said, after she dropped us off, "Last night was lovely, Tony. Thanks for the company." In the silence that filled in behind her as she roared away, I had a dreadful feeling that, once again, something promising had died.

———

The car in the lane was unfamiliar but I recognized the tall man walking toward my door, a lawyer who had been among the several in the courtroom on the day of Strickland's unexpected outburst. "Jones," he said, holding out a business card when I opened the door to him. "Derek Jones. I'm with the Crown. I've been meaning to call you but just happened to be in the area and took a chance I'd find you home. Hope it's not a bad time for you."

"Come in," I said, bending to restrain Birch who had started yapping at the first sound of the lawyer's car.

"That's a Jack Russell," said Jones, crouching.

"Mostly," I said.

"How long have you had him?"

"He isn't mine. I'm looking after him for a friend."

He stood. "I'm here about Dwayne Strickland."

"I guessed that much."

"You know him pretty well, I gather."

I shrugged. "What can I do for you?"

"You can probably help us out by shedding a bit of light on Strickland's time in prison, especially at Millhaven."

"I'm sure you can get access to his records."

"Certain records have been sealed by a judge in Ontario, at the request of Strickland's counsel and CSC."

"What are you looking for?"

"Some of the particulars of a situation in which he ended up in protective custody, in Kingston Pen. It was back in '98 or '99. I think you were involved. Corrections Canada and the lawyer claim it involves institutional security, and his safety."

"Marginally."

"It came up in some discussions we had about resolving this without a trial. It's been mentioned that he could be at risk if he went back inside. I'd be interested in your opinion, now that the case could go ahead."

"Inside is a risky place for everybody," I said.

I could feel his impatience. He was nodding. "I'm curious about the reality ... just how real the risk. How big a factor it could become. We figure he's exaggerating, and we were hoping you could give us a sense of just how realistic his concerns are, providing some context for what, so far, is pretty vague."

"I'd rather stay out of this," I said.

"I understand you know the family of the victim. We want to make sure that whatever we'd agree to is fair for them."

"I also know Strickland."

"We'd cover you with a subpoena if it came to that. Otherwise maybe you could offer some informal instruction. Off the record. It would be helpful."

I laughed. "There's a word for people who do what you're asking me to do."

He seemed puzzled.

"I could tell you that it would in fact be very dangerous for Strickland if he went back inside. In the system he'd be known as a ... an informer. I could also tell you that the system is geared up for that."

"Give it some thought," he said.

"Surely the evidence against Strickland is strong enough to keep the case from being sidetracked by this ..."

"I'll tell you unofficially, the evidence is thin. The guy is dangerous. But the merits of the case against him are ... what they are."

At the door he said, "Frankly, if I was in Strickland's shoes I'd be just as worried about being on the loose around here. There's a lot of strong feeling against him because of what happened to that poor girl."

"I wouldn't be too concerned about that," I said. "The place is pretty civilized."

As I stood at the door and watched him drive away, Birch, beside me, barked four cheerful yaps.

I gave up on the snowbound trail where it crossed the Shore Road and opted for the ploughed track of the highway. Birch bounded on ahead, liberated from the struggle to keep up in snow that, though crusted over, occasionally gave way beneath his weight. He dashed away around a bend. I jogged to catch sight of him then called him back. He obliged and soon we were walking briskly together.

The sun was brilliant and the northwest wind stinging on my cheeks. My legs felt strong. At this rate, I thought with satisfaction, I'll soon have to tighten the belt a notch.

A car passed, someone waved and I waved back. The dog had disappeared again and I heard the car horn up ahead, and in a sudden panic I began to run. There was no sign of him, but after what seemed like miles, I saw his tracks heading up a lane. I followed.

There were other footprints left by large boots. They were partly obscured by drifting snow, so it was probably from someone who had walked up the lane the night before. Then it occurred to me that there were no footprints coming back and when I realized that this was Dwayne Strickland's lane I was walking up, I stopped. I called, "Birch." No response. Wind sighing in the tall spruces around me. "Birch Bark." Still no answer. I walked on.

I remembered the house as being drab and unpainted. But it was a bright shade of yellow, cheerful in the stark contrast of the white clearing surrounded by black spiked trees. The windows glinted. There was no smoke or vapour above the chimney. The dog's tracks veered off in the direction of the woods. The human trail continued toward the house and I followed it around the side of the house, toward a window. It stopped there, where someone had peered in. I pressed my face to the window and I could see in the dimness a television set, a large sagging couch, a couple of overstuffed armchairs and a coffee table. The footsteps moved on toward the back of the house, paused before another window. I looked in on a sparsely furnished kitchen, wooden cupboards, mostly empty shelves, table, stove, a refrigerator that appeared to be from the early sixties. I placed my thumbs on the sash at the top of the window frame and pushed upward. The window moved easily.

The footsteps continued but instead of turning toward the back porch, kept straight, toward the trees. I considered following, but at that moment Birch came trotting out of the woods, struggling where snow had drifted. I called, and he came to me in a leaping run.

I stooped and held his head between my hands. He licked my face. "What did you find in there, old buddy?" I stood and peered toward the trees but the drifts were daunting.

"Let's just go home," I said. He was panting happily. The wind was rising, the sun beginning its quick slide toward the treetops.

At the store next morning Neil was at the counter, elbows on the paper, reading. "They got the heat on now, hunting for Osama bin Laden. Mark my words they'll take him out before Saddam. Anybody want to put money on it?"

Mary said, "Maybe that's why there was a cop car in my lane two nights ago."

"You hiding him up there, Mary dear?" said Neil.

"What time?" I asked.

"Late," she said. "I was letting the cat in. Saw the parking lights. Started walking down and it backed away. But I could see the roof rack, where the flashers are."

"You live across from our most notorious citizen," said Neil. "What do you expect. You're living in a high-crime neighbour-hood." He laughed and turned toward the coffee urn.

It was afternoon when I left to visit Strickland at the regional facility. On an impulse, I drove up Mary's lane. I drove slowly, watching both sides of the road for tire marks. And just before her yard, where the lane widened, they were obvious, on the left. And when I got out of my car to examine them, there were footprints leading up to the tire marks, coming from the direc-tion of Strickland's woods.

—

The visiting area was quiet, one woman leaning close to the screen that separates the public from the inmates, talking intensely into a telephone receiver. A tall guard standing near the door stared silently as I entered. "You're Mr. Breau," he said.

"Yes," I replied. "Here for Strickland."

"Hmmm," he said, still staring. "You wouldn't remember me."

"No," I said.

"Ron Graham," he said. "From St. Ninian originally. You'd have known the old man. Roddy."

"Ah," I said. Remembering. "So you'd be . . ."

"Yes. I don't suppose you remember coming to the school once, talking about this line of work."

I shrugged, recalling something else.

"It was you got me interested." He reached out. We shook.

"So," I said, gravely, carefully. "It would have been your . . . ?"

"Yes," he said. "My two younger brothers." He was nodding, face full of conflict.

"I remember," I said. "And now . . ." Tried to smile.

"It was an accident," he said and shrugged. "But he was a piece of work anyway, your man Strickland. Still is. There he is now." Nodded away from us.

Strickland was sauntering toward his side of the protective barrier. He smiled and waved.

"I'm going to beat this thing, Tony." The matter-of-factness in his voice was a perfect projection of the expression on his face. "I am going to beat it and I'll tell you why."

"Tell me, Dwayne," I said. The other visitor, the woman, was speaking furiously now. The inmate on the other side of the barrier, like Strickland, seemed relaxed.

"Because I did nothing wrong, but more important there isn't a shred of evidence to make a case that I did."

"I thought you were ready for a deal."

"I was. Then the day before the plea I read the agreed statement of facts." He laughed. "Facts. What a joke."

"You could have gone home ... just by saying guilty, to something."

"Maybe, maybe not. In any event, try living in St. Ninian having plead guilty for causing that kid's death."

"I thought the plea would be for bodily injury."

"Same fuckin thing, man. The kid's dead, right. And they need somebody to hang for it. Anyway, the Crown is groping. It'll never go to trial. There's nothing."

"You're prepared to gamble–"

He interrupted, voice intense now, knuckles white on the black phone receiver. "Hey, Tony, how many people have you known ended up pleading guilty for the convenience of the system. Think about it. Deals getting made by lawyers when the con's done worse than what he's pleading to. And sometimes he's done nothing at all, but wants to get it over with, for whatever reason. Come on."

"I hear you but ..."

"It's done, Tony. Hey. I have faith in the system. Okay? Where's your faith? Come on, man." He sat back.

I couldn't suppress the smile. "You've been sitting here for months when you say the Crown doesn't even have a case against you? I'm surprised Sullivan hasn't tried to get you out."

"That was my call," he said. "I'm okay here. It's insurance. Worst-case scenario and they nail me, they'll consider time served. Give the old judge something to work with. And it's a good time to be out of the cold. That old house of mine? Shit, you need your own oil well to keep it warm. What about your place?"

"It's fine," I said.

The young woman stood suddenly. We watched as she headed for the door, hand covering her mouth. The guard, Graham, opened up and let her out. The young man inside sat for a while, studying his hands.

"You know that guard?" I said to Strickland.

He peered for a moment, "Don't think so. But you know what? I think for the sake of the place, it's best that I be away from there while people are understandably upset."

"Yes," I said. "You have a point."

"But when they hear the facts ..."

"You really plan to go back there to live?"

"Where else would you suggest?"

I shrugged, chose my words carefully. "There will always be some who--"

"Don't believe me?" He laughed. "I'm used to that, Tony. I've been blamed for every little thing that's happened there for as long as I can remember. But this time the facts will speak for themselves."

"And what are the facts?"

"Poor young thing shows up at my place looking for somewhere to crash. Unbeknownst to me she has a pocket full of pills. Sometime during the night, accidental overdose. End of story."

"You said she was feeling down."

"I did?"

"Yes."

"Well. She seemed that way to me."

"She didn't say why?"

He held the receiver away from his ear for a moment, scratched. "I hate talking on these things."

"Do you know why she was down?" I asked again.

"Something about a row at home, but I really didn't pay attention. We were sitting at the kitchen table and yes, now that I think back, I got the impression that she was upset. She wasn't crying or anything. Just depressed or distracted. Maybe I should have paid more attention." He looked away briefly. "I suppose I'll always wonder."

In the new silence that now lay between us I could hear distant fragments of old familiar sounds, a loud voice complaining, door buzzer, a metallic slam, all amplified by steel and tile and concrete. I could imagine the bored and wary guards, the inmates looking for attention or seeking to avoid it, everything exceptional, and critical and tedious.

"What did you think when you heard?"

"That she was dead, and at my place? Blown away, man. Obviously didn't connect the dots at first. Half-listening to a story on TV about some kid found dead in suspicious circumstances. Police looking for a person of interest. Had no clue it was me they were talking about."

"Didn't the girl's name mean anything to you?"

"Tell you the truth, no. They were using a name that didn't mean a thing to me. Mary Alice. What was it the kids called her?"

"Maymie."

"That was it. In the media she was Mary Alice. Anyway, the

girlfriend and I were checking in for a flight to Toronto when I got the tap on the shoulder. And there they were. Two big guys in suits and before I knew it I was being marched away in hand-cuffs, everybody gawking at me like I'm Osama what's-his-name. And the girlfriend, clear hysterical. No need for any of it. All they had to do was tell me."

He was shaking his head. "Of course I know it's all proce-dure. All by the book. But when it's happening to you. Wow. Hard to describe."

I believed him, felt almost sympathetic.

"You could help, you know. Your words would have a lot of weight. I want to avoid putting people through a trial. You could make the difference."

"How?"

"If I need a character witness. You'd be great."

"You know where I stand on that, Dwayne."

He looked away, exasperation real.

"What could I possibly . . ."

"You could fuckin tell the world that I'm not poison. Court or no court, I'd like just one person in the place to step up. Say something positive about Dwayne Strickland. Speak up in the store. Write a letter to the editor. Stand up in the court if it comes to that. In my entire fuckin life, I've never heard one person stand up in the crunch and say, like, maybe there's a tiny little streak of something worthwhile in Dwayne Strickland. But you could, Tony. We got a lot in common. It would make a difference."

His face was flushed. It was a Strickland I'd never seen. Then he looked away, chewed his lower lip. "Sorry. I'm just whining. Forget it. All I want is . . . *fuck it*. Never mind."

His eyes were suddenly dark, a slight throb at the temple, near his left ear. The guard walked up behind me. Leaned over me, hand on my shoulder. "Ten more minutes, guys."

Strickland watched him walk away. "I don't intend to beg." Then, distracted: "That guy? He looks familiar."

"He's from St. Ninian."

"Ah."

"Is there anybody looking after your house, Dwayne? Checking in now and then?"

He seemed puzzled, now studying the guard, trying to remember. "No, not really. The place is pretty secure, up that long lane, off the beaten track, nothing there to steal anyway. I hardly ever locked the doors. Why do you ask?"

"I was just wondering."

"Wondering what? Is there something I should know?"

I considered mentioning the footprints, cars at night. Decided not to. "Nothing specific."

"Feel free to check in now and then. I'd appreciate it. That would be good."

"Will do."

"You must find the time long, eh? After years in the rat race. Now retired."

"Not really."

"Why did you take early retirement, Tony?"

"I just felt it was time."

"I remember you getting in touch about Pittman. Asking questions. I didn't know much. But there were rumours afterwards."

"You know about rumours," I said.

"Officer from KP arrived at Warkworth while I was there,

you probably knew him. Steele. Tommy Steele. The guys called him 'Stalin.'"

"I knew him," I said.

"Mad at the world. There's a lot of that in the system as you well know. He took it out on everybody. Then I heard that he'd been demoted and shipped off to Warkworth against his wishes. It was that or quit. Something to do with Pittman. You were there when Pittman got it, I think? You and Steele. I hear there was an internal inquiry."

"You said you didn't know anything about Pittman."

"I didn't know why you were asking. And we were talking on the phone."

"Okay. Now you know."

"Pittman was the go-to guy for drugs in Millhaven when he was there, as you probably knew."

"I didn't."

He looked away thoughtfully. "Everybody knew he was working for a little group of maggots who were running drugs into the population. You must remember the guy who got killed in Collins Bay some years back? Picked off with a high-powered rifle from the tower. Weird, eh? The con was a drug dealer. You knew that."

"No. News to me."

"Anyway, one of the fellas in the yard that night was Pittman. And it seems that Steele was in the tower."

"I never heard that. About Steele."

He stared intensely at my face for what seemed like a full minute. "They never did find out who murdered Pittman, right?"

"Never did."

"Big surprise. Same thing with the poor fuck at Collins Bay."

"What are you trying to say, Dwayne? You got something specific to say about Pittman?"

"You kidding?" He was shaking his head, but his eyes were still intense. Time to move on.

"Hey, Tony . . . that little speech before . . . forget that, okay? That wasn't me talking. I don't know where that came from. Right?"

I stood. "I hear you, Dwayne. Maybe when you're out of here we can have a real talk." I placed the palm of my hand against the screen.

He stood, ignored my hand. He was about to put the phone receiver down. I smiled at him, withdrew the friendly hand. "Actually it was partly because of you that I went out early."

His face now openly registered surprise, and caution. "Me?" he said.

"They said I had a tendency to take the side of inmates in too many situations. Ironic, eh? It was on my file when I got to see it, just before I left. Pittman, Vito. They were both mentioned. But you were Exhibit A. They said that for reasons that were personal I took an inappropriate interest in you when you weren't even part of my caseload. Think about that, Dwayne."

He nodded, but his mind had gone somewhere else. You could see it in his eyes. I've noticed that the most revealing moment in a conversation, whether face to face or on a telephone, can come at the very end, when formalities and niceties are done.

"Good luck," I said. "I mean that."

He sat down again, studied the receiver for a moment, chuckled, then said, "You know, for a minute there I thought you were going to say that you had to retire early because I was fucking your wife."

It took a moment for the words to register. I laughed, a spontaneous reaction, then said, "Not funny, Dwayne."

"It wasn't meant to be."

"You're a sick fuck, Dwayne."

"Anna didn't think so."

"And you're a liar . . ."

"Why don't you ask her . . ."

"I don't talk to Anna." I felt my face turning hot, scarlet.

"Well ask her daddy, ask anybody . . ."

"As if . . ."

"Or ask yourself, Tony, how I managed to go straight from Warkworth to a halfway house."

"I thought it was because you were a fucking rat . . ."

"Oh come on, Tony. Give your head a shake. Anna and her daddy made a deal. Dwayne goes to the street, Anna promises never to see that awful Dwayne again. Daddy writes to the parole board. I guess you didn't know how Anna loves bad boys, did you, Tony. Everybody else did. It was win-win, man. It was over between us anyway. I don't much fancy older women. Too complicated. She was only in it for the ride anyway. Didn't give a shit about Dwayne. Typical old lady, not getting it at home."

Now he was standing. Graham, now behind me, said, "Move on Strickland. Time's up."

"Man to man?" Now leaning, face practically against the screen, turned away slightly, "I felt shitty at first. Figured poor Tony's lost his edge. Then I heard about you and the little shrink. The cute one, Sophie. It was the talk of Warkworth. And I just hadda laugh. 'That old horn-dog Tony,' I said."

And he was gone. I was on my feet. Slamming the phone receiver against the screen, then suddenly being wrestled away by Graham. "Hang on, Mr. Breau. Just give it time. The time will come . . ."

two

In the bottomless night my heart learns to ask:
   where is my friend?
Through the sea of incense
I hear the thunder of churchsong. Joy and threats.
Your eyes look into me, grim and stubborn,
inescapable.

ANNA AKHMATOVA

11.

People who didn't know my particular circumstances, or forgot them, would often comment on how much I resembled my adoptive father or some other MacMillan I'd never known. I had the MacMillan eyes or hairline or was tall, which had been a distinguishing feature of a prior generation of the Mountain MacMillans. Even the dark complexion, which was really a reminder of my Acadian heritage.

It always seemed odd to me, even when I was very young, because it was no secret that the MacMillans weren't my biological parents. It was no big deal at our place. We'd always exchange glances, a secret smile or wink at such careless observations. Once my father remarked to a visitor in a jolly way that I hadn't been so much adopted as kidnapped, then told the story.

I still find it very funny because it's partly true that I was stolen from the orphanage, or at least borrowed and never given back.

"Your dad will never be dead as long as you're around."

I'll never forget the words.

It was late in an evening of cards with an older couple who had been regular visitors for tea and sometimes rum and games of auction. I took the words to mean that, not only did I look like him, but I also had his integrity and toughness. High praise to me, especially at that moment. My father had died in the autumn, suddenly, and I suppose we were all still in a state of shock. It was 1969. I was home for the Christmas break and sitting in for him with Ma at the card table. The woman who made the remark was a close friend of the family and knew the facts first hand. I was flattered and profoundly moved and briefly had to leave the table.

Duncan MacMillan was a quiet man who never seemed to register the stress and disappointment of his daily struggle on the edge of a subsistence life. But from time to time he'd simply disappear for a day and a night or maybe two. We'd fret. Ma would spend a lot of time staring out the kitchen window, or sitting by the stove in her rocking chair, rosary in hand. The house would be very still.

He'd come back bleary-eyed and rumpled, sometimes bruised, and head straight for bed. And invariably, afterwards, there would be a quiet conversation with Ma at the kitchen table, rare moments that excluded me. Once, I remember, the conversation at the table included the parish priest. Remembering that explosive aspect of his personality guided and restrained me in many potentially chaotic situations.

After I left the regional jail I sat in the parking lot for a while rationally processing the significance of what Strickland had revealed to me. I imagined what Duncan would have done. I think that guard would have been somewhat less successful holding Duncan back.

In the reeling emotional reaction to Strickland's revelation, there was one idea that probably saved me from extreme behaviour and its consequences: *We can't be held accountable for what we feel, only what we do.*

Sophie, I thought, *I would call you if I had your number with me.* And I laughed, thinking how I'd tell her that while we were agonizing over poetry and responsibility and guilt, euthanizing something real and good . . .

And then I felt the anger, *whitely passionate.* It was just as the poet had warned, the punishment of memory, a sudden rage that drove me to the verge of tears because tears have always been a cursed feature of my outrage. It was one of the reasons why I'd learned how to control my anger, hold it below the tearful threshold where my weakness is exposed. But sitting alone in the parking lot I let the tears flow freely, allowed myself to shout, *You fucking prick.* Then thought of the absurd significance of those worn-out words, here and now. *Goddamn shit.*

I drove to a hotel and checked in. I ruled out the liquor store. Bad idea. But after sitting numbly in my room for what felt like hours, I found my way to the hotel bar. It wasn't about you, Anna. Oh no, love, once again I'm kind of grateful for the insights gleaned from human failures. Your perversity is on such a scale that mine feels infantile, innocent. I suppose I felt at some dark masculine level a primitive humiliation: bigger, better, younger more attractive dick, and all that stuff. But overall and after long consideration, I felt sorry for you. This is what intimacy and knowledge do—enable empathy in the most extraordinary circumstances.

It was Strickland I wanted to punish, and not for his sexual invasion of my life. These things happen out of human weakness. People rarely fuck your wife to hurt you. It's more likely than not the opposite. They often do it in a state of sentimental warmth toward the betrayed. Okay, pity. Whoever knocked up Caddy—if he thought of me at all, it was probably with some faint sense of guilt. Something in the male psyche causes even the most remorseless of men to identify with the poor slob they're cuckolding. Even twisted Strickland. But to throw it in my face like that? That was not a careless gesture. That was calculated to do damage.

It was while sitting in that hotel bar that many forgotten details of my life on the Mountain Road started coming back to me—like when Duncan, overwhelmed, would disappear for a day or two, the way our dog did from time to time. The logic, I once figured out, was to consciously take himself from a bad emotional place to a worse one. Then returning to the normal situation at least felt like an improvement.

I told the bartender to just keep bringing doubles and I'd tell him when to stop.

———

Just after eight that evening I remembered Birch. I turned away from the other people at the bar, found my cellphone in a pocket. I considered calling Caddy but called the store instead.

"Mary, it's Tony. I need a little favour."

I was enunciating carefully, but she didn't seem to notice.

"I got tied up, won't get home tonight. Do you think you could look in on the dog? The key is under the mat in the porch. Maybe let him out for a minute or two."

"Sure," she said. "Or why don't I just take him home with me for the night? When are you back?"

"Oh tomorrow. Next day for sure. I don't want to put you to any trouble."

"No trouble. He'll know me, from being at the store so often with Maymie or Caddy."

"Of course. Okay then. There's dog food on a shelf in the porch. And you'll need to take his coat."

"His coat?"

"The coat he sleeps on . . . Jack's old coat, but it's his now."

"Jack?"

"Yes, Jack, his . . . I almost said his father." I giggled.

"Hey, Tony. Are you okay?"

"Yes," I said, struggling to strike a tone that was appropriately serious. "I'm great. Just got caught up on some business over here. You're sure it's no trouble?"

"Relax," she said. "He'll be fine with me and the cat."

After I put my phone away, the bar felt different, alien, no longer a haven. I considered paying up, returning to my room, but that option felt worse. The bartender leaned across the counter separating us, wiped in front of me, seemed to be in my face all of a sudden, something on his mind. I had a sudden urge to lash out, pre-emptively. I think he saw something in my look and backed away.

"You're sure you want another?" he said.

"Double," I replied.

Mental math is almost always masochistic but it is irresistible. The math was simple. Anna started spending a lot of weekends at home in Warkworth because she said her parents were having some marital difficulties. And she was up front about Strickland: she told me she wanted to help him improve himself; he was determined to finish high school, had even signed up for a university course, English lit if I recall. Helping Strickland was, she said, actually a pleasant experience compared with the miserable atmosphere at home. She was worried that her parents were on the verge of splitting up. Why would old people do something like that? Strickland on the other hand was full of youthful potential. He had the kind of creative curiosity that could take him places if he had a little help. I agreed. I was disarmed. But I was also feeling guilty. I fell asleep in my hotel room that night struggling with a different mental math equation: attempting to calculate exactly when it was that I first told Sophie that I thought I was in love with her, and whether or not it was likely that Strickland was already banging Anna. And whether one betrayal cancels out another.

———

The day before the Pittman board of inquiry, Sophie called. She suggested a long, quiet lunch.

"Not feeling very hungry," I said.

"You have to eat something. We don't have to talk about tomorrow," she said. "We can talk only about nice things."

"For example?"

"Come on, Tony, I know you're just sitting there, fretting. Tomorrow is very simple. You describe exactly what you saw and heard that day. Factually. And then it's done."

"You know and I know it'll not be done."

There was a long silence before she said, "You're right about that. There will be tomorrow and then the day after tomorrow, and the days after that. And you'll have to live with whatever you say in the course of about an hour tomorrow for a long, long time. But I think you know as well as I do that the truth is always easier to live with than a lie. That's all I'm going to say."

"The usual place?"

"That's my Tony. I'll see you there."

And we kept to the plan, kept the conversation light. I teased her, telling her I was writing a song. "A One-Night Stand in Newfoundland." She blushed, as she always did. "That isn't funny."

We'd had one intense conversation in the days after St. John's, then resolved that while we could not regret what had happened, it couldn't be repeated–for a hundred reasons.

But after that lunch, just outside her office door, she took my hand and said softly, "I love the time I spend with you, Tony. I only wish . . ." I kissed her on the lips then and she put her arms

around me and we stood for the longest time, recklessly cling-
ing to each other.

Turning away from her, reluctantly, I saw Tommy Steele
approaching. He seemed to be reading from a file, seemed surprised to notice me. "I guess we aren't supposed to talk," he said.
"But good luck tomorrow." Nodded at Sophie who had stepped
back from me, arms now folded.

"You too," I replied, studying his face and his expression for
insincerity. I couldn't shake the uneasiness all that afternoon.

After my testimony the next day I felt redeemed, exhausted but
somehow refreshed. Steele was waiting just outside the boardroom. He was to be the final witness.

"Well?" he said, as I walked by.

I said nothing and he grabbed my arm. "Well, well, well," he
said. "You can't even look me in the eye."

"Let go of the arm," I said. He let go, hit my shoulder lightly
with the heel of his hand as if brushing something off my
jacket. It might have been a shove.

He was nodding his head as if confirming a sudden private
insight. "Get a good night's sleep, Tony. We got some hard days
ahead."

The inquiry, when all the paperwork was done, recommended
reprimands for Meredith and Wilson. For Tommy Steele, demotion and a transfer out of Kingston. I knew the question everyone was asking: "How come Breau got off?" I could see the
answer in the eyes of my fellow officers.

———

I woke in the hotel room feeling grim and I remembered that my little happy pills were back at home. I checked the time. Ten o'clock, near the check-out deadline. The thought of the long drive home and my arrival there made me want to throw up. And then I did, gagging over the toilet bowl. I realized as the persistent slime dangled from my lips that I hadn't eaten anything since breakfast the day before, and retched again. *Hair o' the dog,* we used to say. The magic bullet. And there was surprising comfort in the prospect of a drink of something stronger than coffee. The dog, I thought, will survive another day with Mary. I stood, splashed water on my face. Then called the front desk and informed them that I planned to stay another night.

There was a Ford dealership across the street from the liquor store. With my bottles safely stowed in the trunk of the car I stopped in front of it to peer in through the showroom window. But the day was sunny and the light reflected off the glass, making it difficult to see. So I went inside, maybe out of boredom, or maybe it was the cautious instinct to forestall the return to the hotel room. Whatever. I went in and was instantly buoyed by the new-car fragrance as a large, well-dressed salesman bore down on me with a predatory smile.

"I'm just having a look," I told him, but he was anxious to assist me anyway. "We don't have a whole lot in just now," he was saying. "The '03 stock went pretty fast in the fall. What were you thinking of?"

"I remembered that growing up we had a Ford half-ton."

"What year would that be?"

"I recall it was a 1955."

"Yes," he said, clapping his hands together. "Just between you and me, the best Fords ever made were '50 to, say, '56. The cars in '49 were pretty good. But for quality and style, my year would have been '54."

"I wouldn't have thought you'd be old enough to remember," I said.

"That's the thing," he said. "They were made to last. My dad had a '54 Monarch that he drove up into the eighties. Took better care of it than me." He laughed. "I still have it. Keep it in the barn under a tarp. Mint condition. Only take it out for the odd homecoming parade. Now what can I show you?"

"Ah, I'm probably just looking."

"And what are you driving, yourself? Just now."

"Actually it's a Toyota . . ."

"Great car," he said enthusiastically. "What year?"

"Well, it's only three years old," I said.

"Yes," he said. "They last and last, those Japanese cars. The thing is, though, just between you and me, the motors in them are so great that people keep them for a long time. Eh? Not so much turnover. So the dealers have to make the money somewhere, right?"

"Right," I said. "On service."

"You got it," he said. "Engines last forever, but everything else goes for a shit with normal wear and tear. You're going to notice from now on, every time you take it in they'll find something. Big, big service bills, and getting bigger as time goes by."

We'd stopped beside a blue pickup. I peered inside. Console like a jumbo jet. Stick shift. Knobs and buttons. Smell of leather. "They don't make half-tons like they used to," I said.

"You can say that again. But don't be fooled. This thing here is rugged as a bulldozer. F-250. Built for work, though I agree you'd never know to look at it."

I opened the door and slid behind the wheel.

"Lots of memories about the '55 half-ton, I imagine," the salesman said.

"Lots of memories," I said. And got out.

"Were you thinking of a pickup?" he asked.

"No," I laughed. "But if it was red, I might be tempted."

"Well, just by chance we have a red one out back. Do you want to have a look?"

Then we were in the garage amidst the clamour of mechanical activity, wheeze and rattle of pneumatic wrenches, men in coveralls moving slowly and deliberately peering under hoisted cars. Near what looked like a brand-new red half-ton, a smudged mechanic was studying a clipboard. There seemed to be a lot of wires running from a panel into the area of the engine.

"Everything's computerized nowadays," the salesman said. He rapped a fender with his fist. "Just got this in yesterday and he's giving her a total check-up. She's an '02 model, F-150. Guy took it home last fall but unfortunately passed away at Christmas. Low, almost no, mileage. Wife can't drive a stick shift so we took it back, gave her something more appropriate. I could give you a pretty good deal on this baby."

"Ah, I don't know," I said, holding back.

"This here, the F-150 was what replaced the little F-100 you had back in the day. This is as close as you're going to get. Jump in behind the wheel," he said. "Then we'll have a look at what you're driving." He was beaming.

———

We were reminiscing after Duncan died, Ma's eyes red-rimmed. It was unusual, this revelation of emotion where her husband was concerned. "You probably wouldn't remember the time he landed home with the red truck," she was saying. "You'd have been very small."

"I remember. I was seven."

As if she hadn't heard me, she said "You hadn't been here very long, so . . ." And she seemed to drift, obviously forgetting that I was already five when I arrived, but in her mind, newborn.

I was nodding.

"Ah well," she sighed. "Poor Duncan. He was never much for self-indulgence. But that was how it seemed to me when he landed home with that truck. God forgive me. We were struggling but he said, no, we needed something. And I remember saying, 'But red?'" She laughed then and wiped at her eyes. "It'll be so conspicuous. That was what I was thinking. Red. They'll all be talking. And he just said, 'They can talk all they want.' He went away after that, to pay for the truck. To Elliot Lake he went. After that he was more or less back to the mines whenever things got tight financially. Which was a lot."

And I was thinking of how they laughed at me ten years later, when I'd arrive at dances in an old red half-ton, especially in the summer when the parking lot would be full of fancy cars with plates from Michigan and Massachusetts and Ontario, smirking at my truck until the summer night when Caddy Gillis let me drive her home in it.

———

The bank was a short drive away. It took only minutes to get a draft to cover the balance outstanding after a generous offer on the trade-in. It was as if destiny ordained that I would own that truck and I was suddenly lifted by a rare excitement, Strickland, Anna, Pittman forgotten, at least for the moment.

"You can take her out of here tomorrow morning," the salesman said, gripping my hand.

Back in the hotel room I poured a whisky to celebrate my new purchase, admitting that I felt improved. After Duncan bought the little red truck on an impulse that might well have been a lot like mine, he spent the next year working underground to pay for it. I'd gone to a bank for fifteen minutes and had drawn the money that I needed from the settlement I got when my career came crashing down around me. Odd, thinking about it: Duncan getting paid to work, Tony getting paid to quit.

Mary wasn't at the store. Collie told me it was her day off. "You can call her at home." I said I'd just drop by her place, that she was looking after my dog. "Yes," said Collie. "It was all she talked about in here yesterday. The dog. That's some rig outside. New?"

"Second hand," I said quickly. "But new to me. Figured living in the country a fella needs a good half-ton."

"True enough," he said. "And they're comfortable as cars nowadays."

Birch was standing on his hind legs, paws against my thigh, making whining sounds, obviously glad to see me.

Mary beamed. "Will you look at him. You show up and I don't exist anymore. Typical guy." I squatted, scratched between his ears.

"Did you behave yourself?" I asked him.

"Settled right in, he did. Didn't you, Birch." And now she was squatting too, the dog delighted with the double dose of attention. "Only one little slip-up, right, doggie?"

"Oh dear," I said. "What did he do?"

"Nothing at all," she said. "It was my fault anyway. First time I let him out to pee he streaked for the woods toward Strickland's place. I thought I'd lost him but he was only gone a minute. He came right back. You're a good boy, Birch, aren't you?" He licked her hand, nuzzled my face.

"You got a treat for that, didn't you?" He whined briefly. "No. No treats now, not until your next visit."

"Treats?" I said.

"Our little secret," she said. "Just between himself and Mary."

When we were leaving she said, "You can drop him here with me any time you want. Hey, is that a new rig?"

"New to me," I said.

Sitting at my old desk, sorting through the mail I thought: Maybe I've turned a corner. Maybe the truck is symbolic, an emphatic line between who I was before and who I'll be for the long haul. Maybe I owe it all to Strickland, this awakening. Good things often emerge from the debris of what feels like a disaster. And suddenly I felt like calling Anna and saying, "Hey, guess what. *I don't give a shit. I really, really don't give a shit. I don't care that you were screwing Strickland behind my back. You're both pathetic. So carry on, whatever."*

I swung my chair and faced the filing cabinet, opened the drawer and pulled out the legal file and the fat folder marked "Anna." Affidavits, lawyers' letters. Some faded faxes. And I remembered how she'd call on a Sunday night to tell me that she planned to stay a few more days in Warkworth for meetings with some inmate clients there. It never occurred to me to complain, or pry. Absences became the norm. Trust pre-empts anxiety, habit reinforces trust. Dutifully I'd ask about the old folks. Dutifully she'd explain. I suspected not a thing.

Time to get rid of this, I thought. Maybe tomorrow or maybe next week—a little bonfire out back. Time for new beginnings.

"Hey, Caddy. What are you doing?"

"What am I doing? Let me see," she said. "I'm sitting in my hot tub, sipping champagne and reading *Vogue*. How about you?"

"I didn't know you had a hot tub."

"You poor guy. Everybody in St. Ninian has a hot tub. But actually—do you really want to know the truth?"

"Of course."

"I'm knitting."

"Knitting?"

"What's wrong with knitting?"

"I didn't say ..."

"It was in your tone of voice."

"Look, can I come by? I have a surprise."

"A surprise?"

"Something I bought. I want to show it to you."

She walked slowly around the front of my new truck with her arms folded. "Red," she said at last. "It'll sure stand out."

"It's a Ford," I said. "A red Ford half-ton."

She was nodding. "So I see."

Then I realized that she was freezing. We were standing outside in the dim light of an evening at the end of January and she was wearing a light sweater. "Jump in and I'll turn the heat on," I said. She opened the truck door.

"Well," she said. "This is lovely. I love the new-car smell."

"It's actually second hand. Hardly driven. The first owner died shortly after he got it."

"I hope it isn't the *buidseachd*," she said. "I should go in and get the holy water. Wasn't that what the old people used to do? Sprinkle holy water for luck. And put a little cross from Palm Sunday up on the sun visor."

And I felt a sudden welling up, looking at her there, listening to her as she teased. "Let's celebrate," I said. "Let me buy you dinner."

"I don't know," she said.

"Come on," I said. "Enough of the hot tub. It'll just wrinkle you up anyway."

She laughed. "Let me get my coat."

——

Driving through that early winter evening, the western sky in flames, low pink clouds hovering above a claret sea, I felt balanced in a way that had become unfamiliar. Anna exorcised, Caddy beside me in a red truck. Maybe it was just a moment, but I wasn't going to quibble.

I hadn't forgotten Strickland but my anger was gone, though God knows I now hoped the courts would nail him and throw him back into the shark tank where he belonged. That old cliché was running through my mind. "What goes around, comes around."

As if she were following my mental conversation, Caddy said, "I had a call today from the prosecution. The preliminary hearing starts next week. I'll be testifying."

I said, "It'll be good for you, a kind of closure if there is such a thing."

"I'm not looking forward to rehashing a lot of stuff I'm trying to put behind me."

"I can see that. But it's important that they hear from you."

She didn't respond. I glanced in her direction but she was staring out the side window at the darkening sea.

It was mid-week and the restaurant was quiet. As we passed an older couple, the woman reached out and caught Caddy's hand. Caddy introduced me—"My friend, Tony Breau," she said. The name sounded strange coming from her.

Distant relatives of Jack, she explained, after we sat down. Then she whispered, "I almost said MacMillan."

I said I thought Jack was from away. Yes, she said, but he had roots here too. She seemed subdued. I suggested a glass of wine while we explored the menu. She smiled and I ordered.

As she sipped her wine she picked at the tablecloth with a long fingernail that was painted silver. Finally she said, "There's word going around that both sides have approached you to testify and you've said no to everybody."

"You have good sources," I said.

"It's true, then."

"Yes, I'm staying out of it."

She looked away, nodded slowly.

"I'm not interested in helping Strickland's case. And for reasons I don't particularly want to go into, I don't think I could be of much assistance to the Crown."

"I see." She took another sip of wine. "We don't have to talk about it. Actually we shouldn't."

But I had to tell her. "Strickland is going out on a limb. He wants to avoid a trial because he says he'd be at great risk in the prison system. He's considered a rat in that world. And that kind of reputation can get you killed."

"A rat," she said, nodding. "I saw something on television."

"It's the lowest form of life in prison," I said.

"Well." She made an unsympathetic face. "He's made a trial inevitable, hasn't he?"

"Maybe not," I said. "Not if the charges get thrown out at the preliminary."

"How could that happen?" Her expression was dismayed.

"Caddy. They admitted to me . . . the Crown admitted to me that the evidence is thin."

She looked away, nodding. "I suppose I shouldn't be surprised if he wiggles out of it." Then she studied my face for a while, as if I were an interesting stranger. "I sometimes forget that you come from another world. I don't mean that to sound . . ."

"It's true," I said. "It's another world. A hard, hard world."

"And maybe he belongs there . . ."

I examined the tablecloth, struggling to hold on to her, to stop this drift. Then she reached across, squeezed my hand, held it. "Poor Tony," she said. "I'm glad you aren't in that world anymore."

I just nodded.

"Tell me. What would happen to him . . . ?"

"Probably nothing," I said. "There would be a hundred ways to protect him."

"And why can't you just say that?"

"Caddy, his lawyer could make an awful mess of my credibility. Strickland knows as much about me as I know about him."

"What could he possibly know that would damage your credibility?"

"Strickland had an affair with my wife." It was out, inadvertently, the moment suddenly derailed by shock.

"My God." She withdrew her hand. In the silence that followed, the restaurant seemed to have become very busy. People at other tables laughing, clinking cutlery and glasses, background music, waiters enumerating specials. Caddy's eyes now fixed on me, once again the stranger.

"How could you possibly know something like that?"

I laughed. "Because he told me."

"He told you? And you believed him?"

I nodded. "I'm afraid so."

"Why would he tell you?"

"It gives him power. If I'm not going to help him, I'll know the risk of doing damage to his case."

"How could he have an affair with Anna when he was a prisoner?"

"He was in a place where her father was the warden. Anna was there a lot, visiting her parents, inmates who were clients. I told you she's a lawyer. She was also helping Strickland with some courses, to improve his education." I laughed.

"How . . . ?"

"I introduced them."

Once again she slipped her hand over mine, squeezed my fingers.

"So they'd drag that out in court and I'd come off as just some guy with a personal grudge."

"Poor Tony. What a world."

"And he's indicated that he knows some other things related to my work. I can only assume some of the information came from her. In which case he probably knows a lot, especially about a particular situation that became one of the reasons for my retirement. So."

I called the waiter. "Double Scotch, water on the side. You? Another glass of wine?"

She shook her head. "I often wondered why you retired so young, Tony. In every way, still in your prime."

"Maybe that's what it looks like."

"You're a good man, Tony. You were a good man when the rest of us were only children. I always thought that."

"You might not think that if Strickland got his yap going."

"Among other things, he's a liar and everybody knows it."

"And what would you say if he had proof that I'm as bad as he is, causing death by negligence. Or worse–cowardice."

"I wouldn't believe a word of it, not coming from anybody."

I studied her face and the soft shadows tracing lines left there by time and sorrow, but in her searching eyes, there was no shadow, no trace of doubt. I forced myself to smile.

"Have you given any thought to what we're going to eat?"

Sitting outside her place, truck engine running, Caddy said: "I'd ask you in for tea but it's getting late." I examined her face, listened to her tone of voice for some lingering traces of disappointment or embarrassment from my disclosures or from the last time I'd been in her house, the stormy night we shared her bed.

"Thanks anyway," I said. "I really should get home. And of course there's my guest."

For an instant she seemed confused, but then she smiled. "Ah yes. After the court stuff, I'll take him off your hands."

"He's no trouble at all," I said. "He's good company."

"You'll be going to the court yourself, I'm sure."

"I don't know," I said. "I wasn't really planning to." The thought of watching Strickland posturing, manipulating, left me cold. "To tell you the truth the sight of Strickland would be a bit more than I can deal with just now."

"I know what you mean." She continued to sit thoughtfully on the far side of the truck. "I was hoping, though, that you'd be there. It would be good to see you there."

I silently cursed the console between us, the ridiculous cup holders, four of them it seemed.

"Do you know when you'll be on?"

"They've set aside three days," she said. "He told me I'll probably be on the second day, after a policeman and a pathologist and some others. Probably the afternoon sometime."

"What day?"

"Next Thursday, the thirteenth."

"I'll come and get you at noon and we'll go together."

"Ah no, Tony, I wouldn't . . . I didn't mean you have to baby-sit me."

"Caddy, if you want me there, I'll be there."

I woke to a racket the next morning. I'd slept in and it was nearly ten o'clock. The dog was barking and the phone was ringing by the bedside. I half-expected Caddy. I picked it up, struggled to sound cheerful. But there was a computerized female voice on the other end: "You have a collect call from a correctional institution." And then his voice, full of confidence: "Dwayne Strickland."

"If you wish to accept the call," the computer said, "say 'yes.' If not, you may hang up now."

I put the receiver down slowly, firmly.

"Hey, Mr. Breau," the inmate said. He was smiling as if we were old acquaintances. We were on Lower E range. There were two other inmates nearby but too far distant to overhear. He was speaking softly. The name printed on his shirt didn't mean anything to me. Dewolf. "I just came from Warkworth. Somebody there asked me to give you a message." I was confused.

"Strickland?" I said.

"No," he said. "Steele."

I said: "Steele?"

"You're Tony Breau?"

"Yes."

"Steele said you also go by Wentworth."

"Wentworth? You must have the wrong guy."

"No. He said it was your nickname among the coppers, eh, Wentworth. Anyway, he says hello . . . hopes you're well. Says, take care of yourself."

"Wentworth?" I asked in the lunchroom. "That name mean anything to anybody?"

There was an old guard there, memory going back to the fifties. He said: "What about him?" And I said: "Someone brought his name up." And the old guy said, "Only Wentworth I ever heard of was a guard here back in the early sixties. He was making his rounds one night, somebody shanked him in one of the toilets. No witnesses and nobody ever figured out a motive. Eventually there was a suspect, based on information from another inmate. But no proof. Possibly a contract job. Somebody with a beef against poor Wentworth put out a hit on him. Not hard to do in a place like this. Some of these fuckers would kill you for a cuppa coffee."

12.

I remember it was late on a Friday afternoon and I was preparing for an early weekend exit. I was actually standing, stuffing a briefcase, when the door opened and two officers from institutional security walked in.

"Got a minute?"

I sat down. They sat opposite me. I didn't know them well but remembered one of them from the Pittman investigation. He was the larger of the two, with a shaved head. "You know some con by the name of Dewolf?"

"What about him?"

"He's been talking about you."

"So what's Dewolf been saying?"

The smaller of the two looked at the floor for a moment,

then straight at me. "What do you know about him?"

"Not much," I said. "Sex offender. Came here a while back from Warkworth. Out of the blue he made some comments to me that could have been a threat."

"When was that?"

"I dunno. Six, ten months ago. I put it out of my mind. Why?"

"Who did you report this to?"

"Nobody."

"Were there witnesses?"

"There were a couple of cons in the area but I doubt if they heard anything."

"Do you remember who they were?"

"I really didn't take any notice."

"What exactly did Dewolf say?" Now he had a notebook in his hand, flipping through for a blank page.

"He mentioned a name, said it was my nickname. Wentworth. I'd never heard it before. Then I checked it out and found out who Wentworth was."

The larger one, with the shaved head, had his notebook out now too. Mumbled, "So you know who Wentworth was?" I remembered an uneasy feeling from earlier, when this one was asking me questions about Pittman. How he would refer to Steele as Tommy.

"Yes," I said. "I found out."

"And why didn't you report this?"

"As far as I was concerned, Dewolf was just another yappy con. If I took every little . . ."

"It isn't just about you, Tony," the smaller, smarter version said. "This is about the whole place. A potential threat to you is a threat to everybody."

I smiled patiently. "Yes, but there's such a thing as threat assessment."

The big one leaned across the desk. "It's not your place to be making unilateral assessments. Now what was the basis for your beef with Dewolf?"

I looked at him steadily, trying to convey that I knew as much about institutional security as he did. "I never laid eyes on the asshole before in my life. So what has he been saying?"

The smaller one sighed. "Vague remarks. And you're right he could be posturing. But there's enough in what he says about people wanting you taken out that we're taking it serious. So what's the beef about?"

"I have no beef. Not with him."

"Not with him?"

For an instant I considered explaining but an instinct made me shrug and look away from the hard unsympathetic face in front of me. "Not with anybody that I know."

The big one sat back and folded his arms. "So what do you think it was about then?"

I shrugged, pursed my lips, folded my arms too. "Beats me."

"Tommy Steele," he said.

"Tommy Steele," I repeated, trying to seem surprised. Forced a smile. "Tommy. What about him?"

"He's over at Warkworth now. We were wondering if you ever hear from him."

"Ahhh. Right. I'd forgotten that he moved over there. Maybe he's picked something up, about this Dewolf. What do you think? You think it might be worth talking to him?"

The smaller IPSO said: "You and Steele . . . how did you leave things?"

I shrugged. "Who's to know?"

I looked from one to the other, picked up a pen, rolled it between thumb and forefinger, genuinely considering. For a moment I wanted to tell them about the fallout after the inquiry into Pittman's death; the silence and the tension I'd encountered in the day room, among the lockers. Tell them about the hostile glances, the feeling of exclusion, especially after Steele's demotion and transfer to Warkworth. Tell them that Dewolf's message really came from Steele. But I asked myself: Why make matters worse? Why compound the damage done already, why confirm your reputation as a rat? And, really, how could I tell these goons that I now considered my co-workers to be more dangerous than any con? Especially the bald one, who called Steele "Tommy."

At last I said, "I doubt if Tommy knows anything, I'm sure he'd have come forward if he'd heard."

"You and Steele," the big one said quietly. "He couldn't have been a happy camper after the inquiry."

I tried to compose a poker face. "Tommy? We talked things through. What are you getting at?"

The smaller one, seated, now picking at a cuticle, said, "We're all on the same side here, Tony."

I shrugged. "Believe me, I want to help you. But it's likely just some old goof in Warkworth with a grudge. I'm sure there's more than one. I checked Dewolf's history and didn't find anything to worry about, as long as I'm over nine years old." I smiled and dropped the pen.

They stood. The smaller officer leaned across the desk, held out his hand. I grasped it firmly. The skinhead turned toward the door, no courtesies. "We'll be getting back to you," the smaller one said.

"Come on," I said, suddenly feeling the slackness in my smile. "What's to get back about? This is nothing. Dewolf is nobody."

"That'll be for somebody else to decide." And then they left.

It occurred to me to talk to Anna. Get a lawyer's perspective. Should I make a legal move on Steele? Should I be getting ready for a problem with the service? But I let it slide and then it was another summer. We talked about vacation.

"We should really spend a week in the old place," I said. "The place needs some work. What do you think?"

"I think you should go alone," she said. "Give me a chance to catch up on some files. Then maybe . . ."

"St. Ninian without you?" I laughed.

"Oh, I'm sure there are some old girlfriends there to keep you happy."

In the end we decided to postpone a vacation. "We'll take all of January," she said. "We'll get a place in Florida. Just do nothing for a month."

Anna had become extraordinarily busy, away from home a lot. We started referring to time spent together as "dates." A growing legal practice sucks up time and personal attention but I felt no resentment at all. We'd had what felt like a nine-year honeymoon. Now we were both wrapped up in work and

I was happily observing her grow confident and vibrant in spite of all the pressure and professional demands—not to mention the burden of two dysfunctional parents.

"How much longer does your dad have 'til retirement?" I asked once.

"He'll stay in the job as long as they let him. I can't imagine what will happen when all they have is each other. Oh, and by the way, Dwayne may well be heading for a halfway house ..."

"What ... ?"

"You'd be amazed by the progress. He's like a different person. Dad thinks he's almost ready."

Fridays she'd always try to be home early—we tried to keep one evening a week for going out together. And when she did arrive at about nine o'clock on a Friday night in August she seemed to linger in the front hall, slowly fumbling through her brief-case. She finally retrieved a sheet of paper and her glasses.

"I've been in Warkworth," she said, when finally she noticed me. Her face and tone were tense.

"Warkworth," I said. "How are things in Shangri-La?"

She didn't seem to be listening. "Tony, we have to talk about something."

"Sure, what."

"This," she said. She was holding up the sheet of paper, smiling tightly, eyes narrowed.

"What's that?"

"You know what it is. Who the hell is SM?"

"Give it to me."

She handed it over.

In the end Sophie had copied it by hand, added a little note. "The wisdom of experience . . . SM."

"Where did you get that?" I asked. I was hoping that I sounded indignant, to mask the guilt I really felt.

"I asked a question. Who is SM?"

"Sophie MacKinnon," I said. "You've heard me mention Sophie, from work."

"Sophie MacKinnon . . ."

"The psychologist at the RTC."

"That Sophie? I thought she was French."

"She is French." It was a welcome turn in the tone of the conversation and I was about to embark on an explanation of Sophie's fascinating family history, going back to the conquest of Quebec in 1759.

"So what's she doing writing poetry to you?"

"She didn't write it."

"Whatever. You should know, Tony, that I've been hearing embarrassing gossip around Warkworth. Now this? I think you owe me an explanation."

The explanation, under Anna's interrogation, went on for days. Tony on the witness stand, Sophie invisible but everywhere. To be precise, it happened mostly at night as during the day we were both preoccupied with the demands of our professions. For once I felt the elation of relief as the heavy doors of the penitentiary closed behind me every morning.

I considered telling Sophie what was going on at home,

but decided not to. It was best to leave her out of it for as long as possible.

I've had a lot of experience with lawyers so I could follow the trajectory of Anna's strategy, anticipate the inevitable Big Moment: So have you two slept together? And I knew that when the moment came I wouldn't lie. The choice, for me, would be between simplicity and exculpatory context. The value of indignant posturing was dubious, especially with Anna. Looking back and knowing what she was really up to I can only laugh.

I started with a pre-emptive denial. There was nothing between us. Sophie's French, a psychologist, mystical, always trying to see into the soul. And Anna seemed to have been reassured and the discussions became, mercifully, more general–state of our relationship, pressures of work, loss of intimacy, stuff that I could handle easily, stuff that had been front and centre on both our minds, as we discovered.

I carefully measured out my concerns and actually thought that we were making progress. But then on the third evening, halfway through a bottle of Burgundy (I had just remarked on what a great year 2000 was and how maybe we should take our holiday in Burgundy instead of Florida), she said: "Let's get back to Sophie."

"What exactly have you heard?"

She smiled, almost warmly. "I asked the question."

I smiled back. "I didn't realize it was a question."

Her smile died. "Come on Tony, let's not play games. I've heard the gossip. Now tell me, straight out. What's between you two?"

We're friends and colleagues, I explained. I was intrigued by her name the first time I encountered her at a team meeting. She was obviously francophone but the name on the identifying card in front of her, S. MacKinnon, suggested that she was married to someone Scottish, maybe someone from where I was raised. So during a coffee break I introduced myself and she informed me that MacKinnon was her own name. She came from a small place in Quebec where many of the invading British soldiers settled back in the eighteenth century, intermarrying with the French or women from the native tribes, so that there were many there who, though unilingual francophones, had names like MacKinnon, Fraser or MacDonald. And I recall how Sophie laughed at the irony of names–"You have a French name but you're an Anglo."

In meetings we seemed to agree on most issues. I came to rely on her judgement, common sense and, yes, compassion. She believes in people, actually means it when she talks about "correction." We've become natural allies. Drink a lot of coffee together. I laughed. Anna was just listening, frowning. Then I brought Strickland into the narrative, and I might be imagining it now but there seemed to be a subtle change in Anna's posture. I told her how Sophie became a vital connection between Dwayne and me, how Sophie had asked for my help in working to transform Dwayne from con to citizen. I might have grown suspicious but at the time I was simply relieved by her momentary change of mood.

———

Four days into the confrontation that started with the poem, Sophie called my office. "Everything okay?"

"Everything's cool," I said. "What's up?"

"Was just wondering. Haven't seen or heard from you for what seems like years." She laughed. "Isn't that pathetic. I feel like an insecure school girl."

"I'm sorry," I said. "There's a bunch of things going on. Let's have a lunch soon."

"You're sure you're okay?"

"I'm good, Sophie. Thinking of you all the time." And that, at least, was true.

Anna was sarcastic. "So. Coffees and lunches and God knows what ... what *did* you find to talk about in all that time. I've never thought of you as a compulsive conversationalist, Tony. And surely it wasn't all about your convicts."

"Actually it was mostly about work. And her family."

I had asked about the three children who were conspicuous in photographs on her desk. The oldest had just turned thirteen. Her husband, also in a framed photograph, was a carpenter—a very skilled carpenter who built cabinets for the kitchens and bathrooms of wealthy people.

"Her family? What about *your* family?"

"Please ..."

"I can't believe that you would talk about us and our marriage to an outsider. That's appalling."

"What?"

"You expect me to believe ..."

"I never discussed our marriage with Sophie. There was nothing to discuss. I thought our marriage was just fine."

"I can hear the two of you. I can't believe this. So just how far did this little *serial* tête-à-tête proceed, and I want an honest answer."

"I don't know what you mean."

Her laugh was bitter. "My God! Where's your head, Tony? Don't play stupid with me. Did. You. Have. Sex. With. Her."

"Excuse me?"

"Did you *fuck* her, Tony?"

I was—and I can't think of another description—flabbergasted by that ugly, vulgar word. My head swarmed with hot self-righteous answers. Or, I should say, *responses* because all the possibilities came out of a primitive instinct for self-preservation. Lie. Dissemble. But there could be no retreat. Lying and evasion could only make it worse.

"Yes," I said, struggling for dignity. "Once."

She became, I thought—I hoped—very calm and suddenly so did I.

We stared at each other for the longest time and in the silence I felt the love for Anna that I had forgotten because over time it had broken into fragments that had become redistributed in a variety of places. Isn't that what happens to long-term couples? The vast emotion that brings us together eventually gets broken down and packed away in smaller packages. Sort of like the way information is stored in tiny bits on digital devices, ultimately unrecognizable for what they are in aggregate. Sometimes we forget all about them until we stumble across one little package unexpectedly. And I wanted everything to not have happened. For a moment, I wanted my life to not have happened.

Our house was very silent. I ached for a sound. Anything. A crash of something falling, smashing. Heavy metal music. The clash of steel cell doors closing, the terrifying stampede sound of a cell extraction unit. Anything to distract from the inevitability of what would come next.

"Are you in love with her?"

The answers rose quickly, silently to my tongue. Yes. No. "I'm not sure," I said.

"That's as bad as a yes," she said. "A chicken-shit yes."

"What I'm trying to say ..."

She sighed, walked to a window, arms folded across her chest. And eventually, with her back to me, she asked: "So what are we going to do?"

I could have said we could work it out. Maybe I should have said it. Maybe it was true. I could have said: there's nothing between Sophie and me and that was, in physical terms, quite true by then. But emotionally? I suddenly felt emptied out of words and thought. But I knew the unutterable pain betrayal causes–I knew its permanence. I had learned about it the hard way when I was nineteen years old.

I said, "I'm sorry."

"I suppose you are," she said.

From the tone I knew that she'd already moved on. I just didn't know where she was coming from and I didn't have a clue about her destination.

"I'm going to bed," she said finally.

———

I lay awake in the guest room. I desperately wanted to call Sophie, fought the impulse, satisfied myself with an imagined conversation: *You would have been impressed. It was, in the circumstances, surprisingly civil.*

At 2:38 in the morning I tiptoed into our shared bathroom and collected basic toiletries. Razor. Deodorant. Toothbrush. Toothpaste. That'll be enough for now. Motel rooms always have shampoo.

Later, lying in the darkness of the anonymous motel room, surrounded by the impersonal fragrances of commerce and other transient lives, I made a mental note of the date: August 5, 2001. It would be one of the benchmarks in memory, one of the series of existential dots that, when joined together, show the jagged course of a screwed-up life. I'd checked into a low-budget motel near enough to the highway that the night was busy with the hurried sounds of traffic. I noted in the parking lot all the minivans with bike racks and roof racks, the paraphernalia of family adventures. And I thought of Sophie, surrounded by her little clan. Would the outcome have been any different if my answer to Anna's loaded question had been no? If that lovely night in June had never happened, would I be here now, trying to anticipate my future? What if I had been able to clearly, honestly, unambiguously answer yes or no to the logical question, Are you in love with her? But, I told myself, it doesn't matter, does it? Even if this dreadful moment were a consequence of just one memorable evening in an unlikely far-off place, I'd still have no regrets.

———

The motel room was stale and stuffy when I awoke to the sound of children in the parking lot, the consciousness of where I was and why I was there restored by the glare of daylight.

I sat for a long time naked on the side of the bed, staring at the floor. I thought of calling home, decided to wait until the house was empty, leave a message on the answering machine. *I'm okay, in case you're wondering. I'll stop by the house later in the day to pick up some clothes. I hope you haven't changed the locks already.* Tried to sound ironic.

Then I left a message at Sophie's office. *Hi, it's me. It's important that we have that lunch soon.*

It was distressing to find two cars in a driveway I expected to be vacant. I circled the block but they were still there. I parked in front of a van, where I could watch the driveway through the mirror on the passenger side. One was Anna's blue BMW but I didn't recognize the second car, a small red Mazda. After fifteen minutes I was certain that the visitor was there for the long haul. A man friend perhaps? Unlikely. I circled the block again, pulled in behind Anna's car, strode to the door and knocked.

There was no immediate response from inside and I felt my poise begin to wobble from the incongruity of standing on my own doorstep waiting for admission. I had a goddamned key in my pocket. What was preventing me from using it, as I had ten thousand times before? Then I heard that subtle shift in the internal ambience of the house that told me someone was stirring inside and, yes, a heel-strike on the brief expanse of wooden floor between Persian rugs I could imagine clearly. Then the click behind the door.

"Why are you knocking?" Anna asked, pale and puzzled, when she opened up.

Then she turned, and walked briskly down the hallway.

Her visitor was a woman, sitting sideways on the edge of the chesterfield, thighs pressed close together. She was in the act of tugging her tight skirt over her knees. She was attractive, a tumult of auburn hair to her shoulders, a face that might be pleasant in other circumstances. She was smiling but with that cold professional appraisal that conveys tactical interest without the normal human elements of curiosity or self-consciousness. Another lawyer, I thought. She stood and said to Anna, "I'll run along, but you know where I'll be."

"Yes," said Anna. They embraced, sealing my feeling of exclusion. The stranger nodded in my direction and left without another word.

"There's one cold individual. I'd have worn a winter coat if I'd known that she was here," I said, when the door had closed behind her.

"What do you expect?" said Anna, picking up two coffee cups and disappearing into the kitchen. Then she was back. "I'm sure you've heard me mention her. Rita Morgan, from the office."

"Aha," I said. "The specialist in family law."

"She's my friend, that's all," Anna said. "It isn't what you think."

"And what *do* I think?"

She studied me, readjusting her advantages. "God knows,"

she said. "I don't anymore. I thought I knew you. Now I realize I probably never did."

I sighed. "You're reading a lot into a very simple situation."

"Is it really so simple, Tony?"

I sat, stared at my hands. "Do you mind if I have a drink?"

"You know where it is."

I took a chance. "Can I get one for you?"

She hesitated. "No," she said at last. "I don't think so."

There are details that at the time seemed important but they've grown vague. I had three drinks, the last one stronger than it should have been but by then I didn't care—not about my self-control, my rationality, health, or the consequences of saying the wrong thing in such circumstances.

"That poem," Anna said. "I think I know it off by heart." Outside the day was darkening.

"I already told you she didn't ..."

She stood, waved a dismissive hand. "Of course she didn't. I know that. If she could write like that I wouldn't expect to find her in ..." and she abandoned the thought with another wave of the hand.

"It's profound, though," she said. "A warning, as I read it, about the peril of deep emotional involvement when your options are already circumscribed."

"Whatever the hell that means."

"You know exactly what I mean, Tony. You let it get out of control when you should have frigging known there was no place to go with it. That's what surprises me. You were putting a lot at risk. Never mind us. She has a family. You were also risking an important professional relationship. Friendship. Where was your head?"

I couldn't think of a thing to say. I stood. "I just want to gather up some stuff for now. We can continue this another time. Or not."

"No, wait," she said. "Just sit. Here let me get you another little drink."

"I'm driving."

"We'll call a cab."

"I should . . ."

"Tony, I love you. Just hear me out. I deserve that."

I was stunned to silence by the force of her sudden declaration. Then she was beside me on the couch, hand under my jacket massaging my chest. "Hear me out, please. We can get past this."

The details of what she had to say would be interesting if that had really been the start of a happily-ever-after kind of resolution. I don't think I'm ruining the story by disclosing that it wasn't. Far from it. Obviously if that had been the case I wouldn't be where I am now. She was stalling, using age-old tactics. Before long she was undoing buttons, her own as well as mine.

Anna had always been a rather quiet lover, but that afternoon, in wild disarray on the couch, the floor, and later in the bedroom, she became a choir, an orchestra of carnal vocables. I felt like a giant, but later realized that I was really Samson getting a haircut.

That evening over wine and pizza, though, I was a very happy man. The sordid past had been resolved, I thought, my future spread in front of me enriched by a priceless lesson learned. It was a reconciliation that lasted just about a month.

I had warned Anna to leave Sophie out of it. She didn't deserve to have her life infected by a single lapse that was 99 percent my fault. Read that poem again, I told her. It is a reflection of the truth—the relationship was, except for one mistake, platonic. Anna only laughed. "Don't worry," she said. But still I did and on the Monday I went to Sophie's office.

"Close the door," Sophie said.

"How are you?" I asked. She didn't answer.

Then she said quietly, "I know something's happened." And when I didn't immediately respond, I saw the colour rising in her face.

I told her simply. The poem had become the catalyst for a confrontation but the crisis had come and gone, like a summer storm. There had been a very brief separation but now the difficult process of reconciliation was underway and a crucial part of it was a promise to start anew. I was good at crisis management, containing conflict, I said. She had nothing to worry about.

"Is that what you want?" she asked.

I hesitated before I answered, but said, "Yes." Then: "I think so. I think that I should try."

She smiled and the smile told me that she'd read the hesitation for what it really was, a brief moment of doubt before dishonesty that was essentially benign.

She caught my hands, leaned forward and kissed both cheeks.

"You should go," she said quietly. She repeated it, kindly. "You should go. Be good to yourself, Tony."

It was only after I left her office that I felt the full weight of the loss.

It was another Friday–September 7, nearing the one-month anniversary of the grand reconciliation. I actually had hoped to celebrate with a dinner out, wine and romance. It had been a busy month with little of the passionate abandon of that surprising Saturday when she so aggressively and unequivocally inaugurated our physical, emotional renewal. I almost laugh aloud now, thinking back. But in the moment I accepted it for what it was, renaissance and reformation: early to rise, early out the door; long productive days at work; if not passion in the evenings, at least mature collegiality.

I would find her in bed late at night, reading glasses perched on the tip of her nose, duvet littered with briefs and affidavits. Cheek peck, hand squeeze, "night night," shallow, restless slumber. Then morning, and repeat.

I had decided on that Friday, September 7, that it was time for an initiative on my part–a pre-emptive charm attack. I was about to order flowers. At noon she left a message on the answering machine at home. I recall standing there that evening listening, disappointment welling, a bouquet in one hand, a bottle of wine in the other. The message was brief. "Gotta go to Warkworth, hon. The old kids are acting up again. Need mediation. Call you later." There was a kissing sound.

I suppose I might have wondered why she didn't ask me to

go along. After all, I had been part of the Moroz family drama for more than ten years. But I also knew that I really didn't have much to contribute. On the few occasions when I was present for a crisis, it all unfolded in a blizzard of jitterbugging Polish, flying Js and Zs and bitterness. When I'd ask Anna for a précis of what was going on she'd simply roll her eyes. "You really don't want to know."

September 11 was a sunny day. I got out of bed and stood naked for a moment, studying the silent street, suffused by a sense of peace. I hadn't heard from Anna since the Friday. Obviously another crisis in the Moroz household. I wasn't worried about the silence.

I walked to the bathroom, turned on the shower. There was a radio on a shelf above the sink. I pressed a thumb to the power button. A newscast was ending. Then a note of anxiety in the announcer's voice ". . . a report just in . . . an airplane has crashed on one of the towers of the World Trade Center in New York. I repeat . . ."

I left the voice behind me and when I emerged from the shower there was music. But my curiosity compelled me to turn on the TV in the bedroom. It was preset to an all-news channel. I saw a blue sky, a towering building with smoke billowing, crowd voices urgent, excited, people pointing, people running. And then the doorbell rang. I looked out the bedroom window and I recognized the small red car.

Rita Morgan was pale and clearly uncomfortable standing there. I assumed it was from surprise at seeing me in the doorway in a bathrobe, and I was about to tell her Anna wasn't home but she spoke first, as she extracted a thick envelope from a red shoulder bag.

"Tony," she said stiffly, "this is from Anna." She seemed to be waiting for some reaction from me. My mind was blank. Then she turned and walked toward her car. After fishing her keys from the shoulder bag, she turned back to me and said, "It's a legal notice, Tony. You're going to need a lawyer."

I shouted after her, "Hey Rita, you're behind the times. Didn't Anna tell you . . ." but she was gone.

I think I stood and watched her drive away. I'm not quite sure. I became aware that even though it was a warm day I was cold. So I must have been standing there for a while, the package in my hand. I phoned in sick, then went back to bed and watched the horrors unfolding on television all day, the thousands dead. I was haunted by the thought of thousands and thousands of other people walking around at that moment feeling blessed that they weren't in the towers, or in the Pentagon or on the airplanes–but who were nonetheless doomed by what had happened. Thousands and thousands and thousands. People of all ages and ethnicities, linked by a single awful fate that was determined on that day. Nine-eleven was just the beginning.

I phoned in sick again September 12. I was sure that I would hear from Anna. I had no idea where she was. I phoned her parents' place in Warkworth every hour, it seemed. I faxed her father's office. No response. It was as if the world was emptied out.

The phone rang early Friday morning. I had it before the second ring. "Anna, for Chrissake . . ." But it wasn't Anna. It was Arnold, my boss, the assistant warden. He'd heard I wasn't feeling well, but could I drag myself in that day at noon for a meeting? Arnold was a friendly guy, though I would never have considered him a friend. We had a lot of history. We'd shared many laughs, saw eye to eye on most professional issues. When I was called in for a meeting with him, I never really gave a lot of thought to what might be on the agenda. Some new program, a problem with an inmate, maybe some adverse publicity because of someone on my caseload. Problems aren't unusual when you have dozens of troubled, complicated people in your care. Some of the most screwed up and screwed over people in society and I'm supposed to be a counsellor, big brother. You know everything about them and nothing because you don't have time or the emotional reserves to really care about them. There might be one or two exceptions but, for the most part, they are files.

But I knew right away when I walked into Arnold's office three days after nine-eleven that this was different. He was with two others and they were standing, engaged in a conversation that ended abruptly when I walked through the door. They all turned to face me, Arnold and the two IPSOs who had been asking questions about Dewolf. Arnold said, "I don't think I have to introduce you guys." He went behind his desk and sat. They sat off to one side while I took the chair directly in front of Arnold. The room was silent for a while.

Arnold frowned into a file, reading glasses down his nose. Then he pushed the glasses up to the top of his bald head.

"Tony," he said, "I've been catching up on this business about Wentworth and Dewolf. What do you think?"

"I haven't given it a whole lot of thought," I said. "I thought it had been dealt with."

He closed the file and shoved it away as if it had suddenly become irrelevant. I peered at the cover for a name. *Breau, A. D.* I had to think for a moment–Anthony Duncan. Right.

"I'm going to be straight with you," Arnold said. The eye contact was intense, unblinking. "I consider you a colleague and a peer and I have too much respect for your intelligence to try to bullshit you. How old are you, Tony?"

"Fifty-four," I said, surprised.

"And I'm looking at you turning fifty-five," and he retrieved the file and pushed his glasses back down to his nose, ". . . next February 11."

I decided to say nothing.

"And you've been in the service for thirty years now. Jesus Christ, where does the time go?" He removed the glasses and chewed an arm thoughtfully.

"This thing with Dewolf is, like you say, in and of itself, nothing. But viewed in the context of other things . . . I'm worried about you, Tony. These guys are worried about you."

"Worried about what?"

"Your safety, Tony . . ."

"My safety . . . ?"

"Tony, we're in a rough environment. An awful lot depends on solidarity, watching each other's backsides. There's a considerable amount of concern about your safety, Tony. That if push came to shove, you might be in for an unpleasant surprise. Goddammit, I'll be the first to say it isn't your fault, but the fact of the matter is that your vulnerability has become a matter of institutional concern. Obviously we can't penalize you for having done the right thing in the Pittman business, but the fact remains. I want you to give it some thought. Okay?"

He stood. We all stood. The two IPSOs turned toward the door. Arnold said, "Tony, wait. A word in private." The others left and I sat again.

He offered coffee. I declined. There was a long period of silence. He was staring away from me, through a window. I followed his sightline to the high limestone wall, the rolling razor wire along the top, discreet electronic sensors, the corner of a tower. "In many ways you're a lucky guy, Tony. This thing could be a blessing in disguise, you know. Your warrant expiry, so to speak." He smiled at me.

"How so, Arnold?" It was amazing to me how calm I felt.

He pointed toward the window. "That wall ... when you think about it, we've spent more time inside than any convict here. We're prisoners, too, Tony. I'm just talking man to man here. What's said here stays in the room."

"Okay," I said, nodding reassurance.

"In a few months you're gonna hit the magic number, freedom fifty-five."

"I've never really thought about it."

"No? I think about it all the time. This job wears you down. You come in here thinking you can accomplish something the old-timers couldn't–never even tried actually. And then before you know it you're an old-timer yourself. Me ... I've got five more years. Got the date circled on the calendar at home. June 30, '06. Can't come soon enough."

"Retirement is a big step, a big adjustment," I said. "Things are kind of ... busy ... in my life right now. I'm not sure I'm ready."

He didn't seem to hear me. "Tony, this Wentworth bullshit is your ticket out. I've already had some feedback from above. They agree: there is a credible threat. You can get a pretty nice package. Lump sum, full pension. A nice send-off: reception, dinner, speeches. The timing is perfect."

"I don't really feel ready for it," I tried again.

"Let's talk, man to man," he said.

But it took a long time for him to get to the point. I've discovered most bureaucrats are like that. Beating around the bush becomes an art and Arnold was really good at it. With each trip around the bush he got closer to the point, which was: he knew that I was going through a personal crisis and that a workplace relationship was part of it. I think I stood up then, but he waved me down. I recall he stood, walked around the desk, and put a hand on my shoulder, all sympathy and collegiality. Man to man.

"We're all human, Tony. Who among us hasn't made a slip one time or another? But these things don't go down well with senior management. Bad for morale. Did you know she's applied for a position in Ottawa?"

"Who?"

He laughed. "You know who. Sophie MacKinnon."

"I fail to see ..."

"She wants to move to Ottawa. I'm surprised you didn't know that. She asked the warden for a letter of support."

"So that should take care of the problem, if there is one," I said.

"Not necessarily."

"I don't understand."

"The thing is, Tony. We don't want to lose her."

Sophie and I had our last lunch where we had the first one, in a hotel dining room that overlooks the lake. She was hesitant when I called and asked her to meet me there.

I tried to sound casual when she joined me at the table. "I have an update."

"Oh?" she said.

"A glass of wine?" She shook her head.

"By the way, I heard about Ottawa."

She looked downward, face flushed. "I was going to tell you ..."

"No explanation necessary."

"It's best, Tony. A bit of distance. Plus I need a break from this ..."

"I understand completely."

It was unusually quiet for midday on a Thursday. She reached across and squeezed my hand. It's an instinct women have, the hand squeezing, for reassurance or breaking ground for something big.

"I think the kids need it. And Gilles."

"Gilles." And then I realized. A name she rarely mentioned. "I think a change of scene ..."

"Please," I said.

Briefly, we talked about the stress of work. Troubled grown-ups with the needs of children in so many cases. It was then she told me that Strickland was being considered for a halfway house in Kingston. I said I'd heard something like that. She said he was a model inmate at Warkworth—had fabulous assessments from the team there, even a commendation from the warden, Moroz. She laughed and reddened slightly. "I believe you know the warden."

"Anna has started divorce proceedings," I said, watching closely for reaction.

"I heard. I'm sorry. I mean that."

"You heard?"

"You know what the place is like. I really am sorry."

"You don't have to be sorry."

"I know," she said. "But it's always sad. It's a blessing in a way you don't have kids."

"Yes. I've decided to be positive."

She smiled, eyebrows raised. She had her hair clamped high on the back of her head, emphasizing the clean strong lines of her face and brow, small perfectly shaped ears, unadorned by jewelry.

I said, "It crossed my mind that being single will simplify my life. You must have some thoughts."

She shook her head. "It isn't just about you, Tony."

"I think I'm going to have a drink," I said.

"I'm sorry."

"Don't be," I said too sharply. "I'm fucking sick of sorry people."

"I have a meeting." She checked her watch. I ignored the gesture. I waved at a lurking waiter. "My other news," I said, "is that I'll be going away soon, too."

She sat up straighter, tilted her head.

"So you hadn't heard that?"

"No," she said. "I hope ..."

I waved her to silence. "I'm only telling you because you should know your transfer won't be necessary."

"You're assuming a lot," she said. "My transfer is about my kids. Okay?"

The words were like a slap. "I didn't mean ... but I wanted you to know that I'm leaving the service for reasons that are unrelated to ... us."

"I would hope that they're unrelated ..."

I struggled with a sudden billow of despair. I suppose she saw it in my face. I looked away.

"It was futile," she said softly. "It was nice. But ..." She compressed her lips and looked down at the tablecloth.

The despair then turned to anger but the anger was locked in a deep safe place, next to the reservoir of tears. "I actually hoped for a while that it was more than nice."

"Me too," she said. "But after Newfoundland ..."

The drink arrived and I realized that I no longer wanted it. I sipped, poked at ice cubes with my fingertip. A small airplane circled low over the lake under puffy woolly clouds that only seemed to make the sky more painfully blue. "That was awful last week, in the States," she said.

"Yes."

"You think there'll be a war?"

I gulped my drink, ignored her attempt to change the subject. "The timing is right for me," I said. "And I'm sure you know this already, but you're considered to be quite a valuable asset here. They *will* try to block your move to Ottawa. Now that I'm out of the picture."

She formed a modestly dubious expression. "I wouldn't . . ."

"They know about us."

"They brought that up?"

"Yes."

"So the day Steele saw us . . ."

"Yes. And he's been broadcasting it around Warkworth."

"Jesus Christ."

"Speaking for myself," I said, "I was glad. No more deception."

She stared at me for what I later realized was a long moment of disbelief.

Then: "I'm glad for you, Tony. Now I have to go."

"I might stay here for a while." I had a headache. I waved at the waiter, pointed at my glass. I couldn't bring myself to stand. She came around and lingered at my side for a long moment, placed a gentle hand on my shoulder. "Goodbye, Tony," she said softly. And like a ghost she disappeared.

That evening, alone and mildly shit-faced in the silent house–Anna, I had learned, was staying with her lawyer-buddy, Rita–my future appeared to me as a landscape suddenly revealed by the cresting of a hill. It wasn't grim but it was barren and it sprawled endlessly beyond the curve of the horizon. It was a scalding moment, delusions scoured from the surface of reality. Solitude and celibacy, I thought. And, I had to admit, under the alcoholic anesthetic, it didn't feel all that bad.

Even if I reframed the words–made them, say, abandonment and isolation–they still described a kind of freedom. I remember stumbling to bed that night in that paradoxical state of peace that comes with knowing you have nothing left to lose.

13.

After the first full day of Strickland's hearing I watched the early evening news for any mention of the case. There was none. It was all Powell at the United Nations with his slide show, proof that the Iraqis really did have the potential to destroy the planet hidden in their desert wastes. Jesus Christ, I thought, will you give it a rest. I thought you were the honest exception in that cabal.

That night I dreamed there was a woman in the bed beside me. I knew it was a woman by the rich thick hair that fell over an exposed shoulder. I desperately wanted to touch the shoulder, gently stroke the hair, but I was afraid of waking her because I was unsure of who she was, afraid, I suppose, of who she might be.

I woke at dawn and sat up, looked around the barren room. The dog was curled up against my thigh, sound asleep. I asked him, "What do you do when you feel the urge for female company?" He looked up at me and yawned, then jumped off the bed and trotted down the stairs, claws urgent on the wooden floor. Barked once.

I got up, went to let him out. "Good luck!" I shouted after him. He galloped off into the field, squatted. The eastern sky was scarlet. A mild spell that week had reduced the snow to crusty patches in the field, dirty snowbanks on the roadside. I squinted at the white-capped sea, concentrating on its majesty to dispel the hatred that I felt for Strickland.

Pity him, I told myself. He spoke out of fear, made brazen by his poverty of options. Pity is worse than hatred. The injury to him from being pitied would be far greater than anything that I can achieve through hatred. I should have said it when I had the chance, when the time was right: *I pity you.* So I could feel the healing that would begin at watching his hateful arrogance diminishing. Instead I reacted as he would, or any other lousy con.

Birch was back. "Let's hit the trail," I said.

The frosty air was pleasant, refreshing. The trail had been well packed by snowmobiles and reminded me of the mountain road in the days when people still used horses and heavy sleds to get around in the wintertime. Where the trail crossed the road the dog galloped off along the pavement and disappeared.

I shouted, "You get back here," but I was in no doubt about his destination. Mary's place. I smiled at the thought: We have this in common, Birch, that rare feeling of gratification that comes from little acts of human kindness. I jogged after him and eventually caught up to him halfway up her lane, urgently sniffing at footprints and a yellowed hole in the snow where a man had urinated powerfully. It was like a drill-hole and I could see the frozen earth at the bottom of it. The wind was rising, dark trees now sighing and I became intensely conscious of the day's grim purpose.

On the way to Caddy's I stopped at the store for the papers. I was surprised to see Neil there.

"I figured you'd be at the prelim," I said.

He told me he took the morning off to watch live coverage of Powell's presentation to the UN Security Council.

"You should have been watching," he said to me indignantly, when I told him I had better things to do than watch television in the morning. "You wanted proof? It was there in spades. The truth, right out of Powell's mouth."

"Spades?" John Robert chortled. "Didn't realize you were such a fan of spades, Neil."

"It's no fuckin laughing matter," Neil said, face flushed. "He showed the satellite pictures, he's got the intelligence interceptions. I'm just waiting to hear the chicken-shit response from Ottawa."

"It's all bullshit, Neil," I said. "The Bush crowd cooking up an excuse ..."

"There it is," he shouted, waving his hand at me. "The sun shines out of Powell's arse for you liberals until he says something you don't want to hear. I'm disappointed in you, Tony. I thought you had more brains than that. I thought there was more man in you."

Something about the hand, the menace in his tone triggered an old response, cold and cautious, almost angry. I said, "Back off . . . don't wave your hand in my face." He stepped back but I could tell it wasn't a retreat, it was positioning. You could see it in his face, his eyes opaque.

I turned away, but couldn't control the shaking as I dropped the money for the newspapers on the counter. *You're a coward,* I thought, sitting in the truck. *You might as well face up to it. Something's happened to you.*

Then Neil was at the truck window, rapping with a knuckle. I lowered the window, just looked at him.

"Hey man," he said, stooping to bring his face level with mine. "I'm sorry about in there. I get a little riled sometimes. Let's just agree to disagree. Life's too short." He stuck his hand through the window and I grasped it, felt its meaty power. "We shouldn't be letting all this shit get to us. Too much to be worried about closer to home."

I nodded.

"Will I be seeing you at the courthouse?"

"I'll be there," I said.

"I was surprised you weren't there yesterday."

"Did I miss anything?" I asked.

"Ah well, it's all interesting. The prosecution theory–him starting a little sex-and-drugs franchise down there. Plus a lot of technical stuff in the morning. Police investigation stuff and toxicology. Seems she had enough dope in her to kill a horse. There were a couple of teenagers who were supposed to have bought stuff from Strickland but they got all wishy-washy on the stand."

"I see."

"That sleazebag lawyer of Strickland's pretty well took them apart. But everybody's waiting for Caddy this afternoon. She'll have a big impact. And I have a sneaky feeling the Crown has got some surprises up his sleeve. You wait."

"I'll see you there, then," I said.

He stood, rapped the roof of the truck with his oversized knuckles and I drove away.

Caddy was sitting at her kitchen table sipping at a cup of tea. She had her coat on. She'd heard the crunch of my footsteps on the deck and stared at me thoughtfully over the rim of her cup. I waved.

When I came in, she said, "I'd offer tea but I don't think there's time." She stood and kissed my cheek. Then placed the teacup on the table. "I guess there's no putting it off."

"You'll be fine," I said. But she sighed and gave me a look that made me wish that I had simply shrugged agreement. "You're doing it for Maymie," I said. "Keep that in the forefront."

"No," she said. "*You* remember that. No matter what."

In the truck she asked, "Do you think he ever feels anything? Like remorse? Does he ever think of her?"

"I'm sure he has his moments," I said.

"Well you know him better than I do."

"I don't know him all that well."

But there was a time when I cared about him because of the risk he took to prevent what turned into a bloody fiasco. There was a time when I stood up for him, disputed the cynical opinion that he became an informer only to hasten his release from prison. The answer I got from both sides, officer and con: a rat is a rat. Solidarity is key to survival.

The name the court clerk called was unfamiliar, "Mrs. Catherine Stewart," but then she looked at us. We were seated on a bench in the corridor outside the courtroom. "They mean you, Caddy."

She slipped her coat off, grasped my hand briefly, then stood. "You look after this," she said. And I followed her into the courtroom, carrying the coat, feeling grateful for the intimacy of the gesture.

I was surprised by the sparseness of the crowd. Neil was sitting in the last row watching intently as Caddy walked to the witness stand. I felt a strong surge of affection as she went. She was elegant in a simple black dress and mauve cardigan, sleeves shoved up almost to her elbows. The boots she bought in Detroit, and that, one lovely evening, I had helped her to remove, gave her added height and an air of confidence. But when she sat she seemed frail and her face showed the strain of worrying about what lay ahead.

Neil slid along the row of empty chairs until he was beside me. "That's one gorgeous woman up there," he whispered. "I don't know what's holding you back." He nudged my arm. But by then I was trying to get a sense of Strickland, though I could only see the back of his head, could only imagine what was going through his mind.

The judge leaned forward, chin resting on his fist as Jones, the prosecutor, gently introduced the witness, Mrs. Stewart, grandmother of the victim, one of the last people to see her alive. His tone was almost parental as he led Caddy through Maymie's short but obviously active life, the excellence in school, the musical talent, the angelic personality. Both Sullivan and Strickland were intently taking notes as Caddy spoke.

"Now, Mrs. Stewart," Jones said, "I'm going to ask a few questions that might seem a bit insensitive but they're important and I want you to take your time." Caddy sat up straighter, put her hands together, interlaced her fingers. Beside me Neil leaned forward, elbows resting on the chair in front of him.

"Take us back to the last time you saw Maymie, before she left the house. How would you describe her mood?"

"Normal, I would say."

"Normal. She was normally in good spirits I believe."

"Yes. Normally. Though she was a teenager and they can be moody. And she was still suffering occasional depression since the death of her father . . . I should say my husband."

"She was close to your husband."

"Yes she was."

"When you say she was depressed, was there any particular diagnosis or prescription?"

"No. I was speaking generally."

"So the last time you saw her, there was nothing out of the ordinary."

"I'd say that."

The judge peered down at her, "Yes or no, Mrs. Stewart."

"No," she said.

Jones turned and walked a few steps away from her, rubbing his cheek, stopped and peered at some papers on his table, then straightened up and faced her again.

"Now, Mrs. Stewart, there's been evidence that Maymie had consumed a large quantity of a drug called oxycodone that night. You know the drug I'm referring to. Oxycodone."

"I've heard of it," she said. "It's been in the news a lot."

"Do you have any idea where Maymie could have got that drug?"

"I'm assuming from . . ." and she looked straight at Strickland, but before she could finish the sentence, Sullivan was on his feet. "Hang on," he said wearily.

The judge removed his glasses and said to Caddy: "We mustn't assume anything, Mrs. Stewart. If the answer is no, just say no."

"I'm sorry," Caddy said.

Jones said, "So I take your answer to be that you don't know where she got the drugs?"

"I'd only be guessing," Caddy said.

"So that's a yes," the judge said, smiling at her.

"Yes," said Caddy.

Jones continued. "How would you describe Maymie's mood on the evening of . . . last time you saw her."

"She seemed fine."

"Not . . . down."

She shrugged, looked directly at Strickland. "I wouldn't say so. No."

"There was nothing out of the ordinary, last time you saw her."

"Nothing out of the ordinary."

"Did anything in your daughter—correction—your grand-daughter's behaviour ever give you cause to worry that she was using drugs of any kind."

"No. She cared too much about herself. And me."

"That's all for now, Mrs. Stewart. Thank you. I know this isn't easy for you."

For what seemed like a long time Sullivan just sat there, face propped by one cupped hand, staring at the yellow writing pad on the table in front of him, plucking at his mustache.

"Watch this," Neil whispered.

Finally Sullivan shoved his chair back and stood, but remained where he was, leaning on the table. "Your grand-daughter was quite the young lady, Mrs. Stewart. Lovely, bright, talented. The loss of such a bright light is nothing short of tragic. I offer my sincere condolences." He walked slowly around to the front of the table.

"But the question we have to answer here is why a young woman with everything to live for would risk it all just to improve the way she felt emotionally."

"I can't help you there," said Caddy. "But she wouldn't be the first."

"Exactly the point," said Sullivan. "Young people respond to the normal pressures of a complex world by getting high. And sometimes, for complex reasons, they put themselves at risk."

"Or people take advantage of them."

He didn't object, just fell silent, nodding sadly.

"You said that she was very close to your husband who, I understand, died suddenly."

"Yes."

"I'm assuming that she took it hard."

"Yes, she did."

"She was what? Fifteen at the time?"

"Yes." Caddy pulled a tissue from her sleeve, crumpled it in her fist.

"I think we all know from personal experience that people that age have a particularly hard time with raw emotions like grief, loss."

"I suppose."

"I'm sure we can all remember some event in our own experience as children that left us quite at a loss as to how to respond. We just lacked the emotional conditioning, I suppose, that would provide some appropriate response. And so, sometimes, the responses are . . . inappropriate."

"She wasn't like that."

Sullivan turned away, nodding, then stopped in front of Strickland. "You must have known Dwayne Strickland as he grew up."

"I knew who he was. Mostly by reputation."

"Ah. Reputation," said Sullivan. "Yes. A reputation for inappropriate behaviour, acting out. Getting himself into trouble."

"That's for sure."

"A boy, an outsider adopted into a community—and I call this a great virtue of the place—a community with strong traditions, close-knit, clan-based families. A little boy taken in by an older, childless couple, good people, undoubtedly. But I would put it to you, an environment that might have lacked a certain warmth, the kind of nurturing that prepares us for the larger challenges of growing up. Would you agree with me on that?"

"They were lovely people, salt of the earth."

"I'm not saying otherwise. Just that fate, destiny if you will, offered Dwayne Strickland something short of the ideal circumstances for a normal life."

Caddy's face was very pale. She said nothing.

"Just for the record, your granddaughter—Mary Alice—was born in 1985 to your daughter, Rosalie."

"Yes, but I'm not sure . . ."

"And because Rosalie was quite young at the time, just a teenager, you and your husband raised Mary Alice as though she were your own. Is this correct?"

"Yes."

"Mrs. Stewart . . . can I assume that Mary Alice, Maymie, knew that you and your husband were her grandparents?"

"It was never an issue."

"And did Mary Alice know who her biological parents were?"

"She knew who her mother was."

The judge had his glasses off. "I'm not sure of the value of this line of questioning. Why don't we move on to something relevant?"

"I'm interested in knowing if there was conflict or distress relating to the circumstances of the victim's . . . early life, Your Honour." Then Sullivan said to Caddy, "You don't have to respond. I'm just making an observation here."

"Life has unpleasant surprises for almost everybody," Caddy said, glaring at him. "We all have to cope."

"Exactly my point," said Sullivan.

"But nobody has the right . . ." she started, voice quavering, but Sullivan stopped her with a raised hand, and asked her sharply: "Mrs. Stewart, are you familiar with the word 'scapegoat'?"

"Prick," Neil murmured loudly enough to cause several people seated nearby to turn toward us.

During the recess Caddy stood alone, arms folded, studying the floor. "I don't want to talk," she said when I approached her.

"You're doing great," I said.

"He's twisting everything around."

"It's what they do," I said. "The judge understands that."

She shook her head. "It's not right. Trying to make it sound like it was her own fault." She raised a hand to shield her eyes.

Caddy was back on the stand. My shoulders ached, my mouth was dry. I longed for it to be over.

"Mrs. Stewart, I want you to think back very carefully, to the months after your husband's death," Sullivan said. "Do you recall significant changes in demeanor, mood, behaviour of your granddaughter?"

"She was obviously grieving. I thought it was normal and even healthy."

It was probably Sullivan's fifth attempt to corner Caddy.

"I put it to you with genuine regret and sympathy that this young woman for reasons that are tragically common these days, at a time of personal stress, turned to drug use. Perhaps serious drug use, even before Dwayne Strickland showed up in the community, while he was still living in Ontario."

"No," Caddy said. "I mean she wasn't like that. She was just sad."

"You aren't suggesting that drugs only became available in the community after Dwayne showed up."

"I don't know," Caddy said. "I don't know about drugs."

"Well let me tell you a little bit," he said. And he turned to the table and picked up a sheaf of papers. "August 1999, three young local men arrested near the convenience store, charged with selling marijuana. Did you know about that?"

"There was talk."

"Mrs. Stewart, it was in the local newspaper. But anyway. December 2001, a young man home from Fort McMurray, arrested at a local dance in possession of a large amount of crack cocaine. Summer 2002, just past—marijuana grow op discovered on the Mountain Road. You didn't know about any of this? And what about this, Mrs. Stewart—a young man, Jimmy MacLennan, charged with trafficking a year ago after he sold OxyContin pills to an undercover police officer. I think Jimmy was a friend of Maymie's, was he not?"

"Jimmy was long gone when Maymie . . ."

"Ah yes, when Maymie passed away, but the point I'm making is that your granddaughter, if she was a drug user, wouldn't have found it necessary to turn to a stranger, an older man like Dwayne Strickland, to buy drugs. She could easily have got drugs . . . just about any kind of drugs . . . from people she knew, people in her own circle of friends. Wouldn't you agree with that?"

"She wasn't a drug user," Caddy said softly, wearily. "She was a good girl. And she knew who he was." She was staring, nodding at Strickland. "She knew all about him."

"Yes," said Sullivan. "I was going to get to that. In fact, she met Mr. Strickland once before the night she died. And you found out about that. And didn't it become a source of tension, maybe even conflict?"

"I don't know what you're talking about." Caddy wiped her nose with the tissue.

"See, with all respect, I'm going to suggest to you that before she left your house that night, the young woman, Maymie . . ."

"She was just a girl, for God's sake," Caddy, said. "Stop calling her a woman."

Sullivan paused, crossed his arms, studied the floor. Let silence hang in all the empty spaces.

"I want you to remember very carefully. Because I want to suggest to you that there was something bothering her that night," he continued quietly. "She was what I might describe as 'down.' She seemed . . . depressed. And when you pressed her, and suggested that she should stay home there was an argument. And she was angry when she left . . ."

"There was no argument," Caddy said wearily. "I just didn't want her going to his place. I knew about his reputation."

"Ah. There's that word again. 'Reputation.' And in your opinion, what was that reputation based on, Mrs. Stewart?"

Caddy was silent.

"Had there ever been a drug bust at Strickland's place?"

"Not that I know of."

"Well, I'll tell you. The answer is no. In fact, Mrs. Stewart, there's nothing in Mr. Strickland's background to give you any reason whatsoever to be concerned about drugs at his place. Only gossip. A young man living alone, a young man with a troubled background, unemployed. An easy target for local gossip and speculation. A scapegoat . . ."

The judge interrupted. "Mr. Sullivan . . ."

"I'm sorry, Your Honour. But I just want to acknowledge that the accused, Dwayne Strickland, has never claimed to be a saint. But he's also experienced the very human tendency by a small community to form a collective opinion about someone who is, shall I say, different. Or someone who through a few bad choices and a lot of bad luck gets himself identified as a magnet for trouble. And I want to suggest to you, Mrs. Stewart, that this young man, Dwayne Strickland, learned important lessons from his mistakes and went to some lengths to share those lessons with people like your granddaughter."

"For fuck sake." Neil was on his feet, face enflamed. I wasn't sure how many heard him but as he bolted for the door the judge stopped him. "You!"

Neil faced him.

"Another peep out of you and I will bar you from this court-room. Do you understand me?"

Neil nodded, turned and opened the door, closed it gently behind him.

Sullivan seemed distracted for a moment, studying the yellow writing pad. Then he turned back to Caddy, spoke gently. "It's understandable that something like this tragedy creates distress in a place. A peaceful, civil place. We have a deep need for answers. Why? What happened, what caused this aberration, this ... contradiction? But not just any answers—we need *reassuring* answers. It isn't good enough to find an answer that raises larger questions—about the state of our society, of our community, of our families."

The judge cleared his throat. "Mr. Sullivan, do you have any other questions for the witness?"

"Just one, Your Honour."

He came close to Caddy. "Mrs. Stewart—have you or any member of your family ever used OxyContin for any medical reason?"

"I don't know what you mean."

"It's a simple question, Mrs. Stewart. Yes or no. Has anyone in your home ever had a prescription for the drug?"

"I can only speak for myself," she said firmly. "No."

"That's your answer?"

"That's my answer."

"Thank you, Mrs. Stewart."

Caddy stepped out of the witness box and came to sit beside me, rigid. It felt as if I exhaled for the first time all afternoon.

The judge was speaking: "I wonder if you gentlemen can give me an idea of whether it's realistic to anticipate wrapping up by the end of tomorrow."

Jones stood. "I intend to call three witnesses tomorrow."

The judge frowned.

Jones said: "One is an undercover police officer, so obviously I don't want to say too much just now. The other two were friends of the victim." He sat down.

The judge was flipping through a large day-timer. "So obviously we aren't likely to finish up tomorrow."

"In the circumstances I think it would be prudent to assume that, Your Honour,"

Jones said sourly.

"But we can try," said Sullivan.

In the corridor Caddy was quiet, nodding as people whispered comfort, or laid sympathetic hands on her arm or shoulder as they walked by. "It's awful," one said, "dragging you through this all over again." Caddy smiled wearily, shrugged, and after the woman was gone, said, "I have to go to the washroom."

I went to the men's and Neil was there, washing his hands vigorously. "That was something," he said. "I never heard the like. I got the diarrhea listening to it. Honest to Christ. I've been in here ever since. What happened?"

"Three witnesses tomorrow. One of them is supposed to be an undercover cop."

"Great," said Neil. "I was hoping for something like that. The Mounties had to be all over that asshole."

On the highway I reached across and grasped Caddy's hand. "You don't have to be there for the rest," I said. She was silent.

"The undercover cop . . . I want to hear what he has to say. And the others, too."

"You know who they are?"

She was staring at the passing countryside. "One maybe, Angus John," she said. "I heard he was around." She sounded distant. "She had nice friends."

We were at her place then. "Let's do something tonight," she said. "Go somewhere. There's a new bistro in town. Or I could cook something."

"Sure," I said.

"Oh Tony." And then she wept.

Standing by her piano studying her memories, she leaned back, to press her head against my cheek. My arms were loose around her middle, her hands lightly cupping mine. Then she moved my hands to her breasts and I kissed her neck. She turned and kissed me firmly, then more urgently.

"We should go upstairs," I whispered.

"No," she said. "Here. We should stay here."

"The light . . ."

"Leave it on."

Maybe she wanted me—or all the ghosts surrounding us—to see a different Caddy in the glare of light, to hear another Caddy in the sounds she made as she kissed me furiously, hands beneath my shirt, then tugging at my belt and buttons. Of course I responded, at that moment driven more by her expectations than desire. I raised her sweater, unhooked her bra with a dexterity that surprised me. I felt an old familiar surge as the sudden tumble of her breasts released me from whatever inhibition I'd been briefly caught in, sinking to the carpet in that gallery of silent witnesses on top of the piano, hanging on the wall. Jack. Maymie. Maymie. Maymie everywhere. Trousers down, shaken free, buoyed by my rampant readiness in spite of them. Maymie, Jack, Maymie, Jack. But, alas, only briefly rampant.

When we were naked on the carpet I realized that the sensations in my lower body were but tricks of memory. I was limp and my awareness of it guaranteed that there was nothing either one of us could do about it. I cursed the light, the smiling faces of the dead. I could feel her energy diminishing, imagined lust decaying, turning into pity.

No bloody way, I told myself, and in a display of passion that was more angry than erotic, I kissed and sucked and licked my way down the length of her long lovely body, all the way to her painted toenails, then up to where I knew they keep the keys to all their secret fantasies—every woman I've ever known. Hungrily, I banished all the phantoms from the room, even banished Caddy, tried to make her every woman I'd ever loved.

"No, no," she said, suddenly alert. "No, Tony." She had her hands firmly on either side of my head, cupping my ears, then tugging at my hair. "You don't . . ." But it was too late for turning back, too late for either of us.

And then she said, "Oh . . . Jesus . . . *Jesus.*"

I guess I could have stayed the night. In fact, she asked me to. But I felt awkward and quietly declined. "I have to get home. We can't forget about the dog."

14.

Settling into the front seat of my truck on Friday morning, Caddy seemed subdued, an unfamiliar shyness in the look she gave me as she fastened her seatbelt. As we drove away I realized my failure to respond to her glance had caused her mood to swing to sadness, then toward what seemed like irritation. She was staring straight ahead, arms folded as if to stifle a sudden chill.

"I'm sorry," I said.

She glanced at me and said, "For what?"

"I meant to call when I got home last night."

She produced a tissue, blew her nose. "Just as well you didn't. You wouldn't have got an answer."

I reached across and caught her hand. She didn't resist, but closed her fist around the tissue.

"Have you ever wondered," I said, "how our lives would have been if we hadn't been so gullible, way back when?"

"Gullible?"

"Yes. I was anyway. Taking everything literally, about sex and girls. I was amazed to find out later in life how many of us were just having a grand old time while I was struggling to be proper."

She sighed. "You think other people were having a grand old time, do you?"

I realized I'd just made matters worse. I shrugged. "The way they tell it, anyway." And felt the heat increasing in my face and neck as she stared at me, processing and suppressing all the things she could and maybe should be saying.

"About last night," she said at last. "I wouldn't want you to go getting the wrong impression."

"And what impression would that be?" I tried to sound casual, but she didn't answer. Then I became angry, or maybe sorry for myself. Sometimes it's difficult to tell the difference. The day was overcast making the mid-winter landscape seem even dirtier and drearier.

"The friend of Maymie's," I said at last. "I suppose you know him well."

She sighed. "Not really. I know who he is, who his people are. But it's different now. The young ones are hard to get to know. They aren't interested in . . . old people. I think that when we were young, age didn't make such a difference."

And after a long pause, she said, "What was Strickland really like?"

I struggled for an answer that wouldn't hurt. "I'd have to say he's more like we were. Maybe a little old-fashioned. Growing up the way he did, with older folks."

I looked across at her and she was nodding.

She didn't speak again and finally we were at the courthouse. As I aimed the truck carefully into a space between two police vehicles she said, "I think you were fond of Strickland at one time."

I forced a smile. "Umm. I'm afraid not."

Her eyes searched mine, but they were full of kindness. Then she leaned across and lightly kissed my mouth. "I'm okay about everything," she said, eyes wide, eyebrows raised. "Really!"

I could only nod.

I followed Caddy to the third row and sat on the end chair by the aisle. She was beside me, coat folded across her lap, hands clasped together. She still had the balled-up tissue, now a tiny lump I wouldn't have noticed at all if I hadn't seen it in the truck. A sudden wave of tenderness swept through me, scattering misgivings about our past, anxieties about what lay ahead. I touched her hand. She turned her head slightly and smiled and maybe I imagined that she pressed her shoulder a little bit more firmly into mine.

Then two uniformed policemen escorted a third man wearing jeans and a tweed sports jacket up the centre aisle to a place in the front row. Caddy leaned her head close to mine. "The undercover cop," she said. At that moment the clerk ordered everyone to rise.

The judge reminded us all that this was a preliminary hearing to determine whether or not there was sufficient evidence to justify a trial. There was a publication ban on all proceedings but, he warned, the court would be particularly vigilant about the evidence we'd hear today. Then he nodded toward Jones, who stood.

"Your Honour, thank you for the reminder—the evidence today is particularly sensitive considering my first witness. I call Corporal Ryan Jackson."

The man in the sports coat rose from his front row seat and walked toward the witness box, pausing on the way to raise his hand and swear to tell the truth. He was obviously at home on the stand and comfortable with Jones, answering questions with articulate self-confidence. He'd been a police officer for twelve years and it came as no surprise that along with all his special certificates in the forensic sciences he had a master's degree in sociology. His hair was shaggy, collar length. He wore large tinted aviator glasses of a style that had been popular among cool folk in the seventies and he had the kind of mustache that for a while, back then, was commonplace on cops and pimps. Of course I realized, as he was speaking, that the mustache was part of a disguise. Just then Caddy leaned close to my ear. "The glasses are fake," she whispered. "And so is that mustache."

He was seductive in his cautious candour about all the people he had fooled in the course of his undercover work, including bikers. And how, from a biker clubhouse not too far from St. Ninian, he'd picked up three kilos of marijuana on a sunny summer evening for delivery to a local pusher, Dwayne Strickland.

"And do you see Mr. Strickland in the room?" asked Jones.

Jackson nodded in a friendly way toward the middle of the courtroom where Strickland sat behind his lawyer. I could imagine Strickland smiling back at him with a similar, enviable poise.

"And when did this transaction happen?"

"It was in July. I have the exact date in my notes. It was in the evening."

"You may check your notes."

He fished a notebook from inside the sports coat and flipped through the pages. "July 27 at 8:06 p.m."

"And where did this transaction occur?"

"Near Mr. Strickland's residence on the Beach Road ... correction ... the Shore Road."

"You refer to 'a biker clubhouse.'"

"Yes. We subsequently, um, seized a quantity of drugs from there. The charges are still before the courts."

"A quantity of drugs. Various kinds of drugs, we can assume."

"Yes. We ..."

Sullivan was on his feet. "Your Honour, I fail to see the relevance."

Jones said: "I think it's important to confirm that the source of the drugs in question, the drugs delivered to Strickland's ..."

"*Allegedly* delivered," Sullivan said patiently. "We'll have more on that later, but for the moment my friend is on the brink of insinuating ..."

Jones laughed. "Your Honour, I know my good friend here has many talents, but I didn't think predicting the future ..."

"Gentlemen," the judge said wearily, and with a limp wave of his hand, "sit down, both of you." They quickly sat. "I take your point, Mr. Sullivan. But I would like for the witness to confirm that the drugs they found in the raid on the clubhouse included marijuana."

"Yes, Your Honour," Jackson replied. "Quite a bit of marijuana."

"Along with other drugs, presumably including oxycodone."

"Yes. It was quite the pharmacy." An appreciative chuckle rippled through the room. The judge remained impassive.

"Fine," the judge said. "Please continue."

At the break I saw Jackson, Jones and the two uniformed police-men disappear into an office down the corridor. I was about to make a comment to Caddy but Neil was standing beside me and Caddy had slipped away. "They got him by the balls now," Neil said.

"I didn't think you were there."

"I came in near the end, about the drug drop. Sounds like a slam dunk to me. And wait until the next ones."

"And who will they be?"

"You'll see. Final proof that buddy was a fuckin pusher."

I saw Caddy then, re-entering the courtroom. "I'll catch you later," I said, and followed her.

Sullivan took over. He was friendly and respectful, almost fawning, as he probed for details of how the policeman had, in the course of two years, wormed his way into an outlaw motorcycle gang. Granted it was in a small place, nowhere near the peril or sophistication of, say, Quebec, Alberta or British Columbia where, in addition to concerns about police investigations, gang rivalries make the bikers paranoid about people they don't know. But this is a friendly place, and Sullivan and the cop shared a chuckle about how the local bikers even had an annual open house for the general public, free wine and beer and coffee and baked goods supplied by area house-wives. It was how the Mountie first became familiar with the clubhouse, posing as a carpenter who grew up in the neigh-bourhood. Showed up at an open house, made himself avail-able for small renovations—mostly reinforcing doors and other openings, bricking up or barring basement windows. Little things like that, all the while learning the layout, strengths and weaknesses.

"Matter of curiosity," said Sullivan, shuffling some paper. "Would there be any evidence of drug use at these open houses?"

The witness chuckled. "Not a chance. As a matter of fact—zero tolerance. Not even a joint. No, these are public relations exercises in a fairly old-fashioned community."

"I've heard that the bikers actually make good neighbours even in the bigger places. They go out of their way to be helpful."

"I wouldn't go that far," Jackson said, frowning. "But yes, it's in their interests to be neighbourly."

"But there's obviously more going on in their establishments than meets the eye."

"Oh that's for sure."

"Okay," said Sullivan, standing straighter. "Let's go to July 27. But, first of all: Have you ever seen the accused at any of these get-togethers?"

"Not that I'm aware of."

"Had you ever heard of the accused before July 27?"

Jackson frowned. "Can't say that I had."

"But that shouldn't be surprising, right?"

"Right. There are a lot of low-level drug dealers around the countryside who wouldn't normally come up in conversations."

"So you would have considered Mr. Strickland to be pretty 'low level'?"

"I suppose."

"Or maybe 'no level' ... sorry, strike that." Sullivan turned and faced the little crowd of spectators and smiled. Then he continued with his back still turned toward the witness. "But seriously, when was the first time you heard the name Dwayne Strickland?"

"That evening. I asked the other guy that I was with."

"The other guy was a biker."

"An associate. Not full patch."

"Which was why, on the evening of July 27, you didn't immediately arrest the individual identified as Dwayne Strickland. You didn't want to, as they say, 'blow your cover.'"

"It was one of the reasons."

"There were other reasons?"

"Mainly, we wanted to arrest him in his place of residence."

"So yes. Let's be perfectly clear here. The drug drop was not at his place of residence."

"No."

"Can you describe exactly where it happened?"

"Yes. At the end of his lane."

"At the end of his lane, where it joins up with ... the *'Beach'* Road."

"Yes."

"For the record, where did you grow up?"

"Swan River, Manitoba."

"You don't know this area very well, do you?"

"Well enough."

"But you'd never been there, to the *Shore* Road, before that evening, had you Corporal Jackson?"

"No."

"Which is why you aren't even precisely sure of what the road is called, Beach or Shore. Which was why they didn't send you there alone. After all, it was hardly necessary to send *two* gangsters to make a relatively small delivery of pot to a *low-level* pusher in the boonies. You were being trained to be a mule, so to speak."

"I wouldn't consider three kilos . . ."

"Where exactly did you put it?"

"In one of those garbage bins."

"A garbage bin? I'm assuming it had Mr. Strickland's name on it."

"No."

"It didn't? And so how did you know it was Mr. Strickland's garbage bin?"

"We didn't. But it had a municipal number on it and we'd been told to look for that. And to wait to confirm the pickup." He paused, watching Sullivan closely. In the split second before Sullivan would have pounced, he said, "We were pretty certain it was the right place, though, when Mr. Strickland came and retrieved the package from the bin."

Sullivan laughed. "Ahhh. Corporal Jackson, you share my talent for anticipating questions. I'm impressed."

The witness smiled.

Listlessly now, Sullivan said, "The weather was warm that night?"

"It was evening, actually. Before dark. But it was cooling off."

"And what was the individual wearing, the person who showed up to retrieve the package from the garbage bin?"

"I'm not sure, I . . ."

"Very simple question, Corporal. Was he wearing a T-shirt? A tank top? A sweater? Was he wearing anything on his head?"

"I seem to recall Dwayne was wearing a hoodie and a ball cap."

"I see. And you noted that it was a hoodie because, presumably, the hood was up?"

"Possibly."

"In fact, more than possibly. The hood was up."

"I think so."

"So this individual walks down the lane from where you think Mr. Strickland lives . . ."

"He was driving."

"Interesting. You'd have noted his plate number then."

"It wasn't a car."

"No? A truck then?"

"No. A quad. Or four-wheeler, whatever they call them around here."

"So he gets off the four-wheeler, wearing his ball cap the way they do everywhere nowadays, down over the face, his hood up, fishes this package out of the garbage bin, and drives back up the lane toward the house. By the way, could you see the house from the road?"

"No."

"So he drives in the direction of where you think there's a house?"

"Not exactly."

"Then where exactly did he go?"

"He sped off down the Beach . . . the Shore Road, and after about a hundred metres cut off onto a recreation trail and kept going."

"Going fast?"

"He wasn't wasting any time."

"So let me summarize. Somebody who might have been Dwayne Strickland collects a package of marijuana out of a garbage bin that might have been Mr. Strickland's garbage bin at the end of a lane where Mr. Strickland might have lived but you couldn't see a house, and then took off quickly, for somewhere else."

"Well," Jackson said, "I don't think I'd . . ."

"Your Honour, I have a lot more questions but I don't see much point in asking them of this witness. Too much 'might' and 'maybe' in the situation. Not his fault. I think he's done an honest job in trying to be helpful but his usefulness is limited by his lack of particular knowledge. Oh, I have one more question," he said, turning back to Jackson. "Have you or any other officer ever obtained and/or executed a search warrant on the premises of Mr. Strickland?"

"Yes."

"When, exactly."

"I forget the exact date, but it was after the young lady was . . . found there."

"And the search produced what?"

"Drug paraphernalia and a quantity of marijuana."

"How much marijuana?"

"Approximately a hundred grams."

"Not three kilos?"

"No."

"No other drugs?"

"No."

"Oxycodone?"

The witness shook his head.

"I take it that's a no."

"We found no oxycodone, which is not to say . . ."

"One other thing." Sullivan bent down and whispered in Strickland's ear. Strickland whispered back.

"Would it surprise you, Corporal Jackson, that Mr. Strickland doesn't own a four-wheeler and never has?"

"I don't think it surprises me one way or the other."

"Probably not, sir. I don't think I have any further questions."

The judge looked toward the prosecution table. "Mr. Jones?" Jones stood.

The re-direct by Jones didn't amount to much. He helped the officer retrace his steps through the territory Sullivan had vandalized. They admirably emphasized the sinister influence upon society of outlaw motorcycle gangs, the integrated structure of a criminal organization in which a friendly local chapter was part of the same ruthlessness that produced gunfights in public places, massacres of rivals, the corruption of the social fabric—our youth, our public institutions.

The evening of July 27 had been sunny and clear and the sun had set just after nine. There was absolutely no doubt in Jackson's mind that it was Strickland who picked up the package; perhaps more tellingly, he testified that Strickland was well-known to local law enforcement officers as an important link in the regional chain of drug distribution and that in recent months the drug problem in the area had crept beyond the hash and pot that was lamentably tolerated among the older generations; young folk here were developing a taste for more exotic drugs, ecstasy, crack cocaine and the more serious narcotics, oxycodone, Dilaudid, Percocet, even morphine.

Strickland was part of all that, part of an axis of evil–Jones actually used the phrase–that could be shown to have led to the death of a talented and beautiful young woman.

There was a lunch break. The judge was gone, spectators and lawyers milled about, chattering. Caddy had the little ball of tissue at her nose. I put my arm around her shoulders and drew her close.

In the corridor I saw Jones and an assistant slip into a conference room. It's like a hockey game, I thought. Between periods, strategy. The Crown is trailing badly. Caddy headed for the ladies' room and then Neil, as if on cue, was by my side, staring with undisguised hostility at Sullivan who was speaking with the clerk near the entrance to the courtroom. "Lawyers, eh," said Neil. "Make you want to stand up and screech."

Then he grabbed my lapel, put his face close to mine. "See, that's the trouble with a courtroom. The lawyers pack every question full of lies, but it's the poor fucker who has to give the answers who has to swear to tell the truth."

I was surprised by my visceral reaction, a mix of fear and spontaneous aggression. What a cop he must have been, exuding certainty and menace from somewhere deep within the core of him. Growing up he'd been a bully, but this was different. Bullies are, essentially, afraid of something, destined eventually to be exposed as cowards. But there was no cowardice here, no fear, no doubt–his legacy from carrying a gun for thirty years.

"How come the lawyers don't have to swear to tell the truth? Answer that." He let go of my jacket and jammed his hands into his pockets, and stared off into the distance, face scarlet.

Caddy emerged from the ladies', glanced briefly in our direction, then turned away. I was about to go to her when Neil caught my sleeve.

"Anyway, it's a good thing the old judge isn't being fooled by any of the lies and double-talk. Being a lawyer himself he can see right through it."

"You think so?" I said.

"Sure as shit in a dead dog," he said. "I've been watching his face, watching when he takes notes."

"Isn't he always taking notes?"

"You mark my words. I've been in more courtrooms than I care to remember. You get a vibe." And he sauntered off, smiling.

———

The tavern was busy as it always is on court days, being the only public place to eat in the barren months of winter. Caddy was shocked to see Sullivan and Jones obviously sharing a joke near the bar. Earnest Mounties drinking coffee. A young woman and a man from competing media were engaged in a quiet conversation of some intensity. "Look at them all," said Caddy bitterly. "One big happy family. You'd never know what brought them all together."

I groped for a comforting thought. "The older I get the more it takes to surprise me."

"What are you talking about—old," she said, now smiling. "You're far from old."

"About last night," I said, feeling the colour in my face.

"What's that got to do with old?"

I tried to read her expression, the tone of voice. Both seemed neutral.

"Well, let me assure you," she said. But I couldn't let her finish.

"After this is all over we should take a trip somewhere," I said.

"A trip," she said. "What a nice idea. A trip where?"

I hadn't thought it through so retrieved the first memory that came to mind. "Years ago, one spring, I went to the Florida Keys. Very laid back. None of the usual family tourism, or hysterical college students. Lots of quiet gay couples, as I recall, around Key West."

"Gay couples," she said, with a raise of eyebrows.

"They seem to know the best places, tend to be respectful of other people."

"All by yourself you went?"

"It was back in my single days."

"You didn't answer my question."

"I didn't know it was a question."

She smiled mischievously. "Maybe you're gay."

The words were out of me without a thought, "Maybe that's what you think."

"Oh Tony, for Christ's sake." She laughed and grasped my hand: "You look tired."

"I am tired," I said. "I hardly slept a wink last night."

She studied my face for a while, caressed my hand. "Poor Tony," she said. "I slept like a log."

"I call Katriel Pikar," said Jones.

I didn't recognize the witness. "Do you know her?" I asked Caddy.

She nodded, face tense. "Slightly."

She was slim, hair pulled back in a ponytail. She said she was nineteen but looked much younger, spoke softly.

Sullivan turned to Strickland who was leaning forward. They whispered briefly. Sullivan was smiling.

"I think people call you Kat," said Jones.

"Yes," she said, and smiled.

She relaxed as he gently led her through her brief friendship with Maymie Stewart. They met in school. Kat was new to the community. Maymie was friendly, they were interested in the same music, did homework together frequently. That was just after Kat moved here, in 2000, and the friendship flourished through most of 2001, but then diminished.

"You began to see less of each other, I think it's fair to say?"

"Yes."

"And was there a particular reason, a falling out?"

"No, there was no falling out." She looked at her lap, fidgeted with her hands. "She just started hanging out with a different crowd."

"I see. People that you knew?"

"Yes. They were from the school."

"Did you know Angus John MacLeod?"

"A little bit . . ."

Sullivan was on his feet then, "Your Honour–"

Jones interrupted: "Your Honour, Mr. MacLeod will be my next witness."

"Carry on," the judge said.

"Was there any particular reason why you didn't become part of this group?"

There was a long pause. "No," she said finally.

"Miss Pikar," said Jones. "I'm going to suggest to you that there *was* a reason why you kept away from the people she started to spend time with, and that you and Maymie Stewart drifted apart sometime in early 2002 when Maymie became interested in drugs. Am I not correct?"

"I don't know."

"Well let me ask you this. Did you, in 2002, become aware that Maymie had begun experimenting with drugs."

"Yes," she said softly.

"And how did you become aware of that?"

"She told me."

Jones turned away from her, faced the spectators. "You know the name Dwayne Strickland?"

"Yes."

"How do you know that name?"

"People talked about him."

"And what were they saying?"

"I guess that he was home from prison . . ."

Sullivan stood. "I object . . ."

"Withdrawn," said Jones.

"Do you know where your friends would normally go to obtain drugs?"

"Yes."

"That the accused, Mr. Strickland, was the guy who . . ."

From where he sat, Sullivan called out, "Objection . . ."

The judge seemed to smirk at Jones. "I think you might want to ask a question."

"Would you agree that Dwayne Strickland was considered, at the school, as a supplier of drugs to your schoolmates?"

"They said that."

"And your friend Maymie Stewart became part of the group of young people who would go to Strickland's place to . . . socialize."

"Yes."

"But you never went?"

"No."

"And that was because it was generally known that there was really only one reason for people of your age to be visiting a man who was much older and who had a fairly notorious . . ."

Sullivan was on his feet but Jones had already given up.

"No further questions. Thank you."

———

Sullivan turned briefly to Strickland, then seemed to ponder for a while before he walked toward the witness. "Just one or two questions," he said. "Miss Pikar, you say you moved here?"

"Yes. From Ontario."

"You lived in a city in Ontario?"

"Yes. Kitchener."

"Is it safe to assume that there were drugs available in Kitchener?"

She smiled. "Oh yes."

"Lots of drugs, I imagine."

"Probably."

"I'm going to assume that you don't do drugs and don't have much time for people who use drugs."

"I don't judge. But that's my choice."

"Let me ask . . . what brought you to St. Ninian?"

"My dad is the gym teacher."

"And I'm going to suggest your family moved here because it's a healthier, quieter, safer place than, say, Kitchener."

She hesitated.

"You don't have to answer that. Did you know your friend Maymie was going through some personal difficulties when you met her? That she'd recently lost a parent?"

"She told me when her dad died. I was at his funeral. She and I talked about it. Quite a bit."

"You'd say that she was grieving?"

"Yes. They were close. She carried a picture of him in her wallet."

"You've been to Maymie's home?"

"Yes. Once or twice."

"And she's been to your place?"

"Yes."

"I'd say that you and Maymie were *very* close friends there for a while."

"I thought so."

"Let me ask you, Kat. Did you ever see Maymie Stewart use drugs?"

"No."

"How then do you know she did?"

"Well, she kind of told me. But it was mostly from who she started hanging out with."

"She kind of told you?"

"She asked if I'd ever tried weed."

"And you said?"

"No, have you? And she just laughed and asked if I was from another planet."

"And you took that to mean?"

"I guess that everybody has tried it. That I was unusual."

"And do you think that you're unusual?"

She shrugged. "Probably."

"Did you ever hear her mention Dwayne Strickland."

"I don't think so. Well, maybe just that he'd come back here from being . . . from away. Everybody was talking about that."

"I see. I'm assuming that you've never been to Dwayne Strickland's place."

"Never."

"People at the school, I assume, talked quite a bit about marijuana, maybe even used it on school property, between classes, lunch breaks and the like."

"Mmmhmmm."

"That's a yes. And I'll suggest that pot was fairly prevalent around the school when you first arrived here, a time, I'll point out, when Mr. Strickland was still living in Ontario."

"I suppose so."

"Have you ever heard them talking at the school about OxyContin?"

"Not that I remember."

"Are you aware of people using OxyContin for . . . fun?"

"No, not here. But . . ."

"That's all I have, Your Honour. Thank you, Kat."

She sat still for a moment, looking slightly confused.

The judge seemed tired. "You have one more witness?" he said to Jones.

"Yes, Your Honour, and I'm hoping that if, with my friend's indulgence, we sit until five o'clock, we should be able to finish hearing evidence today."

The judge looked toward Sullivan. "What do you think?"

Sullivan shrugged. "Depends on what the witness has to say."

Angus John MacLeod spoke softly, nervously, as Jones spent an hour leading him through the recitation of who he was and what it was like to be a teenager in St. Ninian. He was familiar to me, his manner of speech, his extensive knowledge of family history. But the culture he described could have fit the adolescent experience of any kid in any part of North America—a yearning to be part of something larger and mostly inaccessible, an exaggerated world of glamour, opportunity, excitement.

Angus John came home from a remote oil rig in northern Alberta to testify that he had been a friend of the deceased and that he knew Dwayne Strickland as well as anybody did.

"And what was your impression of the accused ... of Mr. Strickland."

"He was okay, I guess." I noticed that he was looking directly at Strickland with what seemed like confidence or perhaps indifference.

"Would you say that you and Mr. Strickland were friends?"

"Yeah, sort of."

"But you didn't know him growing up?

"He was gone."

"But you knew where he was."

He smiled. "Yup. Everybody knew."

"You're friends now?"

He frowned. "I wouldn't say so. Not since Maymie."

"Not since Maymie?"

The witness stared at Strickland, darkly, nodding, then looked toward Jones, said nothing.

Jones rustled through some papers on the table, as if he'd forgotten something. Then looked up again. "Could you tell the court how you got to know Dwayne Strickland, after he returned here? There is quite a difference in your ages."

"Well. Yes. We'd go to his place. Hang out."

"And was there a particular attraction, at his place? Something that made it a good place to ... hang out?"

"Well." Nervous chuckle. "I don't know ..." He looked toward the judge who seemed bemused. "It was just a place to kick back."

"By 'kick back' you mean relax."

"Yep."

"And to relax you might consume alcohol."

"Sometimes. He didn't mind."

"You'd bring your own alcohol."

"Usually."

Jones turned to face us, smiling broadly. "Mr. Strickland was NOT a bootlegger."

"Ummm, no," said MacLeod. "There's no problem getting alcohol. They got it at Collie's store, even."

"And drugs?"

No answer. There was a long silence in the courtroom.

"I'll repeat the question, Mr. MacLeod. Was Strickland's place known to you and your friends as a place where you could acquire drugs?"

"Yes and no."

"What do you mean 'yes and no'?" Jones snapped.

"Well, if you didn't have your own, Dwayne could provide it."

"He'd provide it. He'd give it to you?"

"Well. No."

"He'd sell it to you."

No response.

The judge said, "You have to answer one way or the other."

"Yes."

"Have you personally paid Dwayne Strickland for drugs?"

"Yes. For weed."

"Weed. Marijuana. But is it fair to say that you could have had other drugs at Strickland's? Wasn't it generally known that Dwayne Strickland was the go-to guy for just about . . ."

Sullivan was on his feet. "Your Honour. My learned friend is asking the witness to indulge in the kind of malicious speculation that I've been talking about. That question is entirely out of order."

"It's relevant," the judge said, "that the accused was known to be part of the drug scene."

Jones was on his feet again. "I think we've established that. Let me move on then. Mr. MacLeod, you were a friend of the deceased. The victim?"

"I was."

"How would you describe Mary Alice, Maymie, Stewart."

He seemed to struggle. "She was nice. Everybody liked Maymie."

"You knew her . . ."

". . . all my life."

"Would you describe her as a girlfriend?"

"Just a friend."

"Would you have described her as a regular at Dwayne Strickland's?"

"Oh no. Not at all."

"In fact, the one and only time she went there, prior to her . . . death . . . you brought her. Yes?"

"Yes."

"You introduced her to Dwayne Strickland."

He nodded. He seemed distressed, looked down at Caddy.

"You aren't accused of anything, Angus. But I want to ask you . . . how did Maymie seem the evening that you both went to Strickland's?"

"She was nervous."

"And what was the purpose of going to Strickland's?"

"We had a six-pack and a video we wanted to watch."

"Any other reason?"

Audible sigh. "We wanted to get some weed off of him."

"You bought drugs from Dwayne Strickland on that occasion."

"Yes."

"And it was *not* the only occasion on which you purchased drugs from Dwayne Strickland?" Jones was now standing, back to the witness, staring hard at Strickland.

The witness nodded. Jones turned around, "That was a yes."

"Yes."

"And on other occasions you have seen others purchase drugs from Strickland."

"A few times."

"I have no other questions." Jones sat down.

Sullivan was on his feet immediately. "Let's be perfectly clear about this. You bought weed from Strickland."

"Yes."

"How much weed?"

"That night, with Maymie?"

"Yes."

"Two joints."

"You bought two joints. Two marijuana cigarettes."

"Yes."

"And smoked them in his presence?"

"Yes."

"And watched a video and drank a few beers."

"That was about it."

"And what was Mr. Strickland doing while this bacchanal was going on?"

"He had a beer. Couple of tokes. Watched the video with us."

"Beer you brought? A toke from a joint you paid for?"

"Right."

Sullivan paced for a moment, suppressing a smile. "And this video, do you remember what it was?"

"A music video. Shania Twain, I think."

"Not pornographic."

MacLeod grinned then. "Maybe a little bit." A chuckle rippled through the courtroom.

"Just a couple of more questions, Angus. You know about OxyContin."

"Uh-huh. Not personally."

"Is OxyContin widely used around here?"

"It's starting. But mostly in the bigger places."

"Were you aware of people using OxyContin at Dwayne Strickland's."

"No."

"Never a mention of it."

"Nothing I ever heard."

"Your friend, Maymie . . . had she ever mentioned OxyContin?"

"No. Not to me."

"Okay. But like the rest of you, she experimented with what we call soft drugs."

"Well. I wouldn't say experimented. She wasn't really into drugs."

"Oh? She wasn't really into drugs?"

"She wasn't all that interested."

"Let me suggest to you that drugs have been, for quite some-time now, freely available here for anybody who *is* interested in acquiring or using them. Am I right?"

"I guess ..."

"In fact, for quite some time there has been a growing con-cern here over the availability of drugs, and the increased availability of drugs like cocaine, methamphetamine and OxyContin."

"I've heard that ..."

"And Angus, would I be wrong in suggesting that one of the reasons for the rising drug abuse problem is the forced migra-tion of so many local young people to jobs out west, jobs that pay a lot of money and enable young men like yourself to come home quite frequently ..."

Now Jones was on his feet. "I have to seriously object to the insinuation ..."

"I'm not insinuating anything, Your Honour, just trying to get a proper picture of what life is like ..."

The judge waved them down. "I'm not *entirely* unaware of contemporary social conditions, Mr. Sullivan. I get the picture. Maybe we could move on to some more specific issues."

"Yes, Your Honour," said Sullivan. He faced the witness, stood silent for what felt like a long time.

"Angus, can you recall for me the last time you saw Maymie?"

Angus seemed to struggle for a moment. "I saw her. That day."

"What day?"

"The day she ..."

"On the day ... before the night she died?"

"Uh-huh."

"What was the occasion?"

"I was leaving for west the next morning. I wanted to say good . . . to say goodbye."

"And what do you recall of that meeting?"

"She was sad."

"Sad that you were going?"

"Oh no, not that. We weren't like that."

"What do you mean by sad?"

His face twisted suddenly and he swallowed. "She cried."

"She cried. And did she have anything to say about why?"

"She said. She said. She wanted to come with me."

"And your response?"

"I thought she was joking."

"And was she?"

"Probably. Though there's girls in the camps, even on the rigs now."

"But she didn't go with you, obviously."

"No . . . I wish though . . ."

"And do you know what happened after that meeting, your farewell meeting with Maymie?"

"I'm pretty sure she went home. She told me she was going home."

"And would you say that she was still sad when she left you."

"Yeah. Yes."

"And did she give you any idea what made her sad?"

He shrugged. "No."

"That's all I have. Thank you, Angus."

Sullivan sat down, staring at the tabletop. The room was silent. Then the judge said, "A brief recess." Then, looking down at Sullivan and Jones, "Gentlemen, we should talk."

Neil was standing near the doorway, arms folded as I walked by. "You know where this is heading," he said. I shrugged. I wanted to go home. I went to the washroom. A homely face stared back at me from the mirror, and yet Sophie told me once she loved it for what she saw there. I could see nothing at all. I'd have made a quiet exit except that Caddy was somewhere in the building and needed me.

I entered a cubicle, closed the door, sat face in hands. Strickland will go free, I thought. Strickland deserves to go free. And his freedom will represent a challenge to the place, and a provocation. It will eliminate a facile answer to a lot of questions, not just how and why poor Mary Alice died but about a mythical community and virtues that we always took for granted—integrity, civility. I had a sense of dread. People do not easily abandon the comfort of their myths and certainties. I longed for someone I could hold and really talk to.

Two men came in and I could hear them talking at the urinals. One was saying: "I saw everybody going back in. They must be ready to go back at it." I waited where I was until they were gone, then followed them toward the courtroom.

I slipped into a seat in the back row as the judge was saying that he would in due course provide written reasons for his decision but for the time being and because the situation was so clear to him he wanted to render a decision verbally right away.

"In the evidence I have heard here, there is no basis for any reasonable expectation that a trial would lead anywhere but to an acquittal of the accused. The Crown has failed to produce evidence that would lead a properly instructed jury to convict. A trial would be a waste of the resources of the court. It grieves me to say that the last few days have been a waste of the court's time."

He paused, stared for a moment at the lawyers in front of him.

"Do you gentlemen have anything to say for the record?"

Sullivan seemed to think for a moment, rubbing his chin. "Nothing to say, Your Honour, except to request that the accused be discharged." He sat down.

Jones stood, and mumbled, "In the circumstances I would not be opposed." And he sat and rubbed his eyes, then leaned back.

The judge frowned briefly at Strickland, then said, "After listening to the evidence and consulting with counsel for the accused and the Crown, I've decided that all charges should be struck. Mr. Strickland, you are discharged and free to go."

Strickland stood and I think he said "thank you," but I couldn't hear for the murmuring and movement of chairs as the courtroom crowd reacted, the atmosphere electric with their disappointment and disdain for the process. Strickland, Sullivan and the sheriff left through a side door. Caddy was still seated, examining her hands. I sat beside her, unsure of what to say or do.

"I'm okay," she said at last. "A trial wasn't going to bring her back."

I put my arm around her shoulder, drew her to me but felt no engagement.

"I hope he'll go away," she said. "He doesn't belong here. He never did."

"How do you like them apples?" Neil said.

"It's the system, for better or for worse."

"Lawyers, eh?"

"I was married to one. I know all about them."

"I thought the old judge had more on the ball than that. 'Properly instructed jury,' my arse. Give *me* five fuckin minutes and I'd instruct them. But in the end, eh, a judge is just another fuckin lawyer. We should talk. Drop by the house some evening. Or I'll come by your place."

"I can't imagine what's to talk about," I said.

He stared at me for a moment, then laughed, slapped my shoulder and walked away.

Caddy was silent on the way home, alone in a lifetime of memories, of people and events I never knew and wouldn't understand.

In her driveway I watched as she fumbled in her purse to find her keys. Then she smiled weakly at me, as if she was embarrassed to discover I'd been watching her. She opened the truck door, hesitated for a moment near the front fender, then walked slowly to the house.

———

Birch seemed agitated when I got back and the moment I opened the door he dashed into the field, squatted, looking at me resentfully. In the kitchen I started to remove my coat, then noticed that the answering machine was blinking. I pressed 'play' then sat, working on my boots. I instantly recognized the voice.

"Hey, Tony. Howya doin'? Tommy here. Tom Steele. I wonder if you could call me. Got something I want to discuss with you. Hope you're well, livin' the life."

He left a Kingston number.

15.

Awoman answered. "Sally?" I asked.

The voice was unfriendly. "Who's calling?"

"It's Tony . . ."

"Shit. Tony! Tony, how are you, it's been God, how long. Hang on, I'll go get him. He's in the garage. My God, Tony, it's so good to hear you. Hang on a minute." The phone was dangling, clunking.

Then it was Tommy, with a hearty "hello." Caution lights glowing inside my head.

"Tom, I got your message . . ."

"Thanks for calling back, Tony. I wasn't sure you would, after everything. I have to tell you that I was shocked as everybody when I heard that you'd taken the package. It was the talk of the place and I wouldn't have blamed you if you'd taken a pass . . ."

"What can I do for you, Tom?" I was working hard to keep a neutral tone. "I'm surprised you found me."

"I called Anna. She gave me your co-ordinates. I don't think we've talked since you and Anna . . . I gotta tell you Tony, Sally and I were quite devastated by that. Sally was saying that if it could happen to you guys, you know what? Made us think hard about what's important to us. So, anyway, how are you doing?"

"I'm okay, Tom. Getting by. What was it you were trying to get in touch about?"

"Well, as you know, ever since that business about Pittman, I've been in Warkworth, doin' my penance, so to speak. And I'm going to tell you straight up, it's been good. Gave me a chance to really do a lot of thinking about things, things that I regret now. I don't mind telling you. I don't think there's a night goes by without me thinking of poor Billy Pittman bleedin' there. And I'm going to tell you, I'm taking ownership. I even wrote to his family, spelled it out. How I fucked up, excuse my French."

I waited. Then I said, "Well that's great, Tom. So where does that leave things?"

"Tony, I've been trying to make it right. But I want *everything* right. Lately I've been having serious conversations with senior management about reinstatement."

Into the long silence, he said, "You're still there, Tony?"

"I'm just thinking, Tom. It's going to be kind of hard to reinstate what Pittman lost."

"That's my everlasting cross to bear, Tony. I can't tell you . . ." He seemed to choke up.

"I hear you, Tom. But I'm not sure what I have to do with any of this . . . now that I'm out of it."

"There's a pretty serious review going on and . . . okay, Tony. I'll come right out with it. I'm going to give them your name as a reference. Would that be okay?"

"I'm trying not to laugh, Tommy. You're serious?"

"I've never been more serious. What do you say?"

"I don't know, Tommy . . ."

"You always said it, Tony. People can change. People can improve . . . even the worst inmate can be rehabilitated. I'm tellin' you Tony . . . and this is a hard thing to say—but I know now that I was as bad as any inmate. But I found rehabilitation—and you were right. It's possible and it's wonderful when it happens."

"If you don't mind me asking, Tommy, how did that come about?"

"Just figuring it out, Tony. Plus I been rethinking the whole religion thing. I was pretty devout in my early days and I've been kind of getting back into it. It's been a great comfort, I can tell you. Sally and me, we've joined a little group. It's done wonders for the relationship."

"I'm happy for you, Tom, I really am . . ."

"Oh, and on that subject . . . another shocker. You'll remember young Sophie, at the RTC. I think she moved to Ottawa around the time you left. Moved the family up there. Then out of the blue, husband walks out on her just last Christmas. Boom. Just like that. Took the kids with him. Couldn't hack the city. Imagine, couldn't hack Ottawa. What's to hack? Hadda be more to it than that. But anyway, that's neither here nor there. I know you guys were close. I just thought you'd want to know that."

I was surprised by the absence of emotion. I felt flat, already weary of his eager voice.

"I know this is a lot of stuff to come at you all of a sudden, Tony. I'm really not asking you to do anything, just maybe let me know if they approach you, which they probably won't. But if they do, maybe we could have another talk. What do you think?"

"I have your number, Tom. I'll call you if I hear anything."

"God bless you, Tony. And I'll tell you in all sincerity, the place misses you. You left a big hole ..."

"Tom, I hear someone at the door ... I'll let you know. Bye for now."

And I wasn't lying. It was Birch barking to get in.

It was mild for early March, and gloomy. I sat with my coffee, staring out the kitchen window at low dark clouds over the horizon, ominous with moisture. By the day's end there would be rain or snow. Birch could sense it and was whining at the door. The sound and the simplicity of his instinct dispersed my mood. "Sure," I said. "Let's go get some cardio."

We stood on the doorstep for a while as if the dog was having second thoughts about our expedition, looking up at me ruefully, shivering. "You're not a dog," I said. "You're a pussy is what you are." He tore off up the lane.

I caught up with him on the trail where he was earnestly sniffing at fresh footprints. I continued on. The other walker had been heading in the opposite direction, which was reassuring. I hated meeting people on the trail, the stopping and socializing, fighting boredom and the chill. Then Birch raced past, tempting me to run.

I started jogging, once again resolving to buy proper shoes.

Running had been a big part of my fitness program once. Anna shamed me into it, reminding me of how certain inmates would take advantage of the confines of the yard for jogging. Round and round they'd go, resolutely plodding, keeping fit for self-esteem or physical survival, or both. She'd say how they'd kill for the opportunity that we had to run along our lovely lakefront past the parks to the conservation trail that went forever. I'd reply that most of them would kill for a whole lot less.

I knew even from a distance that it was Strickland coming toward me on the trail. Something about his hunched shoulders, the trudging gait as he studied the ground, lost in thought. I've seen it a hundred times in the exercise yard, learned from it, the power of concentration, to mentally remove yourself from your immediate circumstances. It would mostly be the solid cons, solitary but never isolated, always aware but from inside a zone of personal autonomy. Plodding purposefully, working on some private challenge. They would never talk to me about their shit, especially not me. I never took it personally. These were the guys I didn't have to worry about.

Though Strickland was preoccupied I knew that he was aware of my presence. He confirmed it when, about thirty feet away, he stopped and stood still, staring at me from deep inside his parka hood, no hint of surprise in his expression. Birch trotted up to him and sniffed his boot. He paid no attention to the dog.

After what felt like a long silence he said, "I have nothing to say to you."

"Cool with me," I said.

I started walking toward him. But as I passed close by, he stooped, extended his free hand, palm down, toward the dog. Birch sniffed and licked, walked around behind him, sniffed his tracks.

"Is this your dog?"

I hesitated briefly. "Yes," I said.

"I'm thinking of getting a dog."

"They're good company."

He smiled, stood straighter. "Living by yourself can get to a fellow in a place like this."

I said, "Let's go, Birch."

As I walked away he said, "About Anna. I tried to call you."

"Don't mention Anna." I walked on.

The daily walks were getting longer and, I noted with a slight trickle of satisfaction, easier. I was near a sparse place where the emaciated coastal evergreens reveal the nearby shoreline. In the rubble of rusty ice floes and tangled driftwood, I could see an abandoned picnic table, a reminder there had been and soon will be a summer, happy voices, nearly naked bodies on a beach, a world that is almost unimaginable in the vast winter gulag. I found myself anticipating sunshine, warmth.

Tommy's call had rattled me–brought back ugliness and bitter calculation, a sleepless night. But I eventually realized that, in a way, it marked the end of the experience that had redefined me and it occurred to me, sitting at that picnic table, that for as long as we are alive and reasonably healthy, an end can also be considered a beginning. Maybe it was really Strickland who inspired the insight. His brief, spontaneous connection with the little dog. "I'm thinking of getting a dog," he'd said. A new beginning.

And Tommy? I smiled. Did he for a second think that I was persuaded by his contrived contrition? His references to Anna and religion? Sophie? It was all suddenly so sad and funny. It was a victory of sorts, Tommy's miserable capitulation, the new spiritual Tommy, his abject surrender to such pathetic needs. I felt suddenly sorry for him: he's been punished and I could punish him again. But I knew I wouldn't. Even Tommy Steele deserved a new beginning.

I stood and I felt lighter. I called for Birch.

St. Ninian was still buzzing about Strickland, how he got off. How he got away with murder. I didn't want to leave the house but I realized it had been days since I'd been at the store. There would be a backlog of newspapers. And I hadn't heard from Caddy since court. I called but she wasn't answering her phone.

The usual half-tons and old cars were clustered in front so I drove on by. The unfinished conversation with Strickland had continued in my head ever since I'd left him standing on the trail. Was Anna just bored, a woman approaching middle age, finding transient excitement with a younger, firmer man? That would be easy to live with—I could pity her for that, the shallow

impulse to deceive herself, to make believe that she was someone younger, more appealing. I could forgive that. But he'd said
she was attracted to bad boys like him. What did that mean?
What if she'd found more than carnal satisfaction? What if she
found in Strickland something that she couldn't find in me—a
missing quality that had also disappointed Sophie and a dozen
other women I could name?

Birch was curled up on the passenger side. "Gotta stop thinking like this, Birch." He yawned. "Wise dog," I said. "Just ignore
me." We were nearing Caddy's driveway so I turned in. But
there was a black car parked there—Neil's Lexus with the
American flag decal on the back window, and the taunting blue
Bush-Cheney bumper sticker. I retreated.

The store was silent when I walked in, the dog behind me.
Mary came around, bent down, held out her hand. Birch
quickly gobbled something, sat, tail twitching.

"What did you give him?" I asked.

"That's between him and me." The dog was staring at her,
head tilted, pleading silently. "One's all you're getting," she told
him. "You come visit if you want more." She stood and went
back behind the counter, leaned down and came up with a
stack of newspapers. "You don't have to feel obliged," she said.

"No," I said. "I've got a bit of catching up to do."

"So what did you make of all that?" a male voice said.

I turned and John Robert was behind me sipping on a cup of
coffee.

"All what?" I said, scanning headlines.

"Strickland. You won't find a word in the fuckin paper about
that." He sounded angry. "He was in here earlier, big as life.

Buying milk. Ignoring everybody. You'd think he was home from Harvard."

"Give him a chance," said Mary.

"Right," said John Robert. "I'll give him a fuckin chance."

Then the door opened and Neil walked in, stamping his feet.

I braced myself for his daily proclamation but Neil just nodded around and walked to the back of the store, then returned with a bag of milk and set it down.

"What's new with you, Neil?" someone asked.

Neil nodded at me. "What's new? You're asking the wrong guy. Ask the fella with all the newspapers. What's the latest, Tony?"

"All quiet, Neil. Even Cheney is keeping his head down."

"Yah," said Neil. "But don't let that fool ya."

"So what did you make about Strickland getting off?" John Robert asked him.

"Ah well," said Neil. "It didn't really come as a surprise to me."

"He was in here before, big as life, buying stuff."

"So he's got a car now, has he?"

"I gave him a ride over," said Mary. "I saw him walking so I stopped."

"Proper thing," said Neil. "That's what makes this place the way it is. Real civil. Right, Tony? It's why me and Tony are back here, refugees from places where civility just gets you ripped off."

"Nothing civil about Strickland," John Robert said. "Mary says he's figuring on staying on at the old place indefinitely, like nothing happened. I can't imagine it, after that poor girl dying on his couch."

"Ah now," said Neil. "The system spoke."

"You've sure changed your tune about the system," said Mary.

"It's all we've got, my love," said Neil, clutching the bag of milk. "And at the end of the day, the system is us. I was just in talking to Caddy. Now if there's anybody with a right to be upset. But Caddy's real resigned. She says we need to put the past behind us. Go forward, she says. And that's good enough for me."

He turned to leave but said to me, "Can I see you outside for a sec." I followed him reluctantly.

"About Caddy. Amazing woman, that," Neil said. "You should call in. She's always been fond of you. Still is. I could tell when your name came up. I'm not suggesting anything ... just a friendly visit." He winked.

It was the wink, I suppose, that silenced me, the presumption of a common cause. I nodded and went back inside to silence, people watching me, waiting.

"Let's go home, Birch," I said.

She still wasn't answering her phone, but when I'd drive by her place her car was there, seemingly unmoved. I even passed by one evening just to see if there were lights on and there was a glow somewhere deep inside the house. After a week I reached a reluctant decision.

"Time for you to go home, Birch." I'm not sure what he understood but he wagged his tail enthusiastically and headed for the door immediately. There wasn't much to bring–his coat, his dish, the leash. "You're an example for all of us, my friend. Admirably modest in your possessions."

I left him in the truck until I was sure that Caddy was home, which was prudent because the day was cold and I spent a long time rapping on the sliding glass door. It was about ten in the morning and I knew she had always been an early riser. And yet the quiet kitchen had the dim tidiness of dawn. There was one teacup on the table near where she usually sat, where I'd surprised her on that sunny autumn day that now felt like such a long, long time ago.

Then she shuffled into the kitchen. She was wearing a man's dressing gown and sheepskin slippers. Her hair was dishevelled from her bed. She waved briefly then paused to tie the belt. "Come in," she said. "I didn't realize it was so late."

She seemed so pale and frail that I momentarily forgot why I was there. Her voice was heavy with sleep or grief or illness. "Come," she said. "Sit. I'll put the kettle on." I studied her back as she filled the kettle at the sink. I knew she was delaying contact, composing her emotions. Then she moved slowly to the stove, turned on a burner and stood there as if lost in thought.

"I'm a bit of a wreck," she said finally, without turning. "I haven't spoken to a soul in days."

"Neil told me . . . he was here," I said.

"Ah, yes. Neil," and she coughed and blew her nose into a tissue she'd been holding in her hand. "Who'd have thought . . . Neil a nursemaid."

"He was worried about you," I said.

"I suppose he was." The kettle started hissing. "I suppose he's around, big as life," she said. "Strickland, I mean. Not Neil." She attempted a dry chuckle. "Bigger than life, that fellow is."

"Strickland seems to be keeping a low profile," I said.

"Ah well," she said. "You've got your own issues with him. I guess we'll all have to just get used to having him around reminding us." Now the kettle squealed and steam rose. She filled the teapot.

We spent a lot of time examining our cups.

"Young Angus John," she said. "I didn't expect it. She was so . . . *there*. In what he was saying. She cried, he said."

She tilted the teacup, swirled the contents.

"I knew she was terribly sad, after Jack. But I never saw her cry. Why, do you think?"

"She was trying to be strong, for you," I said.

"I hope that was the reason." Swirled the cup again.

"I used to be able to read the tea leaves," she said. "That's the trouble with tea bags. They hide the future, don't they? But maybe that isn't such a bad thing."

"Have you thought of maybe going away for a spell?" I said.

"Well, weren't you threatening to take me on a trip?" She smiled at me for the first time.

"Well . . ."

"I'm teasing you," she said. "It's a good thing it's kind of dark in here. I can imagine what I look like."

And then I remembered the dog. "I brought your dog back . . ."

"No," she said, mouth tight, eyes widening. "No, I can't have him around. Not yet."

"He's fine with me. It's just that I thought . . ."

"There are too many reminders already," she said. "I've thought more than once that I'll have to get rid of this place and everything in it. Move, start all over. And then I realize . . .

it's too late. It's too late for starting anything. It's all about finishing things now, isn't it? We've had all our starts and this is
where it's got us. For better or for worse."

"Caddy, that's not necessarily ..."

"I thought maybe if there was a trial, no matter how it turned
out, we'd have a chance to work through all this, bit by bit. And
I might understand things better at the end. But it's ..." She
rubbed her forehead. "But it's like ... she just disappeared. I feel
like one of those people you see on the news whose kid just
vanishes and they're still adrift years and years afterwards. And
Strickland was the last one to see her. And we'll never know
what he knows."

"Maybe he doesn't—"

"I made up my mind to go to see him," she said, interrupting
me. "That's what I was going to do. I still might. Just sit in front
of him. And ask him to tell me."

"I don't know," I said weakly.

"I probably don't have the guts to do it anyway," she said,
staring off over my head. "Let me get you some more tea."

"No," I said. "I'd better go. Poor Birch will be freezing in the
truck."

She smiled. "I'm glad you dropped by. It might take a little
while but ... Where was it you said you went on that holiday?
With all the gay people?"

"The Florida Keys," I said. "Key West. You'd like it there.
We'd just sit around drinking rum punch and watching the
amazing sunsets, reading Hemingway."

"I can't stand rum," she said. "You must remember, the night
I got sick and threw up in the little red truck?"

"I thought that was lemon gin," I said. "But anyway, we can get you something else."

"I'll be thinking about it," she said. And smiled at me again.

There was palpable excitement the next time I went to the store. I could feel it even from the outside, the number of cars and trucks parked in the lot. I could hear voices from the doorstep. And when I stepped inside, everybody seemed to be talking. I went straight to the counter.

"What's the buzz?" I asked Mary.

"You didn't hear what happened? About the big raid at Strickland's?"

"When?"

"Last night. Cops from three detachments. You'd think it was Saddam Hussein they were after. I could see all the lights through the trees so I snuck over to watch."

"What was that all about?" I asked

"Drugs," she said. "Seems they found a stash." She nodded toward the cluster of men around the coffee urn. "Just listen to them."

Then I heard Neil's voice. "Hey Tony, come over here, get a load of this."

He had the inside story. Somewhere near midnight, five police cars raced up Strickland's lane, broke a door as they rushed into his house, armed to the teeth. "I talked to one of them this morning."

They'd been tipped off that there would be a significant drug delivery that night. Maybe the drug mule staying over. They were expecting to find a Hells Angels member there, according to Neil. But their intelligence was flawed.

"There was no Hells Angel, only John Robert's daughter, little Ashley. John Robert and the wife are devastated."

"What happened to her?" I asked, nausea rising in my throat.

"It's what's *gonna* happen to her," Neil said. "She claimed the stash they found belonged to her. Fifty Oxy 80s and a kilo of pot between them on the kitchen table. You imagine."

"Well. Maybe . . ."

"She's fifteen years old," Neil exploded. "That fucker Strickland should be horse-whipped."

"That's the point, see," said Lester quietly. "She's underage so they can't do much. Strickland's claiming the girl arrived out of the blue with that stuff and your fella was giving her a little sermon about how dangerous it was, just having that stuff, never mind using it."

"Where is she now?" I asked.

"They let her come home," Lester said. "They're figuring out whether or not to charge her. It's complicated. Nobody believes it was her dope. You'd have to know her. She's a little far out, like most of them. But a dope dealer? No friggin' way."

"Where the fuck would she get a load like that?" said Neil.

"Some son of a bitch planted it there is where she got it." The voice was controlled but savage. We all turned to see Strickland standing just inside the open door. "And I'd put money on who did it."

Neil moved toward him. "Do yourself a favour and get out of here before somebody throws you out."

"Why don't you try it, you big tub of shit," Strickland said. I noticed he had one hand concealed inside his coat pocket. I moved between them.

"You should leave, Dwayne," I said.

His smile was dangerous. "Right," he said. "I'll leave. But you haven't seen the last of me, Tony. I never thought you'd sink that low."

"You're talking foolishness," I said.

"Really? Who else around here would want to see me back inside but you ... get me out of the way, right? Get me fucking killed if you have your way. All because of Anna, all because ..."

I lashed out at him, fist only half-closed. He stumbled, crashed against the door frame, face contorted. My hand was on fire but I grabbed for him, months and months of anger and confusion, doubt and loneliness surging in one impulse to punish. And then I was struggling to escape the apelike embrace of Neil MacDonald, whose breath reeked of onions and tobacco and dental plaque. I kicked back hard, felt the contact with his shin, then felt myself lifted off my feet and hurled to the floor.

When my head cleared, Strickland was gone and Neil was panting over me: "You idiot, what did you fuckin kick me for?" Then he reached a hand down, to help me up.

"Christ, man," he said. "We're all on the same side here."

My hand was scarlet and swollen, almost the size of Neil's lethal ham-like fist, when I gingerly arranged the ice-packed towel on top of it. I knew the whole place would soon be buzzing with the news. It was depressing how they'd all assume that I'd tried to strike a blow for them and their community and their values and that I was finally, unambiguously, one of them. How little they knew.

Neil called early the next morning to ask about my hand. I told him I thought I'd broken something. He thought it was funny. He'd told the wife what happened at the store and said Hannah was insisting that I come for supper some night that week. What about Sunday night?

I said I was uncertain.

"Better still," he said. "Make it Monday night. It'll be St. Paddy's day. I always break the wagon for St. Pat. We'll be able to have a few cocktails." Laughing, he added, "I think Hanna has taken a shine to you. Says you're a 'fascinating man.' I told her she doesn't know the half of it."

He rang off, still laughing.

I called impolitely late on Friday evening and after perhaps a Scotch too many. I was in a mood of uncommon cheerfulness.

"Neil," I said. "I just realized I hadn't given you a firm answer about dinner Monday evening. I'd love to accept Hanna's kind invitation. What time and can I bring anything?'

"Just bring yourself. Around six." He sounded grumpy.

"I suppose you've been following the news today," I said.

"What news are you talking about?"

"The African uranium that Powell and Bush have been going on about," I said.

"What?"

"It doesn't exist," I said. "Those documents they had were fake. It's all over the news."

"I don't believe that for a minute. Powell wouldn't fall for that. And Bush talked about it in the State of the Union."

"Looks bad on them," I said. "Hard to start a war when one of the main excuses turns out to be bogus."

"Your hole is out," he said. And put the phone down. I stood smiling, remembering Duncan using that same phrase when logic failed him.

16.

Saturday was aglitter with frost and sunshine. The trail crackled under my feet and I had a sense my stride was longer and more fluid. I wanted to believe that perhaps I was emerging from a long dark tunnel of gloom that started in the spring of 2000 with Pittman's death. I wanted to believe I felt better because I was thriving in my solitude. I was part of a community, but somehow above it. I knew that the confrontation with Strickland would become one of the legends of the place. So be it, a brief violent moment that might seal a lasting peace. Tony Breau, the hard man home from a hard place, best not disturbed.

And then I made a decision, on that lovely weekend afternoon with the scarlet sun suspended just above the silent trees, and that decision would, as I see events so clearly now in hindsight, mark the beginning of a change in everything.

I was passing the end of Strickland's lane. I stopped and studied the many tire marks in the frozen snow, trying to imagine the scene earlier in the week, the aggressive urgency of the powerful cars, the squad of nervous, over-stimulated men with guns and body armour, following procedures that apply blindly, regardless of the target—terrorists and hostage takers, or pathetic losers, unsuspecting and alone. And I felt a wave of sympathy for Strickland. It was perhaps a sentimental lapse, identifying with another outsider.

The dog was trotting in circles, sniffing tracks and footprints, and then I realized the raiding party probably had the assistance of a drug dog. "You smell dog, do you Birch?" And he trotted up the lane. Who sent them here, I wondered? It was at that moment I decided to visit Strickland.

There was no sign of life around his house and after knocking several times I almost walked away. But then I heard footsteps descending stairs.

He opened the door and we stared at each other for long seconds before he asked, "What do you want?"

I shrugged. "Old habit," I said. "Checking on parolees. Wondering how you're getting along."

"It has nothing to do with you," he said. "And we have nothing to say to one another." He started to close the door.

"I hope the kid was telling the truth," I said. "That the drugs were hers. Because if they came from where I suspect they came from, you can expect another visit . . ."

"What are you talking about?"

"I'm not going to spell it out," I said. "I don't want to know what your involvement is with the bikers. But you were getting visitors here when you were away. People checking the place out ..."

"You think I'm gonna believe that it was the bikers? Don't make me laugh. They don't care about me because I don't owe them anything. And you know it. You or one of your friends planted those drugs. But it didn't work. And I'm not going anywhere. And you can get off my property right now. I don't ever want to see your pious face back here again. Ever." He slammed the door.

The dog, startled, dashed off toward the trees and I followed him. The woods were dark then, sun almost gone. The hard snow crust broke beneath my feet and I could feel frozen crystals melting inside my hiking boots. Then I found a track broken by someone else and remembered Mary—she'd probably stood among these trees watching as the raid went down. Soon I was in her lane and the dog was nowhere to be seen. I heard him barking and walked around her house to the kitchen door.

"You realize you've got that dog for life," she said when we were at her kitchen table. "I hope you're prepared for that."

She poured coffee. "I could offer something stronger." I declined. I told her we'd been out for a walk when, on an impulse, I decided to call on Strickland.

"Did you believe him?" she asked. "About the drugs?"

"That I planted them there?"

"God no," she said. "But I'm convinced somebody did. There's been enough coming and going around here at all hours that nothing would surprise me. People lurking in the woods. I've been half-thinking maybe it's time for me to move. It's getting hard on the nerves. And now with the talk around the store."

"What talk?"

"You can imagine. People talking about taking things into their own hands. It's *just* talk. But it can get to you. And who knows about the drugs? I'd believe anything."

"Who's talking?"

"All of them. And it's worse now, with John Robert's daughter involved. And I know there have been other young ones over there doing God knows what. It's a bad scene all around, Tony."

"What about Neil? What's he saying?"

"Not much lately. Not since court." She laughed as she poured more coffee in my cup. "Neil's too busy getting ready to invade Iraq."

Urgent news on the television, another crisis meeting somewhere in the middle of the ocean. This time Bush and Blair. Last chance for peace. "What did they do for news before all this, Birch Bark?"

"Yap, yap," he replied.

"Yes," I said. "I agree." And turned the television off. Then as I stood to go to bed, I saw the winking red light on my answering machine.

Her voice was soft and sleepy and at first I didn't recognize her. "I was just thinking about you. Remembering things, out of the blue." Then a long pause followed by a sigh. "I miss our conversations." Another pause. "It's Sophie, just in case you don't remember." She chuckled. "I often wonder how you are, out there. Call me sometime. Have you got a pencil handy?" Then there was another pause before she slowly dictated an Ottawa phone number, and then repeated it.

The dog projected subtle disapproval as I prepared to leave on Monday evening–St. Patrick's Day. He was sitting in the middle of the kitchen, head tilted as I put my coat on. Then he skulked to his coat-bed near the stove, curled up and lay down. "You're getting good at the guilt trips," I said, feeling a real twinge. He lifted his head briefly then dropped his chin to his paws as I turned away from him.

It was a clear, cloudless night, air light with hints of spring freshness and the sky star-spattered. It felt pleasant to be going out, bound for a conventional domestic situation, even one involving Neil.

Driving by the end of Strickland's lane I wondered what might be happening up there. And then I wondered why it mattered. I should be grateful for his hostility. It was liberation, in a way, from my confusion. *You're pissed off at* me, *you sleaze-bag?* But still I felt uneasy. Perhaps it was the unfairness–his belief that *I'd* betrayed *him*. That was hard to handle, so terribly ironic that it made me feel like going up there one more time. But I resisted.

Neil was jolly at the door and the reason was no mystery. Bush had given Saddam Hussein and his two psychotic sons forty-eight hours to leave their country. Neil would be chuffed at the cowboy swagger, the unapologetic assertion of physical force in the cause of a high moral purpose. Something he had done a thousand times in his career, I'm sure—big cop, loaded gun, aggression and control, unsubtle ultimatum.

I kept my sore right hand in my pocket, afraid of what his macho handshake would do to it. He clapped my shoulder and hurried me inside. "Come on in out of the chill. How's the mitt? You pack quite the wallop for a quiet fella." I'm sure he meant it as a compliment.

"Almost good as new," I said.

The air inside was warm and heavy with the fragrances of cooking. We went straight to the kitchen where Hannah looked stressed, juggling two recipe books. "You guys stay out of the way," she said. Neil quickly fetched a whiskey bottle from a cupboard and led me toward the living room.

"Just let me get this out of the way and I promise there'll be no more talk about politics tonight," he said. "What do you think Canada will do when the Americans go in?"

"Well, the government said today we're staying out of it . . ."

"Bullshit political pandering," he said. "When the rubber hits the road I can't believe Canada will stay on the sidelines with the pussies."

"Maybe it's all bullshit," I said.

"Oh, the Americans are going in, man. And surely to hell this country is gonna do the right thing. Think of the embarrassment if Ottawa just sits on its hands. Even fuckin Poland is in the coalition."

I shrugged, smiled. "We'll see." And to change the subject: "I had a chat with Strickland the other evening."

"You did?"

I explained how I had gone there on an impulse, drawn by curiosity about the drug raid–who really owned the drugs, how the police found out so quickly and were so confident of their intelligence they'd mobilized a full-dress takedown. That it seemed strange to me that Strickland would be so careless.

"You know the mentality as well as I do," Neil said. "Cocky. After that court fiasco I'm sure he feels like God almighty. Look at the way he barged into the store, making accusations."

"Come on," I said. "That wasn't strength–that was fear."

"Well he's got goddamned good reason to be afraid," Neil said. "What you did was what anyone of us would have done with the kind of reason you had."

"What are you talking about, Neil . . ."

"Come on Tony, we're old friends. I heard him mention your wife's name. That would have been enough . . ."

"How do you know it was my wife's name?" I was struggling to keep the tone light.

He stood, drained his glass. "I'm sure you mentioned her. Let's go see what's happening in the kitchen."

Generous pouring of wine failed to diminish the tension. I even ventured into the forbidden field of global politics. "Looks like George Bush will get his way after all." Neil ignored me and Hannah remarked that she had no interest in the subject. She was from a family of Democrats and to her Bush was like the aftermath of a bad curry. Something nasty passing through the American digestive tract, a pain the world would have to suffer for another year. No way he'll win a second term.

"I wouldn't be so sure of that," said Neil.

She stood. "I hope you won't mind if I excuse myself," she said to me. "I've been feeling miserable all day."

Neil watched her go, then returned to his dinner. "She's been low for a while," he said. "The long winter got to her. And she hasn't made any friends here. I was thinking her and Caddy, maybe you and Caddy coming here for an evening sometime. Two couples. What do you think?"

"Maybe," I said.

"It's a hard place for an outsider," he said. "Especially in the winter. I'll tell her that. You and Caddy making it an evening here—that might cheer her up."

"Neil," I said. "I have to ask. Who told you about Anna and me? And Strickland."

"Told me what?" he said, eyes narrowed, brow furrowed. "What about Strickland?"

And after some long seconds he looked away and seemed to nod, then we returned to the business of eating.

After dinner and another drink he insisted on listening to a new CD he'd found in town. Local music. But halfway through a tune he stood, walked to a window and peered out, as if expecting someone. He was restless. "That's some rig you got out there. New is it?"

"Last fall," I said. "Hardly driven."

"I was half-thinkin' I need one of those," he said. "I'm constantly hauling stuff for this place. Ruining the car or paying a fortune for delivery. What do you think?"

I shrugged. He sat down across from me, both hands wrapped around his glass.

"I seem to remember you driving a little red half-ton way back, when we were youngsters."

"You have a good memory," I said.

"Your dad, Duncan, what year was it he went?"

"1969," I said.

He leaned back, stared off somewhere over my head. "Strange times, 1969," he said. Laughed at some private memory, then stood and returned to the window, deep in thought.

"Hey," he said suddenly. "I'd like to take that thing for a spin. What do you think?"

"Whatever," I said. "But isn't it a little ..."

"Grab your coat," he said. "I want to see what it feels like."

"It's a standard shift," I said.

"Perfect."

We drove in the general direction of my place and then he turned down the Shore Road. The night was clear and dry and cold. He fiddled with the radio, found old rock music from the seventies. "Those were the days," he said.

Near the end of Strickland's lane he stopped, turned off the engine and the lights, plucked a package of cigarettes from a shirt pocket. "You don't mind me smokin' in here?" Rolled the window down a crack. "Beautiful," he said.

"Why are we stopped here, Neil?" I asked.

"Well, it's like this," he said, exhaling. "A few of us kind of keep an eye on this place, just to be on top of what goes on up there. Some of the ones with kids have some concerns. If the young ones are hanging around up there, the parents like to know. You never know what other visitors he gets. He's got some pretty rough friends. It's a kind of Neighbourhood Watch. A coalition of the village if you like." He was smiling, watching me, waiting I suppose, for some response. A song by Crosby, Stills and Nash with Neil Young was playing softly on the radio. "Like the song says," Neil said, nodding toward the sound. "Teach your children well."

"There's also something about 'teach your parents,'" I said.

He laughed. "That's good." Then he opened the truck door. "You wait here, I'll just be a minute."

"Neil," I said. "This is a bad idea."

"I hear you, Tony," he said. "I admire how you feel after everything."

"After what, Neil?"

He closed the door, sat staring straight ahead for a while. "Okay. Fair enough you're wondering what I know about you and your ex. It's like this. Anything I know originates up this lane."

"What are you talking about?"

"He's been spreading it around. How there was a thing with your wife." He raised a hand. "I'm just repeating what he's been saying."

I stared into the night, suddenly desperate to be home, craving a cigarette for the first time in years.

"Apparently he's been telling the young ones that you're the one stirring the place up against him and the only reason is because, well … anyway, that's what they passed on to their parents when they got some grief for hanging around his place.

I'm just repeatin', Tony. I'm not saying I believe any of it." He stared at me for a while, waiting for a response, then he opened the door again and slipped out of the truck and vanished into the darkness.

I stood on the roadside near the truck studying the stars. Duncan knew the planets and the constellations. Told me once, very briefly, how in late adolescence he had spent a year or so at sea and had become enchanted by the sky during long hours on the night watch. Typically he never spoke of it again. He was like that, delivering brief biographical disclosures that became, after he was gone, a disjointed and confusing memory. I can imagine, now that I have lived longer than he did, that it was how he avoided scrutiny; in his time it was important to avoid discovery of hidden weakness. We all have them, always did. But once upon a time weakness was a challenge to be overcome or hidden. Now we deceive ourselves, thinking that our private weaknesses don't matter. We reveal them freely, sometimes unsolicited, hoping that our disclosure of vulnerability will be interpreted as a sign of trust and will warrant kindness, or tolerance at least, in return. So naive we are, our sad belief in sympathy.

There was a car sound in the distance, a quiet murmur in the stillness of the night. I looked in the direction of the sound, saw a glow.

You should have been more like me, Tony, learned to read the skies. Read people better. But it's too late now.

The car was closer now. Instinctively I moved away from the truck, nearer to the roadside trees.

How did you ever survive all those years in the corrections jungle, Tony?
Truth of the matter? I didn't. Did I, Duncan?

The car was slowing down. Should I step out, wave, acknowledge it. No, nothing wrong, just answering the call of nature. Lovely night though. But the car continued past me, then turned up Strickland's lane.

I got behind the wheel and started the engine, peering into the night to where Neil had dissolved into the silent shadows. Then the truck door opened roughly, and Neil was inside, panting. "Go, Go!" he shouted.

"What happened," I shouted back. Wheels spinning, then the truck jerked forward as rubber caught the pavement, fishtailing slightly.

"Just go."

"What happened?"

"Nothing. He saw me. Drive."

Darkness parting, pale roadside furrowing away before us as we raced through the narrow corridor of light. Neil was staring backward. "Fuck, there's a car behind us."

"What did you do, for God's sake?"

"I did nothing. Just drive."

I'd barely come to a stop when Strickland was at the passenger's window, the car he'd been driving tight behind me, high beams glaring. He was pounding on the glass. Neil rolled his window down. Said nothing.

Strickland shouted: "What the *fuck*..." Then Neil was shoving the truck door open. When he was halfway out, Strickland slammed it back on him, trapping him half in and half out of the cab.

Neil roared in unintelligible rage and heaved outward, sending Strickland stumbling backward.

Then I was outside and I saw another backlit figure in the glare of the car headlights, just a shadow. I backed away, realizing that I was totally exposed. Then Strickland was advancing toward us. Neil turned toward the house. "I'll be right back," he shouted to me. "I know how to deal with this shit." He left the door open when he went inside.

"'You'd better leave now, Dwayne," I said.

"Oh, I'm leaving. But it's all clear to me now, Tony. No doubt left now . . ."

"Just go."

"You're a pig, Tony. Like Anna said . . ."

"Go now," I hissed, looking toward the house where a light suddenly flooded an upstairs room and a shadow moved, bent, searching urgently. "Go, for God's sake, before he gets back."

"She said that down deep you were no better than the rest of them, including her old man . . ."

Then Neil was back, breathing heavily. "Leave this to me," he said. His arm was hanging loosely at his side, whatever he was holding concealed behind his hip. "Move out of the way," he said, elbowing me.

"Pigs," Dwayne said.

I moved directly in front of Neil, blocking him. He shouted, "Get out of my way, goddammit."

"Strickland," I gritted. "Get out of here before my friend puts a bullet in your ass."

——

I remember small details from later that evening–the look on the dog's face when I came in the door, which might have been comical in different circumstances.

"So *I'm* in the doghouse, am I, Birch?" I said. "Great. Move over." And I went to bed but couldn't sleep. Tossed and twisted in the darkness, battering the pillows into human shapes. Holding tight, fighting a sudden disorienting confusion.

Strickland had seemed genuinely pissed, but mostly disappointed.

The next morning I didn't even notice when the dog, after his morning ritual of sniffing at and pissing on the left rear truck wheel, trotted off up the lane and didn't come back. I forgot about him, only noticing his absence when I heard a car outside and didn't hear him bark his customary warning. I felt a sudden sense of panic. Where did he go?

I didn't wait long for an answer. Mary clambered out of her car and the dog hopped out behind her.

"So look who came to visit this morning," she said happily. "There he was, yipping on the doorstep."

"He was mad at me," I said, squatting in front of him. He licked my face, full of forgiveness.

"I was thinking," she said. "Here you've been batching for over a year and I've never once had you up for supper. What about tomorrow night?"

I couldn't think of any reason to say no. "I'm getting to be like Charlie," I said. "Living off the local hospitality."

"No fear of that," she replied. "Anyway, there was no harm in poor Charlie."

———

Neil was at the store early Wednesday morning, poring over the newspaper, jabbing the paper with a stubby forefinger. "Thirty countries in the coalition and guess who isn't. Makes me ashamed to be a Canadian."

"I thought you were an American," someone said. He ignored the comment, kept reading.

Collie winked at me. "Looks like this is gonna be Neil's big day," he said. "Finally, he's got himself a war to fight."

I waited for Neil to allude to the night before, the confrontation in his yard, but he kept his eyes down, scanning headlines. Then he looked up and past me as if I wasn't there.

"See, this is typical," said Neil, gesturing toward Collie. "You think it's all a joke." He tossed the newspaper back on the rack and walked out.

Mary phoned mid-afternoon to confirm that I was coming. "And come early," she said. "I like to eat early."

Her place was an old farmhouse with a huge kitchen that reminded me of my childhood home on the Mountain Road. The walls were unadorned, except for a calendar, a crucifix and clock. The doors to the rooms beyond were all closed. The kitchen was uncomfortably warm.

"I'd show you around," she said. "But the rest of the house is freezing. I suppose you remember the layout anyway, from growing up. I keep threatening to get a furnace but they'd have to tear the place apart."

In the cold deep winter months, all life happened in the

kitchen. One of the doors would lead to a steep, narrow stairway and a bedroom directly above.

"I sleep up there," she said, pointing to the ceiling. "Not that it would matter to you."

I laughed.

"Sit," she said. "Let me get you something."

I calculated that she was in her late thirties. Her face was pretty, hazel eyes that seemed to go from green to grey depending on the light; dark hair with a dramatic streak of white above her left ear.

Over dinner she informed me she'd been working at the store for more than twenty years. She started in her teens, a summer job to earn the money she needed to go away. Then her mother became ill and lingered long enough that Mary lost whatever dreams she had. "You stop noticing time after a while," she said. "It's just one day after another, each more or less the same. Then one day you look back and it's too late for anything else."

We ate in silence for a while. Then she said: "But don't get me wrong. I have no complaints."

"Going away is just ending up somewhere else," I said.

"That's the thing," she said.

Then after another long pause, I said: "So you'd be older than . . . your neighbour."

"A few years," she said. "I was ahead of him in school. But I remember him—he was always getting the blame. Most of the time he deserved it. A little instigator he was, for sure. Teachers used to say it was a shame he couldn't put the brains God gave him to better use." Another long pause. "But I always found him nice enough."

She put her fork down. "Looking back, you start to remem-ber some of the good things. Like, he could be hilarious. He'd come to the store and if it was just me there he'd be mimicking people, the locals who hang around for the free coffee. He'd even be trying to sing popular songs with a local accent–'Hey, hey, get affa my clewd.' You couldn't help but laugh."

And she started to laugh but stopped suddenly. "Sad when you think about it. Collie never wanted him around."

"The incident at the store," I said. "The little fracas."

"Yes," she said. "That was a shocker."

"I meant to apologize. It was just that when he mentioned Anna ..."

"No apology necessary," she said. "But I was wondering. Who's this Anna anyway?"

I laughed. "I thought everybody knew who Anna was, thanks to the gossip ..."

"What gossip?" she said, standing. She walked toward the counter with her empty plate. "Help yourself to more."

"Anna was my wife," I said.

"Obviously not from around here," she said above the sound of running water as she rinsed her plate. Then she turned, looking puzzled. "How would Dwayne have known her?"

I studied her open face for evidence of guile, saw only honest curiosity. "Don't answer if you don't want to," she said, turning back to the sink.

"I heard Dwayne was blaming me for all his troubles in the village," I said.

"Well, I suppose," she said. "He was over here afterwards saying he suspected you for planting the dope. I told him he was crazy, that if there was one person in the village he could probably count on it was you. Then he said something like, 'You don't know the whole story.'"

"That was all he said?"

"That was it."

She squatted by the dog who was sprawled, asleep. "What can we give you, little guy? How about one of Mary's special treats."

Birch raised his head then scrambled to his feet, wide awake.

I said, "I'm surprised you're into cats, Mary. You should have a dog."

She put her face close to his and he licked her mouth. She grimaced. "Cats are great," she said. "A cat'll never let you love him. I never know one day to the next where my old tomcat goes. Just shows up at the door when he needs something."

She rubbed Birch's ears. "I had a dog once, Birch, didn't I? You can get closer to a dog than to a human being. After he was gone I said I'll not put myself through that again, no siree. But you're only a pup, aren't you, Birch. You'll outlast all of us."

At home I poured a drink, turned on the television set. It was strangely silent, a fixed image of a darkened city, sand-coloured, low-rise buildings in the foreground, faintly lit. A broad city boulevard in the middle distance, street lights gleaming but no sign of traffic. In the distant darkness above and beyond the city, soft light flashes. I adjusted the sound, but the picture was still silent as a photograph. Then a car, cautious, solitary, creeping through, hesitant, uncertain as if driving over broken ground. And then a quiet voice from the television told me that the silent city was Baghdad.

How can everybody in the village know and Mary not have heard? Mary didn't seem to know a thing. Then logic spoke: They don't know. And I asked logic: So how does Neil know? Then I remembered, Graham the prison guard. He must have overheard. But how would he know Neil? When and why would he report something that was inconsequential to anyone but me?

From the television came a sudden jarring crash and a flash from somewhere off-screen. The commentary grew more urgent. Coalition forces had landed in the distant desert, were advancing on the silent city. The moment and tomorrow fused. Everything and nothing happening at once. The unseen future now implacable, unthinkable, inevitable.

17.

The dog woke me with his whining. Then he barked once. He was at the door. Someone on the television was calculating how long this newest war would last. I stood, killed the television picture. "Nature calling, Birch?" He whined again and when I opened the kitchen door he dashed off across the porch and into the night. I shouted sleepily after him, "Don't be long," then turned back to the living room and sat. How did I forget to close the outer door? I was completely sober coming home. I yawned.

When I woke again it was daylight, soft and silent, shortly after dawn. I remembered that the dog was still outside, swore silently, opened the kitchen door expecting he'd be huddled in the porch, full of accusation. The porch was empty.

I stepped out. There was a distant truck sound lingering in stillness. A crow and then another crow responding. "Birch," I called. Then: *"Birch Bark!"* No reply. A momentary flash of irritation. "Where did you go this time?" Then I thought of Mary's place. I shouted: *"No more treats for you, asshole!"* I shuffled upstairs, removed my shoes, lay on the bed in my clothes to wait.

Damn. I sat up, looked at my wristwatch –it was just after nine o'clock. I climbed off the bed and ran downstairs, yanked open the kitchen door but the porch was still empty. I walked to the telephone, punched in Mary's number. She answered on the second ring. I said, "Shall I go pick him up or will you drop him off?"

There was a brief silence. "Who are you talking about?" Mary asked.

I felt the first flash of fear.

"The dog, you mean? Lord, Tony. He isn't here," she said, alarmed. "When did you last see him?"

I explained that he'd wanted to go out during the night. Didn't come back. "My God," she'd said. "I hope it wasn't the coyotes. They're getting worse, it isn't safe to let the cat out anymore."

It felt like hours, walking the trail, poking through open spaces in the bush. A light snow falling, feathering the ground, my fearfulness rising with every passing minute. Then I was at Strickland's lane and I considered walking up but knew that if the dog had come this far he'd have gone to Mary's.

I called Caddy.

"Well," she said, "the stranger." Her tone was testy. "I was starting to wonder, how long it would be before you'd surface."

An instant gush of relief. "So that's where he is." I laughed nervously.

"Who?" she said.

"Birch Bark," I said and then explained that he'd gone missing.

"He isn't here," she said. "Why don't you come over? I'll put the coffee on."

"I should stay here, for when he shows up."

Silently I promised: I will *never* let you out of my sight again, you little shit.

"Can you think of anywhere he might have gone?"

"No," she said. "But if he wandered outside of his usual territory it's possible he got confused."

That makes sense, I thought. I know that feeling.

"I think I'll drive around a bit."

"Sure," she said. "But come by later. I'll make you lunch."

The snow was falling thickly then. With a gloved hand I swept it off the windshield. And that was when I saw a yellow notebook page tucked underneath the windshield wiper blade. And at that same instant I saw him, curled up on the seat, on the passenger side. How on earth . . . I rapped on the window. He didn't move. I quickly opened the truck door. He was stiff. And then I saw that his eyes were open, bulging, tongue hanging through bared teeth. And in the fur around his neck, a thin wire tightly knotted.

I snatched the paper from the windshield. One word crudely printed: "Oink."

The truck fishtailed violently as I swung up Strickland's lane, hit the ditch and then bounced back out again, headed for the other ditch. I held the accelerator to the floor and the truck slalomed almost to his doorstep. I still had the paper in my hand as I hammered on the door. The house was silent. I kept hammering. Through the window I could see that the kitchen was empty. The silence of abandonment. There was a rock on the doorstep and I grabbed it, hefted it, then smashed the glass, reached in, unlocked the door. Raced through the house. Upstairs, just the one bedroom was furnished. Unruly bed, clothes piled on a chair. Empty beer bottle on a dresser beside a pile of coins.

Back downstairs I caught up with myself, the other me. It was as if I was meeting myself coming in again, this time, slow and cautious. A moment of confusion, then wary recognition. Thinking crisis in the yard, thinking cell extraction, remembering a hundred situations, now moving with deliberation, brain suddenly engaged. Calm down, I told myself. Get hold of yourself. Breathe deeply. There's nobody here. Think this through.

I sat at his kitchen table, absorbed the room, the silence. A faint odour of kerosene awakened memories. Cold winter mornings at home, Ma at the stove, dousing kindling with the fuel for a quick fire start, quick warmth. And me, shivering over steaming porridge. I was calm then. His absence was the proof I needed. He'd have anticipated my reaction, he'd have savoured the anticipation of my fury. He wouldn't have to see it. I could feel him gloating, somewhere.

I saw the rock that I'd used to smash the window where I'd dropped it on the kitchen floor. I stood and picked it up, placed it at the middle of the table, smoothed the crumpled note, placed it near the rock. There was a pencil on the windowsill. I wrote on the bottom of the note: "You will not enjoy the end of this." Then I put the rock on top of it. I headed for the door, then went back and wrote, "Tony Breau."

I remembered Caddy. Come for coffee, she'd said. I felt the pressure of tears. How can I possibly tell Caddy? I was sitting in front of my house inside the truck. The dog had slid off the seat and was awkwardly on the floor, stiff legs folded, teeth bared. I pounded on the steering wheel until I realized that I might break it. The snow was tumbling softly, the hard ground whitening. "I don't want to remember you like this," I said. I got out, then walked around to the passenger side, carried him to the side of the house where I wouldn't be able to see him. Placed him gently on the frozen ground. Went inside the house and sat with my coat on. I stared at the phone for a while before I picked it up.

She answered cheerfully and I couldn't speak at first.

"Caddy," I said, more to prevent her hanging up than because I had anything to say.

"Tony?"

"Caddy," I said again. And then I told her, bluntly, artlessly, angrily. And she was silent.

"Do you want me to come over?" I asked.

And when she finally replied the voice was distant. "No," she said. "Not right now." And she put the phone down.

The snow continued, a soft blanket growing on the stony shrunken body. I found an ancient pick and shovel in the barn I'd rarely visited. Behind the house the ground was like concrete. And then I remembered a pile of stone near where my field dropped off into the sea. "I'll build a cairn," I said. "It's what they used to do." I returned to the house for Jack's old coat.

Near the edge of the field I scraped the crusted snow aside until the ground was bare and I placed him on the dead grass with the coat on top of him. And I spent the next hour moving the pile of stone until it had become a grave mound. I stepped back and studied it. There was something heroic about the pile. And I remembered a phrase from the ancient language of the MacMillans: *clach air do charn*. A stone on your monument. "And that's what it is, Birch. A monument so I'll not forget this."

The store was empty for a change. Mary covered her mouth with a hand. "I can't believe somebody would do a thing like that," she said.

"I can," I said.

"Who do you think?"

I studied her open, honest face and an old instinct, maybe from that deep aspect of myself they used to call "professional," prevented a reply. I just shrugged. "We'll see," I said.

——

Caddy didn't speak when she saw me on her deck. She hesitated, then nodded her assent so I entered the kitchen.

"The coffee will be cold."

"That's okay."

I saw that with one hand she was manipulating the wedding band she still wore, something I hadn't noticed before now. I wasn't sure if she was trying to remove it or if she was just fidgeting. And then she looked up and met my eyes. I was shocked by the blue unblinking clarity of hers.

"I don't want you to go feeling that this was your fault," she said. "I know it's as big a blow to you as it is to anybody."

My voice was paralyzed. I looked away from her laser stare.

"Tony," she said, almost sharply. I looked back into her face again. "It was just a dog."

"I'm going to deal with this," I said.

"I'd rather you didn't."

I stood.

"Sit," she said. "I'll heat the coffee in the microwave."

"No," I said. "I'll come back another time." I tried to smile. "Don't worry."

"There's too much foolish talk around," she said. "I'm worried about where something like this can lead."

And I blurted, "Jesus, Caddy. You, of all people."

She stood quickly, eyes like ice. "Tony. *Don't.* You. Dare."

Okay, so I drank.

The snow had stopped, the sun had pierced a thin layer of cloud and the ground, except where floes of winter snow survived, was bare again. I'd been sitting alone in the silent house for what I estimated to be hours. Just sitting at the kitchen table, staring out the window, down the field to where a small dark mound of stones now stood outlined against the bulge of the sea and the slope of the horizon.

There was surprising logic in Caddy's reaction, I told myself. Dear pragmatic, unsentimental Caddy. I suppose most of my long reflection at the kitchen table was a reminiscence about that part of Caddy's character. God, how it hurt in 1966, her resolute and unremarked departure. Why? And even after I had the explanation, the harder question: "Why wouldn't she have come to me?" Not because we thought we loved each other, which was probably delusional, but because I was—and there was no doubt about this—her best friend in the world. Lovers always treat each other shabbily, but friends don't.

And then the light outside seemed to be diminishing and at the same time casting a glow on the field and the gulf beyond it. I stood. My body felt stiff from all the sitting. I opened the cupboard door and the whiskey bottle was half-full. I took it with me down the field.

The sun melted, a scoop of butter oozing, briefly delineating the vague separation of lowering sky from rising sea. I was chilled, had another swallow from the bottle, one part of my brain saying this will make you feel warm while the other part, the smaller voice of reason, said go back to the house, this is not warmth—get warm before you make yourself sick.

And then, as if by some unheard command, it was dark. The sudden consciousness of darkness seemed to wake me, and I noticed that the bottle in my hand was empty.

Somewhere in that space of time I lost two days.

By checking back to the timeline of the Iraq invasion I know it was in the early morning of March 20 that someone killed my dog. Yes. *My* dog. And that's why he was dead, because of me. I remember all too clearly what happened two days later, on March 22.

I think I slept a lot on March 21 but it's all vague, except for one unforgettable dream.

I hardly ever remember dreams and Sophie told me once that this is healthy. We should be vigilant about dreams, avoid confusing dreams with memories. Many people make that mistake, she said, finding insights into past experience from later dreams. Dreams are just anxieties, Sophie thought. She was big on anxiety, her view being that most of what we do, including our achievements, rise from anxieties that are rooted in our awareness of mortality. "We are the only species," she told me cheerfully over lunch one day, "with the ability to reflect on the inevitability of extinction."

I asked, sensibly, "So why does the rabbit run away when he sees me coming?"

"That's instinctive," she said. "We have instincts too, to run or fight when the circumstances require us to. But we also have the ability to sit, in moments of relative safety and calm, and think about ourselves as mortal and ultimately doomed."

"Lucky us," I said. "I think I'd rather be the rabbit."

So the dream: I'm on a high rooftop. I'm talking World Trade Center high. CN Tower high. Places I've visited and where I've always sensed that awful feeling of electricity in chest and groin, the watery knees, the irrepressible dread that takes the breath away on the edge of the abyss. And in the dream I was prostrate near the edge and struggling to move away, to the safety of the middle part. But the roof keeps tilting and I have no strength in my arms or legs, and the area of the roof keeps changing shape so that I'm always, when I'm moving, crawling closer to the precipice.

And the odd thing is that I'm not alone on the roof. I see Neil and Collie and John Robert and Lester, the men who hang out at the store, moving around with nonchalance, chatting and laughing. And at one point Neil walks to the edge of the roof and sees something far below and turns toward the group and summons everybody over. In that moment, in the angle and the light, it seems that he is suspended in mid-air, hanging in the fatal nothingness of space. And he is as unbothered as I am terrified, limp in legs and arms and voice, struggling and calling out without movement, without sound. But Neil is in command. The others crowd around him, exclaiming excitedly, unafraid, looking back at me and laughing as the roof continues tilting and shrinking.

I'm drenched. For a moment I'm convinced I've pissed in the bed. And then I realize the sound that woke me was the telephone.

"I heard what happened," Neil's message said.

I thought, How the hell can he know so much so quickly?

"I'm not saying a word about it," he said. "Just let me know if you need anything." Then he was gone.

It's just a dog, Caddy said. Of course, she was right. But that small presence had reawakened something hopeful in me. Fool. Idiot, loving anything. Learned nothing during all those years among convicts and coppers and complicated women. Loved a dog.

I laughed.

The milk had been on the counter, obviously for days, and curdled when I poured it in the coffee. Bread nibbled by the small silent phantoms that owned the house in my absence. I should get a cat, I thought. Then: *You must be joking.* Threw the bread outside. The crows will never let you down. But I hear they have an almost human sensibility so you should be wary of the crows along with everybody else.

Refrigerator empty, but for two cans of Keith's. Stomach lurched at the brief temptation.

Mary was silent handing me the newspapers, totalling the groceries. The papers were full of the invasion of Iraq. The war had started in earnest when I was asleep or drunk or both and was already almost over. The relentless coalition juggernaut advancing through the helpless hapless country.

"I'm surprised Neil isn't in here celebrating," Collie said. "Everything seems to be going just the way he planned it."

"I haven't been paying attention," I said.

"Like a knife through hot butter, the coalition," Collie said.

"Neil must be sick," Mary said with a faint edge of sarcasm. "He hasn't been in here for days."

I ate. Eggs and beans and toast. And I felt ill immediately, and returned to bed.

It was dark. There was a pounding noise. Bam, bam, bam. My head cleared and I realized the noise was coming from the porch. Bam. Bam. Bam.

It was Neil.

"You weren't answering the phone," he said. He was looking at me intensely, face close enough that I could smell a trace of alcohol. "Everything okay over here?"

I switched on the kitchen light. The clock said nine.

"I was sleeping," I said. "What's up?"

"I had a call," he said. "I have to go up to Strickland's. Check it out. I'd like you to come along." He was all business, hands on hips.

"Strickland's?" I grunted a half-laugh.

"John Robert thinks his little girl is up there. He's freaking out. She's supposed to be home, part of the bail arrangement."

"Why doesn't he go and get her himself?" I turned and opened the cupboard where I keep the liquor. There was a half bottle. I retrieved it, held it up.

He shook his head. "John Robert is kind of chicken. What do you think? We'll just go up and knock on the door and take her home. There'll be no problem if there's two of us."

I uncapped the bottle, swallowed, shivered, almost gagged. Handed it to Neil. He held it indifferently for a moment, still studying me. Then swallowed briefly. He was wearing gloves. I noticed the quality of them, soft leather like a second skin. He handed back the bottle.

"I don't think I could face Strickland," I said.

"You could always wait outside," Neil said. "I'd just like to have you there. Moral support, right?"

I shrugged.

"The last thing the place needs is another dead kid," he said. "Maybe last summer, if somebody went there ... but you can suit yourself."

"I'll get my coat," I said.

There was light visible as we drove slowly up the lane. We crept around a car parked in darkness halfway up. "That'll be John Robert," Neil said. So what do you need me for? I wondered silently. We drove on. From the yard I could see the glow in the living room. The flicker of a television screen. We climbed out, closed the car doors quietly.

Neil paused near the living room window, then moved closer, peered in, beckoned. Strickland was asleep on his couch, in the fetal position, hands clasped between his knees.

"He seems to be alone," I whispered.

"She'll be upstairs," Neil replied softly, confidently. Then he was around to the back, easing through the doors. In the kitchen he whispered, "You go wake him up."

I made no attempt at stealth. I just walked into the living

room and ran a hand up the wall just inside the door where I found a light switch. Lit the room.

Strickland was like a cat. Off the couch on all fours and as he rose I saw the baseball bat. He was still half-crouched and coming at me but I but I stepped in and caught him just below the ear. This time my fist was ready for the impact, but still there was a lightning jolt of pain. He fell back, the bat clattered on the floor and I had it then. And then he was coming at me hard. I swung, two-handed and he turned his face away and there was a solid crunch as the bat connected with the back of his head. He went down with a crash. Laughter on the television. Someone talking.

Now Neil was leaning over him, "Grab a leg," he snarled as he grabbed one and started tugging.

I could feel my heart pounding, the terror now a mix of horror and remorse. "Jesus, Jesus."

Then Neil was in my face, shouting, "Grab a fucking leg." For a moment I was paralyzed. "Grab that fuuuuck-ing leg!" And so I did. Struggling toward the kitchen I was desperately looking for a phone. It was on the kitchen table. I dropped the leg, reached for the phone. "I'll call 911," I shouted. Neil was uncapping a quart rum bottle, then pouring the contents on the motionless Strickland. Rum? Then I caught the reek of kerosene. I dropped the phone.

"What the *fuck* are you doing?"

There was the snap of a Zippo lighter and a flash and sudden flame all over Strickland, running along the floor in the direction of the stove.

I remembered the girl.

"No," Neil screamed as I bolted toward the living room, up the stairs, crashing through the empty bedrooms. Cold. Damp. Dark. Musty. Empty. Empty. Empty bedrooms, closets. Looked under beds. Frightened children hide. Nothing, nothing, nothing. Smoke met me, curling up the stairs. I plunged through, head down.

Now more smoke and crackle, burning heat. Coat off trying to smother flames, bare hands tearing at Strickland's clothing, get it off him. Neil nowhere, then his feet on the floor beside Strickland. Then a sudden flash and the wooden floor lurched up and struck my face with a shattering force.

The yard was full of vehicles. The sky sparkled and glowed. There was a crashing sound and the air was heavy with the pungent odour of ancient boards and timber burning. Red and white light strobing slowly, tree shadows, car shadows, man shadows. Voices all around me. I tried to sit up but my head throbbed and I felt breathless. I fell back, now aware of a pillow under my head, a blanket over me. Realized my hands were wrapped in gauze.

Then I heard Neil talking: "There was no stopping him, he just tore off in there, trying to save the guy. I got there just after he passed out with the smoke . . . could only get one of them out . . . didn't think there was any hope for the other fellow anyway."

I closed my eyes, trying to remember. Trying not to remember.

"No big loss, I suppose," someone said.

"Ah well," said Neil, almost sorrowfully.

18.

It was dawn when the doctor told me to go home. My hands were heavily bandaged, mind fuzzy with painkillers. "Take these when you need to," he said.

"What is it," I asked.

"Percocet," he said. "Be careful with this stuff." And he handed me a prescription. "I understand you live alone."

I nodded.

"Is there anyone you could stay with for a few days?"

I shook my head.

Neil was in the doorway of the examining room. "We'll see that he's taken care of," he said. Then John Robert was beside him. "He has a whole village to look after him," John Robert said. The doctor smiled, tapped me lightly on the shoulder.

"You've had quite a night of it," he said.

Driving back through the watery spring light, I asked, "What about Dwayne?"

There was a long silence. "He's gone," Neil said at last. "A hard way to end up."

I was behind him in the back seat and I couldn't see his face. So I waited.

"Like I was explaining to John here, nobody could have done more than you tried to do. And after him trying to take your head off with a baseball bat. You did more than I'd have." He grunted a grim laugh.

I watched the landscape passing. Surely it wasn't so simple. A young man was dead and I had helped to kill him.

"I'll have to give a statement," I said.

"Like I told John Robert. Damned fool was trying to get the fire going with gas or kerosene or something, sees us, drops the bottle, goes for the bat. Something catches. Takes a whack at you but you tear off looking for the girl. He comes after me but now he's on fire and I do like we're trained, knock him down, try to smother it. But damned if he didn't fight me. Then you're back and you're on fire too. So I gotta get you out. By then he's done . . . no way getting back in for him."

"I was waiting in the lane," said John Robert. "I kind of froze there when I saw the fire. In a way I feel responsible."

"She wasn't there," I said. "I checked every room."

John Robert grunted. "The little witch was home. Arrived in after I left. Not a word about where she was all afternoon and evening. I just assumed the worst. Up at Strickland's, on the dope or worse." He sighed. "Hard times to be a parent, Tony. You didn't have any yourself, did you?"

He turned to look at me, arm over the back of the front seat. I closed my eyes, shook my head.

"Wise man," he said. "I never knew how good I had it when I was single."

There was no movement in the landscape, only us passing through it. The sea was flat, pewter grey.

"Bloody shame it had to come to this," Neil said. "But meaning no disrespect to the dead, he brought it on himself."

Then we were in the village and I saw my truck in Caddy's driveway. Neil slowed, then turned in and stopped behind it. "We took the liberty of moving some of your stuff over here," Neil said. "Caddy insisted. And you know what she's like."

"We put your things in the guest room," Caddy said. "I'll show you." She caught my arm, just above the elbow, and squeezed it as we climbed the stairs. Then, cheerfully, "This is it. You'll be here for as long as you have to."

"It's too much trouble," I said. I felt a sensation similar to panic growing inside me. I remembered the rooftop dream, the feeling of vertigo and helplessness. "It's decided," she said. "There will be no discussion." The room was cool, impersonal, multiple pillows on the bed, a thick blue duvet, a large window, drapes drawn. I peered out. The day was brightening. We went back downstairs where the others were waiting.

"All settled in then?" said Neil rising. John Robert was still seated, studying me with an expression that seemed full of unasked questions. Then he stood too. "I'll grab a ride home with you."

After the sound of the car faded I asked: "Whose idea was this?"

She was busy at the sink, washing coffee mugs. "It was a group decision." She turned. "Don't worry, I won't molest you, unless you want me to–for therapy." She smiled at me and turned away again, rattling the mugs in the sink.

"The place will be abuzz," I said.

"It's the twenty-first century," she said. "Even here."

I was sitting on the side of the bed studying my bandages. My hands hurt when I tried to move my fingers, seared with pain as if the skin was splitting, tendons snapping. Then Caddy was in the doorway with a tray piled with gauze and salves and scissors. She set them on the bed, then moved a chair and sat in front of me. Took a hand gently in hers. "I have instructions to change these every day. Okay?" She searched my face. "I know this isn't easy for you."

She worked carefully, in silence. "You're better than a nurse," I said. She just smiled.

When she was nearly finished, she said, "Neil told me what happened so you mustn't feel you have to explain. Nobody blames anybody. It was just a horrible accident."

"Is that what everybody thinks?"

"It's the only way to look at it."

I struggled to interpret the meaning of her comment, finally suppressed the urge to ask her straight out: How much do you know, really?

Then she straightened up, holding both bandaged hands gently, eyes intense on mine. "You always had a tendency to blame yourself for things, Tony. Always too hard on yourself. Let this one go."

I listened carefully for evidence of guilty knowledge, but I could hear only what seemed to be a genuine attempt at comforting. I nodded.

Then she stood, still holding my hands. "Come," she said. She dropped my hands and turned. In the doorway she paused and looked back. "Come," she said. "I'll only be fretting, thinking of you over here alone."

In her bed I whispered, apologetically: "I can't do much with these hands."

"Let me do the work," she whispered back.

And a little later, in the darkness, she murmured: "I liked what you did the last time ..."

I look back on the weeks I spent with Caddy as one of those rare occasions when I managed to banish all consciousness of memory or place beyond that special time with her. I would tell myself: this won't last and I'll have the rest of my life for self-doubt, questions, accusations, guilt. So I let myself sink deeply into the sound and the touch and especially the better memories of her. It became normal, how I settled into the rhythms of her day.

She was an early riser and I awoke each morning to the spatter of her shower. She seemed to become younger, more alive as the days passed, and I allowed myself to think it was my presence, my nightly ministrations to needs that had been long neglected, that accounted for it.

Now I realize of course that the real cause was something else entirely. Strickland's death had closed off an ugly chapter in her life. She was liberated from the menace that he represented and I was part of that liberation. I discovered a Caddy I couldn't have imagined.

"If things had been different back in the sixties, do you think life could have been like this?"

She considered my question for a while then kissed me quickly. "It could have been anything we want to imagine now," she said. "But I don't want to imagine that. It would only make me sad. Okay? I hate regrets."

And she was so right. It is in the fertile gap between how things are and how things might have been that sorrow blooms.

I'd noticed him once at the store, a ruddy-faced man in an expensive leather jacket and designer jeans, cowboy boots that made him seem tall. My trips to the store while I was at Caddy's were perfunctory. Walk in, grab what I needed and get out quickly before authorizing, by some careless word or glance, a torrent of discussion about Strickland's death.

On this visit the stranger caught up before I reached the door. "You'd be Tony MacMillan?"

"Yes."

"I doubt if you remember me, we were in school together a long time ago."

I studied the face. He was probably near my age but the features were commonplace where we grew up. Blue eyes, cropped silver hair, strong jawline. I couldn't come up with a name.

"Jimmy Joe MacInnis," he said. "Dwayne Strickland was brought up at my brother's place on the Shore Road. I grew up there too, in the old house, the place that burned down. I was hoping to talk to you about that when you're feeling up to it."

I could feel my heart rate accelerate.

"I know you now," I said. "Dwayne often talked about you." I fumbled in my heart for words of sympathy, but found only an old cliché. "I'm sorry for your trouble." And then, embarrassed: "I'd shake your hand but mine are still a little tender."

"I expect so," he said. "I appreciate what you tried to do for him. In prison. The night of the fire. Dwayne thought a lot of you. Maybe I could come and see you sometime. Have a coffee. You're in the old MacDougall place on the Shore Road, I think I heard. Old Charlie's."

"I'm not there just now." And I explained that I was recuperating at Caddy's. "You probably remember Caddy Gillis, now Stewart."

"I remember Caddy well," he said smiling warmly. "Saint of a woman, Caddy is."

"So what's new at the store," Caddy asked, as I unfolded newspapers on the table. And checked by an instinctive caution I said, "Nothing. The usual."

And then, "I suppose I should be thinking of getting back to the Shore Road one of these days. These hands are almost useful again."

"I noticed," she said. I couldn't see her face. "I thought you liked it here."

"I do. I love it here. I just don't want to end up like the dog."

She performed an exaggerated double take. "Dead, you mean? No danger of that here, unless . . ." She smiled.

"I meant getting too attached," I said.

"Well, why don't you let me worry about that."

"I think I'll lie down for a bit."

"You do that." Neutral tone, expression.

That afternoon, lying on her bed, it all came back, the awful night, March 22. The images emerged around me slowly like wisps of fog, or smoke seeping underneath a door, small scraps of particular memory hovering—the dazed and desperate expression on his face as he lunged with the baseball bat, the stunned shock when I hit him with my fist, the baseball bat clattering in hypnotic slowness on the floor, the grip end rising slowly toward my outstretched hand, the feral violence in his face, a look I'd seen a hundred times in a hundred faces. And then he was crumpled on the floor and I was standing over him, Neil crouched and roaring: "*Grab a fucking leg.*" And me, dazed, wondering who or what had done this thing. "*Grab that fuuuuck-ing leg!*"

I rose from the bed, struggling to breathe, paced the floor for a while, trying to suppress the rising panic. I breathed deeply several times then walked downstairs. Caddy was at the kitchen table, the newspaper open before her, and looked at me over the top of her reading glasses. "That was an efficient nap," she said.

I sat in what had become my usual place.

"I was thinking of pouring a drink," she said. "Could I interest you in joining me?"

I nodded. And the relief flowed through me, the prospect of a drink or simply being in her healing presence.

I've often asked myself: What makes an ordinary man a killer? But am I so ordinary? Did I intend to kill? I responded to an immediate danger from instinct, training and experience. The baseball bat became a baton. How often have I wielded a baton against a man who believed that by brute force he could gain control of some small aspect of his life or, in extreme cases, an institution by disabling or killing me? The prison system taught me that the margin between life and death is frequently as narrow as a hesitation. Had I intended to kill Strickland with the baseball bat? Another question for perpetuity.

That evening over dinner I said to Caddy, "Sooner or later we'll have to talk about it."

"About what?"

"You know."

Her eyes were full of kindness and she touched my hand gently. "In due course." Then she smiled. "Hey, you didn't flinch when I touched the hand. You must be getting better."

"We're going to have a visitor," I said.

She looked puzzled.

"You remember Jimmy MacInnis? We all went to school together."

It took half a minute for her to work it out. "What does he want?"

"He didn't say. I met him at the store. He said he'd like to drop by."

"I'll be out," she said. Then she stood and started gathering the dishes.

Before we went to sleep that night I asked: "Do you think we could make this work long term?"

"What does 'long term' mean anymore?"

"You have a point."

"How about one day at a time."

"That's good enough for me."

Jimmy MacInnis called three days later, just before noon. Caddy answered, handed me the phone. He asked if two o'clock would be convenient. I covered the mouthpiece. "He wants to come by at two."

"Sure," she said. "I have to go to town anyway."

"You wouldn't consider staying?"

"What would you want me here for?"

"Moral support."

She laughed. "What do you need that for? You're the guy who got half-burned to death trying to save the asshole."

Was that sarcasm or the official story? Was that how March 22 and Strickland's death would be remembered? I felt a wave of nausea.

"Suit yourself," I said and I left the kitchen to sit alone in the living room, watching the road as she drove off toward town.

He arrived in a rental SUV. When he knocked on the front door I led him through to the kitchen. She had put a pot of coffee on to brew before she left and I felt my spirits lift a little.

"Caddy Gillis," he said. "If she's the one I'm thinking of, everybody had a crush on her. Remember how we'd say somebody had the 'notion' for somebody or other. We'd call it the *naw-shun*. Every so often the old expressions come back like that." He shook his head, drifting back through memory. "The old Gaelic people would say that if you were sweet on somebody. We all had the *naw-shun* for Caddy, if I recall."

There was a long silence as each of us attempted to find a place to start, one of the free ends of a tangled piece of rope.

"I don't suppose you had much Gaelic yourself, growing up," he said at last.

"No, it was pretty well gone by then."

"Sad," he said. "Those old people were solid, man. Built this place to last. Integrity was what they had, I guess it's what they left for us. Gave us their example. I suppose we can forgive them for taking the language with them when they went." He sipped his coffee, studied the ceiling for a while.

"I heard plenty of it as a kid," he said. "Hung on to a few fragments but that's about all. Their gumption though, the ability to make something out of nothing. That stayed with me."

"Yes," I said, boredom creeping in around the apprehension.

"Life, eh. Looking back on it I guess that's how it'll seem at the end—a bunch of fragments." He chuckled. Another long silence.

"Anyway," Jimmy said, sitting straighter, taking a sip of coffee. "I'm not here to rake over what happened up at the old place. I've heard enough to get the picture."

I made a dismissive gesture with my pink and scabby hands, but said nothing. Just listen, I thought.

"I talked to Neil Archie. Jesus, he hasn't changed a bit." He laughed. "Neil was telling me how you tried to save poor Dwayne, how you almost ended up . . . yourself."

I shrugged. "I don't remember much."

"I understand . . . but I just wanted you to know, I appreciate what you tried to do that night and before that."

He tilted back, studying his cup. His hands were large and seemed permanently stained by work. "Dwayne used to tell me back when he was doing time that you were one of the few people in the system who took an interest in him as something more than a number. I thought to myself, I hope someday I'll get a chance to express my appreciation, never expecting the circumstances, of course."

I nodded, studying the floor. I glanced over his head at the kitchen wall clock. It said 2:20. "Dwayne," I said finally, "was in many ways his own worst enemy." And I felt an instant flutter of relief at the sound of truth.

"Oh man," MacInnis said enthusiastically. "Truer words were never spoken."

And I realized then that he hadn't come with perilous, unanswerable questions, but to seek some form of absolution.

"I can't begin to tally up the sleepless nights, the pages and pages I wrote to Dwayne, trying, I suppose, to be his dad. No criticism intended, but my brother was old school. Hands-off to a fault, if you know what I mean."

"Yes," I said.

"I mean, we all let him down, one way or another, and we have to live with that. But at the end of the day, everybody, including poor Dwayne, has to face up to the consequences of his own actions. And boy, poor Dwayne had plenty to face."

I stood. "Let me get you some fresh."

"Appreciate it," he said.

And then for a while we relaxed into a comparison of memories of how we left the place, little more than boys. The chat was smooth and easy. How I ended up in prisons, how he, like so many young men from here, found his way to northern Ontario, used a connection from home to get work in hardrock mining. "It was up to yourself then, boy. Some old contractor or mine captain would look you up and down, his face saying, 'If you weren't from home I wouldn't give you the fuckin time of day.' You had one chance and that was all I asked for."

He started as underground labourer, then became a timber man in shaft development. He gradually learned to handle all the complex new machinery for driving drifts and raises, excavating caverns called stopes, but all the time watching and learning bigger things–geology and engineering, leadership. Eventually he won a subcontract from someone else from home, someone big in the specialized work of sinking mine shafts. That was the break he needed and it came at the exact right time.

"I could be as wild as anybody, but right around then I was settling down. Which is what we all do, sooner or later. Right?"

Afterwards he continued the tradition, making it his policy to share his good fortune. "It was just good sense, anyway–guys from here are the best miners in the country. By far. So I was really doing myself the favour, taking on the young fellows from here who'd be showing up like I did with the arse out of their pants. Any more of that coffee?"

I stood.

"I don't know how often I begged Dwayne to come on up, even after the penitentiary, I was ready to give him a chance. He'd have been good at it I know, strong and smart, no lack of initiative there. Brains to burn. But like I always say, a fella can be too smart for his own good. Poor Dwayne. It seemed he was always looking for the shortcut to where guys like you and me got taking the long way around."

The clock now said three o'clock. "Christ," he said. "Look at the time. Let me get to the point of why I came here."

He told me he'd spent a lot of time thinking since Dwayne's death and had concluded that what the place needed more than anything else was a facility that the young people could consider theirs, a community youth centre.

"I love that concept–community," he said. "It takes in everything we've been talking about. The continuity of quality, the gifts the old-timers left us with, all preserved in the community. People getting by, sharing and helping one another. Every chance I've had I've tried to put something back into the community."

Now, he felt, it was time to put some serious money into a community centre for the young people. Maybe save one or two from turning out like Dwayne. He said he'd want extensive local participation because he'd learned that top-down charity never works. People need to feel they have a stake in something. And there's also the practical reality that building something is the easy part. The challenge is the long-term operation, the maintenance, the continuity.

"What do you think?"

I fought the skepticism. I really did. "I think it's a very generous thought."

"Maybe name the place after Dwayne. I was thinking how that would look to people driving through–the Dwayne Strickland Community Centre." His voice broke slightly as he said it.

Mercifully it was nearly over. I could imagine Caddy's response–and heard it shortly after: that plan has about as much chance as a fart in a windstorm. But for the moment, Jimmy Joe MacInnis and I were united in some kind of plan to keep Dwayne's rehabilitated memory alive.

"He was really determined to turn his life around this time," Jimmy said, standing in the middle of the kitchen, ready to leave. "I've learned to read guys, to recognize the bullshit when I hear it. He was serious this time. When I was talking to him, just before he died, he'd decided to move up to Sudbury, take a job there, fresh start. He was genuine. You could see it in his eyes. The eyes don't lie, man."

"You were here just before he died?"

"No, he was up."

"Up?"

"Up to Sudbury, a flying trip to check the place out."

"Do you remember when?"

"I think it was March 19 he arrived. I remember all the talk was about the Iraq business. Dwayne had some interesting theories about that. Yes. It was on the twentieth, him and me and a couple of other guys were in the Nickel Range having a few beers, watching all that go-ahead on television. Next day, March 21, he came back. Never knowing, eh."

"Strickland didn't kill my dog!"

Mary was studying me from behind the counter with an expression of confusion and alarm. "I could have told you that," she said.

"How did you know? Why didn't you tell me?"

"It didn't cross my mind that you'd have blamed him."

"Jesus, Mary."

"I thought you knew. He wasn't even here. He was gone somewhere. He didn't tell me where he was going but he came over and asked me to keep an eye on his place. I know he was worried about people breaking in. He'd mentioned that there were people always snooping around. Then after that business with the drugs, he was really paranoid."

"I was sure he did it."

"No, Tony," Mary said. "Dwayne loved dogs."

Caddy was back from town when I returned from the store and suddenly I dreaded seeing her, telling her what I had learned— and then the story of what really happened, the nauseating truth: how I'd become an accessory to a crime that will haunt me until I die.

I quietly backed my truck out of her driveway and drove down to the Shore Road. My little house had the abandoned look of the many summer places that dot the coastline now. The kitchen door was stuck again. I shouldered through, swearing quietly, resentful of the chill, the dampness, the unimaginative utility of the place. I stood in the middle of the kitchen assessing the haphazard collection of cast-offs that passed for furnishing. The new television screen loomed in the living room, an alien intrusion of modern design and purpose. Old Charlie would have been perfectly at home with all the rest. I sat. I couldn't stay much longer at Caddy's place but living here alone was little more than survival. The worst bachelor dive I'd lived in during my days before Anna had been models of contemporary style and comfort compared to this.

Outside I surveyed the once-lovely vista, now compromised by the accusing pile of stone down where the meadow drops off into the sea. I wandered through the field and as I stood before the little monument I could no longer avoid confronting the awful realization that now screamed for my full attention.

Three people knew the full particulars of the confrontation in Neil's driveway–Neil, Strickland, me. Whoever was with Strickland when he arrived that night had already prudently retreated. Three people knew that Strickland had called me a pig. One of us wrote the note that was under the windshield wiper blade when I found the dog dead on the front seat of my truck. Strangled with a piece of fine wire, the kind we used as boys for rabbit snares. One of us killed the dog and it wasn't me and now I knew it wasn't Strickland.

From her youngest days, Caddy seemed to have the gift of concealing reactions that betrayed emotion. She could absorb shock and surprise with hardly any outward sign. I swear that we could be walking through a fancy room and if I said to Caddy, "Jeez, Caddy, you've got two different shoes on!" she'd walk three more paces before she'd even look down, and then just carry on with a shrug.

"I think it was Neil who killed the little dog."

She was at the sink draining water off potatoes, steam swirling around her face.

"Why would you think that?"

"It could only have been him."

Long silence as she shook the pot, replaced the cover. "But you don't know for sure."

"Not a hundred percent."

"So why speculate?"

"I think Neil set me up, to involve me in a plan to get rid of Strickland."

"Maybe I shouldn't have badgered you into getting that television set. You've been watching cop shows."

"This isn't funny."

She nodded, came close to me, suggested that we have a drink before dinner. And as she poured, she declared, "Well, it would be like something he would do."

"So you wouldn't rule it out."

"Anything is possible."

"Caddy. We murdered Strickland, Neil and me. I was part of it because of that dog."

"Like I said before, it was only a dog. And Strickland is no big loss to the place. Good riddance, I say."

"Caddy, I can't believe I'm hearing this from you."

"It's always been your downfall, Tony, taking too much on yourself. At the end of the day . . ."

"Stop saying that. I hate that fucking expression." My vehemence shocked me, and even Caddy showed surprise.

"*What*-ever," she said eventually. "We're all in this together. Remember that. You, me, Neil, the whole village. It will pass."

"You? What the fuck did you have to do with it?"

"There are things you don't know, Tony. And it's best left that way."

We ate in silence and I went to bed in the guest room. Early the next morning I gathered my possessions and moved back to my own miserable house.

Driving away I reminded myself that more than thirty years before she had shocked me into a state of grief that never really went away. I was always able to find some comfort in the knowledge, when I was in my twenties, that time would save me from despair. Time was on my side back then. In time I'd forget her, outgrow grief and vulnerability. But I never did and now time was my enemy.

Looking back, my decision to place a call to Anna that day stands as one of my more rational impulses. On the other hand it was possibly nothing more than a desire to hear a human voice—even if it might be hostile.

She picked up on the second ring. She sounded friendly, even happy. For an instant I regretted calling, felt sorry for the effect that what I had to say would have on her. Whatever wounded resentment I might have held after what she and Strickland did had long since been expiated. I told her anyway.

"Anna. I'm sorry to have to be the one to tell you, but I thought you'd want to know. Dwayne Strickland is dead."

There was a long unsurprising silence and I used it to think through the rest of what I wanted her to know. She said nothing. I realized that she had nothing to say.

"He died in a house fire."

Still no response.

"It looks like an accident. He was trying to light a fire with kerosene."

"I'm glad you told me," she said. I realized that she had been listening for evidence of an agenda. "You're okay?"

I hesitated. "Sure," I said. "I'm fine."

"You don't sound fine, but I'll take you at your word. Where are you?"

"I'm at the old place. It's peaceful here." Wondering why I added that.

"You cared about him, Tony. You did your best for him. Don't forget that."

And whatever sordid impulse might have compelled me to say what I could have said, disappeared, words never to be uttered—words conveying empty, irrelevant, stupid knowledge that would one day mercifully die with us.

"Thanks for the thought," I said.

"Tony, while I've got you—maybe this is a bad time, but it's something you can think about in the next little while. The dog."

"What?"

"The dog. Jack Daniels—surely you remember your little pal in Kingston?"

"Oh."

"It doesn't really work for me anymore, Tony, having a dog around. There's a breeder interested in taking him but I thought of you, living alone out in the country. It's a perfect place for a dog. I think it would be great for both of you. What do you think?"

I was afraid to speak, unnerved by a sudden congestion in my chest making it difficult for me to breathe.

As simply as I could I ended the conversation. "Give me a little time to think about it. Goodbye, Anna."

———

It became dark outside. I was on my third drink, clear-headed once again. I put the bottle away.

Neil seemed surprised to see me, but motioned me inside. I could hear the rattle and clash of pots in the kitchen as we walked past the doorway, then straight through the comfortable living room to a little room in a back corner of the house. It was, by the look of it, his private space. There was a wall full of citations and awards and photographs. Young Neil the soldier, young Neil the cop, middle-aged Neil the cop, pictures of Neil the host, posing with the guests–identical smile in every shot, the poise of one accustomed to photographers.

He sat in a swivel chair, twisted side to side, hands clasped in front of him, twirling his thumbs. "Can I get you anything?" The tone was wary, but unafraid.

"I don't know why you had to kill the dog, Neil."

He stood abruptly, towering over me, face flushed. "Jesus H. Christ." Turned away indignantly, then back.

"So you're blaming me for that, now," he said. "Where's this coming from? Guilt, is it? You're feeling all guilty because some slimeball meets the end that was–and listen carefully to this, Tony–meets the end that was in the cards for him for a long, long time. Long before either one of us had anything to do with him."

"The dog," I said. "Why did you do that?"

"Oh fuck off with the dog," he said. "A human being–and I'll give Strickland that much–a human being I can understand. But snivelling over a fucking dog? Gimme a break."

I stood. "I'm going to tell the whole story."

"Are you now? And who are you going to tell? The media?" He leaned back in the chair and laughed loudly.

"I'm going to file a separate report with the police. I'll leave it with them."

"I see." He hauled his chair up close to the desk and sat, elbows on the desktop, chin in his hands, like a schoolboy. "And what'll you tell them?"

"Exactly what happened. And don't worry. I'll not minimize my own involvement."

"No. I expect you won't minimize anything. That seems to be your trademark, Tony. Tell the truth. Let the chips fall where they may, knowing that the chips always fall away from the fella with the axe."

"What are you talking about?"

"Chicken-shit whistleblowers, is what. You're all alike."

I turned toward the door.

"It'll be your word against mine," he said.

"I'll leave it up to them."

"Fair enough. But before you go I want to show you something." He was rummaging in the top drawer of the desk. "You know, Tony, cops aren't all stupid and the fellas here, these young Mounties, they've done a pretty good investigation. They haven't talked to you yet?"

I shook my head. "No."

"They'll get around to it. Now sit down. Sit down. Just for a minute."

I sat in the chair nearest the door.

"Remember the night, the little confrontation in the yard here? Well they actually tracked down the young fella who was with Strickland—maybe you don't remember him, he kind of slipped away in the panic. But he was telling them how hot things got between you and Dwayne. He didn't hear everything so they asked me and I was able to confirm that Strickland called you some pretty nasty things, including 'a pig.'"

He was shaking his head now. "If I had a dollar for every time I heard that word. And how you said something about somebody putting a bullet in Strickland's ass. You remember as well as I do, I'm sure."

"And did you tell them that it was you carrying the gun, on the verge of shooting him? Did you remember that part?"

"Gun? What gun are you talking about? Are you trying to say you saw a gun?"

"This is bullshit, Neil. You know it as well as I do."

"I'm just sayin'. But here's the thing. This dog business never entered the picture, as far as the cops are concerned. But it's true. You were pretty upset about what happened to that dog. Very upset."

And from the desk drawer he removed and held up a yellow piece of paper. "And this here is proof of just how upset you were, Tony. You're gonna have to tell them that you found this under the wiper on your truck. Clear evidence for you of who killed your dog." He shook his head slowly, sadly. "Then you head for Strickland's with the dead dog and the evidence and you break in and leave this on his kitchen table. But that's not enough. Oh no. Tony's so upset about his dog that he writes a little love note on the bottom—a threat. A clear, unmistakable threat. And then . . . and then, you fucking signed it."

The expression on his face was one of mockery and pity and contempt. He slapped his forehead in mock disbelief, and slid the paper back in the drawer.

"How did you get that?"

"Huh?" He was through with me, his mind already elsewhere. He seemed weary. "Never mind how I got it. But you know as well as I do, Tony, I can't give it to you. It's evidence. And as a policeman myself I'm sworn and trained to protect evidence by all means possible."

We both stood then and stared at each other, everything that connected us—history, community, the law—now replaced by a single common memory that made us hostages to each other.

"I have to ask you something, Neil."

"Fire away."

"You mentioned my wife. Anna. And Strickland. Where did you hear about that, Neil?"

"Don't you worry about that, Tony. That's between us. We can imagine what the cops would do with *that* but, trust me, some things are just too personal."

"The question was," I said, struggling for calm, "where did you hear about that?"

He put a gentle hand on my elbow, I brushed the hand away. "I'm just curious, how did you connect with Graham? How did you guys end up talking about Anna?"

He straightened up, seemed genuinely confused. "Graham who?"

"You know who," I said.

Now he was perplexed. Studied the floor for a moment. "You're away a head of me, Tony. I don't have a fuckin clue what you're talking about." He caught my elbow again, this time in a grip. "I don't want to seem unfriendly, Tony, but I'm gonna have to ask you to leave."

And he ushered me out of his little office, back through the living room, down a hallway toward the door.

Passing the now silent kitchen, lit only by a vent light above the stove, I glanced in and saw Hannah standing there in the semi-darkness. She was stone still, holding a dishtowel to her face, concealing her expression or maybe wiping something from her cheek.

19.

I needed two days to decide. And it gives me some satisfaction that for those two days I denied myself the comfort, inspiration, stimulation—all the myriad promises—of alcohol. I busied myself around my house. I cleaned. I stored things that didn't have immediately obvious usefulness. I don't think I turned on a radio or the television and I avoided the store. It doesn't diminish the effect of this scene to admit that I was hoping to hear the ringing of the telephone and that I wanted it to be Caddy. But the phone was as silent as the table it sat on.

All the while, my mind processed the images and sensations and potential ramifications of all that had happened to me in the previous month. By late on day two I was reasonably certain what I had to do.

———

For a moment I wasn't sure that she would invite me in when she saw me on her deck. Her face was expressionless. Then she nodded.

"I was about to make a cup of tea," she said.

I sat. I did not presume to remove my coat. "That would be nice." I sensed her uneasiness. I had caught her by surprise and I felt a little bit sorry for her. "I won't stay long," I said.

She shrugged, leaned back against the counter to await the kettle.

"You said the other day, 'We're all in this together.' I want to understand what you meant by that."

"It isn't complicated, we're community. We're . . ."

"Jesus Christ!"

We were both startled to silence by my tone.

"I'm sorry," I said quickly. I stood up and paced, calm resolve crumbling. "I'm starting to hate that word. 'Community.' It's turning into an excuse for everything from mediocrity to corruption."

"Sit, Tony," she said. "Just sit."

She unplugged the kettle and fetched a bottle. It was a fifteen-year-old single malt, unopened. She placed it on the table, returned to the cupboard and found two small glasses. She sat so that we had only the corner of the table between us. She placed her hand on my thigh and squeezed gently. Then she took the bottle, broke the seal and struggled with the cork.

"I found this the other day, after you left. It was with Jack's stuff. A gift from some old friend, or customer when he had his own business. Poor Jack wasn't much for Scotch. Rum or rye would have been Jack's choice." There was a squeak and a hollow thunk as the cork pulled free.

"You don't have to," I said. "Not for my sake."

She smiled. "I think Jack would have loved to see you have a sip of this. You two would have got along."

"I'd like to have known Jack," I managed to say.

"Yes. You're alike, you two." And she poured carefully into the small glasses, then stared deeply into my eyes. "Maybe that's why I loved Jack." She put the bottle down and slowly put the cork back in, never breaking eye contact.

And somehow I knew that the special bottle and the heartfelt disclosure were signals that broken strands of time were about to be rejoined, if only for a moment. She looked down at her glass.

"I read somewhere that you aren't supposed to mix this with anything. Though Jack said once that out west they like to put Coke in it." She swirled her glass, a forearm resting between us on the table. In the late afternoon sunshine, the soft fuzz on her arm seemed to shimmer golden. "Then he'd say, 'Out west, they'll drink anything.' Did you know they put raw eggs in beer out west?"

I smiled at her and we sipped quietly until the drinks were but small puddles in the bottom of our glasses.

"That was another thing. The sense of humour. He was you to a T, my Jack was." Then she stood.

"Help yourself to another. I have to go and get something." She put her coat on and went outside, heading toward the garage and disappearing through a side door.

When she came back she removed her coat and sat where she had been. She was clutching something in her hand. "Do you remember that day in court when the lawyer asked me, 'Have you or any member of your family ever used OxyContin for any medical reason?'"

She drained the little glass and studied it for a moment. Then looked up. "And I said, 'I can only speak for myself . . . No.'"

I waited.

"It was the truth. But there was something nagging at me the moment after I said it." She splashed a bit more whiskey in both our glasses. "After Jack passed, I was tidying his workshop and I found this in a drawer." She held up an empty plastic pill vial.

"I thought nothing of it at the time. He was a construction worker. That work is hard on people, especially out west. Fort Mac, Fort Chip, always Fort something in the middle of nowhere and in the middle of their ferocious winters. And then, even when it's warm, there's the pollution and just the wear and tear on the body." She smiled. "Jack was full of aches and pains, not that he ever complained.

"Anyway, after I came back from court that day I went back to the workshop to see what this was, hoping like crazy that it was Tylenol 3 or something." She handed the vial to me. "Tell me what you see written there. I don't have my glasses."

I read: John T. Stewart, OXYCODONE x 80 @40mg, as required. May 28, 2000. And a doctor's name.

I handed it back. "So Jack was using OxyContin, from a doctor's prescription, for perfectly legitimate reasons. You didn't know that. It was an honest mistake on your part."

She was silent for what felt like a long time.

"Is it really that simple?" she said at last. "Wasn't I under some obligation to correct my mistake? To tell them that I was wrong, that in fact someone in the house had used OxyContin?"

"It wouldn't have changed anything."

"Tony—what if I told you that it was full of pills when I first found it, after Jack was in his grave. And it was empty when I went back to look, that day after court. And there was only one other person, ever, in that garage. After Jack died, she'd sit out there for hours, grieving. I thought."

There was no sound but the sudden hum of the refrigerator, the whir of car tires on the road outside.

"So that's what I meant, Tony. We're all in this together."

Where do I go with this? I asked myself. She's right. We're all in it, all part of this crime. She reached for my glass. "Let me freshen that," she said.

I stood. "No thanks, Caddy."

I wanted to say something reassuring, to seal the compact. And I might have if it were only about Caddy and Tony. I wanted to reach back through time and finally seize the hand she never offered when I was innocent and warm and recklessly in love and needed it. But I couldn't. I couldn't get past that other factor, the brute instinctive pragmatism that Neil, and now dear Caddy, represented.

Turning out of the last bend in the lane to my house I could see a car in front and I realized too late to stop that it was Neil's. *Goddamn*. Adrenaline pumping and mind racing through a dozen reasons for his visit, none pleasant, I pulled up along-side the car. But it wasn't Neil behind the wheel. It was Hannah. I tried to see past her, to the passenger seat. Nobody there. I climbed out of the truck cautiously, surveying the surround-ings. No sign of him. Then I heard the whir of the electric window lowering.

"I'm alone," she said. "Will you get in?"

I nodded and walked over to the car, slid in on the passenger side. Waited. "He's home," she said.

"I see."

"He's been in his bedroom pretty well since your visit. He doesn't always show things . . . like feelings." She looked away, out through her side window. "It's lovely here," she said. "And what a lovely little old house."

"You can come in . . ."

"No. We can talk here." And then she went silent, struggling, I could see. At last she smiled. "He came off the wagon shortly after you left."

"I'd forgotten about his wagon. It was a long fast this time."

"Right after you left he came into the kitchen and saw me there, asked what I was doing. Just cleaning up, I said. I asked if he'd offered you tea or a drink and he just grunted. Then he took a bottle from the cupboard and went to his room." She added, "We have separate rooms."

She waited for a reaction from me, but I had none. I just nodded.

"It's been a very long time," she said, "since we've been what you'd consider . . . married."

"I'm sorry."

"There are worse things. I didn't mind, I guess, until we moved here. But then he kind of disappeared into his own past–at least the pure, innocent part of his history that this place represents. And, of course, I'm not a part of that."

She pulled off a glove and studied the rings on her left hand. "It's very lonely," she said. "And it's worse when people look at your rings and they say to themselves, 'She must be okay, she's got so-and-so.' Isn't that the way it is around here?"

"Probably most places," I said.

She put the glove back on and I thought she was about to leave. But she opened her purse, peered inside for a moment, then extracted a folded, yellow sheet of paper. She handed it over.

"I heard everything the other night. None of it surprised me. But I couldn't stand the thought of him having this power over you, knowing how he'd drawn you into everything. He was just obsessed with that poor Strickland boy. You couldn't talk about it. Strickland was worse than Saddam." She laughed. "I bet if he could have got Cheney and the gang to come up here..." And she laughed again, then said, "I'm sorry. I shouldn't make a joke of it."

I unfolded the paper, folded it again, handed it back. "You can't do this," I said. "He'll know."

"It won't matter. I'm leaving for the States in the morning. He doesn't know it but I'm not coming back. I couldn't survive another week here."

I put the paper in my pocket.

"I'm really sorry it didn't work out," she said. "I'm sure there are lots of nice people here. I liked his idea of getting close to another couple like you and–what was her name?"

"Caddy."

"She sounds Jewish."

"No."

"A lovely person though, I'll bet."

"She is."

"Anyway."

I thought she was about to start the car engine and I was searching for the words, the words of sympathy, concern, regret, gratitude–something human. She sighed loudly.

"How much do you know about what happened in Boston?"

"He told me some."

"He told you about his partner, Donnie?"

"Yes."

"And about how he shot somebody ... and the big inquiry."

"Yes."

"Everything was going well at the inquiry until the lawyer for the criminal who Neil shot made it public that the only drug at the crime scene was a bag of cocaine in Donnie's coat pocket. And that the drug was from the evidence vault. You know what I really think ... ?"

She was shaking her head, tugging at the fingers of her gloves.

"No, Hannah," I said. "You don't have to ..." I reached across and touched her hand.

"I never cared for Donnie," she said. "It had nothing to do with his race. He was just one of those people who make you nervous.

"Then the media made a big to-do about the fact that Donnie and Neil were business partners who owned the crack house where all the shooting happened. The reporters were saying Neil and Donnie wanted the dope dealers out of the house but it wasn't enough just to evict them. They were going to plant drugs there and arrest them, which would get them all put back in prison. Later, Neil told the grand jury he knew nothing about the bag of cocaine that Donnie had with him. They believed him. But I didn't. Not for a moment."

"How much of this did you know before the inquiry and the media got hold of it?" I asked carefully.

"I made it a point never to ask about his work. He just came and went."

I said, "He didn't tell me the outcome—just that Donnie came out the bad guy."

"Donnie, God rest him, had the cocaine on him. And they proved that the bullet that killed the drug dealer came from Donnie's gun. But Donnie was dead—there was a third guy they never found who shot Donnie then escaped out a window. Climbing out the window he managed to shoot Neil just as Neil was firing his shotgun at the other one. The one who lost his arm. You can imagine the story they made of that when the details started coming out. We love our violence when it's happening to other people."

"Neil was never charged with anything."

"No, thank God. He could never have handled that."

"So he retired."

"They went easy on him. He got a good package, generous retirement terms. After all, he'll wear that bullet in his back for the rest of his days and it could cause serious problems at any time. The real problem though was that guy with the arm shot off. He was a brother of the dead drug dealer. Intelligence kept picking up street talk that there was a contract out on Neil and just about everybody connected to him. It just got too hard on the nerves. So we moved here. Even if they thought of looking here, they wouldn't bother."

"Punishment enough, living here." I laughed.

"Exactly."

Down at the bottom of the field I could see the sad pile of stone but beyond it there was sunshine glinting on the endless blue. I realized she was watching me.

"I like you, Tony." She smiled broadly. "You're easy to talk to. Maybe *you're* Jewish ... you never know, being adopted."

I laughed. "At one time I checked. I'm not."

"Too bad. One of my favourite Jews in the whole world is a Tony. Tell me you've been watching him on all those terrible television shows about Iraq. Tony Judt? The historian. He's the only one who ever made any sense, insisting that invading Iraq was a huge, huge mistake we'll have to live with all our lives. You weren't impressed by him?"

"Can't say I recall."

"Darn. If you'd said yes I think I'd have given you a blow job, right here in your driveway."

She ignored the shocked look that I could not conceal.

"In all the hours of TV Neil put me through, with his own running stupid commentaries, the only person who made any sense to me was Tony Judt. But of course, off would go the television when he'd be halfway through his argument, Neil mumbling 'fucking Jewish liberal.' That did it for me as much as anything else."

Suddenly I was laughing hysterically, face down on the leather dash, tears rolling, hands paddling the car seat in helpless spasms, Hannah looking worried.

"I'm sorry," I gasped. Pulled the yellow sheet of paper from my pocket and passed it to her. "Take this back, Hannah. Please. Take it and put it back where you found it. Don't go away. We'll make things work. You, me, Caddy. Just don't go."

"What about Neil?"

"Fuck Neil," I said.

She seemed to think it over seriously for a moment. "That could be a problem. What if it came to that?"

"You can just say no like you've obviously been doing for a while. Lock your bedroom door."

"You don't know Neil very well, do you?"

She eyed me sadly then looked straight ahead, past the steering wheel. "Years ago I tried that. Once. You don't know how easily he'd come through that door. He could make kindling out of any locked door." Handed back the yellow page.

I folded it yet again. "So tell me then, Hannah. What should I do?"

She leaned back and sighed, studied the ceiling of the car. "I don't know, Tony. If you *were* Jewish, I'd tell you to go and talk to the rabbi."

Then, after a long hesitation, she said, "Go to your Caddy. Make it work, you're both from here." She smiled. Removed the gloves again, examining her rings.

"Relationships are strange," she said. "Especially a marriage. Each one, full of secrets, right? Some wise person once said to me—'all intimate relationships are fed by underground streams.'"

She shook her head. "Neil was so insufferably smug analyzing your divorce . . . I felt like slapping him."

Then she looked at me intently. "We both know your Caddy meant no harm. You have to believe that."

"Meant no harm . . . ?"

She pulled the gloves back on slowly. "Anything she told Neil, you can't blame her. Neil just has a way of getting things out of people. I'm sure you understand that. Anything she told him, it was because she cares for you."

"Caddy? I thought . . ."

"Just talk to her." She was smiling, then she reached over and patted my hand.

"Gotta go now. Goodbye, Tony Whoever."

It was the strangest feeling, entirely unfamiliar. I was neither surprised nor angry, just mildly frustrated that I hadn't worked it out before. Simple deduction: Caddy knew because I told her. And I told her because I needed to. And she told Neil because . . . *Neil just has a way of getting things out of people.* Poor Caddy, I thought. You're human after all. But didn't I learn all about that a century ago?

I could tell even in the gloom that they were elderly, the couple seated in the pew near the confessional at the front, to the right of the sanctuary. I stayed well back, not that there was any danger of recognition. I just felt uncomfortable, like someone showing up at a food bank when he could easily afford to buy the groceries. A little voice had nagged, even as I parked outside, "You didn't really believe in this when you had the faith . . . you saw it as free therapy." But the voice of reason replied: So what's wrong with that? *If you were Jewish, I'd tell you to go and talk to the rabbi.* Shouldn't a priest be at least as useful as a rabbi? Confession is their main thing, right?

I sat, examining my conscience as I was trained to do at the age of six in this very place, trying to find language that was explicit and yet sufficiently evasive to prevent a prolonged discussion. I knew that the priest was fairly young–an aberration in these materialistic times–and well liked in the parish for a sense of humour and a pragmatic flexibility where so much of the doctrine as currently interpreted was exclusively rigid.

An old lady emerged from the small curtained space and an old man went in. He stayed considerably longer than she had and I tried to imagine why. What could he possibly have done that would require so much contrition? He eventually emerged, slouched into a pew and knelt. By then the older woman, probably his wife, was at the rack of votive candles up closer to the altar where, I remembered, once there had been a communion rail.

I'd been worried about the formulaic words, but they flowed easily once I was settled on my knees before the screen. "Bless me Father for I have sinned. I confess to almighty God and to you, Father." I stopped there. And after a pause I came clean: "I'm afraid I can't even try to guess the last time I've been to confession." I thought I heard a stir, the priest, perhaps, sitting up more attentively–something out of the ordinary about to happen, something spicier than the routine lapses in charity and self-control that he was accustomed to enduring.

"I guess we're talking years," he said gently.

"Decades," I replied.

"Was there a particular reason for your absence from the sacraments?"

"No dramatic reason," I said. "There was no event or revelation that caused me to lose faith. It all just seemed to become irrelevant."

"I see. So. What brings you back?" He seemed to say it with a smile though I couldn't tell from the little bit of profile that I could see–the strong jawline, well-shaped nose, forehead propped against a hand.

I said, "I don't want to pretend that it's because of a sudden recovery of faith."

He chuckled, shifted position. "Okay."

"I was involved in something, Father, which was wrong. Very wrong. A sin by anybody's definition. I'm not really here to be forgiven but maybe for whatever value there might be in talking about it to someone objective, who will keep it confidential."

"I'm not a psychiatrist," he said.

"I'm sorry."

"That's okay. When you came in, was there anybody else out there waiting?"

"No, I'm the last."

"Okay. Why don't you just get to the point? But first, I have to know–do you have honest remorse for this and all your other failings since your last confession?"

I considered the words. "Remorse would be an understatement."

He laughed. "Good. I had to ask that, just to make sure that we aren't entirely out in left field here. So what did you do?"

"I helped to kill someone."

He was silent.

"It's a complicated story but that's the bottom line. Someone is dead for no good reason and it's partly because of my actions."

"Did you intend to cause this death?"

"No."

"Okay," he said. "We can start there. How did you get mixed up in this?"

"I was manipulated, but that isn't meant to diminish my responsibility."

"Except that, from my point of view, it does diminish your moral responsibility."

"We could argue that. I ask myself why I didn't do more to stop what was going on when it might have changed the outcome."

"And the answer would be?"

"I reacted from instinct. Saving the victim became secondary to—other issues."

"But you're genuinely troubled by the outcome."

"Yes."

"Okay. We're in a good place here. You knew this victim?"

"Yes."

"Was he someone who might have anticipated the circumstances that led to his death? I guess I'm wondering if there was some betrayal here, someone who might have been unaware, perhaps because of trust, of the danger he was in."

"He knew he was in danger. That was what caused the situation to get out of control."

"He was afraid of you?"

"He was afraid. Probably more afraid of who was with me than of me. He knew me fairly well."

"This other person, do you think he—I'm assuming it was he—feels the same kind of remorse that you feel, sees this situation as you see it?"

"Definitely not."

"How would you explain the difference in your responses?"

"I wouldn't know how to begin."

"Well. In any case, it's clear to me that you are genuinely remorseful. And I daresay not likely to commit this particular . . . action ever again. Right?"

"Yes."

"You have to be sincerely determined at this moment that something like that won't happen again. You know that?"

I thought of Neil and the new sense of the depths of his brutality conveyed to me by the woman who knew him better than anybody. *You don't know how easily he'd come through that door.* I couldn't help wondering—what if he comes after me, once he realizes Hannah isn't coming back?

"I guess I have to say I'm human, vulnerable to all the human weaknesses."

"I understand that. We all live with that. I'm interested in your present, honest, state of mind."

"Yes," I said. "I don't ever want to be part of anything like that again."

"Okay. But I have to say that true remorse, real contrition, must be demonstrated by, well . . . a good act of contrition—you know the words—but also by some penitential action. I'm sure you remember that from when you'd come in here as a boy full of remorse for your impure thoughts and actions, bad words and uncharitable behaviour, and the priest would send you out to say a few Our Fathers and Hail Marys. If you'd been a real bad teenager, you might get a turn around the Stations. What we're talking about here is a bit more complicated, right?"

"Yes, Father."

"See, I can offer absolution. But it'll be in the penance that you'll find the comfort both in spiritual and practical terms. Do you follow me?"

"Yes, Father."

"Do you know where I'm going with this?"

"Yes."

"Like I said, I'm not a psychiatrist and I'm definitely not a lawyer. But I think we both know what I'm talking about here."

I sighed. "I'm afraid so."

"So I'm going to use the power Our Lord has invested in me to offer you the full comfort of the sacrament of reconciliation. But for true absolution you *will* have to meditate and I daresay pray long and hard on the proper course to follow. You must faithfully follow the conscience that brought you here, whatever agency it was that intervened to break the long spiritual hunger. Are you with me?"

"I am."

And as we recited the remembered act of contrition and I then listened to his quiet promise of my forgiveness and to his blessing, I thought about 'the agency,' and prayed that she was safely back in her own country, safe from all the perils of the place that was supposed to have been her sanctuary.

——

I sat outside the RCMP detachment for a long time, daunted by the number of police vehicles and other cars and trucks in the parking lot. From the outside the place looked like a hive of enforcement activity, but when I went inside there was only one policeman in view, in shirt sleeves, wearing regulation body armour, gun belt loaded down with walkie-talkie, bullets, mace, taser, handcuffs and, of course, the gun. I stood at the public counter for a full minute before he shoved aside what he'd been reading, and came over.

"So what can I do for you," he said breezily.

"I need to talk, privately."

He compressed his lips, raised his eyebrows, looked around the empty room, and said: "Fine." Leaned on the counter between us.

"I was, uhhh, present at a homicide, a while back. Last month. The Strickland . . . death."

He straightened up, studied me as if I'd just arrived. "What's your name?"

"Tony Breau. I live on the Shore Road." He walked away, down a corridor and disappeared. When he returned he had his jacket and his hat.

The day was warm with a light breeze kicking up the dust and salt and trash until recently suppressed by snow. He remotely unlocked one of the cruisers and said, "Let's go for a drive. Jump in the front seat."

He was silent on the main highway that bypasses the town. Passing the Tim Hortons, he nodded. "If you feel like a coffee, we can grab a quick one." I'd have loved a coffee but I wasn't anxious to be seen in a cop car. "I'm good," I said.

Just past the edge of town he pulled onto a side road that became rutted gravel. I remembered late night summer swimming expeditions somewhere out here. And we were soon stopped on a widening of the road overlooking a pond that I remembered as being considerably larger.

"You're from around here," he said, picking at a cuticle. He removed his hat, put it between us on the console.

"North of here, St. Ninian," I said. "But yes. It's more or less the same place now."

"We drove by where I grew up on the way here," he said. "Gone now, the old house."

"I didn't realize." His name hadn't registered as one that I'd have considered local.

"Grew up with an uncle and an aunt. Lost my parents young, in the States. They brought me back here. A pretty nice place for a kid to grow up, you'd agree." Pointed straight ahead: "Spent summers swimming down there."

"Pretty ideal," I said. And then, "I was adopted and raised by an old couple."

"Yes," he said. "And then you worked as a corrections officer."

I laughed. "You've done your homework."

"After the fatality," he said. "You were on my list of people I had to talk to. I was giving you some time, with the burns and so on. Any day now I was gonna come find you. You're okay now, I can see."

"It was nothing major," I said. "Mostly first degree; there was one they were worried about on the wrist. But it all healed up."

"Yes," he said. "You were lucky."

We fell silent, staring straight ahead at the pond. Then, as so often happens, we both began speaking simultaneously, then stopped together. There was an awkward silence for a moment.

I said, "I was about to say how surprised I was that you guys hadn't come around sooner to hear my version of what went on the night of the twenty-second."

He nodded.

"It was a complicated situation," I ventured. "Do you think this is the proper place for the discussion?"

"Don't see why not." He looked over at me.

"We might want a record of it," I said.

"Of course. But you know how it works. Sometimes an informal ... conversation ... can get a fella closer to the real story than all the formalities of notes and recordings and stuffy little interviewing rooms. So why don't you just start to talk. We can pick up on the important stuff back at the office. I've got a very good memory."

"I'm not sure where you want me to start."

"Why don't you start with how you ended up at Strickland's place that night?"

So I did. How Neil arrived with a story of a teenager whose parents were alarmed that she was at Strickland's, and that there had been a previous incident there involving this particular girl. He was nodding as I spoke. And how when we arrived I was surprised to see that Strickland was alone.

"Working at the stove."

"Well, here's where it gets a bit more complicated than what you've heard."

"How complicated?"

"Strickland was actually asleep when we got there."

"Asleep, you say. You saw him asleep."

"We looked through a window ..."

"But by the time you actually entered the kitchen, he was at the stove, firing it up."

"Well, no. He was just waking up when I arrived in his living room and that was when he attacked ..."

"Yes, I know about the initial attack, but I thought that was in the kitchen."

"No, in the living room."

He seemed exasperated then, wobbling his head side to side as if to say "help me here."

I said, "Maybe if I went back a bit. I take it you know the man I was with, Neil MacDonald. Ex-policeman from Boston."

"I know quite a bit about the context already," he said. "But maybe I can give *you* some context that'll help us get to some mutual understanding. Okay?"

I waited.

"See, Tony ... I'm gonna call you Tony. I mean we're both peace officers and we both grew up around here and are both lucky enough to be living back here again. You know, back in the old days, I wouldn't have had a snowball's chance of ever living back here in God's country. Back then, you remember they wouldn't even let you get married for the first five years you were in the force. And they wouldn't let you do police work anywhere *near* where you might know people or, God forbid, be related to somebody. It's different now. You can actually be a cop in a place you really care about. And that, Tony, is in my opinion what policin' is all about. Havin' a connection with the people, really knowing and caring about the people you work for."

I was nodding because he was right.

"I can see you agree with me."

"I do."

He waited for a while, offered me a Chiclet, I declined. Put one in his mouth, chewed thoughtfully.

"I've been a cop all over this great country. To be honest, this town is probably the biggest place I've ever worked. Mostly little rural places, mostly out west. Places no bigger than where you're living, down the shore. Houses few and far between. One of the first things you learn, when you get to one of those little detachments is that in every case, without exception, you find out that, say, 60 percent of the police work is generated by a handful of individuals, like this Strickland. In many cases there's one fuckin guy—and this one fit the profile perfectly: lived alone, young, smarter than the average bear, did time, figures the rules are for everybody but him. No respect for the law or the officer. Constantly ... I mean *constantly* finding ways to fuck the system, whether its petty theft, taxes, fishin' or huntin' out of season, speeding, dope, bootlegging, sexual perversions. You name it and this guy will be into it. And *fearless*! Loves nothing better than to provoke an officer into a confrontation. Never anything interesting, just some clawing, tearing, rolling-in-the-mud bullshit to get you all sore and dirty. And next morning you're serving the cocksucker toast and jam in the lockup and he's all smiles before he charges *you* with assault."

He was surprisingly calm. "You know what I'm talking about, Tony? 'Cept that in the joint you guys got a bit more flexibility. The con fucking knows the way the system works in there, man. Fuck with the bull and you might get a horn up the arse. Right? But out here, man? It's all about them and their rights."

He was chewing quietly now. "And then, every so often, some young cop, right out of depot, crease on the pants and a shine on the shoes, is walking up to the door of one of these citizens to serve some kind of document with a please and thank you sir or madam, or check out some firearm complaint, or cross dog ... and halfway between the car and the shack ... Blam. Afterwards there's a big national uproar, hand wringing, politicians and red serge and sad faces lined up for miles for the world's prettiest funeral. *Big* speeches, *plans* to make it better, until a few weeks later, when it's back to the routine. Guys like us, and women, too, God love them, drivin' around the back roads with an eye peeled for one of these dudes out doing his thing. Like Strickland."

I decided to interrupt. "I actually knew Dwayne ..."

"Just let me finish, Tony. So here's what was going through my head as I started the file on Mr. Dwayne Strickland, late of the Shore Road in the hamlet of St. Ninian. I'm looking at the facts. Here's a guy lived on the wrong side all his life. Went to the Millhaven finishing school, and you know all about that. Got a fuckin attitude on him that would impress a Taliban recruiter. Sets up shop down there out of sight in your neck of the woods. Builds a customer base among the teenage population. Some young kid kicks the bucket under suspicious circumstances in his livin' room. Buddy gets away with it. And get this, Tony. This guy is so cocky he's been playing silly-bugger with the local bikers' chapter. Taking their dope and selling it and not paying them. And don't you be fooled by their aw-shucks, green-as-grass good ol' local boys hospitality bullshit. These guys are connected all the way into Laval. And he's already told one of their reps to go fuck himself *a couple of times* when they came by to collect their share.

"You know what, Tony? Here's a young healthy guy but say you're an insurance salesman. You gonna write up a policy for Dwayne Strickland? You say so and I'll say you're crazier than he is. Now what was it you were going to tell me?"

"There's a bit more to the story about how he died ..."

"Oh, I fuckin bet there is," he said. "According to you guys he goes after one of you with a baseball bat and a fire starts and in spite of you trying to save his sorry ass, he dies in it. I hate to sound hard, man, but there's something kinda Shakespearean there. I'm trying to imagine what would have happened if you two guys were enforcers for the motorcycle club, eh. He'd been begging for the fire. So what were you going to say, Tony?"

There was a bald eagle on a tree branch high above the pond and a distant contrail inching across the sky. I could feel an internal collapse, but also a sense of release. It was a moment, I realize as I look back on everything, when fate separates the weak from the strong. I was succumbing to weakness. I knew it even as it happened. But I was also asking myself the question: Where does being strong get you when the game is rigged?

"I was just going to ask about the status of the file," I said.

"Oh, the file is staying open, that's for sure. No pressure to close that one."

"Well, you know where I am when you want to add my two cents worth to the paperwork."

"I know that and I appreciate it, Tony."

He started the engine, rolled down the car window and spit out his gum. The eagle lifted off the branch and lazily wobbled off in the general direction of the disintegrating jet path in the sky.

Driving down the lane, the little house looked grim, abandoned. I again had to force my way through the door, finally admitting to myself that I was going to have to soon spend some fresh money on the place, starting with this sticky doorframe. Maybe a whole new kitchen. Or just get rid of everything, pick up and start all over again.

The phone was ringing.

"Hey, it's Neil." He sounded groggy. "Have you heard anything from Hannah?"

"Hannah? Your wife?"

"How many fuckin Hannahs do you know? Yes, my wife."

I tried to mask alarm with fake confusion. "Why would she be in touch with me?"

"She went home to the States for a visit and was supposed to be gone for a week. That was ten days ago. All I've heard from her is some garbled message on the answering machine. I'm not suggesting anything. I just know she has your number because I gave it to her in case anything ever happened to me."

"Sorry, Neil. I can't help you. You sound like you have the flu."

"No. I'm good. What about yourself. You holding up all right?"

"I'm managing," I said.

"Well, just keep on managing. This'll all be ancient history in no time flat. We should get together sometime soon, talk about where we go from here, man."

"What do you mean, go from here?"

"I've been doing a lot of thinking the last week or so. You'd be surprised, the number of phone calls I've had. Word gets around. This isn't the time or the place to talk about it. But let's just say we got a whole lot of fans up and down the country-side. I think we've cranked up some expectations." He seemed to be waiting for a response.

"Let me know if you hear from Hannah, Neil. Good night."

20.

I sat in the gathering darkness and retrieved the yellow paper from my jacket pocket. I spread it on the table, read it, then struck a match and watched it burn until the flame was threatening my thumb and forefinger. At which moment I dropped the remains of it into a saucer.

Later that evening I made two telephone calls, left two messages: The first to Anna, letting her know that I had pretty well decided to take up her offer regarding the dog, Jack Daniels. If it was still on the table I could make arrangements to pick him up in maybe a week when I'd be in the Kingston area on other business. The second call was to Sophie. Wondering if she'd be around and available for lunch or a drink anytime early in the week. I was planning on driving up that way on the weekend and had some business in Ottawa; hoping maybe we could catch up.

Then I turned on the television and watched the president of the United States posing on an aircraft carrier somewhere, dressed in warrior gear, huge banner hanging in the background, Mission Accomplished. And I wondered if anybody ever told him how much he looked like Alfred E. Neuman.

Friday was sunny and warm. I sat on the doorstep sipping my coffee, reconsidering conclusions carefully defined the night before. When all was said and done, my predicament was simple. Neil just made use of what he saw in me, what he knew about me based on his own shrewd understanding of human nature. He just wound me up and turned me loose and I performed exactly as he thought I would.

Well, Tony Whoever, we can't let that happen again. I took a last look around and went indoors.

I stripped the bed, folded and stored the bedclothes. Vacuumed upstairs and down. Then I packed, maybe for a week, maybe for a month, maybe forever. I sat. It was eleven o'clock. I remembered the newspapers—and that I'd have to cancel them. The phone rang. I decided not to answer. Neil again. But when it rang through to the answering machine it was Caddy. I picked up.

"I wasn't sure if you were still around," she said. She sounded weary.

"Actually I'm going to go away for a few days. I meant to let you know."

"That's a good plan, to get away from here for a while. Put things behind you. Not a great time for Florida though."

"Nah. Not Florida. Not in May. I have to do a few things in Ontario."

"Ontario. Oh well."

"Are you all right, Caddy?"

"I'm okay," she said. "Just haven't been sleeping much. When are you planning on leaving?"

"Later today," I said. "I prefer to do my driving at night."

"Hmmm. Maybe you'll drop by for a minute before you go," she said. "I'd like to have a brief chat about something."

"Sure," I said.

I tried calling Sophie once more. Had to leave another message: "Hey Sophie, not sure if you're around at all. Me again. I'll probably be in Ottawa sometime Sunday. I'll try calling again when I'm there. Maybe lunch on Monday. You don't have to worry. Just catching up. No agenda. Okay?"

Caddy was sitting in a lawn chair on her deck, eyes closed, face turned up toward the harsh sunlight. She sat up when she heard my footsteps and smiled at me. "Let me get another chair. Will you have something to drink?"

"No," I said. "I'm okay."

We sat side by side, close enough to touch. She closed her eyes again.

After a long silence: "I think it's going to be an early spring."

"I hope so."

"I went to see the police in town," I said after a while.

"Mmmmhmmm."

"You heard?"

"No, I didn't. What did they have to say?"

"They weren't interested in anything I had to tell them."

"I'm not surprised. Neil is in pretty thick with the local police officers."

"I gathered as much. When you said we were all in it together I thought you just meant Neil and me and you. I didn't realize you meant most of the village, the police and, just for good measure, the biker gang."

She smiled. "This surprises you?"

"I guess not. I guess it surprises me, and it shouldn't, that Neil is so . . . fanatical."

There was another long silence and then she sat up, and began to work at her wedding ring until, finally, she had it off. She held it up to the light as if to estimate its value.

"There's something I should have told you a long time ago, Tony," she said. "It doesn't really make a lot of difference now, but then again it could help you understand a few things."

I waited and after a while I was certain that she'd changed her mind. Then she said softly, almost inaudibly, "Neil is Maymie's grandfather, Tony."

"Neil is . . ." I began.

". . . Rosalie's father," she finished. The pale, pale eyes were blinking rapidly.

I don't know how much time went by after that. I just sat thinking about her disclosure, surprised mostly by just how obvious it should have been to me all along, how unsurprising it really was now that it was out in the open. But isn't truth like that? Unsurprising when we hear it. Of course it was Neil, the warrior about to face a likely death in a far-off land. It made perfect sense. *Neil just has a way of getting things out of people.*

"That would explain why ... Strickland."

"No," she said sadly. "I'm afraid not. Neil doesn't know. About Maymie. When I was pregnant with Rosalie I never told him. I never told anybody."

She raised a cautionary hand. "Don't say anything, Tony, or I'll cry. And I swear I'll never, ever forgive you if you make me cry in front of you. So. Just." She waved the hand again.

And after a long silence: "But there's something else. About Neil. I'm afraid I have another confession ... to do with Strickland ... and your ..."

Her eyes were now brimming, voice gone.

"No Caddy," I said. "There's no need ..."

"I'm just a stupid old woman."

"No, my darling Caddy. You are not."

She was nodding and I had no idea what she was agreeing to.

Gazing at some distant place, she finally asked, "Do you think you'll ever come back, Tony?"

"I don't know," I said.

We stood then, facing one another. "I'm glad you told me about Rosalie," I said. "It always mattered. It still matters."

"Yes," she said. "It always mattered."

She held out both hands and I clasped them. "If you do come back, will you promise that you'll come and see me?"

"Yes," I said. "Goodbye, Caddy."

——

There's a bit of a haze around the rest.

I drove to the store. I know I noticed a vehicle in front, but no particulars. Mary was alone inside. I kept it brief, cancelled the newspapers indefinitely, asked her to keep an eye on my place. I told her I needed a holiday. "I'm not surprised," she said. Then, as an afterthought: "Did you notice those two outside when you came in?"

"No."

"Two guys in a big rented SUV, say they're from Boston, asking for Neil."

"Really?"

"One of them was paying for a pack of cigarettes and when he reached for his wallet I saw a gun under his coat. He saw me looking and that was when he told me–he's a cop, or says he is. I have my doubts. He has one of those mechanical arms. I can't picture a cop with one of those."

I went to a window and looked out. There was a black Lincoln Navigator parked there, windows tinted.

"They asked for Neil?"

"Said they were in the same squad or something. Worked together, were old friends. A couple of what-are-you-supposed-to-call-them nowadays? African-Americans. Anyway, I played stupid. I don't like to give out personal information about anybody around here. Including you."

"I appreciate that."

"You have a safe trip, Tony."

——

The SUV driver's window was down when I left the store and as I walked by a voice asked, "Is that your truck?"

I said it was.

The driver had a shaved head and for all his menacing appearance what seemed to be a kind expression. "I guess you'd need something like that, living out in the country."

"It helps," I said. "You planning a move to the country?"

He shrugged. "Could be," he said, and smiled. His eyes were as gentle as his voice.

The passenger then shouted across, "Maybe you can help. We're trying to find an old friend. Name of Neil MacDonald."

I approached the Lincoln, bent and looked inside. "Well," I said. "It's a very common name around here. You could probably find a Neil MacDonald in every second house. You'd have to be more specific."

"Big fella. Ex-cop," he said. "From Boston. We all worked together in Roxbury. We heard so much about this place from Neil, golf and beaches, music and hospitality, that we decided— hey, let's scout it out, maybe bring the families down here for a summer vacation later on. Anyway, wanted to touch base with ol' Neil. Checked the phone book but, like you said ... MacDonalds, wow." He laughed.

I gave it about five seconds reflection. "I'm thinking," I said. Then five more seconds.

"You know what you should do?" I said at last. "There's a lovely old bed and breakfast a few miles down the road. Beautiful spot, overlooks the sea. The Seaside B and B. There's a big sign on the highway just before you get to it. Check in there for the weekend. Very comfortable. And I'll bet they can help you with anything you need to know about the place."

The driver looked over at the passenger and they nodded at each other briefly. Then he turned back to me. "Sounds like a plan," he said.

As he powered the window up, he said softly, "Y'all have a wonderful day."

I realized that Mary was standing in the doorway of the store, leaning, one arm across her middle. The other arm was raised, hand before her face holding a cigarette, concealing her expression. She puffed once on the cigarette, then dropped it and crushed it with her heel, nodded, smiled slightly, turned and walked inside.

Acknowledgements

I'm grateful to many readers who took the trouble to review early versions of my manuscript—especially Carol Off, Anne Collins and Shaun Bradley, who responded generously in the most primitive stages of the project. Particularly Anne, who struggled with me as the narrative evolved into its final form. I owe particular thanks to Lorne MacDowell, Jill Arthur and my colleague and friend Gillian Findlay for important advice on courtroom scenes. To the extent the courtroom drama rings authentic, those three deserve the credit—where it fails, the fault is mine.

LINDEN MACINTYRE's bestselling first novel, *The Long Stretch*, was nominated for a CBA Libris Award and his boyhood memoir, *Causeway: A Passage from Innocence*, won both the Edna Staebler Award for Creative Nonfiction and the Evelyn Richardson Prize. His second novel, *The Bishop's Man*, was a number-one national bestseller, won the Scotiabank Giller Prize, the Dartmouth Book Award and the CBA Libris Fiction Book of the Year Award, among other honours. The third book in the loose-knit trilogy, *Why Men Lie*, was also a number-one national bestseller as well as a *Globe and Mail* "Can't Miss" Book for 2012. MacIntyre, who spent twenty-four years as the co-host of *the fifth estate*, is a distinguished broadcast journalist who has won ten Gemini awards for his work.